Murder At Melcham Hall

By

Dave Watson

Mirador Publishing
www.miradorpublishing.com

First Published in Great Britain 2013 by Mirador Publishing

First edition: 2013

A copy of this work is available though the British Library.

ISBN: 978-1-909220-63-8

Mirador Publishing
Mirador
Wearne Lane
Langport
Somerset
TA10 9HB

Acknowledgements

Once again, my heartfelt thanks and gratitude to Sandra Coyne, whose support and guidance helped to define the final manuscript.

A special thank you to my dear friend Phil Cowan, who created and manages my website www.davewatson.info

As always, my thanks and gratitude to Sarah and everyone at Mirador. I'm delighted to be working with such a terrific team.

This book is dedicated to Samuel Jeremiah Thorn

1

Annie Griffin cursed the winter months. Her rheumatism played up more than usual and she was frightened of becoming a virtual recluse, isolated from the outside world. Being seventy-two years of age she coped well enough to live alone in Rowan Lodge in the grounds of Melcham estate but would have welcomed more company from time to time. Annie and her husband had moved into the Lodge when Fred became the head gardener in nineteen sixty-five. Following Fred's passing, Sir Clive Melcham, owner of Melcham Hall and the Melcham estate, informed Annie that she would be allowed to remain in Rowan Lodge until such a time that she couldn't fend for herself, and upon his death, had stated in his will that she was to remain there free of charge for the rest of her days.

Built in 1745 Rowan Lodge had originally belonged to the Parker family who historically had owned half the land in the county. But like most families across generations, their wealth slowly declined and they were forced to sell some of their assets. The Lodge was then purchased by the Melcham family whose fortunes had been made by the buying and selling of imported goods from across the channel. The only heating in the property came from the Aga that stood in the kitchen. Large grey flagstones covered the downstairs floor and the only recent improvement to the property was the introduction of a downstairs bathroom and toilet.

Annie shivered as she poked at the dying embers of the coal fire. It was still early morning and the few embers that she had relit before breakfast were beginning to wane. Wrapping her shawl tightly around her shoulders she trudged into the kitchen to retrieve the empty coal scuttle. Slipping into her old shoes she unlocked the kitchen door before stepping outside into the cold morning air. Heavy overnight snow had made the garden pathway almost invisible and clung to both trees and bushes in the surrounding woodland. Holding the coal scuttle in one hand Annie leant on the wall of the house with the other to prevent herself from falling over.

The old wooden coal shed stood behind the house just a couple of yards in front of the now disused outside toilet. Having carefully made her way to the coal shed Annie placed the coal scuttle on the ground, steadied herself and pulled hard on the door several times, each time dragging more snow away. Retrieving the metal shovel from the coal scuttle she prodded at the stack of coal. She had managed to put just three shovel loads of coal into the coal scuttle when she suddenly froze. There, in front of her eyes, protruding from the coal stack was a human hand. Annie dropped the shovel, put her hands to her mouth and screamed.

It was an hour later, after Annie had managed to control her nerves and telephone for assistance, when the police and an ambulance crew arrived.

WPC Mandy Tredwell arrived on the scene to find Annie being comforted by one of the paramedics who winked and put his thumb up to say that Annie was OK. Having been provided with a brief description of the incident by PC William Bell, the desk sergeant at Wells police station, Mandy had left the office straight away and driven out to the Melcham estate. Carefully negotiating the snow laden path she made her way out to the back garden where Jonathan Bridges, a second paramedic was stood next to the open coal shed. A further light sprinkling of snow had failed to cover the exposed hand that was still protruding from the coal, but what stunned Mandy the most was the vacant stare on the face of the victim which had now been exposed by the doctor. Sightless eyes gazed upwards in a look of terror.

'Morning ma'am, I would normally say happy Christmas at this time of year, but it doesn't seem appropriate right now.'

'That's alright.' She returned his smile and knelt down to take a closer look. The hand looked feminine. It was small, and there appeared to be traces of nail polish on the fingernails.

'We haven't touched anything since we arrived,' said Jonathan. 'The doctor moved some of the coals away to see the face but that's all.'

Mandy stood up and extracted her mobile phone.

'Thanks. I'll get the forensic team out here right away.'

The young paramedic nodded and headed back into the house.

As soon as the forensic team arrived Mandy went into the Cottage to speak with Annie. Dr Ian Meadows, the local GP had checked Annie's heart and given her a mild sedative. The old lady was now sat in a large wing-backed chair with a blanket over her legs, holding a cup of tea in both hands.

'Hello Annie,' said Mandy kneeling down beside her. 'Are you OK?'

'I'm fine, thank you my dear. Just a little shaken, that's all. Do we know who the poor person is?'

'No not yet. The forensic team will remove the body and take it back to the lab for examination.'

'I must admit that it did take the wind out of my sails for a moment or two, seeing a hand protruding from the coals.'

'It would mine too,' Mandy replied forcing a smile, trying not to think of the frozen face.

'Oh I've seen worse during my lifetime. I remember watching some of those poor souls who came back from the war. Some of the injuries they had received were horrific. A few of the men were unrecognisable. The physical damage was there for all to see but it's the psychological damage those poor souls had to ensure that was the worst. Did you know that Melcham Hall was used as nursing home for a short while both during and just after the war you know? I'll never forget some of the things I saw back then. It wasn't only the poor souls who went to war, it was the families that were left behind never knowing if their loved ones were coming home or whether those that did would ever be the same.'

She took a sip of her tea then rested the cup on her lap. Mandy could see that the sedative the doctor had administered was starting to take effect.

'Is anyone staying with her?' Dr Ian Meadows whispered as he walked back into the room.

'Yes, I'll stay with her for a while,' Mandy replied, 'but we'll have to organise home help. She can't be left here on her own.'

'Well, she's insistent that she's not going to hospital. I'll pop in again this afternoon.'

Mandy followed the doctor out to his car.

'Have you any idea what the cause of death was, and when the victim died?' she asked.

'I'm afraid it's too early to tell, although my guess would be that the person has been dead for over twenty-four hours. As to the cause of death, there is damage to the back of the head but I can't tell whether that's the result of a fall or whether she was struck with something.'

'OK, thanks doctor. I'd better get back inside. I'll stay with Annie until a home help arrives.'

The moment Annie was asleep Mandy removed the half empty tea cup from her hand and walked out into the kitchen. The room felt cold so Mandy stoked the fire and added a few more pieces of coal, the way her father had shown her when she was a child.

As soon as the forensic team arrived they began the task of removing the body from its coal confines. Mandy watched through the kitchen window as they went about their work. They reminded her of a recent archaeology program she'd watched a few nights previous as the team had painstakingly scraped away layers of soil to expose the skeletal remains of Richard III whose body was found below a car park in Central London. Knowing they would be working outside in the cold for some time she filled the kettle and set about making some hot drinks. It was one of the coldest December's on record and icicles were hanging from gutters and branches alike.

She had just finished speaking with PC Martin Philips on her mobile when there was a knock on the kitchen door. She opened the door to face a rather plump, wealthy looking gentleman who was wearing a burgundy overcoat and black leather driving gloves.

'I'm so sorry for disturbing you, my name is Brian Hargreaves. My wife and I live at Melcham Hall along the drive. We own the Melcham estate.'

Mandy shook his hand and directed him to a seat at the kitchen table.

'I was just driving into the village to pick up some groceries when I saw the police car and the ambulance at the side of the Cottage. Is Annie, I mean Mrs Griffin, OK?'

'Yes, she's fine Mr Hargreaves but she's had a bad shock.'

Mandy explained what had happened and asked him if either he or his wife had seen or heard anything unusual. She noticed that he hadn't appeared shocked at the news that a body had been found and seemed more concerned about Annie's welfare.

'We didn't hear a thing I'm afraid. Melcham Hall sits at the back of the grounds of the estate about a quarter of a mile along the drive. We're so far back from the road and isolated because of the woods it's fair to say we never hear a soul.'

'When was the last time you spoke with Mrs Griffin?' Mandy asked.

He seemed to hesitate before answering.

'It would have been last Wednesday. I go to the market on Wednesdays and always ask Annie if she needs anything. It's rare that she does, but we always ask. She's so independent. She still grows most of what she eats.'

He then went on to explain that Annie had lived alone in the Cottage since her husband had passed away, and that part of his father-in-laws will had stipulated that Annie would remain living in the lodge whilst she could fend for herself.

'Do you know if she has many visitors?' Mandy asked while adding some notes in her book.

Brian shrugged his shoulders.

'To be honest, apart from the young lad who delivers her weekly shopping I don't think she sees anyone. Is there anything we can do?' he asked as he put his driving gloves back on.

'Not for now, but I may need to ask you and your wife a few questions later. I need to speak with Annie first once she's had a rest. She's had quite a shock and I'm not sure she should be left alone.'

'OK, sure. Well, if you need us, just come up the drive.'

Brian Hargreaves made his way out. Mandy watched out of the kitchen window as he got into the black jaguar before driving off. Her gut instinct told her she didn't like the man but maybe it was just one of those days.

It was just after midday when the forensic team loaded the body of a young female into the waiting vehicle. Mandy had already phoned Terry Austin at the pathology lab informing him to expect the body; knowing that the police would want feedback from him as soon as possible he said he'd make his way across town to the pathology lab straight away as the heavy snowfall had blocked a couple of minor roads. Mandy thanked him and said she would touch base with him later in the day. There was nothing found on the body nor in the coal shed that provided any clue to the victims' identity.

PC Martin Philips had arrived at Rowan Lodge just a few minutes before, and was now sat with Annie in the tiny front room.

'Are you still chatting Martin up?' Mandy asked as she entered the room.

'I certainly would have if he'd got here forty years ago,' Annie replied forcing a smile.

Mandy pulled up a chair alongside Annie and asked if she felt well enough to run through the mornings events. Both Mandy and Martin were surprised at how concise the old lady was. She explained that she normally topped up the coal scuttle in the evenings but due to heavy snow falling the night before she had decided to leave it until this morning. She then told them when she first saw the hand sticking out of the coal and how she telephoned 999 a short while after composing herself. She said that the last coal delivery had been two days previous and that although there were no apparent footprints near the coal shed when she'd gone to fill the coal scuttle, any that may have been made the previous day would have been covered by the heavy snowfall.

'Oh, listen to me. I sound like Jane Marple,' she laughed.

'You're doing remarkably well,' Martin commented.

She patted his hand.

'You are a flatterer as well as a handsome young man,' she replied.

Martin Blushed as Mandy winked at him with a broad smile on her face.

'Annie, did you see anyone around here yesterday, or hear anything unusual?' Mandy asked.

'No, no one. The last person I saw was Mr Hargreaves as he drove past the Cottage yesterday morning. He drives that car of his too fast. You mark my words. One day he's going to end up in a ditch somewhere.'

'I understand he drops in every Wednesday on the way to the market.'

'Yes he does, not out of choice mind you. I think it's his wife Lucy who tells him to ask if I need for anything. She's a lovely girl but I haven't seen much of her lately though. I understand she's been quite poorly of late. She married Brian Hargreaves some nine or ten years ago. I think he sponges off her but then that's just my opinion.'

Mandy made a few notes but thought she would speak to Annie at a later stage about her views. Right now, didn't seem the right time.

'So who brings your shopping in?' asked Martin.

'Young Timothy, Mrs Whitlow's boy. He works at the supermarket in the village and cycles here with my shopping once a week. He's a smashing lad.

In fact, he's due today, although I wouldn't be surprised if the roads are almost impassable with all this snow. I ought to telephone and tell them not to bother because I don't really need anything.'

She searched in her handbag for her notebook.

'Let me have the number Annie, I'll give them a call,' said Martin.

A short while later, having left Annie being comforted by a social worker, Mandy and Martin were stood outside the lodge discussing the day's events when Brian Hargreaves jaguar turned into the estate and sped past them along the snow laden track, splattering snow and ice in all directions.

'You don't like him do you?' said Martin watching Mandy's reaction.

'There's something about the man. I don't know what it is yet, but I intend to find out.'

An hour later Mandy was back in the office typing her report when the desk phone rang. She listened as pathologist Terry Austin provided her with an update.

'Hi Mandy, all I can tell you so far is that the victim is female, white Caucasian, age between twenty-five to thirty. Death appears to have been caused by a broken neck although there is a blow to the back of the skull and bruising to the rib cage. Its early days, but my guess would be that the girl fell backwards breaking her neck. I guess you'll have to determine whether she fell or was pushed.'

'A broken neck, have you got any idea when the victim died?'

'I would estimate approximately between twenty-four and thirty-six hours.'

'So the body has been in the coal shed for nearly two days?'

'No, I reckon the body would show greater signs of decomposition if it had. My view is that the body was kept somewhere else before being dumped.'

'OK thanks, Terry. I'm going to be in the office for a while yet if you come up with anything else. I need to catch up a pile of paperwork before the Inspector gets back tomorrow.'

'Yeah, relaxed and sun tanned I expect.'

'He won't be relaxed for long when he hears about this,' Mandy replied. 'Do you have any idea when you will be able to provide us with any more information?'

'I'll know more tomorrow, Mandy. I need to open the body up first.'

Mandy felt queasy, and tried desperately not to think about the girl's body being cut open.

'OK thanks, I'm sure the Inspector will be in touch with you first thing.'

Pathologist Terry Austin and Inspector Wesley had become good friends since they met just over a year ago. Mandy knew that Terry would bust a gut to provide Wesley with as much information as possible at short notice.

PC Martin Philips had stayed back at the lodge deciding he would take a walk around the Melcham Estate to see if he could view anything untoward. The area behind the lodge was densely wooded and even the heavy snow had failed to penetrate some areas of the woodland floor. To his left was the gravelled road that led downhill to Melcham Hall, but instinct told him to remain off-track and cut through the trees and dense foliage of the surrounding woodland. His large size ten boots left a clear trail behind him as he rummaged through the undergrowth looking for anything that he could associate with the murder victim or her killer. He'd only been walking for a few minutes when he approached a small clearing. In front of him the ground sloped away downhill towards a grassy bank. What caught his attention was what appeared to be a single tyre track, still partially visible even though the latest sprinkling of snow had almost covered it in places. Taking a closer look Martin observed how deep the single track was. He followed the track downhill towards an area where the canopy of trees gave way to a grey foreboding sky, laden with even more snow. A hundred yards further on, he noticed two indentations in the ground either side of the track. These appeared again further along. Martin suddenly realised that he was looking at the tracks of a wheel barrow. Now completely away from the shelter of the trees, the tracks were less prominent with the exposed ground gradually becoming a thick blanket of snow again.

At the bottom of the slope stood the imposing Melcham Hall, its drab grey exterior looking sinister in the grey afternoon light. Its grey slated twin turrets and the external brickwork of the portico that sheltered the front entrance were in need of repair. Small lumps of plaster had fallen away in places all over the facade, giving the impression for a long distance observer as if someone had fired at the building with a machine gun.

Brian Hargreaves' black jaguar was parked in front of the property and a somewhat run down looking red fiesta was stood in front of the double garage to the side. Only the tyre tracks in the snow recently left by the Jaguar provided any evidence that someone was at home.

In response to Martin's persistent ringing of the doorbell, the large oak front door was eventually opened by a tall thin woman with long black hair.

She was dressed in a knee length black skirt and a cream blouse that was unbuttoned down to her cleavage. She flicked a strand of her jet black hair away from her eyes and peered out into the cold air. Martin got the distinct impression that she had just woken.

'Good afternoon, how can I help you?' she asked stepping forward.

'I'm sorry to bother ma'am but I was wondering if it would be possible to have a quick word with you and your husband.'

She seemed to hesitate for a moment before answering.

'Is there something wrong?'

'It's regarding the body that was found this morning by Rowan Lodge.'

'Body, what body?'

She put her hand to her neck pulling her blouse close.

'I'm sorry ma'am. I thought your husband would have informed you. A body of a young woman was found dead this morning in the coal shed behind Rowan Lodge.'

At that moment Brian Hargreaves came striding down the wide oak staircase, almost running towards to the front door.

'Hello constable, I'm sorry but when I came home I went straight to my study. I've not spoken to my wife yet.'

'What's this all about?' she asked looking quite shaken.

He placed his arm around her shoulders and pulled her close to him.

'Yeah sorry, I forgot to mention it. I received a business call on my mobile just as I pulled in and it completely went out of my mind. Come in constable. It's cold out there.'

The woman was clearly shaken as Brian Hargreaves led the way into the drawing room. A large Doberman lay next to the fireplace and growled as they entered.

'It's alright boy.' Hargreaves stroked the dog behind its ear and the dog seemed to relax.

Feeling somewhat uncomfortable in the luxurious surroundings Martin sat in one of the divan chairs whilst the woman who he assumed to be Mrs Hargreaves sat in the middle of a large settee, toying with the buttons on her blouse. The drawing room dated back almost two centuries with an intricate plaster moulded high ceiling and huge stone fireplace whose raised hearth now accommodated a wood burning stove gave the room a palatial feel. Several large paintings of hunting scenes adorned each wall.

'I'm sorry to have caused you any distress,' said Martin while they were waiting for her husband to return with the some tea.

'It's just a shock,' she replied. 'I had no idea.'

Martin couldn't understand why her husband had failed to mention the fact that a body had been discovered but decided not to pursue that issue for the moment.

He noticed that she hadn't taken her eyes off the dog since her husband had left the room.

Brian Hargreaves could be heard walking across the patterned oak block floor in the hallway a few moments before he re-entered the room. He placed a silver tray on the tiled coffee table.

'Sorry to have kept you but unfortunately we don't have a maid at the moment. Is Earl Grey, OK with you?' he asked as he began to pour from the teapot.

'Yes fine. No milk or sugar though.'

It was only when tea had been served and everyone was seated did Hargreaves decide to continue. He sat sideways on the settee and placed a hand on his wife's leg who tried to force a smile. Martin thought she looked uncomfortable at her husband's approach but put it down to the fact that she had just been informed of a death.

'I would have told you when I came down, but to be honest I'd received a call from our solicitor saying I needed to answer some correspondence immediately.

You know what it's like. If you don't do these things straight away they can become very costly.'

'But someone has been murdered for God's sake. How can you forget that,' she exclaimed.

Martin gave a polite cough.

'We don't know yet whether or not someone was murdered ma'am, although I don't believe anyone would bury themselves in a coal shed.'

'Oh, no of course not, I just assumed….'

'All we know at present is that a body was found in the coal shed behind Rowan Lodge,' Hargreaves interrupted.

There was an eerie silence for a few seconds.

'I don't suppose you know who the poor person is yet?' he asked.

'No sir, not at this stage in our enquiry.'

'Is Annie alright?'

'I take it that you mean Mrs Griffin. Yes, she's fine. Quite a strong old lady,' replied Martin who quickly finished his tea.

'I appreciate this has all been a bit of a shock but I do need to ask you a few questions.'

'Yes of course,' Brian replied. 'We're happy to help in any way we can, aren't we dear.'

He placed his arm around his wife's shoulder and leaned back in the chair. Martin couldn't help but notice how uncomfortable she seemed.

'How long have you lived at Melcham Hall?'

'My wife was born here and I've lived here for the past nine years. May I ask why you need to know?'

'I just want to get a feel of who everyone is and who knows who in the village. I mean, if you've lived here for several years then I assume you must know most people in such a small community.'

'Well, yes of course, we know most people. Although like anywhere these days there are always people one never gets to meet.'

'Have you or your wife seen any strangers around lately?'

Martin noticed how Hargreaves increased his grip on his wife's shoulder as soon as he asked the question.

'I'm sure I can speak for both us,' he said, 'apart from the lad who delivers the daily papers there hasn't been anyone on the estate except for ourselves.'

Having asked a series of further questions Martin concluded that he wasn't going to get a great deal of information out of either Mr or Mrs Hargreaves right now. He'd skimmed through the notes he'd taken and would follow them up once back in the station. After thanking them both for their time and hospitality he made his way back across the estate, pulling the collar up on his uniform jacket. The snow was falling heavier again and a blustery wind had increased the chill factor. At the top of the hill he turned back to look at Melcham Hall.

Experience told him something wasn't right, but at the moment he couldn't put his finger on it.

2

Wesley put the suitcase down in the hallway while Jane closed the front door. It was the first holiday they had taken since they had moved to Street in the West Country some eighteen months ago. They had just returned from spending ten days with David O'Hara and his family in southern France where conversations had centred more on fishing and vineyards than police work. David and Wesley had met a couple of years previous when as a private investigator David had asked Wesley for help in solving a murder. Un-be-knowing to them at the time, the case was to take them half way around Europe resulting in them coming face to face with the Devil himself. Since then, Wesley had hoped for a quieter life away from London but he hadn't accounted for local myths and beliefs. In his first year as Inspector at Street, in the West Country, he'd uncovered the tomb and resting place of the legendary King Arthur and his wife Guinevere whilst investigating a kidnap case. It was a secret that he'd decided not to share with the public, choosing to allow the legendary king to remain resting in peace.

'It's lovely to go on holiday but it's always nice to come home,' Jane exclaimed as she filled the kettle.

Home now was Jasmine Cottage in the sleepy village of Street. A million miles away from the hustle and bustle of London and the hectic life they both used to live. Wesley was still unpacking the suitcase when Mandy called him to explain the text she'd previously sent, and what had happened since.

'Do we know who the victim is yet?'

'No sir. The DNA doesn't match anyone on record. Terry Austin has said he'll provide you with more information as soon as he can. He estimates the woman to be somewhere in her mid-twenties.'

'How long has she been dead?'

'Again, Terry says it's only an estimate at this stage, but he reckons no more than two days ago. What he is sure about is that the body was only placed in the coal shed overnight, several hours after the person had died.'

'So the victim was moved some considerable time after death?'

'Yes it seems that way.'

'Have we spoken to anyone yet apart from Annie Griffin?'

'Martin had a brief chat with Mr and Mrs Hargreaves. They own Melcham Hall and the estate that Annie's lodge is on. Martin thinks they were very reserved in their reaction to the discovery. Apparently Mrs

Hargreaves said that her husband hadn't even mentioned the incident to her.'

'I find that hard to believe,' Wesley replied cursing as he trapped his fingers in the suitcase.

'Yeah, Martin says he going to talk to you when you're back in the office tomorrow. He wants to interview them separately but wants your opinion on the matter first.'

'OK that's fine. Where's Annie Griffin now?'

'She's at home. She refused to go to hospital for a check-up. Dr Meadows has been in to see her and is going back again this evening. One of the social workers has stayed with her and I'm on my way back there shortly to make sure she's comfortable.'

'Good work, Mandy. Ah well. Back to reality eh?'

'I didn't ask you. Did you and Jane have a good time?'

'Yeah we did thanks. I have to admit we're both a little sunburnt.'

'What at this time of the year?'

'It's hard to believe, but yes. Oh we saw plenty of snow alright, but most days were warm and sunny and we ended up walking everywhere. It was very relaxing.'

'How are David and the family? Have they settled in France OK?'

'They're all fine, Mandy. They love it over there. It's a different world to how they all used to live and his daughter no longer suffers so badly from the asthma that almost took her life when they were living in the pollution of dear old London.'

'Ah that's good to hear. Well welcome home, sir. I'm sorry to have been the bearer of bad news as soon as you arrived home.'

'Don't apologise Mandy, you're only doing your job, and a good one at that.'

Wesley couldn't see her blush.

'Leave a report on my desk for the morning and we'll catch up tomorrow.'

'Sure thing, please send Jane my regards.'

'I'll do that. Thanks, Mandy.'

Wesley hung up and inspected the black looking pinch that had already formed on his finger.

When Wesley re-entered the kitchen he found Jane sat at the table working her way through a stack of mail.

'Look at this lot. We've only been away ten days,' she exclaimed. 'At least we kept the postman busy.'

'I guess it's mostly my fan mail,' Wesley replied with a smirk on his face.

'You wish,' she replied. 'You can make yourself useful by sticking that lot in the washing machine.' Jane pointed to the dirty washing that lay on the floor.

'Who was that on the phone?' she asked.

'That was Mandy. A body was found in someone's coal shed on the

Melcham estate on the outskirts of Shepton Mallet.'

'Oh my God, was it an accident?'

'It's too early to tell yet, the pathologist has said he'll know more by tomorrow. It seems unlikely that it was an accident. You'd have to bury yourself under coal. I know its early days but it sounds like a murder to me.'

'The very thought of just being outside in this weather sends shivers down my spine,' Jane remarked.

Wesley pulled back the curtain on the kitchen window and peered outside. Heavy snow was falling and the grey skies above forebode of more to come. Their pretty back garden was just a white blank.

'If this snow keeps up all night, there's a chance I won't be able to get into the office tomorrow,' he said.

'I hope it doesn't, I'm due back in tomorrow too. It's been nearly three weeks since I was at work, I can't afford to miss another day.'

Following the sale of the bookshop in Glastonbury, Jane had taken a job as a part-time receptionist at the Wells Hospital. It was a world apart from her previous job working in the bookshop in Glastonbury. She now dealt with a multitude of issues relating to peoples operations, injections, health concerns, and births and deaths.

'Oh, am I in luck then? Are you wearing the nurse's uniform tonight?'

'In your dreams, John Wesley, now put that washing in the machine and go finish with the unpacking while I sort out something to eat.'

The drive back to Rowan Lodge took Mandy over an hour. Snow had continued to fall all afternoon making a couple of the minor roads virtually impassable. Fortunately Mandy knew the area well and used her knowledge to take the easiest route available. The A361 between Street and Shepton Mallet was fine as the continual flow of traffic melted the snow straight away but as soon as Mandy turned right into Long Hill, the country lane and path became as one.

As she rounded the second bend, a hundred yards from Rowan Lodge and the entrance to the Melcham estate, Brian Hargreaves' jaguar sped out of the turning heading towards Frome, throwing snow and slush in all directions. Mandy made a note of the car's registration details before putting a call into the station to get the car checked out.

'I'm going to have that bastard,' she muttered to herself.

Mandy let herself in via the back door as requested by Annie. It was a country custom that friends and relatives entered from the back door and not the front, something that Mandy was used to being a country girl. Born in Frome, Mandy was the only daughter of Edward and Margaret Tredwell. Her father Edward was the major business partner in Tredwell and Nugent, the biggest solicitors in Frome. Mandy's parents had always hoped she would follow her father's footsteps and join the practice and were astonished when

Mandy announced she was joining the police force. However, it was an easy decision for Mandy as she couldn't face being sat behind a desk for the rest of her career and the police force seemed the ideal choice. Her father's initial reaction had been to try and talk her out of the idea but he knew Mandy got her stubbornness from him and was never going to change her mind. Since then they had supported her whole heartedly and they were so proud of her when she came WPC Mandy Tredwell.

Annie Griffin was sat in a chair in the front room when Mandy entered.

Annie looked a lot brighter than when Mandy had left her earlier. The room was silent except for the rhythmic ticking of the clock on the mantelpiece.

'Hello my dear,' said Annie putting her knitting on her lap.

'How are you Annie?'

'I'm OK thank you. Pamela here has been a great comfort. She even insisted on cooking me some dinner.'

Social worker Pamela Jenkins appeared from the kitchen. Pamela Jenkins was larger than life, a typical mum Mandy always thought. Their paths had crossed on several occasions over the past couple of years. Everyone in the nearby villages knew Pamela Jenkins. She was always dressed wearing an apron over the top of her cardigan and trousers whatever the weather.

'Hi Mandy, would you care for some tea?'

'That would be lovely thanks.'

'Come and sit down,' said Annie pointing to a chair on the other side of the small fireplace. 'Do we know who the poor girl is yet?'

'What makes you think it was a female?' Mandy asked.

'Well the hand my dear. It was far too small to be a man's.'

'You should have been in the police force,' said Mandy, 'you would have made a good detective.'

Pamela Jenkins placed two teas on the table along with a plate of biscuits and said she was going to visit someone else but would pop in again later.

'I'll close the door to keep the draft out,' she said, leaving Annie and Mandy in the warmth of the tiny front room.

'No, we are waiting for further information from the pathologist, neither the victim's finger prints or DNA exists on record.'

'Do you know how long the body had been in the coal shed?' asked Annie as she reached for her tea that Pamela had just placed in front of them.

'Well according to the pathologist not very long.'

Mandy noticed how Annie's hands were shaking as she held the cup to her lips using both hands.

'Annie is there anything else you can tell us of today's events. I mean, did you see or hear anyone before you found the body?'

Annie placed her cup back on the table.

'I can't say that I did. I didn't go outside at all yesterday because the weather was so bad. It was only because I needed to top up the coal scuttle that I ventured out this morning.'

'I don't suppose you've heard or noticed any vehicles other than Mr Hargreaves' car entering or leaving the estate lately?'

'The only other vehicle belonged to the coal merchant who was here the day before yesterday. It's such a quiet road that one rarely hears a vehicle at all. There is one thing that I forgot to mention. It only crossed my mind this afternoon.'

'What was that Annie?'

'I always slip a block of wood through the loop in the coal shed door handle to keep the door closed. But when I think about, I simply pulled the door open. The block of wood must have been removed. I don't suppose that helps much though does it?' said Annie.

'You never know,' Mandy replied, 'it's worth checking. I'll take a look on the way out.'

When tea had been drunk and biscuits eaten, Annie fell asleep whilst in the process of knitting. Mandy left the room quietly, closed the back door and walked around the back of the building. The door to the coal shed was slightly ajar, wedged in its current location now by a couple of inches of fresh snow. She knew the forensic team had carried out a complete examination of the area so it was extremely doubtful there was anything to be found. She pulled hard on the door to open it just wide enough to allow her to peer inside. There was nothing to see so she leant her back on the door to close it and stood for moment looking at her surroundings. What caught her attention were several small bushes to the side of the coal shed whose lower branches had recently been snapped off. Mandy walked across the uneven snow covered ground, her footprints several inches deep, her shoes getting ruined. Using a gloved hand she brushed away some of the snow from the roots and within seconds caught sight of something. Excavating a little deeper she pulled an object out of the snow. It was a woman's shoe, black with a two inch heel and a simple thin strap that fitted around the ankle. Holding the tip of the strap she carried it back to her car and placed it in a plastic bag for further examination.

When she went back inside, Annie was still fast asleep. Mandy removed the old ladies knitting and placed it on the floor by her side before covering her legs with a blanket. Pamela Jenkins who had a front door key said she would be there for another hour and would make sure the door was bolted before she left.

'I've left my card with my contact details next to the phone if you should need me,' said Mandy.

'Oh we'll be just fine,' Pamela replied. 'Now, where did I put that tea towel?'

3

The following morning Wesley walked into the office accompanied by a chorus of wolf whistles from Mandy and two female support officers.

'Wow, love the sun tan,' Mandy exclaimed. 'A new suit too?'

'Good morning all,' Wesley replied looking rather embarrassed.

'Actually it's an old suit but it's been to the cleaners. I can't afford a new suit on these wages.'

'It must be nice to have a holiday,' said Martin with a smirk on his face.

'It's a shame yours has just been cancelled,' Wesley replied, causing the whole office to erupt in to laughter. 'If you've missed me so much you can go and fetch me a cup of tea.'

The first thing Wesley noticed when he opened the door to his office was how tidy it was. Even the litter bin was empty. He placed his briefcase on the desk and sat down to spend the next hour checking his mail before beckoning both Martin and Mandy to join him.

'Welcome back, sir,' said Martin still smiling.

'So we have a murder on our patch,' said Wesley as he searched his pockets for his tobacco and cigarette papers.

Mandy went over the details again adding that Terry Austin had now confirmed that death was caused by a broken neck.

Wesley nodded as he rolled a cigarette.

'How's this Annie Griffin this morning? I understand she found the body.'

'That's right, sir. One of the social workers stayed with her until late yesterday evening and a welfare officer called on her just after seven this morning. Apparently she seems fine and wants to just get on with things. I have to say she comes across as being both mentally and physically strong for her age. She's seventy-three next year,' Mandy replied.

'Yes and vulnerable, make sure you pop over there today just to keep an eye on her.'

'Yes sir.'

Wesley turned to Martin. 'I believe you're not convinced about the Hargreaves' story. I must admit it does seem strange that Brian Hargreaves omitted to inform his wife of the incident.'

'It's not just that, sir, but I got the feeling they were both holding something back. They continually looked at one another before answering any of my questions. It was almost as if she was frightened to speak.'

'OK, we'll both pay them a visit later this morning. So when is Alison due back?'

'She's back at work next week,' Mandy replied.

'Ah, yes. She's been to Jersey spending time with her parents.'

'Yes, apparently her father's not been too well lately. He had major heart surgery back in the summer.'

'I remember now. Let's hope he's making a full recovery.'

Wesley was about to go into detail regarding the refurbishment plans for the office but was interrupted by the ringing of his mobile phone.

'Inspector Wesley speaking, how can I help?'

'Ah Inspector, its Geoff Dale from the Phoenix public house in Shepton Mallet, you said to give you a call at any time if something was amiss.'

'No problem Geoff, what's up?'

Wesley and Geoff had become good friends over the past eighteen months and Jane and Geoff's wife Maggie socialised at least once a month. Wesley listened as Geoff explained that when he went to open the beer cellar at the back of the pub this morning, one half of the trap door was open and upon closer investigation it appeared as if someone had spent the night sleeping there. He said it could have been a tramp but what with the recent murder he thought he ought to report it. Wesley thanked him for the call and said that he and Martin would be over shortly as they were already planning to visit Melcham Hall nearby.

'Coincidence?' asked Mandy shrugging her shoulders after Wesley fed them the conversation.

'I don't know, Mandy. It could be. Let's face it; hardly anything ever happens in Shepton Mallet does it?'

Although he usually preferred to drive, Wesley allowed Martin the privilege and promised himself that he wouldn't criticize the lad's driving.

Taking the A road from Street they immediately joined a slow moving queue of traffic. Banks of snow were piled up along kerbs and paths and stacked against hedgerows, having been recently shovelled aside by a road sweeper.

'I hear a few of the side roads are still impassable,' said Martin, 'that's why the main road is so busy.'

'It looks pretty enough,' Wesley replied, 'not sure I'd want to be walking about in it though.'

They spent fifteen minutes travelling less than three miles before they reached the junction where they had to turn off to reach the Phoenix. Geoff Dale was stood in the car park at the side of the pub shovelling snow away from the parking bays when they arrived. He greeted Wesley with a firm handshake before being introduced to PC Martin Philips who had trudged gingerly behind trying not to get his freshly polished shoes too wet.

'Let's go inside. I'll get Maggie to make some tea.'

Inside the pub Geoff directed them to a table near a log fire then excused himself while he removed his jacket and wellington boots.

The Phoenix was one of the oldest pubs in the county, dating back to the eighteenth century. It was said that the pub was haunted by a local highwayman who was murdered whilst staying overnight. The story said that he wandered the upstairs corridor at night seeking his revenge. Rows of silver jugs hung the length of the bar and numerous cider barrels were dotted around the lounge bar, being used as tables. To an outsider it probably looked a bit rough and ready but to the locals it was the homeliest and most welcoming pub for miles.

Geoff Dale returned at the same time as his wife Maggie who laid the table with teas and Cornish pasties.

'Tuck into these, they're on the house,' she said. 'You'll need something warm inside you on a day like this. I'm trying an old recipe that my mother used to use so you can tell me what you think of them.'

'Thanks Maggie, that's very kind of you, and much appreciated,' said Wesley.

Martin already had a mouthful of pasty and put his hand up in acknowledgment.

'So you think someone has been sleeping in the beer cellar?' Wesley asked as Geoff took a bite of his pasty.

'At a guess I would say so yes. You see, the last thing I do at night is to make sure the cellar door is shut, even though I simply slide a plank of wood across the loops. Anyhow, this morning the wood was stood against the back wall and one side of the cellar door was open. However, I would think that whoever had slept there left in a hurry this morning. Maybe whoever it was heard Maggie and me walking around in the pub. These old floorboards do creak somewhat.'

Wesley wiped his face with a serviette and took a sip of tea.

'Has this happened before?' asked Martin.

'Actually, yes it has. Several years back we found a young school child hiding in the cellar. It came to light that his step-father had been beating him so he ran away from home.'

'Poor little sod,' Wesley exclaimed.

He had seen some terrible sights working in London, some that he'd never forget. It was where children were involved that he found hard to handle. Grown-ups often fight, but to Wesley's mind there was never an excuse to harm children.

'Let's go and have a look shall we?' said Wesley when everyone had finished eating. Geoff led the way through the kitchens to the emergency exit at the back of the pub retrieving his coat and wellington boots on route. A cold wind blew around the outside of the old building and the pub sign groaned as it swung back and forth. Having carefully negotiated the wooden steps that led down to the cellar, Wesley and Martin waited for Geoff to switch on the naked light bulb that hung from a wooden support in the middle of the low ceiling.

'Mind your head you two. I'm only a squirt so it doesn't bother me.'

'All mod cons I see,' commented Wesley pointing to the single naked bulb swinging on the end of the cord.

'Always believed in having the latest equipment,' Geoff replied laughing.

Pointing to a small recess between the beer barrels at the far end of the room, Geoff walked forward and extracted a small plastic carrier bag and a blue woollen scarf.

'This is where I found these this morning,' he said holding both items aloft.

Wesley carried them across to a small wooden bench where he tipped the contents of the carrier bag out. The items included a pair of grey men's trousers, a short sleeve shirt, a blue woollen scarf, tooth brush and a pair of reading glasses.

'Not much to go on Geoff, but we'll take these away and get the lab boys to go over them. You never know, maybe someone's DNA is on them.'

Wesley replaced all the items including the scarf back into the bag and handed it over to Martin.

'Isn't there a local hostel just up the road?' Martin asked.

'Yeah there is,' Geoff replied. 'What makes you ask?'

'Well it doesn't make sense for someone to kip rough in your cellar when they could have found shelter in the hostel.'

'You've raised a good point there,' said Wesley. 'One can only assume that whoever slept here is in hiding for some reason.'

'You mean someone on the run?' Geoff asked.

'Possibly, people don't usually sleep rough unless there's a damn good reason.'

'It could also have been someone who doesn't know the area,' Martin commented.

Back in the pub car park Wesley thanked Geoff and asked him to tell Maggie that the pasties were delicious. As they drive away, leaving Geoff to continue shovelling snow away from the more exposed areas at the side of the pub Wesley made a call to Bath HQ asking for details to be sent to Street police of any known suspects on the run and a list of missing persons.

Mandy's early morning visit to Rowan Lodge found Annie Griffin busy in her kitchen rolling pastry for a meat pie that she was making. Mandy had just finished a cup of tea when her mobile rang. She listened as Terry Austin confirmed the shoe she had found the previous night as belonging to the victim.

Not only that but the back of the shoe had been roughed up, suggesting that whoever was wearing it had been dragged backwards.

Thanking Terry for the information she hung up.

'You'll wipe the pattern off those dishes,' Mandy said watching Annie searching in a drawer for a clean tea towel.

'You're probably right. Sorry but it's a habit of mine. I always wipe the dishes twice before I put them away.'

'Come and sit down,' said Mandy.

Annie folded the tea towel and laid it on the draining board, then checked the oven temperature on the cooker before pulling up a chair.

'So where is that dishy young constable today?'

Mandy couldn't help but laugh.

'If you're referring to PC Philips then he's on his way to Melcham Hall this morning with Inspector Wesley.'

'Oh, is Brian Hargreaves a suspect?' Annie asked as she raised her hands to her face.

'Everyone is a suspect until we prove otherwise,' Mandy replied.

'Including me?'

'No Annie. We're sure you didn't harm anyone.'

Mandy placed a comforting hand on Annie's arm.

'I would like to ask you a question though.'

'Of course you can my dear. What is it?'

'I was wondering if you knew why Brian Hargreaves' wife Lucy still uses her maiden name and not her married name. It may be nothing but I looked at the owner details of Brian Hargreaves' car this morning and although the car is registered to him, there are two named drivers, Brian Hargreaves and Lucy Melcham. As I say, it may be nothing.'

'I do know the answer as a matter of fact. It's quite an interesting story really. You see, Lucy's father Sir Clive Melcham, was quite a mistrusting man and it was common knowledge at the time that he didn't like or trust Brian Hargreaves. Now although he did agree to their marriage, he apparently made an amendment to his will that stipulated that Brian would only become a part beneficiary of the Melcham estate upon their tenth wedding anniversary. As a result, Lucy said she would continue to use her maiden name until that time.'

'I assume by doing so he implied that Brian would have to prove his love for his daughter and remain married to her for at least ten years.'

'That's exactly right.'

'Have you any idea why he mistrusted Brian Hargreaves?'

Mandy noticed Annie's reaction to this question. The woman seemed to take some time before answering.

'Lucy had been engaged to another young man before Brian Hargreaves appeared on the scene, and I believe there was a bit of trouble when she called off the engagement.'

'What kind of trouble?'

'I don't recall the details but it had something to do with Brian and the other chap falling out. Brian was a bit of a rogue when he was younger and there were rumours that he only asked for Lucy's hand in marriage to help resolve his financial problems.'

'Hmm that's interesting to know,' Mandy replied. 'I have one last question if I may?'

'Of course my dear, ask away.'

'Do you know if anyone is employed at Melcham Hall? I mean, it's a big place to look after.'

'They've had a few people over the last couple of years to do the cleaning. But none of them last very long.'

'Why do you think that is?'

Annie raised her eyebrows and shrugged her shoulders.

'At a guess I'd say it was probably something to do with Brian Hargreaves. As I said, he was rogue when he was younger and I've seen nothing to show that he's changed. That's all I want to say on the matter.'

Mandy reached across the table and placed her hands over one of Annie's frail hands.

'You've been a great help, Annie. What is that you're cooking? It sure does smell good.'

'It's only a meat pie for my dinner. I usually make a selection of fruit pies at the beginning of the week but I really can't be bothered today. I might have to make do with a banana cake I purchased from the local shop. Their cakes are never as nice as my home made ones, although I'd never tell them that,' she replied laughing.

Jane walked through the main entrance to Wells hospital and was immediately conscious of the volume of noise coming from the multiple conversations being held around the reception desk and a voice on the intercom system asking for a Doctor Stevens to report to the Falcon Ward as a matter of urgency. She said good morning to her colleague Rachel who was in mid-sentence of a conversation with a young woman who was demanding an earlier appointment for her x-ray as she was in constant pain and the doctor had informed her that the sooner she had an x-ray done, the better.

Having changed into her receptionist uniform Jane took a seat behind the counter and logged on to a spare computer. Rachel told her she would cover the desk whilst Jane caught up on her mails. She was reading a mail concerning a proposed new shift pattern when her concentration was broken by someone peering at her over the counter. Jane looked up at the friendly bearded face of Gerry Callow. Gerry was known to all his friends as the friendly giant who now ran the bookshop in Glastonbury. When the old bookshop closed and the flat above had been put up for sale he had made an offer to buy the place outright. Some people questioned his decision to pay the asking price at a time when the number of tourists had been on a decline for several years, but Gerry was not only large in size he was large in ambition and saw the shop as a stepping stone to bigger things. He and Jane had met when he first viewed the premises and had become friends ever since.

'Gerry, what are you doing here?'

As she stood up he leaned his huge bulk over the counter and kissed her on the cheek.

'Oh nothing serious, just a quick check up, I had bit of a chest pain a week back so I came in for some tests and today is just a follow-up.'

Jane was reluctant to make any comment about his fitness; he didn't need telling he was overweight and out of condition, and decided not to ask too many questions.

'Are you feeling OK now?'

'Yeah, fighting fit,' he exclaimed and motioned as if he was punching his chest.

'You're looking well, Jane. Where have you been? No one gets that colour around here.'

'Actually, today is my first day back. John and I have just returned from a holiday in France so I'm trying to catch up on my mail. What did we ever do before we had computers?'

'People used to read books and write letters, not all this automated jargon,' he replied.

Jane had forgotten that Gerry was a man who would have preferred to have lived thirty years ago in a time when pen and paper still ruled the world.

'So, when are you coming over to visit? You know you don't have to wait for an invite,' said Jane.

'I know, and it's very kind of you. I promise I'll call at the weekend and pop over if you and John are around.'

'Make sure you do,' she replied smiling.

Gerry blew her a kiss and waved goodbye. Jane watched the gentle giant as he trudged towards the lift area where several other people were already queuing waiting for lifts to arrive. Jane never did understand the hospitals philosophy for making heart patients travel up to the 3rd floor.

4

Melcham Hall looked imposing in the grey light of winter as PC Martin Philips drove the patrol car into the Melcham estate and descended the hill towards the front of the building. Wesley remarked how drab the building looked and pointed to the poor state of the external walls, where several areas of brickwork were left exposed where external plastering had broken away.

'It's different inside,' Martin replied, 'quite a palace really. At a guess, I'd say the owners have just spent a considerable sum in redecoration over the past few years.'

'Hmm let's take a look,' said Wesley stepping out of the car.

'If I'm not mistaken, I'd swear that someone was watching us from one of the upstairs windows,' said Martin as they walked across the snow covered gravel drive towards the front door.

'Yeah, I did notice.' Wesley rolled the remains of his cigarette between thumb and forefinger and let the remains fall to the ground before pushing the doorbell.

After several moments footsteps could be heard inside just before Brian Hargreaves opened the front door looking flustered.

It was Wesley who spoke first.

'Good morning, Inspector Wesley.' Wesley produced his ID to Hargreaves who responded somewhat hesitantly. It was obvious the visit had caught him by surprise.

'Err, good morning Inspector. How can I help you?'

'May we come in? It's pretty chilly out here.'

With some reluctance Hargreaves stood back and beckoned Wesley and Martin into the house.

'I'm sorry to bother you,' Wesley exclaimed. 'I hope we haven't called at an inconvenient time.'

Wesley forced a smile, gauging Hargreaves' reaction.

'Oh no of course not Inspector, I was just a little surprised that's all, especially as I have already spoken with your colleague here.'

'Yes, my constable did mention that he'd called round but as I was already in the area I thought I ought to show face, so to speak. I mean, it's not every day a dead body is found on the estate is it?' Wesley grinned.

Brian Hargreaves gave a nervous laugh as he closed the front door.

Wesley noticed how uncomfortable the man looked as his eyes constantly darted from Wesley to Martin as if he was seeking some form of comfort from somewhere.

'Come through to the front parlour. It's much warmer in there.'

Wesley had to admit that the hallway looked rather grand, with oak panelled walls and an oak panelled staircase that wound its way against the right hand wall turning at the top to open onto a galleried landing. The large flagstone covered floor gave the visitor the impression of a much older property as did the hand pulls hanging by the side of the doors leading off the hallway. A record of time gone by, when one would ring for when servants to provide drinks or nourishment.

Hargreaves led them into the parlour where two large paintings of hunting scenes adorned the side walls. Above the fireplace was a painting of who Wesley assumed to be Sir Clive Melcham. It certainly matched the description he'd been given. A fierce looking man with dark piercing eyes that seemed to follow you around the room. Wesley and Martin sat on the black leather sofa but Hargreaves remained standing with his back to the window. He distinctly gave the impression of someone who was hoping this was a brief visit rather than an extended chat.

'So how can I be of help, Inspector?'

'I understand you and Mrs Hargreaves own the estate. Is that correct?'

'Yes we do, but I don't understand what that has to do with someone being murdered?'

'I didn't say anyone had been murdered,' Wesley replied.

'Oh, I just assumed…'

'The pathologist is still trying to identify the cause of death.'

Wesley looked directly at Hargreaves who coughed to clear his throat.

'You will have to excuse me Inspector. It's all been a bit of a shock.'

'Especially for Annie Griffin who found the body,' said Martin.

'Hmm, yes quite so.'

'Mr Hargreaves. Is your wife at home?' Wesley had already become impatient.

'Yes she is, but unfortunately she's not too well this morning. She suffers terribly from migraines. Dr Meadows has recently prescribed some new tablets that have just come on the market.'

He fumbled with the button on his cardigan. 'The migraines have been getting worse lately.'

'I'm sorry to hear that,' Wesley replied, 'in which case we shan't keep you long. Can I ask how long you have you have known Annie Griffin?'

The question seemed to take Hargreaves by surprise.

'I've known Annie for quite a number of years now, Inspector.' Hargreaves explained how Annie and her husband had come to live on the estate and how she was told by Sir Clive Melcham that she could remain living in the lodge following her husband's death. Wesley had already heard this from Mandy but wanted to hear if there was any resentment in Hargreaves' response.

'I would imagine Annie sees just about every visitor to the estate, especially as anyone would have to pass the lodge on their way in.'

'Yes I guess she does but I still don't see….'

'You see what's confusing, is that Annie says the last visitor she had was the coal merchant some two days. Since then, she's sure no one else apart from you has passed the lodge recently. Which infers that whoever the poor soul is who was found in the coal shed must have come from this side of the estate.'

'What are you trying to say, Inspector?'

Wesley shrugged his shoulders.

'Just seems odd to me that someone could have been on your estate without either you or your wife knowing about it.'

'I don't think I like your accusation,' Hargreaves replied puffing out his chest.

'Don't get upset Mr Hargreaves, I'm not accusing you or wife of anything. I'm just stating the facts as I see them.'

Wesley raised his eyebrows as he stared at Brian Hargreaves who did his best to avoid any eye contact.

'Well if there's nothing else then, I'm afraid I have some business matters I need to attend to.'

Hargreaves walked towards the door. Wesley nodded to Martin and they followed slowly behind. Wesley knew from experience that he was unlikely to get much else out of Brian Hargreaves right now. However, the moment they stepped outside Wesley turned back before Hargreaves closed the front door.

'Just one last question Mr Hargreaves, does anyone apart from you have keys to the main gate?'

'Err, no just me.'

The front door slammed shut as soon as Wesley and Martin stepped away. Wesley looked to Martin who grinned.

'That sure is one happy bunny, sir. He couldn't wait to get rid of us.'

'Yeah, I think we're going to be speaking with Brian Hargreaves again very soon. The chap is nervous for some reason. It's almost like he's expecting us to ask a particular question that he has no answer to. We just need to choose the right question.'

Wesley was back in his office talking with Martin when Mandy entered the room. Both men looked up in admiration.

'Wow, I love the new hairstyle,' Martin exclaimed.

'Yes, it looks lovely. It suits you,' Wesley commented, seeming to blush at the same time.

'Thanks. I thought it was time for a change.' Mandy patted the back of her hair which was now cut into a bob. The long strands of black hair were now gone.

'I went to the new hair dressers in Glastonbury last night. They are doing a special discount for new customers.'

'Perhaps you should go, sir,' said Martin. 'They might be able to get rid of the grey hairs that are appearing.'

'It's a hair dresser not a magician,' Wesley replied causing laughter all round.

Mandy provided them with a brief update of her chat with Annie Griffin.

'She's not a bad judge of character,' said Wesley when Mandy had finished.

'That Brian Hargreaves seems dodgy to me too. Let's put it this way. I don't trust the man and I've only met him once. He couldn't wait for us to leave.'

Wesley walked over to the wipe board where he'd already scribbled a few notes. Luckily for Mandy and Martin they'd learned how to read his scribble by now so could follow most of what was written.

'Mandy, will you check the missing persons list and anything else that's relevant. We still don't know who the murder victim is. Someone must have known her. Spread the net if you have to. I want to know who she is.'

'Martin, I want you to pay a visit to Hooper's coal merchants. Here's the address.' He handed over a slip of paper that he'd torn from his diary.

'They're based in Wells, so shouldn't be hard to find. The owner is a chap named Gary Hooper. He took the business over from his father some years back. Find out how often they deliver coal to Annie, the date and time of the last visit, and did the driver see anything unusual. You know the drill.'

Wesley walked back to his desk where he retrieved his tobacco and papers and began rolling a cigarette.

'I'm going to pay a visit to the council offices. I've already spoken with Jim Hansen. He's going to provide details relating to the ownership of Melcham Hall and the estate.'

Wesley found a used match to poke the tobacco ends into the roll-up.

'Any questions either of you?'

'You may want to ask if they keep any records of people working at Melcham Hall as well,' said Mandy.

'Yeah that's a good point. I doubt it but it's worth a try. That new haircut has certainly got you thinking,' Wesley replied with a smirk on his face.

A rusty blue and white metal boarding slumped against a slatted wooden fence at the end of the industrial estate was the only signpost to *'Charlie Cooper's Coal Merchants'*. Martin pulled up alongside the entrance to the site and exited the vehicle. The moment he stepped outside the car he was immediately greeted by a fierce looking Alsatian dog that suddenly appeared from behind the wrought iron gate. Martin took a step back before he realised the dog was chained up and couldn't get any closer to him. The animals barking had alerted the occupant who now strode across the courtyard.

Martin flashed is ID through the gate at who he assumed was Gary Hooper, seeing as the man's face and hands were already blackened by coal.

'Sorry about that but we used to get coal stolen on a regular basis. That was until we employed Bruno.' He stroked the dog's ears as the animal seemed to relax. Martin waited for the man to unlock the gate before gingerly entering the site. He'd always had a fear of large dogs and couldn't hide his discomfort.

'Don't worry about him. He won't hurt you now I've let you in.'

The young lad extended his arm to shake hands.

'Gary Hooper's the name. Charlie was my father. He passed away a few years back so I took the company over. How can I help you, officer?' he asked as he led the way across the forecourt towards an old portakabin.

Martin looked down at his soot covered hand before replying.

'We're following up on a possible murder enquiry.'

Gary stopped in his tracks and turned to face Martin.

'Do what? A murder enquiry you say?' Christ, how am I involved?'

'Let's go inside and I can provide you with some details.'

Every inch of space in the portakabin was covered in either box files, magazines or what appeared to be piles of invoices. Gary picked up a huge pile of papers from an old leather chair and added them to another pile on top of a tall grey filing cabinet.

'Take a seat. You'll have to excuse the mess, but I never get time to do much paperwork. As long as I invoice people I don't worry too much.'

He slumped himself down in a moth eaten swivel chair on the other side of a small wooden desk.

'So what's this all about?' Gary asked a he lit a cigarette.

'I understand you deliver to Annie Griffin, Rowan Lodge, in Shepton Mallet.'

'Old Annie, yeah I do, been delivery coal there since I was a lad. Is she OK?'

'Yes she's fine, but the problem we have is that she found a dead body in her coal shed yesterday.'

Gary stubbed the remaining half of his cigarette out in the ashtray.

'Come again. Are you serious?'

'I wouldn't kid you about something like that,' Martin replied.

'Bloody hell poor old Annie. That must have been some shock for her.'

'Yes it was. Although the body was found yesterday, we believe the person was probably murdered a day or two before that. Are you able to tell me when you last made a delivery to Rowan Lodge?'

'I can tell you without looking at the book. It was on the 20th, around four-thirty in the afternoon. I made the delivery myself. I only have one person working for me, Jamie Kearns, but he's taken the whole week off. It's ideal for me as it's usually quiet in the week leading up to Christmas believe it or not. Most people have pre-ordered their winter supply long before now. On top of which, I don't get another delivery to the yard until the New Year.'

Gary scratched his head and reached for another cigarette.

'Oh my God, do you think the body was already there when I threw another few bags of coal into the shed?'

'No we don't, Mr Hooper. It's the pathologist's view that the body had been placed in the coal shed not long before Annie Griffin found it.'

'Poor old, Annie.'

'Can you cast your mind back to when you made the delivery? Was there anything that seemed unusual? Or was there anyone about that you didn't recognise?'

Gary Hooper rubbed his soot covered hand across his face and screwed his nose up before answering.

'There was certainly no one else around. Annie waved to me out of the kitchen window before coming to the back door. I told her to stay indoors because of the weather. She wished me and the family a happy Christmas before I drove off.'

'So you saw no one else?'

'Nope, the place is pretty desolate at the best of times. Do you know who the person is?'

'No, not yet I'm afraid.'

Martin stood to leave.

'OK, thanks Mr Hooper. If you do think of anything though, please give me a call.'

Martin handed him a card across the table.

'Don't worry, I'll see myself out.'

As he crossed the yard Martin stopped to take a quick look at the tyres of Hooper's coal lorry and made a note of their make and size. The Alsatian was now spread out on the floor and didn't take any notice of him.

Wesley sat in the car park of the local council offices and remembered when he'd last visited the place some eighteen months ago. That day he and council employee Gary Knowles agreed to keep a secret, a secret that if leaked would have changed the face of Glastonbury forever.

Since then Gary had changed careers as was now studying to become a full-time archaeologist.

'So, Sir Clive Melcham's father had Melcham Hall built then?'

'Sure did, Inspector.'

Wesley was sat with Jim Hansen in the council records office. There wasn't a building in existence in the whole of the county that Jim couldn't provide the history to.

'How did the man make his money?'

'Back in the late1800's his own father owned several dairy farms in

Somerset and Devon which he then sold when land started to become more valuable. That's when the family moved to Shepton Mallet and had Melcham Hall built. Our records show that part of the original estate at Melcham Hall was used for farming right up to the 1950's.'

'So where was Sir Clive Melcham born?'

'He was born at Melcham Hall. He was their only child. Lord Melcham's wife died during childbirth. Following her death he sold the remaining farms and invested his money into stocks and shares for his son. Sir Clive and his wife Maria, she was Italian by birth, then had two children, both girls, Lucy and Kate.'

'I assume Sir Clive and his wife are both deceased?' asked Wesley.

'Actually no, Sir Clive passed away from pneumonia ten years ago but following their earlier divorce, Maria moved back to Italy. It was quite an amicable break-up and I understand she returned home quite a wealthy woman. If she is alive she'll be in her nineties by now.'

'So the estate was left to Lucy and Kate?'

'Yes sort of.'

'What do you mean?'

'It appears that Lucy and Kate are like chalk and cheese. Lucy is the business woman who always stayed at home whereas Kate is the born again hippy who decided she was bored with home life and told her father she was going to travel the world. When he threatened to remove her name from his will everyone thought she would back down and remain at Melcham Hall. However, she did exactly what she had said she would do. She bought a camper van, packed her bags and drove off into the sunset.'

'And where is she now?'

'The last I heard she was living somewhere in France on some hippy commune. I only know that because until a couple of years ago she used to stay in touch with my daughter. You see, they all went to school together.'

Wesley put a hand to his forehead, a habit when he was confused.

'So let me get this right. Lucy is now married to Brian Hargreaves.'

'That's right,' Jim Hansen replied, 'but she still uses her own surname.'

'OK Jim, I give up, another twist?'

'Rumour has it that Sir Clive didn't like Lucy's choice of husband. She married Brian Hargreaves just weeks before Sir Clive passed away. It was no secret that Sir Clive viewed Brian Hargreaves as a bit of a rogue, and off the record he was probably right. In any case, in his will Sir Clive stipulated that none of the estate or in fact none of his assets would ever be passed down to Brian until Brian and Lucy had been married for ten years. He wanted Brian to show that he loved Lucy and would remain faithful to her.'

Wesley sat back in the chair and crossed his legs.

'So let me get this right. With Kate Melcham excluded from Sir Clive's will and Brian Hargreaves excluded until his tenth wedding anniversary, Lucy Hargreaves inherited everything.'

'That's correct Inspector. Lucy Melcham is one very wealthy lady.'

'One last thing,' said Wesley, 'I understand Melcham Hall was used as a nursing home during the war and for a short period afterwards.'

'Yes it was. From nineteen forty-three to about the end of forty-six I believe. It was really a hospice for the terminally ill, those whose war injuries were beyond repair.'

'Where was Sir Clive living during this period?'

'Oh, he and his wife lived in the annex. She was a nurse you know. When the last patient passed away, Sir Clive paid for a complete refurbishment of the local hospital so they could take in any future patients who had suffered during the war. Shortly after that he had Melcham Hall restored to what you see today. The refurbishment cost him a small fortune at the time.'

'What's the estate worth?'

'That's a difficult one,' said Jim. 'At a guess I'd say the whole estate is probably worth somewhere in the region of £2.5 million.'

'Phew,' breathed Wesley. 'A nice few bob then.'

'It sounds great, Inspector. The problem these days is the cost of the upkeep of something so large. It's really not a viable proposition for most people. I mean, there are over twenty rooms in Melcham Hall and at the end of the day as far as I know, there's only two people living there.'

'Yeah I see what you mean. Couldn't they open the place up to the public?'

'They could for sure, but that comes with a cost. I'm led to believe that a considerable sum of money would need to be spent on restoration work before they did that.'

'Hmm, it becomes a bit of a vicious circle doesn't it?'

'That's the problem, Inspector. Although Brian Hargreaves is well known for being a bit of a rogue with his financial dealings in the city, I believe they're actually struggling to maintain Melcham Hall right now.'

'Hmm, that's interesting. Ah well, thanks for the information, Jim. I appreciate you giving me your time.'

'As always it's a pleasure, Inspector. Send my regards to your good lady.'

Mandy had spent most of the afternoon trawling through the missing persons list when a call came through to the office.

'Hello, WPC Mandy Tredwell speaking.'

'Good afternoon, this is PC Mark Harris speaking from Wells police station. I believe you may have found one of our missing persons.'

PC Harris read out the description of the murdered victim and it was virtually an exact match. Only the hair colour was different.

'So do you have a name for me?' Mandy asked.

'Yes, I believe the girl may be Felicity Morgan. She's twenty-one years of age and was born in South Horrington. Her parents say she left college a few months back and is believed to have been temping as a housekeeper somewhere in the Wells area although we don't have an agency or job address. Apparently she used to keep in touch with her parents on quite a regular basis, phoning them twice a week and at weekends but they haven't heard from her for over a fortnight.'

Mandy sighed. The thought of another young girl becoming a statistic was a sad thought and changed her mood.

'Can you fax me the details of the missing girl and the parents contact details,' she asked.

'Sure. They're on their way.'

'Have the parents been notified of the situation?'

'No, I thought it best to wait until we had some kind of match and confirmation of the details from you first.'

'OK, leave it with me. I'll get in touch with them.'

'Thanks Mandy.'

'Yeah thanks.' She hung up.

As soon as Mandy received the fax details it was obvious it was the same person so she put the wheels in motion for the parents to be brought over to Street to identify the body and made arrangements to meet them at the mortuary. She also spoke with Terry Austin, the local pathologist who agreed to meet her before the girl's parents arrived. Mandy knew from experience how good Terry was handling distressed parents and relatives.

Wesley was busy sifting through a pile of paperwork when he heard a commotion in the hallway outside his office. He opened the door just as Martin was about to knock.

'What on earth is going on down there?' Wesley asked pointing to the far end of the building where the prison cells were situated.

'Archie Black, sir.'

'Excuse me?'

'Archie Black. He escaped from Prenton prison a few days ago. He got into a fight outside a pub in Wells last year where he knocked the guy senseless. He was given six months for GBH. He's got previous form too, several minor offences for burglary and theft.'

'How did he get in here?' asked Wesley returning to his office, beckoning Martin inside.

'We received a call from a Mrs Tanner from the village bakers this morning who said he was seen stealing food from behind the counter. We radioed two of our lads who were patrolling in the area to have a word with him. When they started to question him he started to kick off so they brought him in.'

'Go on, there's more to the story,' said Wesley, 'I can tell from the smirk on your face.'

'It would appear that it was Archie Black who spent the night sleeping in the beer cellar at the Phoenix. When I asked him what he was doing in the area he suddenly burst out with "You can't do me for it. I never touched the girl". So I asked him to explain what the hell he was talking about. He says that the night before last he was making his way across woodland from Prenton to Shepton Mallet when shortly after jumping a hedge and entering what he believed to be the grounds of a stately home, he tripped and fell.'

'Go on,' said Wesley rolling a cigarette.

'Well this is the interesting bit sir. He says he fell over someone's leg.'

'What?'

'The lad says when he stood up and looked down to see what he'd tripped on, he saw the body of a young girl lying on her back. He said the look on her face told him she was dead. He was scared and as he was already on the run, no one would have believed his story.'

'So he just ran away.'

'That right, sir. The lad says he panicked and ran for a couple of miles or so before he crossed a main road where he came across the Phoenix pub.'

'What time was this?'

'Around eight o'clock in the evening.'

'OK, good work Martin. Ask Terry Austin to fax a photo across of the girl found in Annie Griffins' coal shed. I hope to God it's the same kid otherwise we have two murders on our hands. At the same time get Archie Blacks prints sent over to Terry to see if they match up with anything on her clothes or body.'

'We're pretty sure we know who the victim is now, sir. Mandy's just taken a call from Wells police. It looks like the woman's name is Felicity Morgan. Mandy's arranged to meet the parents with Terry Austin later today.'

'OK, good work. Let Archie Black stew for a while. We'll talk to him later.'

Mandy returned to the waiting room in the mortuary to face Felicity Morgan's distraught parents. Having just confirmed her identity the couple were still in a state of shock. Mrs Morgan held a handkerchief to her eyes whilst her husband sat staring at the floor. They hadn't spoken much except to ask how she had died. Mandy informed them that Felicity had died as a result of a broken neck but omitted to mention that there was also bruising on her body. She didn't think it was necessary to cause them more grief.

She left them for several minutes to grieve, before returning to ask a few brief questions. She always found this the hardest part of the job asking people to think clearly when obviously their minds were elsewhere.

They explained that after finishing her Arts degree, Felicity wanted to take a year out. However it was her mother who said she would just be wasting her life so why not do something completely different for a while until she decided upon the career she wanted. As a result, she'd taken a couple of temporary posts, firstly working in a bar then housekeeping for someone.

They said she'd been sharing a room with a friend named Janet Moore, somewhere in Wells, but they didn't know the address. Apparently she'd known Janet from college. Mandy realised there was nothing to gain by pressing them further right now and arranged for a police vehicle to take them home.

As soon as she arrived back at the station she set the wheels in motion to trace a Janet Moore, the girl Felicity had been staying with.

Mandy had been through this process with grieving parents on two previous occasions and it was never easy but this time she came away with the feeling that something was missing from the interview. Something was unsaid.

It was early evening when Wesley called Mandy and Martin into his office.

'I appreciate it's been a long day but I just want to recap what we know so far about the Felicity Morgan case. Somehow the local press have got wind of the murder so the story is bound to be on local news later tonight and probably therefore in the national press tomorrow.' Wesley paused as he started to scribble some notes on the wipe board. While he was doing so, the phone rang which Martin answered.

'Who was that, anyone for me?' Wesley asked as Martin replaced the receiver.

'Not directly, sir. But as you requested, the desk sergeant showed Archie Black the faxed photo of Felicity Morgan and he's confirmed that it's the same girl he saw in the woods.'

'I guess it is good news in the respect that his confirmation tells us we're looking at one murder and not two,' said Mandy.

'Yeah if there is such a thing as good news and murder,' Wesley replied.

Wesley spent the next half an hour going over the course of events and the information they had to date. When he eventually looked up at the two exhausted faces staring back at him he couldn't help but smile.

'Okay, let's call it a day. I'll leave a few bullet points on the board for us to action tomorrow morning. Good work team. Go home and get some rest. We have another long day tomorrow.'

After Mandy and Martin had left the room Wesley opened the window and lit a cigarette giving some more thought to the next day's actions. It was nearly nine o'clock when he closed the office door, having satisfied himself that he'd covered everything for the day. His notes on the wipe board read:

1. Speak with Terry Austin to get a clear understanding of how the neck was broken.
2. Archie Black DNA and fingerprints?
3. Mandy to check that Annie Griffin is OK.
4. Locate Janet Moore.
5. Take Archie Black to the spot where he saw Felicity Morgan's body.

By the time Wesley arrived home Jane was asleep on the sofa. Trying not to make a noise he crept out of the front room and into the kitchen where he found his dinner in the microwave, the usual place for a policeman's dinner.

He ate the spaghetti bolognaise in a minute and was so absorbed in the newspaper that he never heard Jane until she appeared in the doorway.

'Well good evening Mr Inspector, sir,' she exclaimed.

Wesley pushed the newspaper to one side, stood up, walked around the kitchen table and placed his arms around her before kissing her passionately on the lips.

By the time Jane stood back her face was crimson.

'What on earth brought that on?' she exclaimed. 'Usually all I get is a grunt and a pat on the forehead.'

'Then it's well overdue.'

Wesley reached for the kettle and filled it with water as Jane sat herself at the table.

'So how has your day been?'

Jane yawned as she was about to respond.

'Oh that busy eh?'

'Sorry John, I don't know why I'm so tired. Perhaps I need another holiday.'

Wesley was stood with his back to her making tea so didn't see the smirk on her face.

'I think half the population of Wells was in the hospital this morning. They were actually queued just trying to get to the reception desk at one point.'

'Why, is there an outbreak of something?'

'I was beginning to think so. I have to say most people are quite pleasant but you get the odd or two who are so damn rude. They want to jump the queue, expect a doctor or consultant to see them immediately and if they don't like what you tell them they want to speak with someone else.'

'That reminds me,' said Wesley as he placed the teas on the table. 'I need to ask a favour. Will you make an appointment for me to see the dentist? One of my back teeth hurts like hell, I'm not sure I haven't broken it.'

'I'll phone in the morning and see what appointment I can get. I think Alistair's on holiday all over the Christmas period so you might have to wait a while.'

'I'm sure you can smooth talk the receptionist,' he replied.

The look on Jane's face told him she wasn't impressed.

'Gerry Callow came in today. Apparently he's been having a few chest pains lately.'

'Is he OK?' There was genuine concern on Wesley's face.

'He says he's feeling better but I want to keep an eye on him. You know what he's like. He doesn't exactly look after himself does he?'

'He sure is carrying a lot of weight,' Wesley replied.

'I saw on the news that you've identified the poor girl who was found on the Melcham estate.'

Wesley looked up in surprise.

'It's on the news already?'

'Yes it was on the eight o'clock news. They gave her name as Felicity Morgan and said where she'd been found and that her parents had identified the body but were too distressed to speak.'

Wesley slammed his cup down on the table.

'Some of these reporters are the pits of the earth. What on earth do they expect someone's parents to say when they've just identified their kid in a mortuary? They make me sick.'

Wesley stood up, searching his pockets for his mobile phone and his roll-ups, and headed for the back door.

'I'm just going to phone the station. If I see one reporter outside the station tomorrow morning he'll feel the weight of my boot.'

Jane reached out to place a hand on his shoulder and lent forward to whisper in his ear.

'Don't be long, I'm awake now.'

5

The Half Moon café had stood in Street for many years and was a favourite of some of the older town folk so Wesley had been surprised when Terry Austin had suggested meeting him there rather than at the mortuary. It was the first time Wesley had ever seen him away from the mortuary and without his white pathologist coat smelling of disinfectant.

'Well this is a pleasant change,' said Wesley standing up to shake hands.

'Actually it's a rare day's leave, that's why I suggested meeting here,' Terry replied. He was wearing blue straight fit designer jeans, a black polo neck top and carrying a small denim jacket.

'It's good of you to spare me the time when you're not working,' said Wesley after ordering two coffees.

'It's my pleasure, Inspector. I had to come into the town this morning, I've actually got a dentist appointment later. The old gnashes are playing up and I've been putting it off for ages.' He pointed to the back of his mouth.

Wesley waited until the young woman had placed two mugs of coffee on the table and walked away before answering.

'It's funny really,' said Wesley, 'I've witnessed some horrific things during my career but a visit to the dentist still scares the hell out of me. I actually asked Jane just last evening to make an appointment for me.'

Terry smiled until he took a sip of coffee when he grimaced as the pain in his tooth emphasised the reason for his visit.

'I guess you don't have a murder suspect yet for Felicity Morgan,' Terry asked.

'No, that's what I want to talk to you about. In your expert opinion is there any way the girl could have just fallen? Or are you positive someone murdered her?'

Terry pulled a face as he took another sip of coffee.

'It's always possible for someone to fall and break their neck but in this case I would have to say that bruising around the chest and ribs suggests that when she died someone fell on her at the same time.'

Wesley blew into his coffee cup.

'So we can rule out any possibility that it was an accident. I mean, she wasn't on her own.'

'She definitely wasn't on her own. I suppose it's feasible they could have both stumbled but the bruising on her chest suggests that she was punched.'

'I guess there's no way of knowing whether her attacker was male or female.'

'Not really although whoever punched her did so with considerable force.'

'I know it's a silly question, but did we check for any DNA other than the girls?'

'Yes I checked personally,' Terry replied, 'although there were a few microscopic particles of skin other than Felicity's on her clothing, there's no DNA match to anything we have on record. That includes Archie Black by the way.'

'So Archie Black didn't kill her?'

'I can't say for sure obviously, but from the evidence we have I would say it's highly unlikely.'

Wesley ran his hand across his eyes. He'd only just arrived back from holiday but he felt tired already.

'Terry, in your expert opinion, did Felicity break her neck by falling over or was she murdered?'

Terry placed his coffee down on the table before answering.

'My gut feeling is that the girl fell to the floor after receiving a blow to the ribs, but I don't think we'll ever prove that.'

'Was she…?'

'No, there was no sign of sexual assault.'

Using a matchstick Wesley prodded stray pieces of tobacco into each end of his roll-up.

'Ah that's interesting. That tells me that her attacker had a different motive.'

'I think you have to ask the question what she doing in the woods on the Melcham estate in the first place,' said Terry.

'Do you know, sometimes you're so boringly right,' Wesley replied laughing.

'Well, I'd better be off. The dentist waits for no man.' Terry drank most of his coffee in one gulp and stood to leave.

'I appreciate your time and feedback, Terry. Is there anything else you can tell me?' Wesley left the money for the coffees and followed the pathologist to the door.

'There is just one more thing, Inspector. Felicity Morgan was in the early stages of pregnancy.'

WPC Mandy Tredwell had telephoned Annie Griffin to ask if it was OK for her to pop over. She didn't want to turn up unannounced in case Annie had other visitors, although she said she seldom did these days. When Mandy arrived the back door was already open so she knocked hard, listening for a reply from within before entering.

'Come in my dear,' Annie answered. 'Please close the door after you.'

Mandy stepped straight into the kitchen and closed the door behind her.

'Oh my, that smells good,' said Mandy.

There was a smell of freshly baked bread drifting through the entire house. She followed Annie back into the kitchen where Annie extracted two freshly baked loaves from the oven. Mandy was reminded of the days when her own mother used to take her to her grans. Her gran would always dust herself down, wiping flour off her apron before reaching out to give Mandy a big squeeze. Annie did exactly the same.

'It's good to see you,' said Annie, 'I hope you're looking after that handsome young colleague of yours.'

Mandy couldn't help but laugh, at the same time as discreetly wiping a tear from her eye.

'Yes we are,' Mandy replied looking somewhat embarrassed.

'Sit down at the table,' said Annie, 'the kettle has just boiled.'

The two women sat talking for half an hour. Mandy was impressed just how well Annie coped on her own and how independent she was.

'Have you been able to identify who the poor girl is yet?' Annie asked as she laid the table with to two cups, sugar and milk.

'Yes we have, her name is Felicity Morgan. She left college last year and has spent the year temping. I can't tell you much more at the moment,' Mandy replied.

Annie sighed, 'such as waste of life.' She poured tea into the two cups and produced a box of cakes from the breadbin.

It was when Mandy approached the subject of Melcham Hall that Annie jumped at the chance to reminisce. She pulled open a drawer in the welsh dresser and extracted a plastic bag that was wrapped with two rubber bands. Opening the bag Annie tipped the contents onto the table. The bag was full of old black and white photographs. She showed Mandy photos of her and her husband when they were courting on holiday in Cornwall, and photos of Annie's mother standing in the doorway of a picture postcard looking thatched Cottage. What caught Mandy's eye was a photo of a group of people standing outside Melcham Hall. Annie pointed to everyone in turn explaining who they were. The crowd was made up of all the family members along with servants and household staff. It was Brian Hargreaves' wife Lucy who caught Mandy's eye. She was nothing like the person who she had envisaged Brian Hargreaves to be married to. She and her sister Kate both stood taller than the rest of the family. They both wore long evening gowns which Mandy imagined as being blue and pink. They both had shoulder length black hair, long thin necks, and a figure to die for. "Something I'll never have" Mandy thought to herself as she took another bite of cake. It was almost as if Annie could read her mind when she said, 'The twins were so pretty. It was almost impossible to tell them apart in those days.'

'Where does Kate live now?' Mandy asked.

'Oh somewhere in France I believe. She fell out with her father just before he died. She was such a free spirit that girl. Unfortunately I don't think Sir Clive appreciated the talents she had. You see, he expected her to stay at home and rear a family in Melcham Hall, but she wanted a different lifestyle altogether. She wanted travel, excitement, danger even. She was the tomboy of the two.'

'But Lucy and Brian have never had children have they?' said Mandy.

'No, it wasn't to be. I believe it's Brian who can't have children although Lucy has always blamed herself.'

'Didn't you say that Lucy hadn't looked well the last time you saw her?'

Mandy noticed how Annie seemed to hesitate before answering.

'That was a couple of months ago. There was a time when she popped in for a chat nearly every day, but not now.'

'If you don't mind me asking, do you know the reason why she stopped her visits?' asked Mandy.

Annie toyed with the tea towel.

'I think Brian Hargreaves knows the answer to that,' Annie replied.

Another heavy snowfall meant that the country lanes were almost impassable in places. Wesley allowed Martin to drive as he knew the local roads better and sat in the back of the vehicle with a subdued Archie Black.

Turning away from Shepton Mallet they passed the entrance to Melcham Hall then took a left turning that most people would have missed. Following a single lane track for over half a mile they then passed under a railway bridge before Archie suddenly pointed to a spot just ahead.

'That's it, just there. I ran across the road into the shelter of those trees before jumping the hedge.'

Martin pulled the car into the nearest layby. Before they had left the station Wesley had informed Archie that he would put a good word in for him if he helped them with their search so the lad wasn't handcuffed as he lead the way through the undergrowth.

Having safely negotiated their way across a ditch where the small trickle of water had now frozen into one solid mass, Archie then pointed to a break in the hedgerow which had been damaged when he'd previously scrambled through.

The snow was several inches deep here and with the mixture of long grass and bracken, all three soon had soaking wet feet.

'Just here!' Archie shouted, pointing to spot in between two gorse bushes. He stood back as Wesley and Martin took a closer look. Although there had been further snow fall it was apparent that the long grass had been recently flattened and a small ridge in the woodland floor leading down the slope on the other side gave the impression of something heavy being dragged away. Being careful not to tread anywhere where any evidence may still have existed Wesley followed the trail until he left the canopy of overhanging trees where the trail disappeared from view under the fresh layer of snow.

'Where are we exactly?' he asked Martin.

'Well if my bearings are correct I would guess we're on the edge of the

Melcham Hall estate with the house being at the bottom of the slope about a mile further on.'

Archie Black nodded his head. 'That would be the house I passed, big stately home.'

'OK let's get back to the car,' said Wesley looking down at his sodden shoes and trousers. 'We'll get forensics up here to take a good look around. I don't hold out much hope but you never know. I suggest you come up here with them Martin. Your trousers are already wet.'

Martin caught the smirk on Wesley's face as they trudged back through the undergrowth.

Jane tried to hide her yawn. It was only her second day back at work yet she felt as if she'd never been away. Yesterday she'd spent nearly the whole shift either answering the phone or talking face to face with patients, it had been non-stop. Today was a little quieter and Jane was able to take a fifteen minute break. Making directly for the hospitals refreshment area she almost collided into someone who had stopped abruptly in front of her to allow paramedics push a wheelchair patient through from the accident and emergency area. As Jane peered over the woman's shoulder to get a glimpse of the patient her heart nearly missed a beat. Gerry Callow, covered in a blanket from his shoulders to his feet was slumped forward in the wheelchair.

'Excuse me, I need to get through,' said Jane almost pushing the woman aside.

She hurried after the paramedic who was walking briskly towards one of the vacant cubicles. She managed to catch up just as a nurse was pulling the curtain across.

'How serious is it?' Jane asked, almost shouting.

The nurse recognised Jane's uniform and said she would come out to her in a minute. The minute seemed like ten by the time the nurse reappeared from behind the curtain. She beckoned Jane to follow her down the hallway.

'I gather you know the patient?' she asked.

'Yes, his name is Gerry Callow. We've been friends for over a year. Gerry runs a small bookshop in Glastonbury. What's wrong with him?'

'Someone walked into the shop this morning and found Gerry clutching his chest. Apparently he's had a couple of bouts of chest pains in recent weeks.'

'Yes I know he was here yesterday for a check-up.' Jane realised she was almost crying.

'Don't worry, we'll look after him,' she replied reassuringly. 'I'll tell him you were asking after him. Why don't you pop back down when you've finished work? I'll leave a note for you at the A & E counter.'

'Thank you so much, that's really kind,' said Jane.

Deciding that she no longer had time to queue for a tea she made her way back the reception desk, knowing that it was going to be hard to concentrate on anything else.

6

With WPC Alison Bolt still on leave and PC Adam Broad currently on secondment to Bath HQ assisting with a major drug enquiry, Wesley was short staffed and had to spend more time than he would have liked carrying out the day to day chores of running a local police station. He had just finished opening mail in the post room when his mobile rang. He recognised the caller's number straight away.

'Good day Mrs Wesley. For what do I owe the pleasure?'

'Hello John, sorry to bother you I've just read something in the local paper that I thought you may be interested to hear.'

Following the change of ownership at the local bookstore in Glastonbury some six months previous, Jane had decided to seek employment elsewhere and now worked as a part-time receptionist in Wells hospital and was sat reading the local newspaper during her break.

'I was skipping through the job adds in the local paper when I saw an advert for a part-time domestic helper, someone to go in three mornings a week.'

'Well that's interesting but I don't see why you would think I would necessarily want to know.'

'Hold on, let me finish. When I telephoned the agency they told me that the vacancy had already been taken but they'd forgotten to remove the advertisement from the paper.'

'Jane, where is this all heading?'

'Oh John, you are so impatient. The vacancy was at Melcham Hall.'

'What? Really?'

'I thought that might interest you. That was where the woman's body was found wasn't it? On the Melcham estate I mean.'

'Yes it was. I guess it could just be coincidence but I'll check it out. Is there a contact number or email address?'

He jotted down the details as Jane read them out.

'Thanks, Jane.'

'It's going to cost you, you know that.'

'In that case I'll be home early,' he replied laughing.

Leaving the post room Wesley walked up the stairs back to his office, passing the open plan office that housed all the other staff based at Street police station. Martin was sat at his desk busy typing up a report when Wesley walked up.

‘Do me a favour, Martin. Ring this number for me,’ he said handing over a slip of paper. ‘It’s an employment agency, advertising for a position at Melcham Hall. I want to know when the advertisement was placed, who placed it, and what happened to the previous employee.’

‘Sure thing,’ Martin replied taking the details.

‘Oh and there’s one other thing.’

‘Yes Chief?’

‘Take those wet shoes off the radiator.’

Mandy looked again at the address Wesley had given her. Felicity Morgan’s parents lived in South Horrington, a small village on the outskirts of Wells.

Leaving Shepton Mallet, Mandy headed towards Wells before taking the Old Frome Road towards the picturesque village. Even though she knew the area quite well, the narrow high hedged country lanes were difficult to navigate when snow blanketed the area. She put the car in second gear making the uphill climb away from Shepton Mallet and was soon beginning to wish she hadn’t used her own car. Her Ford Fiesta was great for nipping in and out of traffic but not powerful enough for some of the steep inclines, especially in the slippery wintery conditions she now faced.

‘The Brackens’ was a spacious looking bungalow that sat back off the main road. It was situated at the top of the hill that provided for magnificent views across the local landscape. On a clear day Glastonbury Tor could be seen in the distance. Mandy had already telephoned to ensure someone would be at home so that she wouldn’t have a wasted journey. As she turned the car into the drive she noticed the curtains twitch at the house next door. Gathering her things she thought of Felicity’s parents and knew that neighbours would be gossiping about recent events, some trying to help, others just being nosey. But she was experienced in these situations and knew exactly how to approach both the parents and neighbours alike. Even though snow had been swept away from the path to the front of the property her shoes were still soaking wet by the time she got to the front door. She rang the doorbell and waited for someone to answer.

Henry Morgan opened the door almost immediately and squinted into the grey cold light. Mandy could see he had been crying and looking unshaven and dishevelled she knew this was going to be a difficult meeting. Henry beckoned her into the hallway and closed the door behind her.

‘Shall I take your coat?’ he asked almost in a whisper.

‘Thank you.’

‘Please go through to the lounge, my wife is in there. I’ll make some tea and join you in a second.’

Mandy entered the spacious tastefully furnished lounge to find Sally Morgan staring out of the patio doors that provided a view of a large landscaped manicured garden.

'She used to love playing out there when she was a child. She would have friends over and they would play in the orchard at the bottom. She was so happy.'

Sally turned to face Mandy and started to cry. Mandy walked across the lounge and wrapped her arms around Sally Morgan and held her until her sobs started to fade.

'I don't think I can handle this,' Sally said when she eventually stepped back.

She wiped the tears away with a linen handkerchief.

'Come and sit down,' said Mandy and led Sally to a rose patterned sofa where she sat down beside her.

'I'm so sorry, I'm just a complete mess,' said Sally looking up.

Mandy looked into her eyes and saw the emptiness there, that vacant look of sorrow and despair. She'd seen it too many times before. It wasn't a situation she enjoyed although everyone told her how good she was at handling such circumstances.

'There is no need to apologise Mrs Morgan, I do understand.'

'Please, call me Sally.'

Mandy noticed how much she was shaking so reaching out she took one of Sally's hands in both of hers. At that moment Henry Morgan entered the room carrying a wooden tray with silver handles. He placed it on the small mosaic tiled coffee table. It looked to Mandy as if the tea had been poured into their best china tea cups.

'Thank you,' she said.

Henry sat opposite them on a single seated cushioned chair. Mandy could tell from his body language just how stressed he was.

'So have you come to tell us that you have caught the bastard?' Henry suddenly exclaimed. His left hand gripped the clenched fist of his right hand so tightly his knuckles were white.

'I'm afraid we have made little progress so far,' Mandy replied, still holding onto Sally's hand. 'It's no excuse but the weather hasn't helped us. Fresh snowfall has covered most the area around where Felicity was found.'

'Well it's not good enough…'

Sally released her hands from Mandy's. 'Oh shut up, Henry! It's not the poor girls fault. The police are doing all they can,' she shouted.

'Well perhaps they should try harder,' he replied and stormed out of the room. A few seconds later they heard another door slam on the other side of the hallway. Henry's sobbing could be heard throughout the bungalow.

'He's not usually like that,' said Sally. 'He's such a gentle man but like me he's finding this hard to accept.'

'I know, I know.'

Mandy handed a cup to Sally which she took in both hands. In the short silence that followed Mandy could sense Sally beginning to relax. She took a sip of tea herself before speaking.

‘This is a lovely place you have. How long have you lived here?’

Sally stared at the fire place where the coal had been set for lighting later in the day. A brass poker and a set of tongs lay on the tiled surround.

‘Henry had the bungalow built back in nineteen seventy-three. In those days most of this area was just orchards. When he first brought me here I couldn’t imagine living here, everywhere seemed so desolate. However, the next time he brought me over three or four other bungalows had also been built at the top of the hill here. The place looked so lovely and I fell in love with it straight away. Oh I admit that it took me a while to get used to being in the country so to speak. I was born in the centre of Oxford, which even in those days was quite built up compared to around here. Felicity was actually born right here in the lounge one Sunday morning. My waters burst just after Henry had left for work. I managed to telephone for assistance before collapsing on the floor. The ambulance crew had to enter via the French doors as it was then. A lady named Margaret delivered Felicity just ten minutes after arriving. They were scared I was going to lose the baby as the head was already visible when they arrived.’

Mandy took the cup from her as she started to sob and placed an arm around her shoulders.

‘Sally, I know it hurts but I do need to ask you a question.’

‘I understand,’ she replied sniffing and retrieving the handkerchief from her lap.

‘Do you know if Felicity had a boyfriend?’

‘A boyfriend, I don’t think so? I mean, she never mentioned anyone. Why do you ask?’

‘Were you aware that Felicity was pregnant?’

Because of the influx of students staying at Wells University it was a long and laborious job trawling through the list of rented accommodation in the area.

Wesley slammed the phone back into the receiver and reached for his tobacco.

It had been a long time since he’d had to do so much digging himself and couldn’t wait for WPC Alison Bolt to return from holiday.

Uniformed officers had already been despatched to scour the local town and villages showing a photograph of Felicity when one of officers struck lucky. Handing the photograph around in a local café close to the University, a young female said she recognised Felicity and said the last time she spoke with her she was sharing a room with a flatmate, name of Janet Moore. She wasn’t sure whether Janet was a fellow student but she was able to provide an address because she had recently been there when Janet had organised a party. PC Barnes placed the call through to Wesley who jotted down the address and agreed to meet him there in half an hour. The property was typical of the area, a three storey house that had once belonged to one family but was now divided into half a dozen one bed apartments.

PC Barnes led the way up the steps to the front door. The solid blue painted door was situated between two full length frosted panes of glass. On the left hand wall just inside the entrance to the porch was a list of names and push buttons inside a plastic casing. Wesley read down the list of names. Felicity Morgan wasn't listed but Janet Moore was. He pressed the buzzer and waited for a reply. After three attempts Wesley was about to give up when the front door opened and a scruffy looking lad appeared.

'Oh sorry, I was just on my way out.' He looked at Wesley, then PC Barnes who was in uniform. 'Is there something wrong?'

'I'm trying to find Janet Moore,' Wesley replied, 'and you are?'

'Pete Evans. I live in Flat 2. Janet lives in Flat 6 at the top of the second flight of stairs. Is she OK?'

'I hope so,' Wesley replied and squeezed past.

The old house had obviously not been decorated in years. Flock wallpaper covered most of the walls but strips of it were missing where either notice boards or posters had once been placed before being torn down. A pay-as-you- go telephone was fixed to the wall at the top of the first flight of stairs. By the time they reached the top landing Wesley was out of breath.

Flat 6 was at the back of the building at the end of a short corridor.

Wesley banged hard on the door and waited. He was about to knock again when he heard a shuffling movement inside the flat.

'Are you in there, Janet?' he shouted.

'There's definitely someone inside,' said PC Barnes listening with his face close to the door. He knocked again and called out.

'This is the police, open up!'

A few seconds later they heard a sound like the scrapping of a chair.

'Are you really the police?'

It was a girl's voice, a girl who sounded scared.

'Yes, Inspector Wesley and PC Barnes. Can you please open the door?'

A chain rattled and a bolt was slid across before the door was slowly pulled back. Wesley looked at the face of a petrified Janet Moore. In the same moment he showed her his ID she stepped forward and collapsed into his arms.

'Quick, grab a chair,' Wesley said to the young PC.

Having managed to sit Janet on the chair, Wesley knelt down on one knee in front of her as PC Barnes went to fetch some water.

'Hey what's going on?' Wesley asked. He placed his hand under the girls chin so that she would look up. It was clear that the poor thing was scared to death and that she had been crying. He extracted a handkerchief from his coat pocket, placed it in her hand and laid a hand on her shoulder until her breathing seemed to slow.

'Come on, tell me what this is all about,' said Wesley as he stood up and pulled up a chair alongside her. The girl took a few more seconds to compose herself before speaking.

'I'm sorry Inspector, I'm so scared. Until a few days ago I'd been sharing the flat with Felicity Morgan.' Wesley sat silent as Janet began to sob. She took a sip of water before continuing.

'I was beginning to wonder where she had got to when I saw the evening news on television and listened to the news reporter saying that the body of a young female found on the Melcham estate had been identified as Felicity Morgan.'

'Janet, I know how difficult this must be right now but do you have any idea where Felicity was working?'

'Oh yes, she'd been working at Melcham Hall, only part-time. She got the job through some agency in Wells. But she left there about a week or so ago. She said she'd seen something that had distressed her but didn't say what it was. It had obviously disturbed her because she was scared.'

'So where had she been for the past week?'

'She spent most of her time in the flat but a few days back she said she'd thought of an easy way to earn a lot of money.'

'Do you know what she meant by that?'

'No, that morning was the last time I saw her. It was the day before her body was found. After making a quick telephone call from the telephone out in the hallway she grabbed her coat and disappeared. I've not seen her since.'

Wesley looked across the room at PC Barnes before asking his next question.

'Janet, do you think Felicity was on the game?'

'No I don't! She wasn't like that at all.'

'Okay calm down. I have to ask these questions.'

The tears welled up in her eyes.

'Who could have done such a thing to her? Felicity wouldn't harm a fly.'

'That's what I'm trying to find out, Janet.'

'I need another glass of water, I feel sick,' said Janet and walked across to where the kitchen area was located at the end of the lounge.

'Is this just a one bedroomed flat or two?' Wesley asked looking around.

'Two, they're both off the hallway on the right. The first one is mine, the second is Felicity's.'

'Do you mind if I take a look?' asked Wesley.

Janet shrugged her shoulders. 'Sure.'

Wesley nodded to PC Barnes who remained with Janet.

The bedroom was tiny. There was just enough room for a single bed, a small bedside table and a single wardrobe. He looked in the wardrobe first. A couple of long flowery dresses, a denim jacket, two shirts and a couple of tee-shirts were the only clothes hanging up. Underwear lay on one of the three small shelves in the corner, along with two scarves and several paperbacks.

Wesley made a quick search of the bed, looking under the quilt and pillows before opening the single drawer to the bedside unit. This was obviously where Felicity had kept her worldly possessions. He found a passport, a few items of jewellery, some loose change and a small, almost empty bottle of perfume. But what caught his attention was a plain white envelope that looked to contain something. He picked it up and sat down on the bed to inspect the contents. Inside was a single sheet of paper that had been folded twice. Wesley unravelled the paper to view the content. It was a letter written by Felicity to her mother. Having read the details, he refolded the paper and placed it back in the envelope which he slipped into his pocket. It was something he would have to hand to Sally Morgan, when the time was right.

Wesley returned to the living room where he found PC Barnes copying down names and addresses from a phone book that Janet had handed him.

'I'm afraid there are only a couple of names I can give you, Inspector,' said Janet. 'Felicity never got to know any of my friends.'

7

'Pregnant! My Felicity! Never!'

Sally Morgan stood up and walked over to the patio doors holding her hands to her face. Mandy was trying to understand the emotional turmoil the poor woman was going through.

'Are you sure?' The look on Sally Morgan's face was total bewilderment.

'Yes, we are. The pathologist confirmed that Felicity was in the early stages of pregnancy.'

Sally Morgan turned away from Mandy to stare out towards the back garden.

'What did we do wrong?' she cried, 'what did we do to deserve this?'

Mandy watched this usually mild mannered woman struggle with her emotions, and could feel her pain.

'I guess you're too young to have children?' Sally asked turning to face Mandy.

'I lost a child in childbirth.'

Mandy was surprised how quickly she responded and how easily she answered. It was something she hadn't spoken about to anyone for a long time.

'Oh, I'm sorry. I didn't realise.'

'Sally, it's OK. It's something I've come to terms with.'

The two women faced one another for several moments as if both were searching for answers.

'I can't believe Felicity was pregnant. I didn't even know she had a boyfriend,' Sally exclaimed.

'Do you want me to speak with Mr Morgan?' Mandy asked.

'No. No, I would prefer to tell him myself.'

Mandy stood up and walked across the room to stand beside Sally. There was never a good time to ask a parent if she could look at their son or daughters room but it was something she had to address.

'Do you think we could take a look at Felicity's bedroom?'

'Yes of course.'

Sally wiped her eyes with a handkerchief before leading the way into the hall. She opened the last door on the left at the back of the bungalow. It was quite a small room, no more than ten feet by eight. The lower half of one wall was painted white with a colourful border that ran across the middle, with the top half painted deep blue. The far wall was different though. It was covered in polystyrene tiles that were almost completely masked by posters of pop groups and semi naked men. It was the right hand wall that caught Mandy's eye. The whole length of the wall above the border had been hand painted. It was a mural of a little girl walking in the woods. There were rabbits, butterflies and an owl. It all looked so peaceful.

'Felicity painted it when she returned from University,' said Henry Morgan who was now stood in the doorway.

'It's lovely,' Mandy replied.

'I'm sorry for my behaviour earlier. I don't know what came over me,' he said.

'You don't have to apologise Mr Morgan. I understand. May I take a look around Felicity's room in private?'

'Yes, of course you can.'

Henry Morgan took his wife's hand a led her into the hallway before closing the door. Mandy began to search through all the usual places. What was apparent was that Felicity enjoyed dressing up. There were expensive designer dresses and shoes, along with underwear to match. Mandy tried in vain to remember the last time she had made such an effort, maybe it was time she started spending more on herself. The only thing of interest that she found was an old address book which she found in a bedside drawer.

Returning to the lounge Mandy asked for permission to take the address book away then bade her farewell saying she would return it in a day or two. Before leaving, she dropped a card with her contact details on it on the coffee table.

'Please give me a call if you need me for anything or if you think of anything I ought to know. It doesn't matter what time of day or night.'

'Thanks,' replied Henry.

'Thank you Mandy,' said Sally and kissed her on the cheek.

Mandy jumped into the car and drove it around the corner where she parked up again. She took a tissue from her handbag just as the tears began to flow.

She thought she had got over the loss of her own baby. Maybe she needed more time. Maybe she would always need more time.

PC Martin Philips entered the 'All's Wells' job agency. Two young women were seated on a bench seat just inside the door, obviously having just completed their registration forms and waiting to be interviewed. A blonde haired woman dressed in a silk cream blouse, dark blue pencil skirt and wearing heels that she seemed to falter on rather than walk on, approached from the back of the office.

'Good afternoon constable, I'm Shirley Pemberton how can I help you?'

'Good afternoon. Is there somewhere we can talk in private?'

'Yes of course. Please follow me.'

She led the way past a small bank of desks where another woman wearing a headset appeared to be in conversation with a client.

Stepping into a small back office Shirley Pemberton closed the door behind her and directed Martin to a seat before sitting opposite him.

'Would you like tea or coffee?'

'No I'm fine thanks. I won't take a minute of your time,' Martin replied extracting a small notebook from his top pocket.

He estimated Shirley Pemberton to be in her mid-twenties and wondered why he'd never met her in one of the local bars or clubs around town. It was a thought he had to put aside for the time being.

'Do you run the agency, Mrs Pemberton?'

'No, the agency actually belongs to a Mrs Clement but she's on holiday at the moment but I suppose I'm the next in line, and by the way it's Miss and not Mrs Pemberton.'

'Ah that's good,' Martin replied blushing almost immediately after he'd made the comment.

When Shirley Pemberton smiled back at him the room temperature seemed to increase dramatically. Martin gave a polite cough as he tried to compose himself.

'Being the main job agency around here that provides employment for housemaids on either a full-time or part-time basis I'm hoping you might have a young woman registered with you, name of Felicity Morgan. Is that correct?'

Shirley Pemberton placed her elbows on the table and put her hands over her mouth before replying.

'What's happened to her?' she asked nervously. 'We haven't heard from her for over a week and she hasn't come in to collect her last pay cheque.'

'I'm afraid I have some bad news Miss Pemberton. Felicity is dead.'

Retrieving a tissue from the desk drawer the woman dabbed her eyes, a look of genuine shock on her face.

'Oh dear Lord what happened?'

Martin gave a brief explanation of events missing out the cause of death.

'So you had no idea?' he asked.

'No officer, none at all. My sister and I, that's the lady sitting outside, are running this place alone at the moment. We're here fourteen hours a day just to make it pay. I never get time to watch the television or catch up on local news.'

'Do you keep a file on everyone you employ?' Martin asked.

'Yes, yes we do. We actually make up a file for everyone who comes through the door.'

She stood up and walked over to a range of filing cabinets and working her way along stopped at the one marked 'k-n'.

'Now let me see. Here we are, Felicity Morgan.' She closed the cabinet drawer and walked back to the table. Opening the buff manila folder she flicked through a couple of pages before she found what she was looking for. Turning the folder around to enable Martin to view the particular page she pointed to the address shown.

'There you are. That's where Felicity was working.'

Martin read the address out loud, 'Melcham Hall.'

'Can I assume you have not received any contact from Brian Hargreaves?'

Shirley turned the folder around again and checked the contents.

'No nothing. I certainly haven't heard from Mr Hargreaves and if my sister had received anything or taken a call she would have noted it in the file. See here, we list the date and time of all conversations and correspondence on the inside of the folder.'

Martin rubbed his forehead.

'Don't you think it's strange that neither, Mr or Mrs Hargreaves have telephoned to ask why their house maid hasn't turned up for work?'

'I would say it's not only strange but very unusual for a client not to advise us if someone has failed to report for duties. That's the first thing they normally do, if only to remind us not to make claim for a day's pay.'

Martin asked for photocopies of all the paperwork on file before thanking Shirley Pemberton for her help. He stopped in his tracks just as they approached the front door.

'Just one other thing, I would be obliged if you didn't call Mr Hargreaves about my visit. I'll be paying him a visit first thing in the morning and would like to speak to him first.'

'Of course, I understand.'

Just as Martin turned to walk away Ms Pemberton handed him her card.

'That's my contact details, if you need anything else. By the way, my name's Sandra.'

It was midday when Jane finished her shift and less than fifteen minutes later when she reached the doors to the Falcon Ward. The nurse had kindly left a note in A & E saying that Gerry Callow had been admitted for further tests and had been taken up to Falcon Ward where he would be monitored for the next twenty-four hours. Jane pushed open the door not knowing what to expect or whether she was even allowed in. She caught the eye of Sister Andrews who was wheeling a trolley towards her stacked high with medicines.

'Good morning, Sister. I was wondering if you could help me. A friend of mine was brought in this morning complaining of chest pains. Would you happen to know how he is? His name is Gerry Callow.'

Sister Andrews noticed that Jane was still wearing her receptionist's jacket and was able to read Jane's name from her name tag.

'Hello, Jane isn't it? Yes, Mr Callow was brought up this morning. He's quite comfortable, we've had a heart monitor attached to him all morning and there haven't been any signs to particularly worry about. The doctor is coming to see him this afternoon and if there's no change then he will probably be allowed to go home in the morning although the doctor may well prescribe something for him.'

'Would I be allowed to speak with him?'

'I would rather he slept for the moment, Jane. He was quite exhausted when he was brought in. I will tell him you enquired after him though.'

'Oh I do appreciate it,' Jane replied, 'You see, he's a good friend of the family. Would you be so kind to ask him to phone me once he's back at home?'

'Of course, I'll let him know,'

'Thank you, that's very kind.'

Leaving the hospital Jane felt more relaxed knowing that her friend was OK.

But she knew she was going to lecture him about his diet.

It was Jane's first night out with friends since she and Wesley had returned from holiday. The quiz night at the Phoenix pub in Shepton Mallet wasn't quite as exclusive as some of the places they had recently visited in France, but it was both warm and welcoming. The pub was busier than usual and the quiz master had called a break so people could go to the bar to refill their glasses. Maggie, whose husband ran the pub, had just returned from the bar with a tray of drinks.

'This is supposed to be my night off,' she laughed as she handed the drinks around.

'You could have taken a peek at the answers for the next round while you were behind the bar,' said Jessie Taylor.

'Now, now, I can't be seen cheating in our own pub, can I?'

Everyone at the table laughed. The evening wore on and everyone was having a good time. Jane thought it hilarious that her team had only managed one answer from the last round of ten. When the quiz was over and the scores counted they were pleasantly surprised to hear their team had ended up a respectable fourth.

Mind you, there were only six teams.

'All I can say is that two of the other teams couldn't have answered a bloody question,' stated a rather merry Muriel Hopkins who had managed to spill most of her wine across her lap.

'Oh do come upstairs and take a look at our Christmas decorations,' Maggie pleaded to Jane as people started to make their way home. 'Geoff made a real effort this year for our son.'

Jane followed Maggie behind the bar and up the narrow wooden staircase that took them straight into the upstairs lounge. The room ran the whole length of the pub, with two bedrooms and a bathroom at one end and a small kitchen at the other. The low ceiling did nothing to hide the age of the building but there was a homely feel to the place. Maggie led the way to the smallest of the two bedrooms. She put her finger to her lips as she lifted the latch door.

'Harvey is asleep. Jessie Taylor's daughter Rebecca has been baby-sitting while we've been downstairs.'

As she quietly opened the door, sufficient light shone into the room from the lounge to enable Jane to marvel at what she saw. The whole room had been decorated to look like a manger. A painting on the far wall showed a stable where shepherds were flocked around baby Jesus. Another wall showed two donkeys feeding in a barn and on the ceiling a large white star took centre stage on a blue background.

'That is so beautiful,' said Jane after Maggie had closed the door. 'How old is Harvey now?'

'He'll be two in April.'

'It's such a shame that babies have to grow up,' Jane remarked.

The two women spent several minutes discussing the time when the young infant would start play school before Jane said it really was time she made a move for home. They had just reached the bottom of the stairs when they heard a rumpus going on at the far end of the bar.

'I'm not serving you any more drink. You've already had enough. It's time for you to go home.'

Maggie's husband Geoff was shouting at Brian Hargreaves who had become aggressive when Geoff had refused to pour him another beer.

'Come on Brian, you've outstayed your welcome.'

Geoff Dale escorted Brian Hargreaves to the door, handing him his jacket on the way. 'Are you sure you don't want me to order you a cab?'

'I told you, I'm walking home alright!'

Brian Hargreaves stumbled out of the door, making his way across the car park towards the main road. He could be heard swearing to himself for several minutes.

'That's the third time in about a week,' said Maggie as she helped Jane put her coat on.

'Has he always been like that?' Jane asked.

'No just recently. I don't know what's got into him but he's sure drinking a lot these days. Maybe he's got problems at home. Who knows? We get to hear all the reasons running a pub.'

'Doesn't he bring his wife to the pub anymore? I'm sure she used to accompany him. If not, she always picked him up.'

'Haven't seen her in ages,' remarked Geoff as he came through the bar.

'Sorry you had to hear me raise my voice but it's becoming a regular occurrence.'

'Oh I've heard a lot worse,' Jane replied patting him on the shoulder.

'Thank you both for a lovely night. I'll offer to give him a lift on the way home if I pass him. These country paths are still covered in snow. It would be so easy for him to slip over.'

'Especially in his condition,' Geoff replied.

Having wiped the sprinkling of snow away from the passenger window, Jane turned right out of the car park and drove slowly along the badly lit country lane. A mile further on, having just passed the entrance to Melcham Hall, she turned back at the mini roundabout to head towards Wells before taking the B road to Street. There was no sign of Brian Hargreaves anywhere.

8

Lucy Hargreaves sat staring at the needle marks in her arm. How many times had she been drugged? One of the last things she remembered was Brian walking into her bedroom asking if her migraine had eased before he poured her a coffee. That was the last morning she had spent in Melcham Hall, over two weeks ago. Since then she had been confined to a solitary room where her only visitor called upon her twice a day to leave a tray of food and drink and ask the same question over and over again. The room she was now confined to was sparsely decorated with a bed, standalone wardrobe, a wooden coffee table and a single chair. The flowered wallpaper was faded and torn and black damp patches were dotted along the bottom of the every wall.

She walked across to the window and gripped the metal bars that had long ago been added, either to prevent burglaries or more sinisterly to prevent inmates escaping. She had no recollection of the journey to the place. She could be in a different country for all she knew. She reached through the metal bars as far as she could reach to touch the window with her fingertips. The outside world looked so close but seemed so far away.

The large Georgian house lay back from the road and was almost totally obscured by trees and dense shrubbery. Lucy stared at a pair of jays that were sat on a nearby branch, envious of their freedom. She kept asking herself the same question, day in day out, "why did I not go to the police?"

Lucy was dressed in the same clothes as she had worn the previous day and the day before that. Although there was a small collection of her clothes in the wardrobe she had already worn most things twice. Someone had removed the clothes hangers so her few possessions were stacked at the bottom of the wardrobe. There was no clock in the room so Lucy had no idea what time of day or night it was except for the daylight that came through the window. Just as she slumped back on the side of the bed she heard the key turn in the lock. Lucy quickly lay flat on the bed pretending to be asleep. She couldn't face more questions today.

Having had a restless night's sleep Mandy sat yawning in front of the pc when Martin entered the office. 'Did you have a late night?' he asked winking.

'I'm sorry to say no I didn't. Just didn't sleep well. You seem all perked up this morning though. Not sure I want to ask why.'

‘Do you remember that blonde bird from accounts?’

‘Can we change the subject now,’ said Mandy interrupting before Martin provided her with a more detailed version of his evening.

‘How did you get on at the job agency yesterday?’

‘Do you know they had no idea that Felicity Morgan was dead? It still amazes me how many people don’t listen to the news.’

‘Could they confirm where the girl had been working?’

‘Oh yes, that’s the interesting thing. She was employed at Melcham Hall. In fact that’s exactly where I’m heading this morning.’

‘It seems to be the popular place right now.’

Mandy and Martin both turned around as Wesley walked through the door.

‘Hello, sir,’ said Martin, ‘how is Jane this morning? I hear she was at the quiz night last night.’

‘How on earth did you find that out?’ Wesley asked.

‘Some of the lads popped in last night after football training. They didn’t stay long as Geoff kept asking them to keep quiet.’

Wesley nodded his head in acknowledgement.

‘What time are you going over to Melcham Hall?’

‘In about half an hour, as soon as I’ve caught up with a few bits of paperwork. Why, are you coming with me?’

‘I may follow you over there. I’ve got to pop over to forensics first. I’ll catch up with you in a while.’

Wesley had been sat at his desk for five minutes when he called Mandy into his office.

‘Close the door, Mandy would you.’

Mandy closed the door and stood by the desk.

‘Take a seat. This won’t take a minute.’

‘What’s up, sir?’

‘How are you?’

Mandy was taken back from Wesley’s direct question and stammered a quiet response.

‘OK.’

Wesley produced his cigarette papers and tobacco and leaned back in the chair as Mandy watched him expertly roll a cigarette.

‘Mandy, I’ve known you for over two years now, and I think I’m a pretty good judge of character.’

Mandy didn’t reply but simply stared at the desk in front of her.

‘You need a holiday little lady.’

‘But, sir, we have a murder on our hands and with Alison being away and Adam being on secondment we’re at full stretch already.’

‘Alison is back from leave tomorrow. Fill her in on everything that’s going on and book some leave.’

‘Can I ask why, sir?’

Wesley stood up, walked around the desk, and sat on the edge in front of her. 'You look tired. You may not think that I notice, or care, but I do.'

She bit her lower lip, unsure what to say.

'I'm also aware that little Jack would have been two years old this week.'

Mandy looked up, tears welling in her eyes. Wesley stood up and held out his arms. Mandy leapt up from the chair, buried her head against his chest and began to sob.

'It's OK, let it all out.' He held onto her until she stopped crying. By the time he let go they were both blushing.

'Sorry, sir, I thought I could handle it,' she said, 'but the loss never goes away.'

'It never should and never will,' Wesley replied, motioning for Mandy to sit down. He knew that Mandy's son Jack had died when he was just a day old and her boyfriend at the time left her shortly after her loss. There was an accepted silence between them for several minutes before Wesley spoke.

'Back in the summer of 2008 my world fell apart. We had been married just a few months when Christine was killed by a drunk driver. She was walking home along the Embankment towards Chelsea Bridge when the vehicle mounted the kerb.' He paused to compose himself. 'She died before I got to the hospital. You see, Mandy. That was five years ago but the pain in still there, it will always be there and something inside of me wants it to be there. Does that make sense?'

'Yes,' she replied looking across the table to where Wesley was trying to ignore a tear running down his cheek.

The journey from Street to Shepton Mallet was less difficult now that some of the snow had turned to slush on the main roads and Martin arrived at Melcham Hall just after ten o'clock. The sound of ice cracking under the cars wheels prevented him from making a surprise visit and by the time he had exited the vehicle Brian Hargreaves was already stood on the steps outside the front door.

'Good morning, constable. I hope this is a quick visit, I have a busy day.'

'Good morning, Mr Hargreaves.' Martin ascended the steps to the front door. 'I think it's better if we talk inside, don't you?'

Brian Hargreaves sighed, his body language showing his obvious displeasure. Martin closed the door behind him and followed Hargreaves into the front parlour who immediately sat himself on a sofa without inviting Martin to sit down.

'May I?' Martin asked looking towards the chair opposite. Hargreaves motioned by nodding.

'Can we get on with it?' said Hargreaves.

'Why didn't you report Felicity Morgan as being missing from work?'

The question seemed to catch Hargreaves by surprise, rocking his nonchalant behaviour.

'Why would I report the girl missing just because she failed to turn up for work? I mean, it was only a part-time job. I mean, my wife and I just assumed she decided she didn't like the job.'

'But that doesn't explain why you didn't contact the job agency to let them know, or even more to the point, why you didn't contact the police when the poor girl had been identified as being murdered.'

'We never watch the garbage on television. It was only yesterday when I read the national press that I realised it was the same girl,' Hargreaves replied defensively.

'Have you any idea what Felicity Morgan would have been doing wandering around your estate Mr Hargreaves?'

'I thought she was found in the coal shed behind Rowan Lodge?'

'She was, but prior to that she'd been seen dead in the woods up on the slope. Why would she have gone there?'

Hargreaves shrugged his shoulders in a careless manner.

'You're the copper, you tell me.'

Hargreaves crossed his legs and pretended to glance out of the window trying to look disinterested.

'Is Mrs Hargreaves at home?'

'What?'

'Mrs Hargreaves. Is she at home right now?'

'What's my wife got to do with all this?'

'It's a simple question, Mr Hargreaves.'

'I don't like your attitude young man!' Hargreaves stood up.

Martin didn't reply but sat looking him in the face. The stare off between them lasted less than a minute before Hargreaves looked away and returned to his seat. He sighed and shrugged his shoulders before speaking.

'Look, I'm under enormous pressure to get a deal done right now. I can't spend my time worrying about some stupid girl who gets herself killed.'

'I appreciate you have business to attend to Mr Hargreaves but you see when a body is found it's my business to find out what happened. Now I'd appreciate it if you answered my question.'

'My wife has gone back to bed. She is under medication right now.'

Martin waited for him to continue.

'As I mentioned before, she suffers from migraine and has been undergoing a series of tests to ascertain the reason. Check with Doctor Meadows if you don't believe me.'

Martin stood to leave. It was quite apparent the conversation wasn't going anywhere. 'I'm sorry to hear Mrs Hargreaves feels unwell. Please pass on my sympathy.'

Martin let himself out but turned around as he descended the steps at the front of the house.

'Oh one last question. Did Felicity Morgan seem happy when she was working here?'

'Happy? I wouldn't know.'

As Hargreaves closed the door Martin looked up at one of the bedroom windows where someone was looking through the curtain.

The forensics lab was a hive of activity when Wesley strolled in. Catching the eye of a tall brunette through an observation window, he held his ID up to the glass. She walked across the room, glanced at his ID and beckoned him along the corridor to the door.

'Hello Inspector Wesley, good morning.'

Wesley was taken back with the tall slim figure, long blond hair and a smile that had certainly melted many a man's heart.

'I received a call this morning to say that a knife had been found near to where Felicity Morgan's body was originally seen,' he stammered almost apologetically.

'Ah yes, that was me, Inspector. Do come in,' she said closing the door behind her.

'Let me introduce myself, I'm Mel Harris, I only started here a week ago.'

They shook hands before she led him over to an oblong shaped metal trolley that was stood up against a row of glass cabinets.

'This is the item we found.'

Mel held up a clear plastic bag that contained a solid silver carving knife.

'Where was this found exactly?' Wesley asked.

Mel squinted at the small tag that was attached to knife by a piece of string.

'Found in the grounds of the Melcham estate, fifteen feet from where it is believed the victim originally died. There are a number of miniscule coat hairs from the cardigan the murder victim was wearing on the handle.'

'So what you're saying is that Felicity Morgan had at one time been carrying the knife.'

'I can't be positive as there are no clear fingerprints buy yes that would be a safe assumption.'

'Is there anything distinctive about the knife? I mean anything that's not immediately obvious?' Wesley asked.

'Not really, Inspector. It's the usual form of carving knife although I would say it's not one of the normal run of the mill mass production items.'

'Oh, what makes you say that?'

'The coat of arms indented stamp on the handle.' Mel reached for a magnifying glass and held it out in front of her over the handle of the knife.

Wesley extracted a pen and notebook from his coat pocket.

'It's OK Inspector I've already pencilled a little sketch for you.'

Mel laid the knife back down on the trolley and walked over to a small wooden desk where she extracted a slip of paper from the top drawer.

'Here you are.' She handed it across.

Wesley examined the sketch which was expertly drawn.

'Thanks very much Mel. I must say this drawing is almost like a replica. How did you manage to copy it so precise?'

'Three years at art school before I changed careers.'

Wesley looked again at the sketch before slipping the paper into his notebook.

'You've been a great help Mel, thanks.'

'You're welcome, Inspector.'

'Please, call me John.'

Mel smiled as they shook hands.

Wesley stood in the car park drawing deeply on his cigarette. Something about the coat of arms looked familiar but he wasn't sure why.

Jane was in a happier mood today as Gerry Callow had left a message on the answer phone to say that he was back home and feeling better. She hopped off the bus and began the short walk to the hospital. The morning had started cold and crisp with just a light flurry of snow but by the time she reached the entrance to the hospital it was snowing heavier and she had to shake the snow from her clothes before entering the building. Having discarded her coat for her receptionist's jacket she realised she still had another ten minutes before her shift started so she sat in the back office and selected Gerry's number from her mobile.

Gerry Callow answered almost immediately.

'Ah, my guardian angel,' he exclaimed laughing as soon as he heard Jane's voice. 'Bless you for popping in to see me yesterday. I think I gave the nurses a fright, seeing my big lump slumped on the bed.'

Jane couldn't help but laugh at Gerry's description of himself.

'You gave us all a fright you big pudding. How are you feeling this morning?'

'Much better thanks, Jane. I think I over did things. As you know I've been trying to spruce up the shop a bit and probably did too much too soon.'

'Well don't,' Jane replied sharply. 'You were told last year to slow down.'

'Sorry mum.'

Jane sniggered. Did she really talk to Gerry Callow like a son?

'Listen, I finish at midday, so I'll pop in on the way home to make sure you're OK.'

'Jane, my dear, Glastonbury High Street is not exactly on your way home is it?'

'So I'll take the longer route home. Is there anything you want me to bring in?'

'I don't suppose you're going anywhere near the bakers are you?'

'No, Gerry Callow, I'm not. No more cakes for you. I'll bring you in something healthy.'

Jane was still laughing when she hung up.

9

Having worked her way half way through Felicity Morgan's address book Mandy came across a telephone number she was surprised to find.

Simply out of curiosity, she dialled the number and waited for a reply.

The phone rang four times before it was answered. The woman's voice sounded hesitant.

'Hello, this is Lady Hargreaves speaking.'

'I'm so sorry,' said Mandy, 'I've dialled the wrong number,' and hung up.

Replacing the receiver, she gathered her notes together before slipping them in a drawer. Twenty minutes later Mandy pulled into the main car park at the far end of Street's shopping mall. Even though the recent snow had made travelling difficult, many shoppers appeared to have made the effort to get out and the small town shops were doing a good trade. Passing one of the local bakeries Mandy was tempted to grab a large cream slice but resisted temptation, thinking the extra few pounds around her waist would detract her from wearing her swimsuit in a few days from now. Entering the travel agency she was immediately greeted by a young shop assistant who gave the appearance of having just left school. His acne was only partially hidden by the bum fluff around his face.

'Good afternoon, how can I help you?'

Mandy almost laughed when she spotted his multi coloured trainers, which certainly didn't match the rest of his clothing of white shirt and grey trousers.

'I'm looking for a short break, somewhere warm where I can get some sun to my body,' Mandy was sure the lad blushed when she smiled at him.

The young assistant proved to be extremely helpful and diplomatic as he steered Mandy away from some of the livelier locations after deciding that although Mandy was still only in her mid-twenties she probably wouldn't have felt comfortable being surrounded by a load of drunken teenagers.

Having just agreed the deposit for her January holiday in Tenerife Mandy was searching through her handbag for her purse when her mobile rang. She checked the caller's number before answering. It was Wesley. Mandy motioned to the young lad that she would take the call outside then return.

'Hello sir, sorry I was in the travel agency.'

'Ah good, I'm pleased you've taken my advice. Mandy, can you pop over to see Annie Griffin. She's just phoned the station saying she's just remembered something that may be important. It may be nothing but can you check it out.'

'Sure, will do. I'll be on my way in five minutes.'

'Thanks Mandy. Where are you going for your holiday?' Wesley asked.

'I'll show you the place I'm going to later,' she replied sounding excited.

'Yes please do, but don't tell Jane otherwise she'll be asking to go on a holiday too.' Wesley couldn't see the smile on Mandy's face.

'By the way, sir, I was looking at Felicity Morgan's address book earlier and came across a phone number that might interest you. It's a mobile, belongs to Lady Hargreaves.'

'You mean Brian Hargreaves' wife?'

'That's the one.'

'Well, well. Now why would Lady Hargreaves give Felicity Morgan her private number?

'I don't know, sir, but it seems strange doesn't it?'

'Hmm. Mandy, do me a favour. After you've spoken with Annie see if Lady Hargreaves is at home. Make some excuse about already being on the estate to see Annie so you thought you'd pop in. You know the drill. I'm interested to hear what she has to say about Felicity having her mobile number.'

'Sure thing, sir, see you back at the office later.'

Mandy placed her mobile back into her coat pocket and headed back into the travel agency.

Wesley looked up from his desk as Martin entered the office.

'How did your meeting go with Brian Hargreaves? Mandy is popping over there later to speak with Lady Hargreaves. Apparently Felicity Morgan had Lady Hargreaves' mobile phone number in her address book.'

'They are certainly a strange couple. I still haven't met Lady Hargreaves yet. To be honest I can't work Brian Hargreaves out. He said he had no reason to report Felicity as missing simply because she failed to turn up for work. I wouldn't go so far as to say he was rude but he got very defensive when I asked him about his wife. He said she's on medication for migraines and had gone to have a lie down. She seems to live her life lying down.'

'Do you believe him?'

'I'm not sure to be honest. I was going to speak with Dr Meadows, he's their doctor. He'll confirm one way or the other whether Lady Hargreaves is under medication.'

'Yeah, like you, I'm not sure about Brian Hargreaves or his wife,' Wesley replied. 'Let's see what Mandy comes up with.'

Mandy was sat in Annie's kitchen looking at the homemade apple pie that Annie was slicing up.

'Are you sure I can't tempt you?' Annie asked.

'No honestly, I'm fine thanks Annie. Just a cup of tea would be fine.'

'I'll wrap a piece up so you can take it home.'

Mandy smiled as she watched Annie place a slice of the pie in grease proof paper. It was something Mandy's mother used to do.

'Annie, you telephoned the station to say that you'd remembered something that you think may be of interest to the police.'

'Now let me think. What was it?' Annie rested one arm on the worktop and squinted at the bread bin. 'Oh yes, I remember.' She left what she was doing and sat down at the table opposite Mandy.

'Do you remember that I told you that Brian's wife Lucy used to visit me quite regular?'

Mandy nodded.

'Well, the day before yesterday I thought I know what I'll do, I'll phone her just to see how she is. The funny thing is, when she first answered the phone I didn't recognise the voice straight away. Oh this is hard to explain,' said Annie scratching her forehead.

'Go on, you're doing fine,' Mandy replied encouragingly.

'When she first answered the phone she said "Lady Hargreaves speaking". Well, I've known Lucy since she was a child and she never referred to herself as Lady Hargreaves even though she's entitled to. She always answered saying "Hello this is Lucy, with whom am I speaking?" You see the difference?'

'Yes, but I'm not sure what you're getting at,' Mandy replied.

Annie swallowed as if she was nervous about what she was going to say next.

'People might think I'm an old fool these days and I admit I'm not as switched on as I used to be but I've just got a funny feeling, here in my stomach,' she said holding her hand to her belly.

Mandy remained silent allowing Annie both time and space to finish what she wanted to say.

'I don't think the woman who answered the telephone to me was Lucy Hargreaves.'

'Why, Annie, just because she answered the phone in a different manner?'

'No not only that. I told her I hadn't been able to attend to Fred's grave recently because of the weather.' Annie paused for a second. 'She replied, don't worry Annie he'll understand. I'm sure you'll be able to get over there when the weather brightens up.'

Mandy looked confused.

'I don't get it.'

Annie leant forward on the table, concern showing in her eyes.

'My Fred was cremated. The real Lucy Hargreaves would have known that.'

Wesley and Martin were enjoying a pub lunch and Wesley was particularly impressed with the Shepton Tribute bitter that Geoff was trialling.

'These fish and chips are real tasty,' said Martin taking another mouthful.

'Just the job,' Wesley replied, 'pass some salt over please.'

The Phoenix was renowned for its fish and chips.

Martin handed the salt across the table knocking his fork on the floor in the process.

'I'll get it, it's on my side,' said Wesley.

He handed the fork back to Martin then suddenly grabbed Martin's arm.

'Hold on a second, let me take a look at fork.'

'Why is it dirty or something?' Martin asked looking bewildered and handing it back. Holding the middle of the fork Wesley raised it up to the light.

'Yes! I thought so,' he exclaimed.

'Sorry sir but you've got me, what are you looking at?'

Wesley turned the fork around so that the rounded end was facing Martin.

'Take a look at the handle. Just there,' he said pointing. 'Do you see the crest? That's the same crest that's on the knife that was found near where Archie Black says he saw Felicity Morgan's body. I knew I'd seen it somewhere before.'

Wesley leapt from his chair and went to look for Geoff or Maggie. One of the part-time barmen informed him that Geoff was in the cellar changing a barrel but Maggie was 'out back' helping with the food orders. He was reluctant to allow Wesley to duck under the bar until Wesley showed his ID.

Maggie and two middle aged women were busy preparing food orders.

'Maggie, I appreciate you're busy but can I have a quick word?' asked Wesley standing in the doorway to the kitchen.

She was just about to retrieve a couple of large potatoes from a box on the floor.

'Hi, John, what's up?'

'The cutlery you're using. How long have you had it?'

Wesley could see the puzzled look on Maggie's face.

'Sorry, can we go somewhere quiet and I'll explain. I promise it won't take a minute.'

'Sure, follow me.'

Maggie led him into a small oblong shaped store room that was packed from floor to ceiling on either side with drinks bottles and food stuffs. She flicked a switch which slowly lit a six foot long fluorescent tube that gave out a minimal arc of light to the room.

'John, you do realise that you're carrying a fork in your hand,' she said moving a box to the floor so she could sit down.

'Oh yes. Look I know this probably isn't making a lot of sense right now but I'd like to know where and when you purchased this cutlery. There is a crest on the end of the handle.'

Maggie scratched her head and swept her hand back through her mass of jet black hair.

'We bought it just after we took over the pub, just after the refurbishment finished. I think Geoff managed to get it cheap from somewhere. John, what's the matter?'

'It's the crest,' Wesley replied pointing to the fork handle.

'What about the crest? I don't understand.'

'It looks like a coat of arms. It's an exact match to the knife that was found near where the body of Felicity Morgan was first seen.'

Maggie raised her hands to her mouth.

'Oh my God, are you sure? That means…..'

Wesley placed his hand on her shoulder to calm her down.

'All it means at this moment in time is that it's an exact match. It doesn't mean it couldn't have come from somewhere else.'

At that moment Geoff's voice could be heard from the kitchen.

'Geoff, we're in here!' Maggie shouted.

Geoff appeared in the doorway stinking of ale.

'Sorry for the smell. Bloody barrel split.' He looked across at Wesley then back to Maggie.

'What's up?'

Wesley repeated the story then asked Geoff the same question.

'I bought the whole cutlery service from a stall holder down at the market in town about a year ago. I only paid fifty quid for the lot.'

Wesley shrugged his shoulders.

'So we don't know where they originated from.'

'Yeah we do,' Geoff replied, 'I bought them off Bill Taylor. He bought them off Brian Hargreaves. Those markings are the Melcham family crest.'

Wesley and Martin were still sat in the pub finishing their beer when Geoff joined them at the table. The pub was nearly empty again now following the lunchtime rush.

'I've collected up the cutlery and we're missing two knives, three forks and a couple of spoons from that particular collection,' said Geoff. 'Occasionally we'll bin a knife or fork if it's damaged or just looks too used if you know what I mean. Sometimes people steal them. It's impossible to tell when the knife might have gone missing.'

'I appreciate you checking, Geoff, I wonder why Hargreaves decided upon selling the lot in the first place?'

Geoff raised his eyebrows and looked across the table at Wesley.

'There's been rumour around here amongst the locals for some time now that Hargreaves is not as well off as he pretends to be. I hear he recently sold a couple of grandfather clocks too.'

'Do you think he's in debt?'

Geoff shrugged his shoulders and stood up to leave.

'I wouldn't know John, but I'll tell you this, he's one strange character. I don't think he would still be living there if old Lord Melcham was still alive. Rumour has it the old man didn't like him. I think he would have booted him out long before now.'

'So what's our next move?' asked Martin.

'I think you ought to buy me another pint of Shepton Tribute and then we'll assess the situation,' Wesley replied holding his empty glass aloft.

Henry Morgan stood poking at the embers of the bonfire. He was so engaged in what he was doing he never heard his wife as she approached. He seemed to have gone into a shell from the moment Sally had told him that their murdered daughter was in fact pregnant.

'Henry, what are you doing out here and what on earth are you burning?'

Henry had lit the small bonfire at the bottom of their garden as soon as he'd returned home from work.

'Just a few of Felicity's things, I mean, she won't need them will she?'

'Oh, Henry you've got to stop this! It's almost like you're cremating our daughter. Every day since she's been gone you've burnt something of hers in this bloody garden. This has got to stop.'

'It's my way of handling it OK!' he shouted throwing the pitch fork to ground.

Sally tried to put her arm around his shoulder but he shrugged her off.

'Why don't you speak to the doctor? I'm sure he'll prescribe something for you,' said Sally.

'Bloody doctor doesn't understand. How could he?'

He marched back toward the bungalow leaving Sally Morgan standing alone to watch the flames eat away at a bundle of clothes. Wrapping her arms around her waist she began to sob as the tears rolled down her face blurring her vision. She looked up as she heard the family car start up and peered down the side of the property just in time to see Henry pull out into the street. Another occasion when she knew he would return home drunk, if he came home at all.

Sally went back into the bungalow and made her way to Felicity's bedroom. She was almost scared to open the door as if by doing so she would be sucked back into a world she knew she could never be a part of again. It was obvious that Henry had been in the room. All of Felicity's teddy bears had been lined up on the bed against the wall as if they were waiting for Felicity to come home.

Sally walked across the room and pulled open the wardrobe door. There was only one dress still hanging up and Sally recognised these as the dress Felicity wore on her prom night. Closing the door Sally slumped back on the bed and let out a piercing scream that would have been heard for miles around.

Mandy was sat in the car outside Annie's Cottage as the implications of what Annie had just told her began to sink in. She selected Wesley's number on her mobile and waited for him to reply. He answered in two rings.

'Hi, Mandy, you OK?'

'Yeah fine thanks, sir. I just wanted to bring you up to date with a chat I've just had with Annie Griffin.'

After repeating the conversation she'd just had with Annie, Mandy finished by saying she was on her way to Melcham Hall to question Lucy Hargreaves to ascertain why her mobile phone number was found in Felicity Morgan's address book.

'Alright, but do me a favour. Ask her if she knows when and why her husband sold the cutlery?'

'The what, sir?'

'The cutlery. It seems that Brian Hargreaves has been selling off the family hair looms recently including cutlery and grandfather clocks to mention but two. I'll explain more a bit later but there are two grandfather clocks for sale in the antique shop in Wells. I've just spoken with the owner and apparently Hargreaves is desperate to sell. He's been selling quite a number of items.'

'It sounds like he's struggling for money,' said Mandy.

'Yeah, that was my immediate thought too. See if you can find out what's going on.'

'Sure thing, is that all, sir?'

'Err yes. Just be careful at Melcham Hall. I've got a feeling that not everything is as it seems over there.'

'OK will do. I'll call you later.'

Mandy hung up and replaced her mobile in her handbag. She was so looking forward to her holiday.

The gravel pathway leading through the estate down to Melcham Hall was still icy even though most of the snow had melted in the exposed areas. Mandy turned the car around outside the building before bringing it to a halt. She had been trained to always leave the vehicle facing away from the property in case she ever needed to make a quick getaway. Looking at the crumbling blocks that stood guard to the front porch she now understood why Martin had said the property looked in need of repair. She'd been thinking about Martin a lot lately but dismissed it from her mind before getting out of the car. Mounting the four stone slabs she pressed the buzzer next to the imposing front door. The body language of the person who answered suggested the woman was carrying the world on her shoulders. Her back was arched, her head seemed to have dropped into her neck and she continually rubbed her hands together. Her hair had been tied back in a bun but several loose strands were hanging either side of her face.

'Lady Hargreaves?'

'Yes, what do you want?'

'I'm WPC Mandy Tredwell. May I come in?'

The woman seemed to study Mandy for several seconds before slowly pulling the door back and gesturing for her to enter. Closing the door behind her she turned to face Mandy motioning for her to lead the way into the first room on the right of the hallway. Mandy stepped into the front parlour with its paintings of hunting scenes and dark flock wallpaper that gave the appearance of being trapped in time.

'Please take a seat.'

Mandy sat in one of two wingback chairs that stood closest to the window.

She studied Lady Hargreaves as the woman gingerly sat in front of her.

'So how can I help you? My husband has already spoken to one of your colleagues about the incident outside Rowan Lodge. I don't see how we can be of further help?'

Mandy crossed her legs and leaned back in the chair trying to create a more relaxed approach.

'I actually came to ask you about Felicity Morgan.'

'Who?'

'Felicity Morgan. She was the young woman who was housemaid here for a short while. The young woman who was found murdered.'

'Sorry but I didn't know her name.'

'That's strange, Lady Hargreaves. Can you tell me why then, she would have had your mobile number written in her address book?'

Mandy noticed the whites of Lady Hargreaves knuckles as the woman constantly rung her hands.

'I really have no idea.'

'So you don't recall ever providing Felicity Morgan with your mobile number?'

'Certainly not, why would I give her my number?'

'That's what I'm trying to ascertain, Lady Hargreaves.'

'Could your husband Mr Hargreaves have given her your number?'

At the mention of her husband, Mandy noticed the woman become even more rigid in her manner.

'I think Brian would have told me if he'd given anyone my number.'

'In that case do you have any other idea how Felicity came to have your number?'

'I do have a habit of leaving my mobile lying around the house, maybe she took the number having found the phone somewhere. I can't think of any other explanation.'

Mandy re-crossed her legs to stop the pins and needles in her foot.

'I understand from the job agency that you haven't asked for anyone to replace Felicity?'

'Err, no, my husband says it's an opportunity for us to see if we can cope without any domestic assistance.'

Mandy smiled trying to get her audience to relax.

'I guess the cost of having someone in domestic service is expensive these days?' she asked.

'Very possibly, you would have to ask my husband about that. He deals with all the finances.'

'Ah, so he's probably the best person to ask about grandfather clocks.'

'Pardon me?'

'My father is interested in buying a grandfather clock and I understand there are two for sale in the antique shops in Wells, both belonging to your husband.'

'Oh, is there? I'm afraid I don't get involved in that side of things.'

Mandy thought she would try one last approach.

'Just one last question if I may?'

Lady Hargreaves toyed with her skirt running her fingers up and down the pleats.

'How well do you know Annie Griffin?'

'Annie? Oh she's like one of the family.'

'So you've known her a long time?'

'Since the day I was born.'

'It's such a shame that she lives on her own in that lodge isn't it? It must be very lonely at times. I understand you used to visit her quite regularly.'

'Yes, yes I did, and I ought to make more effort to see her these days.'

'How long has her husband been gone?'

'Oh, several years now, I can't exactly remember when. Time goes so quickly.'

'What was his name now?' Mandy asked giving the appearance that she was trying to remember.

Lady Hargreaves sat staring into space for some time before turning back to look at Mandy.

'Sorry but for the life of me I can't recall his name. As I say, the years go by so fast.'

As Mandy stood to leave she handed Lady Hargreaves her card. 'Please give me a call if you think of anything you think we ought to know about. You can reach me directly on this number.'

Lady Hargreaves stared at the card and gave the impression she was about to speak before changing her mind. Mandy noticed how Lady Hargreaves had never once looked her in the eye.

Having left Lady Hargreaves standing in the doorway, Mandy stood by the car looking back at the house as the weak winter sun began to disappear over the rooftop casting an eerie shadow on the front of the property. As she got in the car she felt a shiver run down her spine and was happy to hear the sound of the automatic door lock. She now understood why Martin had said he'd felt there was something not quite right about Melcham Hall.

10

The sky was a dull grey and melting snow had left dirty slush piles on kerbs and pavements alike, and a cold northerly breeze meant that the temperature only remained just above freezing. Wesley stood in the alleyway alongside the station drawing deeply on his cigarette. He had upturned the collar of his jacket and pulled it close to him for warmth. This was only his second winter away from London and he struggled with the extreme cold. Buildings and people are always more condensed in the inner cities leaving one less exposed than the rural areas. He remembered walking the beat during his early days as a young constable, being sent out in all weathers for several hours at a time. He specifically remembered the day when he'd been called upon to undertake traffic duty when the traffic lights at Westminster Bridge had failed. It had been a cold January morning with the temperature just below freezing. The kind of day when you could see your breath and the clothes you were wearing felt both damp and wet. An old lady from the corner drink stall had taken him over a cup of coffee as she felt sorry for him but by the time he had the opportunity to take a sip, the coffee was stone cold and a layer of ice had formed on the top.

He watched two young lads trying to skid along the opposite pavement and remembered the days when his mother used to cuff him around the ear for trying the same. "You'll wear the soles out of your shoes and then your father will tell you off" she used to say. Wesley smirked at the memory, rubbed the remains of his cigarette between thumb and forefinger and made his way back inside the police station where he found Mandy sat with her coat on, her hands gripping a hot cup of tea.

Jane had just phoned him to say she was visiting Gerry Callow in the bookshop in Glastonbury and would therefore be home a little later than usual, just in case he wondered where she was. Wesley knew she missed working in the bookshop and thought it was only a matter of time before she said she was going back.

'You look as cold as I feel,' said Wesley, 'come into the office. I'm just going to grab a drink myself.'

Mandy closed the door behind her and sat opposite Wesley as he toyed with the tea bag in his mug.

'So you've booked a holiday then?' he asked without looking up.

'Yes sir, a week in sunny Tenerife. I could have done with a few weeks to lose a bit of weight, but have had to buy a bigger swimsuit.'

Wesley smirked as he dropped the tea bag in the bin.

'The break will do you the world of good.'

'Can I just say thanks, sir,' Mandy replied biting her lower lip.

'Thanks, what for?'

'For understanding.'

She was sure he blushed as he searched amongst paperwork on his desk for the file he wanted.

'So, it appears that both you and Martin think there's something odd about Lady Hargreaves' behaviour?'

Mandy explained how Lady Hargreaves had seemed so vague with her answers to the questions she'd asked, especially her seemingly lack of knowledge about the items her husband had been selling and her lack of interest in both Annie Griffin and Felicity Morgan. Wesley leant back in his chair considering his next move.

'Mandy, you know some of the locals. Ask around the village and get a feel for the local gossip. We know that Lady Hargreaves has always been supportive of the local community. According to Jim at the council she's treasurer of the Women's Institute and Chairlady of the local Bowls club.'

At that moment Martin knocked on the door and entered. He sneezed twice before pulling up a chair.

'I don't want your cold thanks very much,' said Wesley.

'And you can keep away from me too,' Mandy commented laughing, as he sneezed again. 'The last thing I need is to be having a cold when I'm sat by the swimming pool.'

'Sorry, I must have picked it up from someone in the Phoenix earlier.'

'Oh so you two have been out for a pub lunch eh?' Mandy asked.

'Only on business,' Wesley replied with a grin. 'We were talking about Lady Hargreaves and the concerns you both have.'

'Hmm got another one too,' Martin replied blowing his nose. 'I've been speaking with Lenny Harris. He looks after the grounds of Melcham Hall these days. He's only been there for a just over a month. Apparently Brian Hargreaves sacked the last fella calling him a lazy so and so.'

Both Wesley and Mandy remained silent waiting for him to continue.

'Anyhow, Lenny says that he's only met Lady Hargreaves a couple of times and only spoken to her the once although he's seen her loads of times walking around the estate with that Doberman of theirs. When I asked him if he'd seen any change in Lady Hargreaves' manner he replied no except that when he last saw her only a few days ago she was having trouble controlling the dog.'

'What's that got to do with anything?' Mandy asked.

Martin blew his nose again.

'Well Lenny says that the boys down the pub all say that the dog normally follows Lady Hargreaves wherever she goes and obeys her every command, but when Lenny saw her last she was chasing after the dog because it had ran off. Lenny says he could hear her swearing and cursing as she tried to catch it. He said when he did see her with it, the dog was on a lead and Lady Hargreaves looked almost scared to touch it.'

The three of them sat in silence for a few moments. It was Mandy who was the first to speak.

'I get the feeling we're all thinking the same thing but not saying it,' she said looking first at Wesley then at Martin.

'See what else you can find out from the locals Martin, I'll make a couple of phone calls from here,' Wesley replied before turning to Mandy.

'I think you ought to stay inside for a couple of hours my dear. We don't want you getting a cold before you go away. Phone Felicity Morgan's parents first will you. I believe her cremation is the day after tomorrow, find out the exact time. I want two of us there. When you've done that see if you can ascertain what telephone numbers have been dialled from the pay phone at the place Felicity was renting from.'

Wesley passed a slip a paper across the desk. 'That's the pay phone number.'

Two hours later, still sat at his desk, Wesley pinched the bridge of his nose screwing his eyes up at the same time. Jane had telephoned to say she had just returned from the bookshop where Gerry Callow looked to be in good spirits and seemed to be taking the doctor's advice by slowing down a little. She said that just as she was passing the hairdressers she was accosted by Wendy Barnes, the shop owner. Apparently Wendy had read the article about a body being found on the Melcham estate and went on to say that the last time Lady Hargreaves had visited to have her hair cut she'd noticed that the woman was losing her hair and had looked rather drained. Jane said that maybe it something of nothing but worth mentioning. He thanked Jane and hung up before dialling the number she had given him. A woman answered sounding rather flustered.

'Good afternoon Principals hairdressing.'

Wesley thought it was a strange name for a hairdresser's but didn't want to get into that line of conversation right now.

'Good afternoon, this is Inspector Wesley speaking from Street police. Who am I speaking with?'

The woman seemed to regain a little of her composure.

'Oh good afternoon Inspector, this is Wendy Barnes. How can I help?'

'Wendy, I'm sorry to bother you and I know you're busy but can I just ask you a quick question?'

'Of course you can, Inspector.'

Wesley couldn't see Wendy patting the back of her hair to make sure she looked OK even though she was only on the telephone.

'Jane informs me Lady Hargreaves is one of your clients. Is that correct?'

'Yes, Lady Hargreaves has been coming to us for several years. What is it you would like to know Inspector? I mean, she is OK isn't she?'

Wesley reassured her it was only an initial enquiry as to people's whereabouts over the past few weeks following on from the discovery of a body on the Melcham estate.

'Oh I see,' she replied twirling the telephone cord around her fingers.

'When was the last time Lady Hargreaves visited the salon?'

'Let me take a look in the book, I can tell you exactly when Lady Hargreaves' last appointment was.'

Wesley could hear the rustle of papers in the background and the sound of something being dropped before the woman came back to the phone.

'Ah here it is. It's five weeks to the day when Lady Hargreaves came in.'

'Do you know who attended her?' Wesley asked.

'Why yes, it was me, Inspector. Lady Hargreaves has always been rather a fusspot if I may say so. You know what I mean. Everything from the time she arrives, including her haircut and the coffee cup she drinks. Everything is always the same.'

'Tell me Wendy, the last time you saw Lady Hargreaves, did she act different in any way? Was there anything odd about her appearance or manner?'

'Well I don't like to speak about people as a rule, as your good lady would tell you, but there was one thing that struck me as odd.'

'And what was that?'

'She was losing her hair.'

'Wendy, forgive me for being naïve but aren't we all slowly losing our hair?'

Wesley ran his hand across his own head, aware that his hair was thinning a little these days.

'Oh yes, Inspector, of course we are, especially as we get older.'

'So what makes Lady Hargreaves any different?'

'Quite simply, that when I combed her hair it was literally falling out in clumps.'

'And this had never happened before?'

'I've been in the hairdressing business for over twenty years and I've not seen anything like it except when poor old Miss Bracknell lost her hair when she was being treated for cancer. Even then, she was in her seventies and Lady Hargreaves is only half her age.'

'So you don't know of any other medical reason that could cause this?'

'No I don't. At the rate her hair was falling out I would take a guess that the poor woman will be bald in a month from now. We did have a bit of a laugh about it at the time but Lady Hargreaves didn't seem too concerned. In fact, I'd go so far to say that she seemed to have other things on her mind.'

'How do you mean? Can you give me an example?'

'Not really, Inspector. I mean, nothing specific, but for the whole time she was here it was almost as if her thoughts were elsewhere.'

'Has she got any future appointments booked?'

'Let me look.'

When she spoke again Wesley could hear the uncertainty in her voice.

'That's strange. There's nothing in the diary, Inspector. And Lady Hargreaves has always had a couple of bookings in advance.'

'Well, perhaps you're right. Perhaps she did have other things on her mind. Thanks for the information, Wendy. You've been a great help. Do me one more favour would you?'

'Of course, what is it?'

'Just let me know when you next hear from Lady Hargreaves.'

'Yes of course.'

Wesley thanked the woman for her time before hanging up and making another call, this time to France.

The phone rang several times as Wesley patiently waited for someone to pick up. Eventually a gruff voice answered.

'Bonjour, who is it?'

'Hey my friend, how are you?' Wesley laughed, 'such a warm welcome from sunny France, spoken in your best French.'

'Wesley? Is that you?'

'Sure is. Sounds like I woke you up.'

'Actually you have, it's my day off, but as it's you I'll forgive you.'

O'Hara yawned and stretched his legs. He'd fallen asleep in the armchair watching a movie with his daughter who was curled up alongside him.

'Is everything OK? It's unusual for you to phone so early in the day. I mean, the pubs aren't even open yet.'

'They've just opened over here. I'm just queued to get in.'

The two friends shared a private joke. Since moving to France and retiring from being a private detective, David O'Hara's lifestyle had completely changed. He and his family were now settled into a rural part of France where his daytime job involved driving into the local village to sell fruit and vegetables from a market stall from six in the morning until two in the afternoon four days a week. Not only had his lifestyle improved but also had the health of his daughter who two years ago almost died following a series of asthma attacks. Not helped by the abundance of fumes she inhaled daily living in Central London. Now she competed in sports and was fast becoming a good athlete.

'David, I need a favour?'

'What, so soon? You only left France a few days ago. I thought you said you were looking for a quieter life in the country?'

'I am but tell that to the villains of this world.'

'Yeah I understand, ask away.'

'If my geography is correct the town of Perpignan is not that far from you.'

'That's right, it's just on the coast from here, about twenty kilometres away. Don't tell me there's been a murder in the town. The whole place is as quiet as a library at the best of times. The only thing that makes the front pages in Perpignan is the snail race they hold every year in the square.'

Wesley couldn't help laughing at the mental vision he had of life in Perpignan. 'No, seriously I would like to ask if you could visit an apartment in the town. The address is 15 Rue des Fleurs, apartment 4.'

'A pretty young blonde I assume eh? ' O'Hara asked with a smirk on his face. 'I hope Jane knows about this.'

'That's just wishful thinking. The person I'm looking for is Kate Melcham, daughter of the late Sir Clive Melcham, or Lord Melcham as he was known around these parts. This is her last known address.'

'What's the reason for finding her?'

'I'm just inquisitive. I've got a hunch that you won't find her living there anymore.'

'John Wesley, you work in riddles. You want me to drive to Perpignan to search for a woman who you believe isn't there.'

'That's correct. You see, I have a feeling the woman has returned to the UK but I need to be sure of the facts before I make my next move.'

'If it was anyone else asking I'd say they were completely bonkers. Do you have a photo of the woman?'

'I've got an old photograph from a local newspaper so I'll scan it over to you.'

'OK, that gives me something to go on. I'll drive over there this evening. The roads will be quieter then.'

'That would be great, David. I do appreciate it.'

'You won't appreciate my invoice,' O'Hara joked. 'What's the story, or shouldn't I ask? I'm just thinking if the woman is there what should I say?'

Wesley gave him a brief run down on recent events.

'If she's there just pretend you're a salesman or something. Take some of your fruit and veg to sell,' Wesley replied trying not to laugh.

'I should have known you'd be so helpful. I'll call you from Perpignan.'

'Love to the family,' Wesley replied before hanging up.

'This is interesting,' said Mandy entering Wesley's office. 'I stopped at a local newsagent in Shepton Mallet and got talking to the shop keeper. When I mentioned the Melcham estate she said that a strange thing occurred last Sunday. Apparently the young lad who delivers the newspapers to them saw Lady Hargreaves standing by the garage so he called out to her as he'd done several times before. However, this time she just stared at him as if she didn't recognise him. She said he was kind of spooked by it.'

Wesley nodded his head and explained to Mandy that he'd just telephoned

O'Hara asking him to confirm whether Lucy Hargreaves' sister still lived in France.

'Are you suggesting that the woman at Melcham Hall is in fact not Lucy Hargreaves but her twin sister Kate?'

'I'm not suggesting anything yet,' Wesley replied. 'I'm just trying to tick a number of boxes.'

Martin was sat in the police canteen dipping a large slice of uncut bread into a pea coloured soup when Wesley caught up with him. 'Your face looks the same colour as that bloody soup,' Wesley remarked sitting opposite.

Martin's sniff and nasal reply answered the question.

'Man flu? This is not to the place to be if you need sympathy.'

Wesley grinned as he took a bite of a bacon sandwich.

'Any luck with British Telecom about calls being made from the payphone where Felicity was lodging?'

'I've just received a printout from them,' Martin replied wiping soup from his chin. 'I'll take a look at it in a while.' He pushed the remains of his soup away and blew his nose. 'By the way the funeral is at eleven the day after tomorrow.'

'Funeral, I thought Felicity Morgan was being cremated?'

'I just assumed so too but she's being buried in the local church in South Horrington. Mrs Morgan said that several years ago she and her husband paid for two plots to be used for when they passed away, but now they've agreed that Felicity should be buried there.'

'Oh I see,' Wesley replied with a sigh. 'I can't imagine what it's like to have to bury your own child.' His thoughts suddenly turned to Mandy who he knew was still finding it difficult to cope with the loss of her daughter.

Wesley pulled up outside Jasmine Cottage and switched off the car engine.

Outside the grey sullen sky had already given way to a dark moonless evening and the only light visible through the car windscreen came from the reading lamp in the window of their front room. This was only the second year in their new home since he and Jane had moved to Street, although London already seemed a lifetime ago. Wesley took a moment to look at the picture postcard scene in front of him, the thatched Cottage whose roof was still mostly covered in snow, the robin standing in the porch seeking both food and warmth and the knowledge that this was now home. They had purchased Jasmine Cottage the day they first saw it and Jane had burst into tears when Wesley said they would buy it. Now it had become their home and they had already made plans to have a small extension built in character with the existing building.

As soon as Wesley opened the front door the smell of newly baked bread caught his attention, reminding him he was hungry.

'Shut that door, I can feel the draft coming through to the kitchen,' Jane called.

'That's what I like, a lovely warm welcome,' he replied stepping into the kitchen.

'And take those dirty shoes off,' Jane exclaimed.

'I love it when you talk to me like that,' said Wesley after placing his shoes on the mat by the back door and taking Jane in his arms. He gave her a hug and kissed her on the cheek.

'Get off you big lump and go and wash your hands. Dinner's ready.'

The oblong shaped kitchen at the back of the Cottage acted as their dining room as long as they didn't have company, when they used the back room through the adjacent door.

'So tell me about your day,' asked Jane once they were seated.

Whilst eating his way through homemade steak pie with potato and vegetables Wesley explained the intrigue surrounding Lucy Hargreaves' behaviour and their current lack of being any further forward in identifying Felicity Morgan's killer.

'You mentioned something about Mandy too, as you left this morning,' said Jane as she raised a glass of wine to her lips.

'Yeah, I was wondering if you could give her a call sometime. You know, just ask her how she is. She's a bit down at the moment and I'm worried about her. Its two years this week since she lost her baby.'

'Oh my word, doesn't time go quick. Yes of course I'll phone her and arrange an evening out.'

Wesley reached for his wine glass, wiping his mouth with a napkin at the same time.

'I know she's just booked a holiday but I think she needs company right now.'

'Has she not got a boyfriend? I don't recall her mentioning anyone.'

Wesley shrugged his shoulders.

'I don't know, I don't think so. If she has she certainly hasn't told anyone.'

'I'm not sure I'd want you lot knowing details of my social life,' Jane remarked with a smirk on her face as she pushed her plate away.

'I'm only concerned about Mandy's welfare,' he replied, 'she's a hard kid but she broke down in the office. She's only human.'

Jane reached across the table and placed her hand on his.

'You're a big softie really John Wesley, and I love you for it.'

11

Lucy Hargreaves woke and leaned across the bed to look at the time. Seeing that neither the bedside alarm clock nor the bedside table were there she slowly came back to the daunting reality of her situation. She rubbed the sleep from her eyes and stared at her surroundings. She had become a prisoner in the dingy room. Lucy tried to recall how many days she had been held captive. At first it had been easy to keep count, but now she wasn't sure if it was still days or weeks since her confinement. A breakfast tray had been placed on the table at the end of the bed containing tea and toast. After addressing to her toiletry needs she sat on the edge of the bed and took a bite of the cold toast. She felt the tea cup; that was cold too. Hearing the key turn in the lock, Mandy looked up as the kidnapper entered the room.

'Good morning, Lucy. I hope you slept well. I was wondering if you had changed your mind about signing the papers. It seems such a shame to keep you locked up like this when you could be out enjoying yourself.'

Lucy picked up the tea cup and hurled it across the room at her visitor, where is smashed to pieces against the far wall.

'What a pity, I was hoping we would make some progress today, I'll come back when you're in a better mood.'

She heard the door close and the key turn in the lock before burying her head against the bed quilt as the daily tears began to flow.

As it was her day off, Jane had spent the afternoon helping out in the bookshop, making sure that her friend Gerry Callow was doing exactly what the doctor ordered, and that was to rest. There were fewer tourists around this time of year so it was the ideal time to make changes to the layout of the shop. Jane cleared away a mountain of empty boxes that littered the back office and set about opening others that contained the latest editions of a number of magazines. Even though the bookshop concentrated mostly on second hand historical books and novels, the latest editions of a few well known magazines always caught the eye, tempting people into the shop.

Gerry Callow felt slightly embarrassed at leaving Jane to do all the manual side of things he wasn't used to being fussed over. When he appeared with a tray of tea and biscuits, Jane immediately took the tray from him, placed it down on a chair and removed the biscuits.

'No biscuits, Gerry. Remember what the doctor said.'

When Jane left at five o'clock the shop looked tidier than it had done for months. There was a new window display advertising a mixture of old and new books, old on the left, new on the right. Inside the shop, Jane had removed all the cardboard boxes of new stock, filling shelves and rearranging sections to make them look more attractive.

'There you go,' she said as she put her coat on. 'People can actually walk around the shop now, and get to shelves that might be of interest to them.'

'Thanks, Jane. I don't know what I would do…'

'Be quiet you, just do as the doctor said,' Jane replied grabbing her handbag.

'I'll give you a call at the weekend and pop over if I get the chance.'

'Jane, please don't put yourself out. I'll be OK.'

Jane smiled and kissed him on the cheek.

'Phone if you need anything,' she said closing the door behind her.

A bitterly cold wind blew along the High Street almost blowing Jane off her feet. With a flurry of snow swirling under the street lights and pavements still slippery from an earlier snow fall, Jane was relieved to reach the bus garage in one piece. As the bus chugged its way up the hill and out of town, Jane looked across at the Tor and recalled the time when Wesley had found himself exploring underground tunnels in search of a kidnap victim. She shivered at the thought of being enclosed underground and tried to wipe the thought from her memory.

Brian Hargreaves pushed the dinner plate across the table.

'For God's sake get a grip woman,' he shouted.

Lady Hargreaves sank her head into her hands. 'You didn't tell me you'd murdered the girl,' she cried.

'That's because I didn't murder her, I didn't touch the girl.'

Lady Hargreaves looked up, tears running down her face.

'Then who did? She was found dead on the estate. Look, it's in the bloody newspaper. It says she was stabbed to death.'

'I've read the bloody paper. I don't know who killed her but it wasn't me.'

Brian Hargreaves reached for his cigarettes, realised the packet was empty and threw it on the floor.

'I heard you arguing with her the last day she turned up here.' You stood at the top of the stairs telling her to mind her own business about something or other. What was that all about?'

He seemed to hesitate before answering.

'She was asking questions about you, if you really want to know. She said you didn't know where the cleaning agents were kept or where the key to the broom cupboard was. She said you acted as if you didn't know anything about your own house.'

'Do you think she suspected something?'

'It makes no difference now, the dead can't talk.'

He reached for his jacket and grabbed his car keys.

'Where are you going?' she cried standing up.

'I'm going into town to buy cigarettes. Is that OK?'

'What about me? I'm stuck in this damn place. I can't go anywhere without people staring at me. Even Annie Griffin is stood by the bloody window all day. I can't even go for a bloody walk without her seeing me.'

Brian Hargreaves walked across the room and grabbed her roughly by the arm.

'You've got everything you ever wanted. You've got this place and your hands on the inheritance. What the hell is wrong with you? I told you from the start you need to be patient. Don't give me a hard time. You knew what you were getting into.'

He slammed the door behind him, leaving her staring into space.

The drive from Cabestany to Perpignan took O'Hara less than thirty minutes.

He used to hate driving in London and often took the tube instead, but driving in the French countryside was quite pleasurable. After driving through a couple of small hamlets he took the main road towards Perpignan which still only compared to a B road in the UK. He had only passed two other vehicles before he parked the Citroën in the main square. After switching off the ignition he looked at the slip of paper again to check the address. He located the Rue de Fleurs with ease. The narrow cobbled street ran downhill, away from the main square. Its ancient, tall white washed buildings leant so close to each other on either side of the narrow cobbled street that he was sure the overhead balconies were almost touching. The solid wooden door to number 15 had a gothic look with its arched top and single brass knocker. Apartment numbers were displayed on the right side of the door alongside letter boxes inbuilt into the ancient stone wall. The only street lighting came from the main square a hundred yards back and the jutting balconies from the old buildings cast long shadows down the street. He pressed the buzzer for apartment 4 and waited. He was about to try for a third time when the front door was opened by an elderly man wearing thin striped trousers supported by thick leather braces, a white collarless shirt and a cravat. The deep cragged lines on his weather beaten face gave the appearance of scars crisscrossing his entire countenance. The old man looked up at O'Hara then at the buzzer that was lit for apartment 4.

'I'm trying to contact Madame Kate Melcham I believe she lives in this building,' O'Hara stated using his best French accent.

The old man shrugged his shoulders and muttered a guttural reply that he couldn't translate. He held on to the door to prevent it from closing behind the old man and wait for him to shuffle away down the street before slipping inside the building. The dimly lit hall had a musty smell giving the visitor a feeling of intrusion. Small chequered black and white tiles covered both the floor and the lower half of the surrounding walls, with the vast majority being worn and cracked. There appeared to be two apartments on each floor so he made his way up the stairwell to the top floor. Apartment 4 was located to the right of the stairwell at the front of the building. Squinting in the gloomy recess of the doorway he realised there was no bell push. He rapped hard on the door, the sound echoing throughout the old building. No one answered the door and there was no sound from within the apartment. He was about to try and force entry using a multi bladed pocket knife when he heard the rattle of a chain and a bolt being slid back, before the door to the next apartment was slowly opened. A white haired lady who O'Hara guessed to be in her late seventies or early eighties, peered through the gap that the chain allowed.

'Who are you looking for?' she asked in a rasping voice that was almost a whisper.

'I'm sorry to have disturbed you,' O'Hara answered, 'I'm looking for Madame Kate Melcham.'

'She's gone,' she answered waving her arm in the air.

As O'Hara knitted his eyebrows she could see the confused look on his face.

The old woman released the latch and pulled the door open a fraction wider. She leaned heavily on a gnarled walking stick and had difficulty breathing. 'I've not seen her for two weeks,' she said.

'Does she live on her own?' He was conscious not to scare the woman by making it obvious he didn't know the girl.

'Never seen anyone else,' she replied eyeing him. 'What is she to you?'

'I'm a friend of her father, she's not been in touch with the family for several weeks so he asked me to pop by to see if she was OK.'

Her neighbour hesitated before seemingly coming to the conclusion that she could trust him.

'She left without saying goodbye to anyone. Speak with Pierre who owns the bistro in the square. She used to work there.'

She shuffled her feet awkwardly moving backwards into her apartment.

'Thank you Madame,' O'Hara replied, 'I appreciate your help and I'm sorry to have disturbed you at this time of the evening.'

He listened as the door was bolted and the chain put back before descending the stairwell. He knew he may need to gain access to Kate Melcham's apartment but now wasn't the right time.

Pierre Arcand walked with a stoop. O'Hara wasn't sure if this was down to old age or the fact that he appeared to stand taller than the low ceiling café. He looked unhealthily thin and the veins in his neck and arms were pronounced. His black waist coat hung limp on his shoulders and perhaps fitted him better in years gone by. O'Hara sat at the counter and ordered a brandy and a black coffee.

'It's quiet in here tonight,' he commented trying to start a conversation.

Two elderly gentlemen sat playing dominoes were the only other occupants.

'We're only busy at weekends. Are you on holiday?'

He didn't want to explain that he only lived in a neighbouring village so ran with the tourist idea.

'Yeah just driving across France, staying wherever the wheels take me. A well- earned break.'

The bar tender smiled.

'We all need a break sometimes.'

He watched Pierre as he laboriously wiped dry a row of glasses.

'I've been trying to find an old friend while I'm here. Her name is Kate Melcham, she lives just across the square.'

'You know Kate?' Pierre eyed him with a quizzical look.

'Yeah, we were at university together back in the UK but I lost touch with her when she moved to France.'

'Are you a friend of the family then? Pierre asked putting the dirty tea towel on the counter.

'I know the family, but can't say as I'm really a friend. I know Kate didn't see eye to eye with her father.'

Pierre nodded as if he'd just received confirmation that O'Hara was legit.

'I understand he wrote her out of his will before he died,' Pierre replied.

'I didn't know that, however I understood they never got on that well.'

O'Hara knew little of the woman's background, only what Wesley had told him so didn't want to get dragged into an historical discussion about the Melcham family and why Lucy ended up in France.

'She worked here for a while,' said Pierre pouring himself a brandy into a small glass tumbler. 'I miss her too. She told me she had to leave as something had happened back home.' Pierre raised the glass to his lips and downed the whole contents in one gulp. 'I never thought she would ever return to the UK. She seemed settled here.'

'She's gone back to the UK? When did she leave?' O'Hara pushed his own glass across the counter motioning for him and Pierre to have another brandy.

'On the 10th of December. She came to the café that morning and said she had booked a ticket on the local ferry and was leaving that night.'

Pierre poured two brandies and pushed O'Hara's glass back across the counter. O'Hara was sure the old man's eyes had glazed over.

'Well, here's to Kate's good health.'

O'Hara raised his glass and drank the brandy in one go, the fluid burning the back of his throat. Pierre did the same then standing up and wiped his hands on his apron.

'I'm sorry you have had a wasted journey.'

Pierre gave the impression he wanted to say something else but decided not to.

‘Ah well, I have to get on,’ he said. ‘It was good talking to you.’

‘How much do I owe for the coffee and brandies?’ O’Hara asked as he searched his jacket pocket for change.

‘Nothing monsieur, it’s on the house. A friend of Kate’s is a friend of mine.’

O’Hara thanked the man and made his way to the door. Just as he opened it he had a gut feeling there was more to be learnt before he left Perpignan.

‘Is there anywhere around here where I can crash out for the night? I’ve been driving nearly all day and need some sleep before I move on.’

Pierre nodded in the direction of the square.

‘The hotel Aragona on the opposite side of the square, try there. It’s the only hotel around here. It’s pretty basic but I’m sure you’ll find a room there.’

O’Hara nodded and smiled and headed across the square. Pierre stood behind the lace curtain watching the visitor before he disappeared into the hotel entrance.

12

Wesley had called everyone into the office for an early start. After welcoming WPC Alison Bolt back from her holiday he ran through the course of events of the past few days so that she was up to speed with the murder enquiry, with Alison asking a few questions along the way.

'I've just spoken with the employment agency where Felicity was employed and put forward a plan with which they have accepted. The agency will telephone Brian Hargreaves this morning to advise him they have a replacement for Felicity. That replacement will be Alison.' Wesley waited for a reaction.

'Isn't that putting Alison in a dangerous situation?' asked Martin.

'I did speak with Alison before the meeting to make her aware of my suggestion and she was happy to agree. With Alison having just returned from leave neither Brian Hargreaves nor the woman he's living with will know her. She'll be a total stranger with a CV that provides her with a new identity. If Hargreaves accepts the appointment we'll have someone on the inside. I'm not sure what's going on at Melcham Hall but something is amiss.'

'When are we expecting an answer from Brian Hargreaves?' Mandy asked.

Wesley looked at his watch. 'The agency should be telephoning him now.'

'Have we made any progress locating Kate Melcham?' Martin asked.

'I'm waiting for feedback from O'Hara. Her last known address is in France not far from where O'Hara now lives. He was going to pay her a visit last night. I'll give you an update as soon he touches base. If that's all, I'll be back in the office around eleven.'

'Where are you off to, sir? Just in case we need to contact you,' asked Mandy.

'I'm off to the dentist,' Wesley replied stretching his jaw. 'I've had a bloody toothache for over a week.'

'I'm surprised you still your own teeth at your age,' Martin replied causing laughter all round.

'Who was that on the phone?' Brian Hargreaves asked closing the front door behind him. He'd been to the village shop to buy cigarettes, something that was becoming a daily habit.

'It was a lady from the employment agency. She says she has someone who will replace Felicity Morgan and will send the girl around later today for you to interview her unless she hears from you first.'

'About time too, it's taken them a few days to get another cleaner sorted out.'

'Do we really need a maid?' she asked placing her hand on his arm.

'We need someone to help clean this place that is unless you want to spend every day cleaning Melcham Hall.'

'Tell me everything will be OK,' she said wrapping her arms around his waist, trying to soften him up.

'Just a few more weeks, that's all. Then we can sell up. You know I have to wait for the full term of the marriage to be reached before I gain the inheritance. Then all I need is to produce a signature.'

'I just want to get out and get away from here. I feel like a prisoner.'

'Be patient. We've come this far, let's not throw everything away for the sake of a few more weeks.'

'What if the solicitor wants to see me personally? I mean, he's been the family solicitor for years.'

'All he needs from you is a signature and your sister will supply that. Now stop worrying. I need to do some work. I'll be in the study if you need me.'

She was still standing in the hallway when he closed the door to the study. The moment she heard him turn the key in the lock she crossed the hall and headed for the staircase. It was time she started making a thorough search of the house. There were things that she needed answers to before she made her move.

Wesley stuck his head around the door and called Mandy into his office.

'I've just had a call from PC Reid at Wells police. They arrested Felicity Morgan's father for being drunk and disorderly in Glastonbury town centre last night. Apparently it's the second time he's been picked up in the last few days. Strangely enough, the first time was the day before Felicity's body was found.'

'Do you want me to pay him a visit?'

'Yeah, he was let out this morning so I assume he's gone home. Just say you popped in to check that he and his wife are OK. You don't have to mention anything about his arrest. Their daughter's funeral is tomorrow so let's go softly-softly on this for the time being.'

'What does he do for a living?' Mandy asked as she turned to leave.

'To be honest I have no idea. See what you can find out.'

A few minutes later Wesley almost bumped into Mandy as he came out of his office. She seemed to be in a hurry and was carrying a small suitcase.

'I didn't realise you were starting your leave today,' he exclaimed looking down at the suitcase by her side.

At first Mandy appeared lost for words and seemed to be rather flustered.

'Are you OK?' he asked.

'Oh, I, err, I'm just dropping this off at the charity shop,' she replied holding up the suitcase.

'Don't tell me your holiday clothes don't fit.'

'Err, no, these are baby clothes,' Mandy replied before disappearing down the stairs.

'Shit!' Wesley thought. 'Why did I have to ask?'

Having rushed home to get changed, WPC Alison Bolt decided that it was safer to jump on a bus to Shepton Mallet rather than make the short walk to Melcham Hall. The bus stopped two hundred yards before the entrance to the Melcham estate, just past the Phoenix Public House. Alison found herself feeling a little exposed as she entered the grounds to the estate on foot. She passed Rowan Lodge where a small plume of black smoke drifted lazily from the top of the chimney. She could see a light on in the kitchen at the back of the property and imagined Annie Griffin standing there baking sumptuous pastries and cakes. She'd heard all about Annie's cooking. Smiling to herself, Alison trudged on down the hill following the gravelled drive until she saw Melcham Hall in the distance at the bottom of the hill. The expansive building looked jaded and in need of some repair. She remembered Martin saying that the place looked almost neglected on the outside but was vastly different inside. She had just mounted the steps to the front of the building when she heard another door open and a man's voice call out.

'Come here Apollo! Come here!'

Alison turned around to see a large Doberman making its way towards her. Having kept dogs in the family since she was a little girl she hadn't grown up frightened of them but still she couldn't help but feel a little uncomfortable.

Brian Hargreaves came running up behind the dog which now stood a few feet away at the bottom of the steps, its low growl seeming to vibrate off the building.

'Sorry about that,' Hargreaves panted as he caught up with the dog. 'Don't worry his bark is louder than his bite.'

'I'm glad to hear it,' Alison replied leaning back on the front door.

Hargreaves held the Doberman by its collar and escorted it up the steps.

'You must be Miss Harris. My wife informed me that the agency phoned to say they were going to send you over.'

'Yes, Alison Harris, I'm pleased to meet you. I understand you have a position vacant for a housekeeper?'

'Yes we do. Come this way.'

Alison followed Hargreaves into the hallway keeping a steady distance away from the Doberman who never seemed to take its eyes off her. To her relief Hargreaves shut the dog in the kitchen before leading Alison to the front parlour.

‘Please, take a seat.’

Alison sat back in the large green chesterfield sofa, her feet only just touching the floor.

‘So what housekeeping experience do you have?’ he asked sitting on the arm of the small settee opposite which provided him with a somewhat elevated position to look down on her, his eyes continually reverting to her breasts.

Alison could tell that Brian Hargreaves was someone who was used to being in charge so she was happy to go along with that for the time being. She explained how she had had to nurse her mother when she was younger, and look after the family home. Since then she’d worked at two other domestic properties with the most recent as a ‘live-in’ housekeeper looking after two young children before the family had decided to immigrate to Australia. Brian Hargreaves seemed quite impressed with her response and agreed to show her around the house, after which she could decide if she still felt she could take on the cleaning chores of such a large establishment.

Some twenty minutes later, having seen a number of the rooms and been given a thorough insight into the workings of all the wash appliances and locations of linen cupboards and utensils, they moved back into the parlour.

‘So, if you’re happy with what you’ve seen, when would you be able to start?’ Hargreaves asked.

‘What about tomorrow?’ Alison replied.

‘Splendid. Now is there anything else you would like to ask?’

Brian Hargreaves seemed relaxed and gave the appearance that he was quite enjoying himself so Alison thought she would tread carefully.

‘May I ask if there’s a lady of the house?’

The question seemed to catch him off guard but he quickly composed himself.

‘Err, yes there is. Lady Hargreaves usually has a nap this time of day, that’s why I haven’t called her down. I’m sure the two of you will get on just fine.’

There was an awkward silence for a few moments until Alison stood up to leave.

‘Well, that seems to be it. Thank you Mr Hargreaves. I look forward to working for you and I’ll be here at nine a.m. sharp in the morning.’

Alison reached out to shake hands.

‘Please, call me Brian,’ he replied, holding onto Alison’s hand for a little longer than was necessary.

As soon as she returned home, Alison called Wesley to tell him how her visit had gone.

‘Ah good, so at least we’ll have someone on the inside from tomorrow. You’re going to have to tread carefully, Alison. Don’t put yourself at any unnecessary risk, just carry out whatever chores are needed but keep your eyes and ears open to what goes on.’

'Sure thing, sir.'

'Oh, by the way. Did you get to meet Lady Hargreaves?'

'No, apparently she was lying down. Well, that's what Brian Hargreaves told me.'

'Hmm, that's the same line virtually every time we've been there.'

'Really? Well hopefully I'll see her tomorrow.'

'Yeah I hope so. I suggest you keep a low profile today so stay at home unless you hear from me. The last thing we need is Hargreaves spotting you near the police station.'

Wesley put the phone down and made his way down to the police canteen as his stomach was rumbling. He found Martin sat on his own with a pile of folders on the table in front of him.

'What on earth are you doing?' asked Wesley.

'Hi sir, I thought I'd come down here to get some peace and quiet. I have a lot of paperwork to catch up on.'

'I can see that. Do you want anything to eat I'm just going to grab a sandwich.'

'Oh well, if you're paying I'll have bacon in mine,' Martin replied with a smirk on his face.

When Wesley returned with food and drinks Martin placed some of the folders on the floor to create space. Wesley watched him eat his food as if the boy hadn't eaten in weeks. Knowing that Martin had recently moved out of his parent's home into a one bed flat in Wells, Wesley wondered how he was coping with independence.'

'So, how's your new place? Have you settled in OK?' Wesley asked as he took a bite of his cheese and onion roll dropping crumbs all over the table.

'Yeah it's good. I haven't had a lot of time to do much to the place yet and I have to admit being the world's worst DIY man so I'm hoping dad is going to give me hand.'

Wesley wondered whether that a physical hand or simply money to pay for someone else.

'Are you staying in the flat over Christmas or are you going to stay with your parents?'

'The plan was to stay at the flat so I could start getting it into the shape I want but apparently mum has already told dad to remind me that I'm expected over for Christmas dinner.'

Wesley had finished his roll and now started to remove the cellophane from a Cornish pasty.

'Are you hungry, sir?'

Wesley grinned with a mouthful of pasty. Flakes of pastry were strewn across the front of his shirt.

'Jane's out later for a girlie night out and I don't fancy cooking.'

With food and refreshment finished Wesley left Martin to plough through paperwork and made his way back to his office where he slumped down in the chair behind his desk. Martin wasn't the only person with a mound of papers to deal with.

Glastonbury town centre was busy with people out rehearsing their drinking skills for the Christmas period. Jane met Mandy at the bus station and they took a slow walk into town heading for the Star and Garter pub. After eventually finding a couple of spare seats in the far corner of the lounge bar, Mandy set off to order some drinks. The Star and Garter was one of the oldest pubs in town and even Mandy had to duck her head in places to avoid the beams running across the low ceiling. When she returned to the table with drinks she found Jane talking to two other women.

'Let me introduce you to Mel and Yvonne. They run the party shop in the High Street,' Jane exclaimed.

'Pleased to meet you,' said Mandy taking a seat at the end of the table and hoping that Jane hadn't mentioned that she was a police woman. People never meant any harm in telling friends about her job but she was looking forward to a night off, away from discussing local gossip and murders.'

'Mel was just telling me that sales are down this year,' said Jane.

'Oh really, but the town always seems so busy every time I drive in,' Mandy remarked as she took a sip of wine.

'I think it's just the fact that a couple of our usual customers don't appear to be organising parties this year. We usually hire out twenty to thirty fancy dress costumes for New Year's Eve but this year I think we've hired out two so far this year.'

'I expect it's the university crowd that hire that sort of stuff isn't it?' Jane asked.

'Oh no, most of the students go home for Christmas and New Year. Usually it's the people working at Sainsbury's, for the past two years they've had a party at the village hall. Then it's the crowd who attend the annual fancy dress party at Melcham Hall,' Yvonne replied.

Mandy's ears pricked up at the mention of Melcham Hall. Hoping Jane wouldn't give her away she tempted fate by asking a couple of discreet questions.

'I gather there's always been a New Year's Eve party at Melcham Hall then?' Mandy enquired, trying not to sound too interested.

'Oh since I can remember,' Yvonne said as she reached for her own glass of wine. It was obviously not her first.

'Have you any idea why they're not going to have a party this year? I guess even the wealthier people are finding times a bit tougher these days,' said Mandy.

'Well, as you know Jane,' said Mel, 'I'm not one to gossip but it did seem a bit strange.'

'What did?' Jane enquired.

Mel sat upright in her chair, seemingly pleased to be the centre of attention.

Then leaning across the table as if to share a secret she whispered that she'd taken the liberty of telephoning Melcham Hall to speak with Lady Hargreaves to enquire as to whether they were holding a New Year's Eve fancy dress party as she wanted to ensure she would have sufficient stock of costumes and other fancy dress regalia.

'But do you know, when I spoke with her she seemed to know nothing about it. It was mighty strange. It was almost as if I'd dialled the wrong number and spoke to a complete stranger.'

'Perhaps she was just embarrassed at not giving a party this year,' Mandy exclaimed trying to play down the information.

The conversation then turned to the money the council were supposedly wasting on a new by-pass to help ease the amount of traffic running through the town. At this point Mandy excused herself and slipped out into the cold night air where she made a phone call to Wesley.

'The mystery gets deeper and deeper,' said Wesley after listening to what Mandy had to say about Lady Hargreaves. 'I've just put the phone down to David O'Hara who says that Kate Melcham, Lucy's twin sister, hasn't been seen in France for some weeks either. Apparently she just packed up her bags and left for the UK.'

'If we're thinking along the same lines then that sounds too much of a coincidence to me,' Mandy replied.

'I agree Mandy. Anyhow, thanks for the update. Go and enjoy your evening but don't get my wife too drunk.'

'Probably too late for that I'm afraid,' she replied laughing.

O'Hara entered the hotel foyer and immediately understood why Pierre said they would probably have vacancies. The dimly lit foyer failed to hide the grubby décor. Cream painted walls, cracked in several places and only decorated by a couple of cheap faded paintings gave the whole place a neglected, unwelcoming look. He walked across to the small reception desk and pressed the bell on the counter and wouldn't have been surprised if 'Lurch' from the Addams family had appeared. Instead, a rather plump woman, deceptive of age, entered the foyer from another door at the side of the staircase.

'How can I help?' she asked in an accent so harsh it was almost threatening.

'I'm looking for a room for the night,' O'Hara replied.

The woman seemed to assess him before she answered. It was almost as if no one ever asked her that question.

'Is it just for the one night, monsieur?'

'Yes please.'

She shuffled her feet across the threadbare carpet and went behind the reception counter where she extracted the hotel register.

'Please sign there,' she said pointing to the next free line in the book.

'It's thirty euros payable in advance. Breakfast is extra.'

O'Hara paid her the thirty euros but decided against breakfast. If breakfast looked as appetising as the hotel then it was best avoided. Having placed the money in a drawer under the counter she handed him a room key.

'Room 6 is on the first floor. Take the stairs and turn left on the landing. The bathroom is at the end of the corridor. Have you not got any luggage?'

Bringing an overnight bag wasn't something O'Hara had thought of.

'Err, no. Travelling light,' he replied forcing a smile.

The woman didn't return the smile and had already disappeared again before he had started to ascend the stairs. The dim lighting seemed to be a trend throughout the hotel, not helped by the fact that each bedroom door was painted dark brown and the carpet less floorboards on the first floor were almost black through wear. O'Hara opened the door to Room 6 and switched on the light. A single naked bulb hung from the centre of the room casting dark shadows in all corners. Apart from a single bed against the far wall, the room contained a standalone single wardrobe and a wash basin that stood underneath the back window. O'Hara walked across to the wash basin and turned on the tap.

A trickle of cold water dribbled out even when the tap was fully open.

He ran a handful of water across his face and looked for a towel but there wasn't one. Pulling back the net curtain he peered out of the window into the inner square below. There was nothing to look at other than other windows and brickwork. He tried to open the window to let some air into the stale room but realised the window had been screwed shut.

Kicking off his shoes, he then laid his jacket on the end of the bed. He was tired, the mattress was uncomfortable and he tried to ignore the broken springs. It was going to be a long night.

13

WPC Alison Bolt made one final check in the mirror. She wasn't sure if she looked like a house keeper, or come to think of it, what a housekeeper looked like. Dressed in a knee length grey skirt and black woollen jumper she grabbed her coat and handbag before leaving her apartment and making the ten minute walk to the bus stop. A north easterly wind made the crisp morning air feel colder than usual. Alison pulled up her coat collar and began to regret the decision to take the bus. It really was too cold to be standing around. By the time she eventually stepped off the bus in Shepton Mallet a slow drizzle made her journey even more arduous. Putting her head down against the wind and spray, Alison started the brisk walk to Melcham Hall.

She had been walking for less than a minute when a car horn tooted and Brian Hargreaves' black jaguar pulled into the grass verge just ahead of her. The passenger window was wound down as Brian Hargreaves beckoned her towards the car. Alison recognised the voice immediately.

'Good morning, Mr Hargreaves,' she said as she sat in the passenger seat beside him. 'How did you know it was me?'

'Ah, that's easy my dear. No one walks along this part of the country lane at seven-thirty in the morning unless they're visiting Melcham Hall. I mean, there's not another property within half a mile except for the Phoenix Public House and it's a little too early for that to be open.'

Slipping the car into gear he placed his hand on her knee.

'Good to see you're on time though. There's one thing I do expect of my staff, that's punctuality.'

Alison adjusted her skirt, forcing him to move his hand. She wondered why he was out and about so early in the morning.

'Have you been visiting someone?' she asked trying not to sound too intrusive.

'No, I just popped into the village to buy some cigarettes. A nasty habit I know and I will give them up one day.'

'We all have our vices,' Alison replied.

'And what would yours be?' he asked with a glint in his eye.

Alison thought it best not to get into the conversation so she looked the other way as they turned into the estate.

'What a lovely little place,' she said pointing at Rowan Lodge.

'Err, yes. It's owned by the estate but we don't use it any more.

Historically it was the estate keeper's accommodation but we just have someone pop in once or twice a week these days.'

'Does anyone still live there?'

'Yes, Annie Griffin. She's an old lady. Her husband used to tend to the estate. Unfortunately he passed away but my father in-law allowed Annie to stay on.'

'Oh I see.'

Alison could tell by the tone in his voice that he didn't really approve of the arrangement. When they arrived at Melcham Hall, Hargreaves was the perfect gentleman, opening the car door and helping Alison out of the vehicle. Once inside the house he led the way into the kitchen.

'There you go, you know where everything is. The only rooms that are out of bounds are the two bedrooms in the north wing. Lady Hargreaves manages the rooms herself.'

'OK thanks,' Alison replied unsure what she was expected to say.

'Would you like me to make tea or coffee?' she asked.

'Not for me thanks, but be sure to make something for yourself.'

Alison waited until Hargreaves had left the kitchen before removing her coat, which she hung on the back of the kitchen door. Before getting started she checked that her mobile was on and that she had a signal. She had agreed with Wesley that she would text the message *Melcham* if she needed assistance. After choosing a selection of cleaning agents from one of the cupboards she made her way out into the main hall. The house seemed eerily quiet. Deciding she would start the cleaning upstairs she mounted the wide staircase that wound its way up to a spacious landing where two leather wingback chairs stood either side of a custom built sideboard that extended the full length of the landing.

A thin deep pile carpet ran the length of the whole top floor leaving exposed polished floorboards either side. A cleaner's nightmare, Alison thought to herself. The first door she came to in the south wing was a small bathroom. Once inside Alison opened the door to a wooden cabinet that hung directly above the toilet. The cupboard was virtually bare except for an unopened tube of toothpaste, a half empty mouthwash, a small bottle of aspirins and a dirty looking face towel. The room was clean and tidy although it was apparent that no one had used it for some time. After dusting over the top of the cupboard Alison closed the door behind her and made her way along the corridor to the next room. She opened the door to a spacious bedroom where a four poster bed stood against the right hand wall and a large Victorian fireplace took centre stage against the left wall. Closing the door quietly behind her she made a quick search of the room, unsure what she was looking for. Again, the room gave the impression that no one had used it for quite some time and a thin layer of dust covered the furniture. Several expensive looking dresses hung in the wardrobe along with half a dozen pairs of shoes.

Alison was just closing the wardrobe door when Brian Hargreaves burst into the room.

'What are you doing?' he asked standing just inside the doorway with his hands on his hips.

'I assumed you would want the beds changed so I was looking for fresh linen,' Alison answered.

'No one uses this room, so leave it as it is.'

He stepped to one side indicating that she should leave the room.

Picking up her box of cleaning agents, Alison exited the room turning left along the corridor towards the other bedrooms.

'Actually there's no need to clean up here today, my wife gave everything a quick dust over yesterday,' Hargreaves called out behind her. Alison heard him turn the key locking the door to the bedroom.

'Oh, OK sir. I'll go back downstairs and start with the front parlour. I expect some polishing is required.'

Hargreaves didn't answer or follow her but Alison knew he was stood at the top of the stairs watching. As she entered the front parlour she noticed she was sweating. Standing next to the sideboard she placed her hand in the middle of her tummy and took three deep breaths to control her growing anxiety.

There was a strange atmosphere in Melcham Hall, she wasn't sure what was causing it but she was determined to find out.

Closing the door, Alison surveyed the room. She didn't like the hunting scenes that hung on two of the walls and the ghastly look on the faces of the animals being chased or caught, but what interested her were a couple of small black and white photos that stood at each end of the mantelpiece above the grand fireplace. Alison stood viewing the first photo, at the same time running the duster along the edge of the mantelpiece just in case Hargreaves reappeared.

The photo was of two young girls playing on a swing in the back garden of Melcham Hall. She guessed them to be Lucy and Kate when they were seven or eight years old. A woman was standing behind the swing with the two girls sat in front. Although the picture was faded, Alison was pretty sure that the lady was Annie Griffin. The other photo showed the two young girls, again about the same age, playing croquet with a young boy. The boy was stood sideways on so only half of his face was visible. Alison extracted her mobile phone and quickly took a couple of close-up snaps, not knowing whether anything would actually show up.

A dark wood mahogany bureau stood against the far wall next to a row of shelving. Alison ran the duster along each shelf in turn, glancing at the book covers at the same time. Medical books completely lined the top shelf, the middle shelf contained works by Shakespeare and Benjamin, amid a number of books on poetry and drama. The third shelf contained a whole collection of novels written by Agatha Christie. Alison moved along to the bureau and polished the deep brown mahogany with care. Being careful to listen at the same time, she pulled on the drop down flap but it was locked as were the two drawers at the front. Something she would have to work on when no one else was around. Instead, she grabbed the hoover and began to sweep the machine over the thick pile carpet. She was almost finished when she heard a door slam somewhere upstairs, followed by footsteps overhead. Alison switched the hoover off and stood still, straining her ears to listen. There were definitely two voices and the conversation was becoming quite heated although she couldn't catch what was being said. A moments silence followed before a door was slammed shut and footsteps could be heard on the stairs.

Alison switched the hoover back on making her way slowly towards the front window. A few seconds later she watched Brian Hargreaves stride across the gravel drive and get into the jaguar before he spun the wheels throwing an array of stones and mud in all directions before speeding out of the estate.

Unplugging the hoover, Alison returned it to the kitchen, pulling the door close behind her. Extracting her mobile she text Wesley to tell him that Hargreaves had just sped out of the estate.

Wesley and Martin were sat talking about recent events when a call came through for Wesley from the reception desk.

'Hi sir, it's PC Westlake speaking. I have a lady named Mel Harris on the line from forensics who wants a word with you.'

'OK put her through.'

Wesley listened as Mel Harris confirmed that coat hair analysis had proven that the fibres found on Felicity Morgan's clothing came from a Burberry trench coat and not anything that the victim was wearing. Wesley hung up after thanking her for the information.

'That's one of them expensive looking coats that upper class business men wear,' Martin commented after Wesley had informed him of Mel's comments.

'Yeah it is. Not the kind of clothing you'd expect someone to be wearing when committing a murder,' Wesley replied. 'Martin can you do me a favour? Get on to all the local dry cleaners. Find out if anyone has taken one of these coats in for cleaning over the past couple of weeks.'

'Sure will do, anything else?'

'Yeah, put a call out to the guys over at Wells. Alison says that Brian Hargreaves has just sped out of the Melcham estate. Ask them to keep a lookout for his car. I want to know what that man is up to.'

Having already telephoned to make sure someone would be at home, Mandy waited patiently for an answer after ringing the doorbell.

When Sally Morgan invited Mandy in she noticed how dishevelled the woman looked compared to the last time she'd visited. She took a seat at the small oval shaped kitchen table as Sally filled the kettle.

'So how are you, Sally?' Mandy asked as she watched the woman place two cups on the worktop, chinking them together as her hands were shaking so much.'

'I'm OK. The doctor has given me tablets to help me get through this,' she replied reaching for an oblong shaped box of tablets that she held up for Mandy to view. 'Have you caught anyone yet?'

'No we haven't. But I can assure you that we will get the person responsible for Felicity's murder.'

Mandy knew her reply sounded far too rehearsed but there was little else she could say. Neither woman spoke while Sally poured the tea. Mandy thought that if she gave Sally time she would eventually open up. The woman needed someone to talk to.

'Do the police believe there's a link between Felicity's murder and her pregnancy?' Sally asked.

Mandy shook her head.

'We've nothing to prove that either way. We've spoken with Felicity's doctor and made enquiries to several other local health centres but they all say that Felicity had never been to see anyone about the pregnancy. In fact, Felicity's doctor said she hadn't seen Felicity for over a year. I have to say Sally, I'm somewhat surprised, given how slight Felicity was that no one noticed the fact she was pregnant.'

'My Felicity wasn't one for wearing tight clothes,' Sally replied. 'She was a bit of a hippy really. You know what I mean, flowered dresses and all that kind of stuff.'

'What's also strange is that her flatmate says she never saw her with a boyfriend either,' Mandy exclaimed.

Sally held her cup in both hands and sat staring into space.

'I can't imagine my Felicity ever falling in love with anyone. She was a wild child in many ways. She liked to live life to the full if you know what I mean.'

'Yes, I know what you mean and I don't wish to sound coarse but she didn't need to be in love with anyone to become pregnant,' Mandy replied.

'Did Felicity ever say why she was unhappy working at Melcham Hall?'

'No, but then we didn't even know where she was working. She only told us that she'd got work and that she was OK and would pop over to see us when she settled in, except that's never going to happen now is it?'

Mandy put her cup down on the table and placed a hand on Sally's shoulder.

'May I ask where your husband is?' Mandy asked.

Sally looked up and stared at Mandy as if she didn't understand the question.

'Your husband, Henry, I was just wondering where he is?'

'He's gone to play golf.'

Mandy could not help but look astonished.

'Oh, I know what you're thinking. How could he leave me alone at a time like this? It's his way of handling things. At least he's not out getting drunk again.' She paused as if giving herself time to think.

'You see, we've never been close, Henry and I. In many ways Felicity kept us together. He has been a successful business man most of his working life in the insurance business. He was always away from home for days at a time, the result being that Felicity and I got to spend a lot of time alone together. I know Henry loved Felicity as much as I did, in his own way, but he finds it hard to express his love, if you know what I mean.'

'What was his reaction to Felicity being pregnant?'

'He still refuses to believe it. I don't think Henry ever wanted his little girl to grow up. He always saw her as a seven or eight year old, dependent on her daddy.'

'How do you think he would have reacted to a boyfriend asking for her hand in marriage?'

Sally smirked. 'He'd have probably shot him.'

Having just left the dentist, Wesley was walking back to his car when he recognised the person coming towards him.

'Terry Austin! Well I never. What are you doing in Street?'

The two friends shook hands.

'Another visit to the dentist I'm afraid. This is quickly becoming an expensive hobby.'

'Tell me about it. That's where I've just come from,' Wesley replied with half of his face still numb. 'I didn't know you came out this way?'

'Yeah, my parents lived in the village for years before they retired and moved down to Poole. I've been going to the same dentist in Street since I came out of college. However, Dad's into yachting in a big way these days so my parents spend most of their time around Poole harbour.'

'I think this is only the second time I've seen you out of your white coat,' Wesley remarked.

'I have to admit being more comfortable in the pathology lab than in a dentist chair,' Terry admitted. 'I can dissect other people's bodies all day but I get squeamish when someone's trying to drill a hole in my tooth.'

'I need to ask you a question about Felicity Morgan before you go,' said Wesley.

'Sure, what is it?'

'You said that she was in the early stages of pregnancy. Is it at all possible to be more precise? I mean more exact?'

'It's a difficult call John. Felicity Morgan was a small woman, quite underweight even though she was carrying. I'd go so far as to say that she might not have been aware she was pregnant.'

'Are you serious?'

'It happens.'

'What makes you say that about Felicity Morgan though?'

'When I opened her up, her tummy was virtually empty. She hadn't had a solid meal in several days which is extremely rare for someone who knows they're pregnant.'

'Hmm, good point.'

'However, in answer to your question, given the size of the foetus I would take a guess that she was somewhere between eight and ten weeks.'

Still dribbling down his chin from the effects of the injections Wesley thanked Terry for the feedback and wished him well at the dentist.

Doctor Ian Meadows welcomed Wesley into his surgery.

'Come in John, it's good to see you. I hope you're keeping well.'

'Apart from an abyss and two fillings I'm fine,' Wesley replied wiping his mouth with a handkerchief.

The doctor directed Wesley to a small two seated settee that sat below a large bay window overlooking the village green. Sitting himself on a single cushion covered chair opposite, he sat back and folded his arms.

'I don't believe for one moment this is a social visit, or that you've come to wish me a pre happy new year. So how can I help?'

'You already know me too well,' Wesley replied, 'I'll come straight to the point. I need to ask you about one of your patients, Lady Hargreaves.'

'Go on.' The doctor looked down his nose over the top of his half rimmed glassed that hung precariously to the end of his nose.

'I'd like to know if Lady Hargreaves is in good health.'

'You know that I can't disclose personal information relating to any patient don't you.'

'I understand that, Ian. Let me ask another way. When was the last time you had reason to see Lady Hargreaves?'

'I can tell you without looking at my notes that Lady Hargreaves came to see me about two months ago. She was a little under the weather and was in need of a pick me up.'

Wesley ran his hand across his jaw as was his trait when deep in thought and winced as he remembered the fillings.

'So you believe her to be in pretty good health?'

'As far as I'm aware, John yes. May I ask the reason for your questions?'

'Since the murder of Felicity Morgan, whose body as you know was found on the Melcham estate, we've had reason to visit Melcham Hall to speak with both Lord and Lady Hargreaves.'

Wesley was about to reach for his cigarette papers and tobacco when he remembered that the doctor wouldn't approve.

'Several people who have known Lady Hargreaves for some time have expressed a concern that her mannerisms and behaviour are out of sorts.'

‘I don’t understand, in what way?’

‘The fact that she didn’t recognise someone she’s known for many years, and hasn’t been answering the telephone in her normal manner. Also it seems that she appeared to know little about Annie Griffin, or show any concern about the old lady’s welfare.’

‘Hmm, maybe she’s got other things on her mind. It happens to us all at times if we feel under pressure or we’re simply snowed under with other things.’

‘I understand that, but surely what has the woman got to worry about? She doesn’t work; she simply helps to run the estate. Surely that can’t be too demanding can it?’

‘We all react differently to different kinds of pressure, John. What may seem unimportant to you can be a major headache for someone else.’

‘OK but I’m not alone in thinking that things aren’t quite right at Melcham Hall. I can’t put my finger on it, but something doesn’t jell.’

‘So what do you want from me?’ asked the doctor.

‘Would you be able to pay a visit to Melcham Hall? You know, just say it’s a courtesy call in light of recent events.’

Doctor Ian Meadows stood up and looked out of the window and ran his fingers through the mass of grey hair that belied his age.

‘I’ll pop in to say hello. But I have to warn you John, if there is something medically wrong with Lady Hargreaves then I cannot break confidentiality to advise you of her ailment.’

‘I understand.’ Wesley stood up to leave.

‘I appreciate your help, Ian. I’m dealing with a murder enquiry here and if you come across anything you think I ought to be aware of…’

‘I’ll call you straight away,’ Doctor Ian Meadows replied. ‘Now, before you go I have something for you. You’ve saved me the trouble of dropping it off.’

He walked over to a small dark mahogany writing bureau, opened the top drawer and extracted an envelope.

‘Don’t worry it’s not a prescription. It’s an invitation to our New Year’s Eve drinks party. I do hope you and Jane can come, Anne and I would love to see you.’

‘That’s very kind,’ Wesley replied taking hold of the envelope, ‘we’d be delighted. ‘Hopefully by then I won’t be dribbling over everyone.’

Martin had drawn a blank phoning local dry cleaning stores to see if anyone had taken a Burberry trench coat in to be cleaned. It seemed that very few people owned a Burberry trench coat as nearly everyone he asked said they had never had one taken in to be cleaned. He was on his way down the stairs towards the police station reception desk when he heard the phone ringing back in the office. He ran back up the stairs and grabbed the phone before the caller hung up.

'Good afternoon Street police station.'

'Hi, is that Inspector Wesley?'

'No this is PC Martin Philips. How can I help?'

'Martin, this is PC Phil Robbins over at Wells. Can you pass on a message to Inspector Wesley? Tell him that Henry Morgan, Felicity Morgan's father is in intensive care. He tried to commit suicide.'

'What!'

'Yeah, he tried to gas himself in his car. He was parked in his local golf club's car park but someone spotted him and managed to drag him out just in time. Apparently the engine was still running and a rag had been stuffed into the exhaust.'

'Christ, that's a turn up. OK, thanks I'll pass the message on.'

Martin immediately thought of Sally Morgan. The poor woman was already in a desperate state without her husband trying to top himself.

'I don't suppose there has been any sighting of Brian Hargreaves anywhere?'

'Nothing reported I'm afraid. I'll give you a shout if he is spotted.'

14

Having finally returned all the cleaning utensils to their appropriate places, Alison was stood in the cupboard at the back of the kitchen. It was a small walk-in cupboard where three of the walls were covered in shelving containing a mixture of products ranging from cleaning fluids to medicinal items such as boxes of Migraleve and aspirin along with boxes of weed killer and rat poison. She was reading one of the labels affixed to a large bottle of bluish fluid when she heard voices out in the hallway. Closing the cupboard door behind her, Alison picked up a tray of dirty cups and plates and carried them over to the sink and turned on the hot water tap. One of the voices belonged to Brian Hargreaves, the other, Alison assumed was his wife. It was quite apparent they were arguing. Placing the crockery one piece at a time into the sink she strained her ears to listen to what was being said.

'Why didn't you tell me the new woman had already started?'

'What difference does it make?' Brian Hargreaves replied.

'We have a stranger walking around the house and you can't even be bothered to tell me,' the woman shouted.

'I don't see what all the fuss is about. She's only a bloody cleaner!' Hargreaves replied raising his voice. 'Come with me and I'll introduce you before you have another bloody migraine.'

Alison increased the hot water tap pretending to wash some of the clean cutlery.

Brian Hargreaves almost burst into the kitchen with Lady Hargreaves who was trying desperately to keep up with him. Alison assessed Lady Hargreaves body language as her husband made the introductions. The woman seemed nervous, almost agitated and refrained from looking Alison in the face. Alison noticed how she constantly rubbed her hands together. Something about her hands seemed strange but Alison couldn't fathom what it was. Apart from 'hello,' Lady Hargreaves never spoke, allowing her husband to rabble on trying to sound as if he was in charge of the situation.

She finally breathed a sigh of relief when they left her alone again in the kitchen. After putting away the clean crockery she laid the wet tea towel on the worktop next to the sink and slowly opened the kitchen door listening for the sound of voices or footsteps somewhere in the building. The house was silent and Alison shivered as if someone had just walked over her grave. The vast hall with its dark mahogany wood panelling and high ceiling held an eerie atmosphere. As she walked across the uneven flagstone floor she almost felt as if she was intruding into time gone by. She could imagine young children running around in their Victorian clothing playing hide and seek in and out of the rooms, a maid on her hands and knees scrubbing the floor, shouting at the children's muddy footprints. The old house now seemed somewhat neglected, unloved. A doorway under the main staircase stood almost invisible, being made of the same dark mahogany wood. Alison crossed the hall and slowly turned the handle, wincing as she waited for the sound of the lock to turn. As she pulled the door open a cold draft hit her in the face taking her breath away. Inside was complete darkness. Alison felt along the wall for a light switch. The single naked bulb hung a few feet in front of her from the low ceiling, pointing the way to a flight of stone steps that seemed to lean against the cold stone wall. The light wasn't strong enough to enable her to see what lay at the bottom of the stairs. She assumed this must be the cellar and was intrigued at what she may find but decided that it would have to wait for another day. Being caught in the wrong place twice on her first day might be construed as being more than nosey. She switched off the light and stepped back into the hall before closing the door quietly behind her. She looked up at the grand staircase. Was it her imagination or did someone's shadow just disappear on the landing above?

With her days work done, Alison couldn't wait to get out of the house.

After sending another text to Wesley to say that Brian Hargreaves had returned home she set about gathering her belongings to make a hasty retreat.

Wesley stood next to the bed as the nurse administered the bedding surrounding Henry Morgan. An oxygen mask was fitted over the man's nose and mouth and a drip was attached to his arm. If it wasn't for the slow rise and fall of the bed sheet an onlooker could have mistaken him for a corpse.

Wesley had forgotten how many times he'd seen people in this situation, but never understood what drove someone to attempt to take their own life.

'Do we have any idea when he's likely to regain consciousness?' he asked.

'I'm sorry, Inspector. The doctor saw him again some thirty minutes ago but didn't say anything. I do know from experience that patients who have tried to gas themselves in this way often take several days to recover, that's if they cover at all.'

'Was he conscious when he was brought in?'

The nurse looked down at her notes. 'No, apparently he was unconscious when he was admitted.'

Wesley sighed and nodded his appreciation of the situation. He reached into his coat pocket and extracted a card which he handed to the nurse.

'Has Mrs Morgan been in to see him?'

'Yes, she was here a short while ago. I believe a friend has taken her home to get some rest. She wanted to stay, but we persuaded her to go home and said we would phone her the moment there was any change.'

'OK, please give me a call too, the moment his condition changes,' he said.

The nurse looked at his card, reading his name aloud to herself.

'Of course Inspector, we'll let you know the moment there's any change.'

Wesley left the hospital and made his way across the visitors' car park where he sat on the small metal railing alongside his car. He noticed how his hands were shaking as he rolled a cigarette. He hated hospitals, had done ever since the day he'd lost his wife. He always remembers seeing her laid out on the bed, knowing that he was never going to have the chance to speak with her again and feeling guilty that he hadn't made it in time. The day the drunk driver ended her life, ended a period of happiness for Wesley that at the time he felt he would never find again. However, people say time is a good healer, and in his case the healing had been helped when Jane re-entered in his life. He'd met her several years earlier before their paths crossed again when he visited Scotland Yard.

Jane was working as secretary to Chief Superintendent Hemmings who Wesley reported to. Un-be-known to Wesley at the time, the case he was on would bring him into contact with Gerry Holland, Jane's husband. It was during the course of the investigation that Gerry Holland was shot dead, leaving Jane a widow.

As soon as his mobile phone vibrated Wesley read the text from Alison and immediately forwarded it to Martin with a footnote to advise Wells police.

Lighting his roll-up he made his way over to his car and sat behind the wheel thinking about Henry Morgan. Why on earth would the man try and take his own life knowing he would be leaving his traumatised wife all alone. What was it he was trying to run away from? Yeah sure, he'd lost his daughter but he still had a family. Wesley was still deep in thought when another ambulance sped into the hospital grounds heading for the accident and emergency entrance.

'Looks like someone else is going to have a crap Christmas,' he said to himself.

Brian Hargreaves opened the door to find Dr Ian Meadows stood on the worn steps with his coat collar turned up against the cold.

'Good afternoon Brian, I hope you're keeping well. I was just passing and thought I'd pop in to say hello and hand you and your dear lady an invite to our New Year's party.'

'Oh thanks doc,' Hargreaves replied accepting the envelope. He hesitated before inviting the doctor into the house.

'I'm sorry, I'm being rude. Do come in.'

He stood aside and beckoned the doctor inside. Closing the door behind him he took the doctor's coat and hung it on the coat stand.

'Please come into the front parlour. It's warmer in there.'

Hargreaves led the way taking a seat on a single wingback chair and directed the doctor to a seat on an adjacent, identical chair, next to the fireplace. The two men exchanged pleasantries with the doctor expressing how nice it was to sit in front of a coal fire.

'So how's the good lady? I haven't seen her for a while. I expect she'll be in need of another prescription soon.'

Dr Meadows noticed the hesitancy before Hargreaves responded to his question.

'Err she's OK, thanks doc. She's having a lay down at the moment. As you know she suffers from the occasional migraine. Too much brandy if you ask me.'

Hargreaves forced a smile trying to make a joke of the matter.

'That's a shame, I would have loved the opportunity to say hello.'

Hargreaves didn't reply and sat staring into the fire. Dr Meadows got the distinct impression that Hargreaves wasn't going to invite him upstairs to see his wife.

'Ah well, let her know I popped in and asked after her. Is that your new housekeeper I just saw walking along the drive?'

'Err, yes. That would be Miss Harris. She only started today, she's replacing…'

'Yes I heard about Felicity Morgan,' said Dr Meadows, 'I do hope they catch whoever is responsible. It was such a waste of life, especially in someone so young.'

Brian Hargreaves stared at the doctor without making a response.

'Ah well, I best be off.' The doctor stood up to leave.

'I'm sorry it's only a fleeting visit. I also need to pop in and see Annie Griffin before I start the rest of my rounds.'

'How is the old girl?' Hargreaves asked helping the doctor with his coat. The change in his voice made it apparent that he was delighted the subject had changed to Annie Griffin.

'Remarkably well considering her age,' the doctor replied with a grin.

Having said goodbye to the doctor, Hargreaves lent back against door and sighed. He knew he had a few decisions to make and fast.

Annie Griffin raised her weary body from the armchair and made her way painfully through to the kitchen. The cold weather played havoc with her joints, today was no exception and her whole body seemed to ache. She looked at the little calendar that was hanging from the door handle above the kitchen worktop and tried to force a smile. It was Christmas Eve but she sure didn't feel very festive. She poured herself a tea and sat at the kitchen table, her mind wandering back to when she a little girl and the fun times they used to have at Christmas. Her father used to make her wait in her bedroom on Christmas morning; he said he had to check to see if Father Christmas had been before she was allowed downstairs. Annie would wait to hear him whistle before leaping off the bed and hurtling down the stairs, straight into the front parlour where the Christmas tree always stood. Her presents were always the ones at the base of the tree. Her parents always insisted their presents to be left on the dining table to be opened after a morning sherry and before dinner. Annie especially remembered her new bike and how the stabilisers had been left sticking out of the wrapping and her father saying that Father Christmas had obviously ridden the bike to their house.

She was still dreaming of days gone by when her thoughts were suddenly distracted when she heard a noise outside the Lodge. After placing a dirty cup in the sink she wrapped her cardigan around her at the same time as a shiver ran down her spine. Annie pulled the net curtain back a little and wiped the condensation off the window to peer out just in time to catch a fleeting glance at someone's shadow as they passed the window. She stood silent for a few moments trying to calm her nerves and listen for any further sound. Closing the curtain she stood the plant pot on the draining board and made her way through towards the front of the house. Just as she reached the front door she heard someone trying to push a key into the lock. Whoever it was, tried several times before realising that the door was locked from the inside. Annie stood nervously trying to contain her fear. Silence followed before she heard the visitor walk away from the door. Annie took a deep breath to compose herself before entering the front room where she peered out of the side of the new lace curtain she'd recently purchased at the market. There was no one to be seen. Although clumps of snow still clung to both the hedgerow and bushes, the path leading to the front door was now just a muddy track making it virtually impossible to decipher one person's footprints. Trying not to make a sound, Annie manoeuvred herself past the armchair to reach the small table where the telephone stood. She picked up the card that Mandy had left her and dialled the number. Mandy answered almost immediately.

'Hi, this is WPC MandyTredwell speaking. Who's calling?'

'Is that you, Mandy?'

'Yes, who is it?' Mandy didn't recognise the quiet nervous voice.

'It's Annie Griffin from Rowan Lodge.'

'Hello Annie, are you OK?'

'I think someone is trying to break in,' Annie whispered.

'What?'

Just then there was the sound of breaking glass. Annie jumped and dropped the phone.

'Annie, are you OK?' Mandy shouted, but the line had gone dead.

It was less than twenty minutes later when the first patrol car screeched to a halt outside Rowan Lodge. Mandy was joined almost immediately by both Martin and Wesley as they pulled in directly behind her, each in their own vehicle.

'Take a look around outside,' Wesley directed Martin, pointing to the back of the property. 'Mandy, you come with me.'

Wesley knocked hard on the front door and called out to Annie. At first there was no answer but just as he was about to call again they heard Annie crying from the front room. Wesley was about to break the door down when Martin called from inside.

'Hold on, Chief. I've come in the back way.'

When they entered they found Annie sat in the armchair, tears streaming down her face.

Mandy rushed over and knelt down in front of the old lady.

'It's OK Annie, we're here.'

Mandy placed her arms around her as the woman sobbed. She signalled to Wesley that Annie was unharmed.

'Let's take a look around,' Wesley said to Martin.

As soon as they stepped into the kitchen Wesley saw the broken window.

'There are a few footprints out back,' said Martin, 'but where the snow has melted it's almost like a swamp. However, there's a brick on the back doorstep underneath the window which I guess is what was used.'

'How did you manage to break in?' asked Wesley.

'I didn't have to,' Martin replied. 'I remembered Annie telling me that you have to turn the handle and press the latch otherwise the door won't open.'

Wesley sighed and scratched his forehead.

'I'll put a call in to forensics and get someone over here to check for fingerprints and then see how Annie is. While I'm doing that, have a wander around the estate to see if you can pick up any tracks.'

'Oh I see, get my trousers and boots wet again,' Martin remarked with a smirk on his face.

When Wesley re-entered the front room he found Mandy stood next to Annie, talking into her mobile.

'Hello Annie, are you OK now?' Wesley asked pulling up a chair to sit beside her.

'Yes I'm fine. I'm sorry, Inspector. I'm just a silly old fool. I don't know why on earth I screamed.'

'Because you were scared, and what's more because you're entitled to.'

Wesley took hold of one of Annie's hands and reassuringly clasped his two hands around her tiny fingers.

'Have you any idea who was trying to break in?' he asked.

'No, I mean why would any sensible person want to break in here? There's nothing of any value,' Annie replied trying to force a smile.

'So you never actually saw anyone, just a shadow?'

'No, I think as soon as I screamed whoever it was, ran off. He or she certainly never came into the house.'

'I wonder why they never tried to open the back door. Martin says the door was unlocked.'

Annie gave a nervous laugh.

'I never lock the back door, Inspector. Oh I know I should but it's something I was brought up with. No one in the country used to lock their back door. Visitors were even expected to come in through the back way.'

'Unfortunately times change, Annie, I would recommend you keep the door locked from now on. I'll get someone over to repair the broken window.'

'I've put a call in to Dr Meadows,' said Mandy replacing her mobile back into her pocket. 'He's only just left Melcham Hall so he should be here in a few minutes.'

'Oh you needn't have gone to all that trouble. I'll be fine, really I will,' said Annie.

'I'm sure you will but it won't do any harm for him to check you over,' answered Wesley.

Mandy left the room to make Annie a hot drink while Wesley asked Annie to explain step by step exactly what happened. Mandy found Martin in the kitchen picking up a few pieces of broken glass.

'Who the hell would want to do this?' he asked dropping pieces of broken glass into a plastic bag.

'We don't know,' Mandy replied, 'but what worries me is something that Annie just said.'

Martin knitted his eyebrows as Mandy leaned close to whisper. 'If there's nothing in here of any value then that only leaves one other object.'

'You mean, Annie?'

'I hope I'm wrong,' said Mandy.

Wesley and Martin were back at the station having left Annie with Mandy and Dr Meadows.

'I was wondering, sir,' said Martin, 'do you think that whoever killed Felicity Morgan believes that Annie may be a witness?'

Wesley rested his head in his hands.

'It's possible for sure, but would you take a chance and go back to the murder scene? Wouldn't you want to be as far away as possible?'

'Maybe, but not if you lived nearby,' Martin replied shrugging his shoulders.

'What are you getting at?' asked Wesley now sitting back in his chair.

'Think about it. Annie's place is off the beaten track so not many people even know it's there. If a stranger was seen hanging around, people would ask questions wouldn't they? But what if the person wasn't a stranger? I mean, what if it's someone who's often seen around those parts.'

'What are you trying to say?'

'Brian Hargreaves?'

Wesley placed his arms behind his head.

'You don't like him do you, Martin?'

'Do you?'

'Not particularly, but I'm not sure he's capable of murdering someone. Oh he comes across as being loud and aggressive I know, but I think if you or I shouted at him he'd back down straight away. In any case if it was him why would he run away simply because Annie screamed? Why wouldn't he have simply knocked on the front door? Come to think of it, surely he would have known how to open the back door?'

'Hmm, I don't know,' Martin sighed, 'but I had a good look around outside and there were no new car tracks at the entrance to the estate, or evidence of a vehicle being parked along the roadside and if anyone had run across the estate, off road, their footprints would have been easy to spot.'

'So you think that the suspect made their way back into the estate, back to Melcham Hall?'

'That's my guess.'

Martin walked across the office to peer out of the window leaving Wesley sat deep in thought.

'OK, it's going to be dark in another hour or so. First thing tomorrow take young PC Bradshaw with you over to Annie's and take another look around. I'll call Mandy so that she can inform Annie. That way she'll be expecting you. Just stick your head in the door and make sure she's alright.'

'Do you think Annie will be OK on her own tonight?' Martin asked as he turned to leave.

'Yes she'll be fine. Mandy is staying with her until later and I've arranged for the night patrol to keep an eye on the place,' Wesley replied.

That afternoon Brian Hargreaves stepped off the train at Charing Cross. He hated trains at the best of times and this afternoon had been no exception. The carriage had been full and although he'd taken an aisle seat he had been continually lent upon by a rather large woman standing in the crammed aisle. After exiting the pay barrier he made his way across the concourse towards the taxi rank where he boarded one of the many cabs that were queued waiting for customers. Jumping into the back of the cab he handed the driver a business card that contained his destination address. The driver glanced at the note and raised his eyebrows.

'Certainly sir, I'll have you there in no time.'

Even though the cab driver obviously knew his way around London, the traffic was busy as they made a slow crawl towards their destination. Hargreaves looked out at the hoard of people everywhere. He hated the city, the throngs of people, the enclosed spaces, and still held a boyhood fear of being trampled underfoot. He couldn't wait to get back on the train and away from London.

He noticed he was shaking by the time the cab pulled up outside the hotel. After paying the driver he was immediately greeted by a doorman who directed him to the reception desk where upon his arrival an attractive brunette immediately escorted him to the private lounge.

'Please, follow me,' she said leading the way.

Hargreaves followed in her footsteps ogling at the woman's curves in her tight fitting pencil shirt. The plush surroundings of the private lounge were further enhanced by the wall to wall wood panelling and the leather seated furniture that adorned the room. At the far end of the room the receptionist pushed open another large door which led to the bar. As soon as Hargreaves stepped inside a butler directed him to the person he was looking for.

'Ah Hargreaves, there you are. Can I offer you a drink?' his acquaintance shook his hand in a vice like grip. The man was immaculately dressed, of medium build, but muscular and had the looks of an ex-boxer. Not someone you would want to argue with. Having requested a brandy, his associate called a waiter over and ordered two large brandies.

'So what news do you have for me?' his asked as he directed Hargreaves to a small green leather chair opposite. They were sat either side of a large open fireplace where a log fire was giving out an enormous amount of heat. Although his acquaintance seemed unperturbed, Hargreaves was sweating profusely.

Just at that moment the waiter reappeared to hand them each their brandies from a silver tray. Hargreaves waited until the waiter was out of earshot before answering.

'I might have a problem,' he exclaimed before taking a large sip of brandy to calm his nerves.

He looked across at his acquaintance who was staring into the fire.

'There's no such thing as a problem. There are only answers to questions,' he replied as he swirled the brandy around in his glass.

Hargreaves was unsure how to continue and a deafening silence followed until his colleague spoke.

'Tell me. What's the answer to this thing that seems to bother you?'

Hargreaves was trying hard to control his nerves and a small pulse seemed to vibrate across his temple.

'Felicity's body was found. The trouble is; the police are now swarming over the place. It won't be long before they…'

'Stop!' The man sitting opposite simply raised his hand in command. It was obvious he was used to giving orders. Hargreaves almost dropped his glass.

'You assured me that you had dealt with the matter. So what are you concerned about?'

'Well the police for sure, because they've been searching the grounds for clues. I don't see what the problem is if you didn't leave any clues.' The man took a sip of brandy and stared at the fire for several seconds before continuing.

'I'll make a few phone calls and find out what the police know. In the meantime make sure they don't find anything else. I assume Lady Hargreaves is coping with all this?'

'Yeah,' he replied as he downed the remains of his brandy.

'That's good. We wouldn't want any more complications would we?'

The man raised his glass in a salute before finishing his drink and stood to leave.

'Don't get up. Leave ten minutes after me. There will be a cab waiting for you outside. I don't expect to hear from you again before our business has concluded. When the time comes I'll contact you.'

'What about the police?' pleaded Hargreaves, but his associate was already halfway across the room. Hargreaves waved his hand to catch the attention of the waiter and ordered another large brandy to calm his nerves.

15

Having made his way through the overgrown foliage the stranger eventually stopped at the edge of the woodland and looked down at Melcham Hall. The building looked pretty much as he'd remembered it, although there were now a few gaps in the stonework at the front of the building where the interior brickwork was showing and lumps of concrete had fallen away. Leaning against a tree for support, he decided to rest up for a few minutes. He allowed himself to daydream of years gone by. Picnics on the lawn, croquet and badminton, playing hide and seek with the girls, but especially the dancing. They would waltz on the front lawn, covering every blade of grass, his body close to hers. His thoughts were disturbed when a rook suddenly took flight from a nearby tree, causing a flurry of snow to fall in front of his eyes, bringing him back to reality. Should he simply walk up to the front door? No, that would be a mistake. He needed to bide his time. He'd only been back in the country a few days and had so far managed to avoid being recognised by anyone. He had changed though. Once upon a time he was tall and slim with the build of an athlete and could out-dance anyone, but time hadn't been kind to him. Now he was balding and middle aged, chain smoked, and had a beer belly that some Englishmen would be proud of. He lit a cigarette and pondered his next move. He knew he had to make his move soon. He couldn't stay around the village indefinitely using a false name and ID. As he took another long drag on his cigarette, he turned around upon hearing the sound of a twig snap. His reactions were too slow.

It was past eight o'clock in the evening and Wesley was still sat at his desk slowly working his way through a pile of paperwork when his mobile phone vibrated on the desk causing several folders to fall to the floor. He cursed as he made a grab for his mobile. It was the nurse from the hospital.

'Hello, is that Inspector Wesley?'

'Yes, Wesley speaking, how can I help?'

'Hello Inspector, this is Nurse Bradshaw from Wells hospital. I've just taken over the night shift. I thought you would like to know that Henry Morgan has regained consciousness and is asking for you.'

'Thank you, nurse. I don't suppose I could pop in and see him on my way home?'

There was a muted silence as Nurse Bradshaw contemplated Wesley's request.

'I'm sure it wouldn't hurt, but just for two minutes. The man is still extremely poorly.'

'That's very kind, I understand. I'll be there within the hour.'

It was dark and bitterly cold by the time Wesley pulled into the hospital car park. Another heavy snowfall around teatime had obliterated all the parking bays and there were far too many cars crammed into spaces that didn't exist. Wesley parked right in front of a no-parking sign, and resigned himself to finding his car clamped when he returned.

Nurse Bradshaw was in the process of replacing the saline solution drip going into Henry Morgan's arm when Wesley entered the room. She gave Wesley the briefest of smiles that seemed to say, you've got two minutes and no more.

'How are you doing?' he asked seeing that Henry was awake.

'Better now, thanks.'

Although his lips were dry and cracked and his skin looked grey and drawn, Henry Morgan looked OK for someone who had just tried to gas themselves.

Wesley waited until Nurse Bradshaw had finished her duties before continuing.

'So, tell me what happened?'

'Don't think this is a habit of mine, Inspector, because I can assure you that it's not. I don't know what came over me, except to say I've never felt so down in my life. I'd had a couple of drinks at the golf club and when I returned to my car I suddenly thought to myself, I can't handle this anymore. My daughter's dead and I can't bring her back. I know I've got Sally at home but it didn't seem enough.'

With some effort he pushed himself back on the bed so that he was sitting more upright. Just that small amount of movement seemed to tire him greatly.

'It's Felicity's funeral tomorrow, Inspector. I have to be there.'

Wesley tried to consider the implications although he knew that the consultant would have the final say. At that moment Nurse Bradshaw re-entered the room.

'I'm sorry, Inspector. Mr Morgan really ought to get some rest now.'

Wesley acknowledged her request and asked if she could give him just one more minute. When she had reluctantly left the room he leaned across the bed to speak with Morgan.

'I'll see what I can do but please understand that the final decision has to be made by the doctor.'

'Thanks.'

'One other thing, you and I need to have a little chat about a few things once you're out of here.'

As Wesley reached the door to leave he turned back to look at Henry Morgan.

The man looked frightened out of his life.

O'Hara woke to a pale grey light filtering through the shabby curtain. He sat on the side of the bed holding his back which had been punished by the broken springs of the bed. He wearily walked over to the hand basin and splashed his face with water. His mouth felt like a sandpit and he desperately needed a drink but refrained from taking a chance on drinking the tepid looking water running out of the tap. He checked his mobile as he put his shoes on. There were no calls. Leaving the hotel he crossed the square to the café where Pierre was busy wiping down tables in expectation of new customers.

'Good morning my friend, I hope you slept well.'

'I feel like I've slept in a hammock filled with stones.'

'In that case you'll be in need of a coffee. Take a seat and I'll bring one over.'

'Thanks, could I have a croissant with cheese to go with it. I haven't eaten since yesterday lunchtime.'

The small café started to fill up as O'Hara ate breakfast. He tried to listen to a couple of conversations that were taking place at other tables but he couldn't get to grip with the accent. He'd learnt to speak broken French since moving to France but the dialect changed considerably from town to town.

With breakfast out of the way, he took his first cigarette of the day before asking Pierre for another coffee. He'd noticed two men sat at a table in the far corner of the café near the counter. They'd arrived shortly after he had and had hardly spoken over a single cup of coffee. Each time he glanced across the room one of them seemed to be looking his way. O'Hara took a long drag on his cigarette, blowing the blue smoke high into the air. Maybe it was his imagination but he had the gut feeling they were watching him. He tried to convince himself he was just tired and paranoid but the gut feeling wouldn't go away. Stubbing the remains of his cigarette in the ash tray he placed twenty euros under the saucer before waving goodbye to Pierre who was busy serving.

O'Hara was pleased that his car was parked at the end of the square, his whole body ached and he was glad to slump his weary body behind the wheel. As he switched on the ignition, he wound the driver's window down to let in some fresh air. Slipping the car into gear he drove slowly past the café heading towards the main road. The two men were both watching him. One of them had a mobile phone to his ear. He was tempted to turn around and drive past the café again so he could take a quick photo of them on his phone but changed his mind at the last moment. Whoever they were, it would only antagonise them and he wasn't looking for trouble.

Felicity Morgan's funeral was definitely one of those days that Wesley wished he was elsewhere. Having been given permission by Henry Morgan's doctor that he could attend his daughter's funeral, Wesley had sent two young constables to escort him to the church where they stood either side of him throughout the service. Felicity's father never uttered a word all through the ceremony. However her mother was inconsolable throughout the service and had to be supported by two members of the family. Wesley noticed that the Morgan's never even looked at one another in the church. It was only when the coffin was being lowered into the ground did Henry Morgan show any sign of emotion. As the vicar read the final sermon Henry slumped to his knees and began to sob.

'I'm so sorry,' he cried. 'Please forgive me my angel. I'm so sorry.'

He buried his head in his hands and wept for forgiveness. Wesley tried to look away. Whatever the man had done, he found it hard to watch.

As the congregation began to disperse, Mandy along with the assistance of one of the relatives helped Sally Morgan into the car. Mandy said she would pop back to the family home a short while later. Meanwhile Wesley and Martin stood a little way back from the grave to allow Henry Morgan time to grieve. After several minutes Wesley rubbed the remains of his roll-up between thumb and forefinger and motioned Martin to follow him. Henry Morgan was now standing next to the grave staring into space. He jumped as Wesley placed his hand on his shoulder.

'Oh Inspector, I thought you would hang around.'

'I'd like you to accompany us back to the station Mr Morgan. I appreciate this isn't a good time but I shan't keep you long. The doctor wants you back at the hospital later.'

Looking like a man who was about to hang, Henry Morgan walked in-between Wesley and Martin back to the unmarked police vehicle. A single local news reporter stood nearby and reached to undo the cover on his camera as they approached. Wesley left Martin to assist Morgan into the vehicle and went to speak to the reporter. He raised his hand before the man could speak.

'If I see one word in print from you about police presence at Felicity Morgan's funeral it will be the last report you ever write,' Wesley stated. The reporter looked as if he was going to reply but thought better of it, turned, looking totally dejected and walked away down the country lane.

Back at the station Henry Morgan had been taken into Wesley's office by Martin whilst Wesley stood outside the building to make a quick call to Mandy to explain the situation. By the time Wesley entered his office it was obvious that Henry Morgan had been crying.

'Please, remain seated,' said Wesley as he walked around the desk to sit opposite Henry. Placing his elbows on the table and his hands under his chin Wesley came straight to the point.

'What made you so angry to strike your daughter?' he asked.

His direct approach had an immediate effect.

'I don't know what came over me Inspector. It's something I'd never done before,' he stammered, 'I just lost my temper.'

Wesley could see that the man's bottom lip was quivering and that it wouldn't take much to push him over the edge. The doctor had warned him not to push Henry too far.

'How did you know?' he asked.

Wesley sighed before replying and rubbed his hands across his face.

'It was just an assumption Mr Morgan. Maybe experience, I don't know.'

For a moment there was silence as Wesley stared across the table into the eyes of a distraught father. It was Henry who broke the silence.

'Felicity came home one evening. Oh she had already moved out, and we weren't expecting her. My wife was actually at a friend's house and knew nothing about her visit. Felicity told me that she was pregnant. I asked her if she had had a pregnancy test but she just laughed and said she didn't need one. She said she was a woman and just knew. I asked her who the father was and that's when she started crying.'

'Go on,' said Wesley.

'She said she couldn't tell me, but because of who it was she couldn't keep the child. That's when I lost my temper.'

'Do you mean that's when you hit her?'

'Not straight away. I shouted at her and demanded that she should tell me who the father was. I said there's no way you're going to have an abortion. It's something my wife and I are strongly against. Felicity laughed at me and said, "You don't understand. I knew you wouldn't understand".

Henry had bitten his lip, so much so that a trickle of blood ran down his chin. 'That's when I walked across the room and physically dragged her out of the chair. She screamed at me and told me that she'd made a mistake by telling me and should have realised that I'd react the way I did. I pleaded with her to change her mind, Inspector. I knew the mental damage she would cause to her mother if she found out.'

Henry stood up and trudged across to the window to peer down onto the street below before continuing. From experience Wesley knew it was best to give the man a bit of breathing space. When Henry turned around to face Wesley, his face was ravaged with guilt.

'Felicity reached for her coat and said she was leaving. She said not to worry but she would sort things out on her own. As I reached out to her she slapped me across the face. Oh she apologised straight away and started crying, but when I grabbed her arm she swung at me again. This time there was so much anger in her face.'

'What happened next?' Wesley asked.

'That's when I hit her, only once, in the ribs. As soon as I'd realised what I'd done I begged her for her forgiveness but she pushed me away and ran out of the room. That was the last time I saw her alive.'

Wesley puffed out his cheeks while he gathered his thoughts.

'How do you explain the bruise on her arm?'

'I guess that's where I held on to her,' Henry replied. He began to sob, his whole body seeming to rake with the pain of his confession.

'Can I ask you one question?' said Wesley.

'Sure, go ahead.' Henry looked back across the room at Wesley.

'At that time, did you know where Felicity was working?'

Henry shook his head.

'No, but I've since been led to believe she was employed at Melcham Hall.'

Wesley nodded, but he wasn't convinced.

Henry walked back to the desk and sat opposite Wesley.

'So what happens now, Inspector? Am I under arrest?' he asked placing his hands on the table.

Wesley stood up and walked across the room and opened the door.

'I suggest you go back into hospital until the doctor discharges you, then go home and comfort your wife. She needs you right now,' he said.

Grabbing his jacket from the back of the chair Henry Morgan walked across to where Wesley was standing.

'Thank you, Inspector. Thank you so much.'

Having escorted Henry Morgan downstairs to the reception desk and arranged for a constable to take him back to the hospital, Wesley went back upstairs in search of Martin who he found in the outer office chatting up one of the new police cadets who was on a training course.

'Come on son, it's your turn to buy the drinks,' said Wesley.

Martin couldn't help the disappointed look on his face as he went in search of his overcoat.

'He'll be back in the office tomorrow morning,' said Wesley winking to the young cadet who was checking her hair in a mirror.

Wesley got Martin to drive out to the Phoenix, as Wesley wanted another quick chat with the landlord, Geoff Dale who had sent him a text. He also fancied another pint of Shepton Tribute which he'd taken a liking to.

'So, what's Brian Hargreaves up to now?'

'Not really sure,' Geoff replied while he was pulling a pint.

'Graham Taylor, mate of mine who runs a stall down at the market says that Hargreaves has been asking around the market looking for someone who might be interested in earning a few bob.'

'Has he said what's involved?'

'Apparently not, but he gave Graham his contact details and said there was a drink in it for him if he found someone. Obviously it may be something legit, but knowing Hargreaves, I doubt it.'

Wesley held out a ten pond note for the drinks.

‘Na, those on me, it’s my birthday,’ said Geoff who went off to serve another customer.

‘So, if Henry Morgan didn’t kill his daughter, who did?’ said Martin taking a sip of his orange juice.

Wesley puffed out his cheeks.

‘Good question. I think it’s time we started talking to some of Felicity’s friends.’ He extracted a crumpled piece of paper from his jacket pocket and pushed it across the table.

‘There’s a list of names there that Janet Moore, the girl who was living with Felicity provided. See if you can contact any of these people. Someone must know something about her.’

Later that evening, Jane was sat at home watching the local news on television when her attention was caught by a news reporter standing outside Annie’s home in the grounds of the Melcham estate.

‘Police are continuing to investigate the murder of Felicity Morgan who was found murdered on the Melcham estate last week. We understand that although her father, Henry Morgan, had been taken in for questioning he has since been released by the police. Felicity Morgan was buried today, just two days before her 24th birthday. In what may be a related incident, there was an attempted break-in at Rowan Lodge today. The property stands at the entrance to the Melcham estate where Felicity’s body was found. Although the police have refused to comment, a local source tells us that the break-in may well be related to the recent murder. This is Alan Douglas reporting for Wells News.’

Jane switched off the television and grabbed her mobile phone. It took only two rings for Wesley to answer. Jane told him of the news report and expressed her disgust at the bad timing and lack of thought for both the parents and poor Annie who would have seen the reporter and the TV crew outside her Cottage.

Wesley was furious.

‘Thanks for letting me know, Jane. I’ll speak with them now. These people can be the pits of the earth. I’ll get Mandy to pop in and make sure Annie’s OK.’

Wesley explained the call to Martin who was just as annoyed.

‘That Alan Smith fella makes me sick,’ he said. ‘He’s just moved down from London where he had a reputation of being a pain in the arse with ill-timed broadcasts. I’ve spoken to a couple of the guys over at Wells and no one seems to like him.’

‘People like him, either don’t think, or are just plain insensitive. Does he not realise that not only was Felicity Morgan buried today but Annie Griffin, an old age pensioner lives on her own in the lodge. She must be terrified with all that lighting and camera equipment outside her window,’ said Wesley as he selected Mandy’s number on his mobile.

Mandy answered straight away and said she had seen the evening news and was already on her way to Annie's.

'If the idiot is still there, please oblige him with my number,' said Wesley. 'I want everyone away from Annie's place, and no one, I repeat no one, is to go anywhere near there unless authorized by me.'

'Yes sir, I understand,' Mandy replied.

Wesley motioned to Martin that it was time to leave the pub.

'Wait in the car while I speak with the newspaper,' said Wesley once they were outside. 'I don't want anyone else to hear what I'm going to say to them.'

Deciding there was nothing more they could do today, Wesley got Martin to drop him home. He was sat watching TV in the lounge as Jane entered with tea and biscuits.

'You shouldn't eat cheese at this time of night,' she said placing the tray on the small coffee table.

'A man has to have one luxury in life,' Wesley replied reaching forward to slap Jane on the bum. 'Unless that is, you can think of a better way to finish the evening my dear.'

'Just eat,' Jane replied with a grin.

Wesley often discussed the day's events with Jane without divulging anything confidential, but tonight he needed her advice. He extracted the envelope from his pocket. The one he'd found in Felicity's bedroom.

'Take a look at this love. Tell me what you think.'

Jane sat down on the settee and opened the letter. She placed the fingers of one hand over her mouth as the realization of what she was reading began to hit home.

'Oh my, that poor girl, what on earth must she have been going through?' Jane exclaimed with a sigh. 'Have you shown this to her mother?'

'Not yet, I'm not sure this is the right time.'

'John, I don't think there will ever be a right time.'

'I know. I guess I'm just putting it off. I'm not sure there's any benefit by giving Sally Morgan the letter. It can only cause her more stress than she has now.'

Jane handed him back the letter knowing John faced a difficult decision.

'How is Annie Griffin?' she asked, changing the subject.

'Yeah she's fine. Mandy called me just before I arrived home to say she was already with her. The old lady seems strong as an axe. Apparently the TV reporter knocked on her door to ask her for an interview but she told him to sling his hook.'

'Good for her. There should be a law against these reporters pestering people like that.'

'There is,' Wesley replied trying to stifle a yawn. 'The trouble is they know just how far they can go before breaking the law.'

Jane knew he was tired but decided that now was the best time to ask the burning question she'd been bottling up for a couple of days.

'John, you know I went over to the bookshop to help Gerry get the place in order, well, it got me thinking. You see, I miss working in the bookshop and I was wondering what you would think if I asked Gerry if I could help him out one afternoon a week. I know we agreed I would start to slow down a bit and work fewer hours but I really would enjoy being over there. I....'

Wesley leaned over and placed his finger to her lips. 'So long as you're happy,' he said.

Wesley must have fallen asleep in the armchair because he was awoken by the sound of his mobile phone vibrating on the coffee table. He sat up straight, trying to release the crook in his neck and reached across for his phone. The first thing he did was to check the time. It was two a.m.

'Wesley here,' he said as he tried to gather his thoughts.

'Hello, sir, desk sergeant, Bill Coombes, here. I'm sorry to bother you at this hour in the morning but I thought you ought to know there's been another body found.'

'What? Where is it, Bill?'

'It was found down one of the country lanes between Shepton Mallet and Doulting. Not far from the Melcham estate. Dave Hopkins, a local milkman, was driving his milk float on his way to Horrington Village where the depot is, when he saw the body in a ditch along the side of the road. The ambulance crew got there about twenty minutes ago but called us straight away. The fella was already dead. I've told them not to touch anything and I've taken the liberty of contacting the doctor and calling forensics out, both are on their way. PC Barker from Wells was in the area so he's on his way too. Is there anyone else you want to call?'

'Err no, thanks, Bill. There's no point in calling anyone else at this time of night. Tell Barker I'm on my way.'

Wesley gingerly stood up, his back was killing him. It happened every time he fell asleep in the armchair. Grabbing his coat in the hallway he slipped into the kitchen to leave Jane a note before quietly leaving the house. He hoped the noise of the car engine wouldn't wake her.

Twenty minutes later Wesley turned into a layby fifty yards past the scene so that his car wouldn't cause an obstruction on the bend of the narrow country lane. He locked the car and pulled up the collar of his jacket. The overnight temperature was probably somewhere around freezing and you could see your breath in the cold night air. As he approached the scene, PC Barker came walking towards him.

'Good morning, sir. Sorry you had to be called out,' said Barker shaking hands.

'What can you tell me?' Wesley asked as they trudged towards where the body lay.

The forensic team had already cordoned off a large area from the footpath and across the ditch to the hedgerow.

'The victim is male. I'd guess late thirties or early forties. Casually dressed, but there's no ID.'

'That's a pretty basic description,' Wesley thought to himself.

'Is there any sign of a fight?'

'There is considerable bruising on the face, and by the looks of it I would guess the nose is broken. It looks as if the body was dumped there. Trouble is it was raining earlier and it's hard to see any tyre tracks. There's nothing obvious though.'

Wesley extracted a pair of plastic gloves from his jacket pocket as they reached the cordoned off area.

'Wait here, Barker. Make sure no one else enters, OK.'

'No one will get past me, Inspector.'

Wesley slipped under the plastic cord and dropped down into the ditch where the body lay slumped on the grass. A member of the forensic team who was kneeling beside the body looked up as Wesley approached.

'Good morning, Inspector.'

Wesley was taken by surprise. The young woman had piercing blue eyes, blond hair tied back in a bun under a hood and a smile that must have melted the heart of many a man. He immediately asked himself why someone so good looking would want to spend their life handling corpses.

'Good morning,' Wesley replied kneeling down on the other side of the body.

'Mel Harris. We met last week.'

She held out her gloved hand which Wesley took in his. 'It's nice to meet you again. Sorry it has to be in such awful circumstances.'

'Something I'd better get used to,' she replied with a grin and shrugged her shoulders.

'So what have we got?' Wesley asked.

'White male medium build, late thirties to early forties at a guess. Has been dead a couple of hours I would say. Doctor Meadows has just left, he agreed with me.'

'Anything else you can tell me right now?'

'I would say that the victim suffered a rather heavy beating before he died. There's bruising showing above the eye and his nose is broken too. I'd guess that he has several broken ribs but it's difficult to be precise until we get him back to the lab.'

'What's that in his hair?' asked Wesley pointing towards the back of the victims head.

Mel leaned forward and extracted what appeared to be a strand of yellow foliage. She looked at Wesley and shrugged her shoulders.

'You're the local here,' she said. 'Looks like gorse to me but I couldn't tell you where it came from.'

‘I think I might know,’ Wesley replied. ‘Can you bag it up and take it back for examination.’

‘Sure, will do, Inspector. I didn’t realise you were a bit of a horticulturist.’

‘I’m not, Mel, but I’m sure I’ve seen something very similar growing around here.’

She pointed to the chequered waistcoat the victim was wearing.

‘He’s not exactly dressed for being outdoors is he? My guess is that he was roughed up before his body was dumped here.’

‘Do you believe he was dead by the time he was left here?’ Wesley asked.

‘I would say so, not for long though, a couple of hours at the most.’

‘OK thanks, Mel. Once you’ve finished here ask the paramedics to help you bag the body. I’ll be in touch.’

‘Nice to meet you again, Inspector, I’ll provide you with a full report later today.’

Wesley stood up and began walking away as Mel Harris placed a couple of medical instruments back into her medical kit bag.

‘Oh by the way, Inspector, “Happy Christmas”,’ she called.

Wesley turned around with a surprised look on his face. He hadn’t even realised it was Christmas Day. Leaving instructions with PC Barker that someone was to remain onsite until forensics had finished their work, Wesley made his way back to the car. He switched on the engine and turned up the air con before rolling a cigarette.

“This is going to be another long day,” he said to himself.

He took a slow drive to the station where the desk sergeant was surprised to see Wesley walk through the door just before four a.m.

‘I thought you’d go home to get a couple of hours sleep,’ he said as Wesley took his overcoat off.

‘I still might do, Bill, but I need to write up a quick report while everything is fresh in my mind. Not only that but I thought there was more chance of you making me a coffee at this time of the morning than Jane.’

They both laughed as Bill raised the counter to let Wesley through to the back office.

‘I’ll go and make it now,’ Bill replied.

A weak early morning sun was just breaking through the clouds when the telephone on Wesley’s desk woke him up. As he reached across the desk he knocked over the remains of his coffee that had gone cold.

‘Wesley speaking,’ he answered in a sleepy drone.

‘Good morning, Mr Wesley. I’m sorry if I’ve disturbed you. I appreciate that it’s Christmas Day but I thought it was important that I call you. My name is Margaret Whitlow, Timmy’s mother.’

For a moment there was silence between the two of them as Wesley tried to gather his thoughts and Margaret Whitlow considered how best to explain herself.

'I'm sorry, Inspector, let me explain.' she continued. 'Timmy delivers groceries and newspapers to most people in Shepton Mallet. When he was delivering the local evening paper last night he saw the photograph on the front page from yesterday's funeral of that poor girl who was murdered.'

'You mean, Felicity Morgan,' Wesley replied still trying to fully wake up.

'Yes that's the one. Well, my Timmy says to me, "Look at the man in the photo mum. I know him". So I asked him to point the man out to me. The sentence under the photo describes the man as being Felicity's father.'

Wesley ran his hand across his face to wipe the sleep from his eyes.

'Oh yeah, so where does he know him from?'

'My Timmy says he's been a regular visitor to Melcham Hall recently.'

Wesley sat up straight in his chair.

'Is he sure? I mean, I've spoken to Mr Morgan several times but he's never mentioned visiting the Hall before.'

'Oh yes, Inspector. Timmy says that he's seen Mr Morgan there on a number of occasions when he's been delivering the daily newspaper or weekly groceries and apparently his car has been there most days.'

'That is very interesting news,' Wesley replied. 'Please thank Timmy for bringing this to my attention. It may just be coincidence but it's something we'll look into.'

Mrs Whitlow hung up, a broad smile on her face. She felt so proud of her son.

Wesley on the other hand, was pensive. What was Henry Morgan doing there and why on earth had he not mentioned any of this during any of their conversations?

Wesley stuck his head outside of the office door looking to see if Martin was in yet. Sure enough, he was sat talking to the young police cadet who had taken an eye to him the previous evening.

'Happy Christmas you two, Martin, could you spare a minute?' Wesley called across the room. Seconds later an embarrassed looking Martin entered Wesley's office.

'She's nice isn't she?' said Wesley sitting behind his desk and motioning for Martin to pull up a chair.

'Oh, err…yes,' Martin stammered.

Wesley smirked as he reached across the table for his tobacco.

'If I were you I'd try and find some mistletoe.'

Martin looked down at the desk as his face reddened.

'I've got a job for you. I want you to pop over to Wells and speak with PC Mark Hayles. I've already spoken with his superior, Inspector Drearden, so Mark will be expecting you. It's come to my attention that Henry Morgan has been spending a lot of time over at Melcham Hall.'

Martin raised his eyebrows in surprise at the news.

'Yeah, it's news to me too,' Wesley remarked before continuing.

'Fill Mark in on all the details surrounding Felicity Morgan's murder, her father's visits to Melcham Hall, and the mysterious behaviour of Hargreaves' wife. Don't forget to mention the fact that Alison is already working there undercover as a housemaid. I want Mark to tail Henry Morgan for the next few days and I want to know where he is at any one moment. I know Morgan spent the night in hospital under observation but they expect him to be released this morning. Tell Mark to call me if he sees anything suspicious but not to intervene.'

'Is there anything else, sir?'

'Yes, we have another murder on our hands. A fella was found dead on the road between Shepton Mallet and Doulting in the early hours of this morning. He'd been beaten up.'

'Christ,' Martin replied taking in a deep breath. 'Have we been able to identify the victim?'

'Not yet. I'm going to pop home to get some breakfast as I was called out at two a.m. this morning, then I'm heading over to the pathology lab. Give me a call later when you've spoken to some of Felicity's friends, assuming you can get hold of them over the Christmas period.'

'Yes sir.'

'Once you've spoken with Mark I suggest you go home to spend a few hours with the family. I mean, it's Christmas Day. I'll call you if I need you.'

'Thanks, sir. Happy Christmas.'

16

Christmas Day passed without any further incidents except for a drunk causing a fight outside the Phoenix pub after the lunchtime session. Wesley had arrived home to the smell of roast turkey cooking. He found Jane watching a movie so grabbed a bottle of wine and two glasses and sat beside her. These moments were too far and few between.

'Before you get comfortable, your Christmas present is on the bed,' said Jane.

'On the bed or in the bed,' he replied with a smirk on his face.

Wesley jumped up just in time as Jane's attempt to thump him on the shoulder missed by a fraction. The rest of the day was spent with Wesley wearing his new clothes (minus tobacco stains) and Jane admiring her new diamond ring.

Gerry Callow and his mother joined them in the evening and Wesley had to no choice but to listen to Gerry explain in great detail just how much Jane had done to improve the layout of the bookshop.

By the time they left that evening Wesley could have drawn the layout of the shop from memory even though he hadn't been in the place since Gerry had bought it.

On Boxing Day they were invited to lunch with their neighbours, the Harrington's. Keith and Dawn Harrington were both retired school teachers and now spent most of their time enjoying the peace and tranquillity that village life provided. Having both spent their careers in the teaching industry and being involved in a multitude of schools plays, they were keen thespians and now ran the local amateur dramatic society. Their thatched Cottage had been lovingly renovated and provided for all their comforts. Wesley enjoyed their company because even though they knew the job he had they never ever talked about work. Wesley was admiring their new extension which had been sympathetically designed to look as if was part of the original building.

'I'll give you the builder's number,' said Keith when Wesley mentioned that he and Jane had been discussing the possibility of extending their own kitchen.

The Harrison's daughter was staying with them for the Christmas period and Jane spent an hour or more talking to her and her mother about her favourite subject, books. Amelia was training to become a veterinary surgeon and explained how difficult it was to find the 'complete' book to help her with her studies. Meanwhile Keith and Wesley sat discussing the education system with Wesley stressing the difficulties that new police recruits faced trying to balance work with education.

That evening, back in their own place, Jane and Wesley commented on how lucky they were to be living in such a lovely village with such nice neighbours in such an idyllic location.

Still full of too much Christmas dinner WPC Alison Bolt now faced her second day working as a housemaid at Melcham Hall. She had to wait over an hour for the bus to Shepton Mallet and was convinced that the bus company were still running a Sunday service even though the driver said they were now running as normal. She let herself in with the spare key that Hargreaves had given her and hung her coat on the stand in the hall. She still felt spooked around the place and as usual there was no sign of Lady Hargreaves. Alison headed for the kitchen where she found a note from Brian Hargreaves saying he had to pop out and would be back later. She was still in the kitchen assembling a variety of cleaning agents when she heard a crash in one of the rooms directly overhead. She ran across to the kitchen doorway and peered up at the grand staircase but there was no one in sight so she called out.

'Is anyone there? Are you OK, Lady Hargreaves?'

Having been told that the part of the building above the kitchen was out of bounds Alison was hesitant in running up the stairs to investigate. She called out again but again, there was no reply. Deciding that she ought to take a quick look she climbed the stairs stopping at the broad landing. There was no sign of anyone on the landing or along the corridor to her right. Knowing that Lady Hargreaves' room was to the right of the corridor and that Brian Hargreaves had gone out Alison assumed there was no one else in the house.

There were four doors leading off the left hand corridor, the first was a small broom cupboard, the second a bathroom and toilet. Alison made her way along to the next door and turned the handle. The room had obviously once been used as a bedroom but now it was crammed with wooden crates, the kind used when one is moving house. Deciding not to spend too much time upstairs Mandy thought she would take a quick look in the last room before going back downstairs. The door was locked. Extracting a small leather pouch from her trouser pocket she opened it up to produce what appeared to be a bunch of different shaped hairclips hanging from a thin metal bar. However they were actually specially designed lock picks that a colleague had presented her with as a present shortly after she joined the police force. Alison tried the first couple, twisting them gently in the lock but to no avail. Then, triumph! As she twisted the third one in the lock there was a click as the door lock opened. Alison placed the lock picks back in her pocket before slowly turning the door handle. Opening the door just wide enough to allow her to peer in the room she quietly slipped inside, closing the door behind her. The room was in darkness so Alison searched for a switch and flicked on the light.

Heavy drape curtains prevented any daylight from entering the room where time seemed to have stopped. Everything in the room was covered in cobwebs. She walked over to the dressing table which had obviously been untouched for some considerable time, a thick layer of dust and cobwebs covered every ornament in sight. For fear of disturbing anything on display she turned her attention to the first of the three top drawers. The first contained expensive looking ladies underwear, the second, stockings, tights and socks, the third however was locked. Again Alison went to work with the set of lock picks and soon had the drawer open. At the front were several different shaped bottles of perfume and a couple of handkerchiefs but what caught her attention were the small pile of letters wrapped in a crimson silk bow.

Annie Griffin sat reading the article in the local paper that referred to Felicity Morgan's funeral. 'What a waste of a life' she said to herself shaking her head.

WPC Mandy Tredwell had just left Annie after sharing tea and toast and Annie had settled into her favourite chair preparing herself for her usual morning siesta. She had been dreaming of days gone by when she and her husband had spent time on the estate having picnics, just lying back listening to the sounds of birds singing and the breeze as it whispered through the woodland trees. She recalled times when the only thing they had to think about was what to choose for dinner, the times when they made love in the woods when the rest of the world seemed a lifetime away.

A sharp rap on the front door brought her back to reality. "Oh I wonder who that can be now. I hope it's not that damn reporter again," she thought.

Keeping the safety latch on Annie opened the front door to peer outside.

Brian Hargreaves was stood on the doorstep.

'Oh it's you, what's up?' asked Annie.

'I'm sorry to bother you Annie, but my car is stuck in the ditch just along the main road. Do you think I could borrow your phone to call a breakdown vehicle?'

'Why, yes of course,' Annie replied.

She closed the door again to enable her to slip the safety latch before pulling the door open and gesturing for Brian Hargreaves to enter. As soon as he stepped into the hallway Annie could see how flustered he was. His face was red as if he'd been running and his shoes were covered in mud. Hargreaves noticed Annie looking at his shoes and apologised before taking them off and placing them on the doormat.

'You know where the phone is,' said Annie, 'I'll be in the kitchen if you need me.'

'Thanks,' he replied stepping into the front room.

Annie pulled the kitchen door close without shutting it and could hear Hargreaves talking. She couldn't make out what was being said but it was obvious from his tone of voice that Hargreaves was arguing with someone.

As soon as she heard him hang up Annie quickly sat herself down at the kitchen table.

'I'm sorry to have bothered you,' Hargreaves said as he poked his head around the door.

'I hope you managed to get through to them,' Annie replied.

'I'm sorry?'

'I was saying I hope you managed to get hold of the breakdown people.'

'Oh, err…yes, yes I did, thanks. I'll leave you in peace now. I'm going to walk back to the car to wait for them,' he replied.

As soon as Annie heard the front door close she left the kitchen and made her way to the front room window. Hargreaves had gone. Wrapping a shawl around her shoulders Annie made her way back into the kitchen and out through the back door, closing it quietly behind her. It was a bright crisp morning and for the first time in several hours it had stopped raining. Annie made her way slowly around the side of the house and rather than heading towards the gated entrance to the estate she took a short cut through the woodland following the boundary along the main road. Treading carefully, so as not to slip on the woodland floor she eventually came to gap in the hedgerow some two hundred yards from the Cottage. From this vantage point Annie could view a long stretch of the road that ran past the estate. Just as she thought, there was no sign of Hargreaves' car anywhere. Back indoors Annie gave herself a couple of minutes to regain her strength before she dialled WPC Mandy Tredwells' mobile.

'Hello, is that Mandy?'

'Annie? Are you OK?'

'Yes, yes my dear, I'm fine. I just thought you ought to know something.'

'What is it?' asked Mandy pushing aside a pile of folders on her desk.

Annie explained how Brian Hargreaves had asked to use the phone saying that his car had broken down, how harassed he seemed and the fact that he appeared to have been arguing with someone on the phone.

'I'm sorry,' said Mandy after Annie had explained the events, 'but what is it that concerns you?'

'It's just that Brian Hargreaves said he had broken down in his car a few hundred yards away from here but I've taken a look down the lane and there is no car in sight.'

'So you believe it was just an excuse to use your phone for something else and he was lying about the car?'

'Yes but not only that my dear, he knew where the telephone was.'

'Sorry, Annie I don't understand.'

'You see, the telephone has been hanging on the wall in the hallway for the past twenty years but when I told him he could use the it he went straight into the front room to pick it up. Don't you see? He knew where it was.'

'Annie, are you trying to tell me that you think Brian Hargreaves has been in your front room without your knowledge?'

'I'm convinced of it,' Annie replied.

'OK, I'll see if we can put a lookout for his car. In the meantime don't answer the door to anyone other than me or Inspector Wesley. I don't know what Brian Hargreaves is involved in but it sure seems that he's up to no good,' said Mandy.

Wesley was sitting in his car outside the pathology lab having a cigarette when the call came through from Mandy who explained events at Annie's place.

'OK, pop in when you get the chance. Make sure she's alright. See if BT can identify where the call was made to from Annie's phone. I'm just going into pathology to see if we can gain any more information on the latest murder victim. I have a meeting arranged with Alison, in Wells at midday, after she's finished her morning stint at Melcham Hall. Keep me updated though.'

'Will do,' Mandy replied gathering her car keys and logging out of her pc. One of her colleagues had saved a photo of the hotel she was going to be staying at as her screensaver, a constant reminder of warmer days to come.

She needed to pop into Glastonbury to obtain some euros and pick up a couple of items from the dry cleaners first then she'd pop in to see Annie again.

It was while she was driving to Glastonbury that a thought suddenly struck her that Annie had been calling her a lot. Mandy felt uncomfortable that she felt the way she did. Obviously the old lady needed her otherwise she wouldn't call. Would she?

Mel Harris and Terry Austin were bent over the naked corpse examining an area of bruising on the man's chest and neither noticed Wesley enter the room. Wesley gave a polite cough as he closed the door quietly behind him.

'Ah, good morning,' said Terry as Wesley approached. 'You've met Mel haven't you?'

'Morning again, Mel,' Wesley replied. 'Yes, we met on Christmas Day, about two in the morning along a dimly lit country lane.'

'I do hope your dear wife Jane knows about your little rendezvous,' Terry replied with a smile.

Mel looked at Wesley with the faintest of crimson in her cheeks.

'If she didn't I'm sure you'd tell her,' said Wesley grinning but now feeling rather uncomfortable with a naked corpse stuck under his nose. He watched as Terry Austin made a long incision down the front of the body, removing vital organs with precision and lining them up on the side like a butcher dressing his shop window. Although Wesley was now a veteran at watching this procedure it still made him feel sick. He stood silent until Terry had finished.

'So what have you got for me?'

'Well it's different to the last killing,' Terry replied. 'Whoever killed this poor chap here beat him to death.'

Wesley could taste the bile rising in his throat as Terry pulled back the chest cavity to reveal the remaining organs.

'The guy would have died from internal bleeding. A nasty blow to the side of the head, one of his lungs is crushed, several broken ribs, broken nose, damage to the spleen and a burst artery under the heart. Whoever did this used something heavy. My guess is a blunt instrument, wooden, something shaped like a mallet.'

Wesley took a step back as the feeling of nausea got worse.

'I asked Mel to take a look from a forensic perspective as there is something else quite interesting. Let me show you.'

Pulling on the arm of one of the circular lights above the corpse he shone it directly onto the skull.

'Take a close look at the guy's hair. It's full of these tiny yellow particles.'

'Is that the same as you noticed earlier?' Wesley asked Mel.

'Yes, it's gorse. Strange that someone would have it in their hair unless they've been lying in a gorse bush. These bits are seeds.'

'Doesn't make sense to me,' Wesley replied looking first at Mel then Terry.

'Maybe it's just a coincidence, or maybe the two bodies were in the same vicinity at one time?' Terry suggested.

'What makes you say that?' Wesley rubbed his chin looking perplexed.

'It's the same match as particles found on Felicity Morgan's clothing,' Mel replied.

Wesley puffed out his cheeks. 'So what we're saying is that at some point both of our victims were in the same place?'

Terry shrugged his shoulders.

'Possibly, I don't know of another explanation,' said Mel.

'Is there anything else you can tell me about this fella?' asked Wesley.

Mel Harris reached for a clipboard that was lying on the metal tray under the trolley that the corpse was on.

'Male, aged between late thirties early forties, five feet ten inches tall, has a scar where his appendix was removed several years ago. No distinguishing marks except for a small tattoo shaped like ۞۞۞ on his left wrist. I've drawn it for you.'

'OK thanks,' said Wesley accepting the pencilled drawing.

'Have you any idea who he is?' asked Terry as he started to crudely stitch the torso back up.

‘Not at the moment. We’ve put out the usual missing persons brief but I guess its early days yet. The only thing we’re pretty sure of is that the guy isn’t a local. If he was, someone would have recognised him by now.’

Having decided there was nothing else to learn from his visit Wesley thanked them both for their time and made his exit. The clinical smell of the pathology lab was making him feel queasy again.

Standing in the street outside the building that housed the pathology lab, Wesley stopped to roll a cigarette. As he searched his pockets for his matches his mobile phone vibrated. It was a text from Mandy saying that Annie was OK. He replied to confirm he’d received it then put a call through to Martin to see if he had come up with anything. Martin said that no one had been reported missing since last night and that so far, door to door enquiries between Shepton Mallet and Doulting hadn’t revealed anything either, adding that the area where the body was found was such a remote location that it’s quite feasible that no vehicle other than the milk float and the killer may have travelled along that stretch of road for several hours. He said he was now on his way to speak with a couple of Felicity Morgan’s friends who he’d managed to track down.

Wesley agreed to meet back at the station later and said he was on his way there himself. He wanted to download a photo of the victim from his mobile onto his laptop. The plan was then for a number of local officers to take the mug shot around the local villages to see if anyone recognised the victim.

Mandy was sat with Annie when the telephone started ringing in Annie’s front room.

‘I think that will be BT for me,’ said Mandy. ‘Do you mind if I answer it?’

‘Of course not, go ahead my dear,’ Annie replied.

Mandy took the call and scribbled down some numbers as a BT engineer provided her details of where Brian Hargreaves’ call was made to. When Mandy re-entered the kitchen, Annie could see the concerned look on her face.

‘What’s wrong love?’

‘I don’t know to be honest,’ Mandy replied with a quizzical look. ‘I’m not sure we haven’t stumbled upon a hornets’ nest. The phone call that Brian Hargreaves made was to a call box on the corner of Whitehall and Downing street.’

‘Do you mean the Downing Street where the Prime Minister resides?’ Annie asked.

‘Yes, that’s the one. What’s more, we also have CCTV footage of the person taking the call.’

‘Oh really, and do you know the person?’

‘I think most people in this country know the person,’ Mandy replied.

Having ensured she had locked the door to the bedroom WPC Alison Bolt sat on the edge of the bed and began to untie the silk ribbon from the collection of letters she'd found in the drawer. It was apparent they had been kept in date order so she began to read the oldest letter first. Some fifteen minutes later, having finished reading the third letter, Alison placed it down on the bed and began to contemplate what she'd discovered. Looking at the dates, the letters were all written over fifteen years ago and were intimate in detail. They were written to a lover who was apparently living in France. As there were at least another dozen letters to be read Alison decided she ought to return the letters back to the dressing table drawer from where she could retrieve them at a later date. Ensuring that she relocked the drawer she switched off the light and left the bedroom. Alison began descending the stairs when she suddenly gasped with surprise.

'Oh Lady Hargreaves, I didn't see you standing there.'

Downstairs in the entrance hall Lady Hargreaves was leaning against the library door looking up at the staircase. Her eyed appeared glazed as if she was going to faint at any moment.

'Could you fetch a glass of water up to my room,' Lady Hargreaves answered stepping forward to clutch the bannister.

'Are you sure you're OK?' Alison asked as the woman struggled to mount the stairs.

'Yes, yes I'm fine.'

Alison descended the last couple of steps and turned to cross the hall towards the kitchen. Just as she reached out to open the kitchen door she heard a shriek from behind her. She turned around as Lady Hargreaves tumbled backwards down the stairs. Alison ran back across the hall and leapt to the floor where Lady Hargreaves' body was slumped. She immediately felt for a pulse and was relieved to find one, albeit quite weak. A minute later Alison was speaking with 999. It was twenty minutes before the ambulance crew arrived. They immediately gave assistance to Lady Hargreaves who although now conscious, wasn't making any sense at all. While they attended to her, Alison slipped out of the front door to phone Wesley.

'So where's Hargreaves?' he asked after Alison advised him of events.

'Don't know, sir. I haven't seen him this morning. When I arrived I found a note in the kitchen saying he'd had to go out.'

'Do you want me to stay here or go with Lady Hargreaves to the hospital?'

'Stay there, Alison. Even a confused Lady Hargreaves might wonder why her housemaid accompanied her to the hospital. I'll make my way over to the hospital in a while to check on her. If there's no sign of Hargreaves take a look around, see what you can come up with.'

'OK, sir.'

She told him about the letters and he agreed that she'd been right in leaving them where she found them.

'Do you want me to send someone else over to stay with you?'

'No sir, I'm fine.'

'OK, but be careful. I don't trust Hargreaves.' He told her about the call Hargreaves had made from Annie Griffin's place and that there was no evidence of a breakdown recovery vehicle being requested.

After Alison hung up, Wesley sat with his elbows on the table and ran his hands across his jaw. He didn't feel comfortable with Alison being at Melcham Hall on her own but he needed someone on the inside and knew that she could handle herself. Although Alison was probably the smallest person in Street police station she held a black belt at karate and represented the police in a number of martial arts exhibitions around the West Country. Some of her colleagues nicknamed her 'Bruce' after the famous Bruce Lee.

Shortly after leaving Rowan Lodge, Mandy arrived back at the station to find even more paperwork on her desk. Just as she picked up the top folder, Trish Matthews the young police cadet came running across the office.

'I do hope you didn't mind me leaving the folder on your desk, Mandy. It's the list of local vehicle breakdown services you asked for. I've telephoned every company on the list and no one has a record of Brian Hargreaves requesting assistance.'

'Oh, thanks very much,' Mandy replied, rather taken back by the young girl's enthusiasm.

'I did speak with the AA, RAC and Green Flag too, but they hadn't assisted him either,' Trish exclaimed.

Mandy nodded her head to acknowledge the girl's comments.

'Good work, Trish. You've been a great help.'

A proud Trish Matthews walked back to her with a confident swagger and a beaming smile on her face.

PC Mark Hayles sat pretending to read the newspaper on the table in front of him as he sipped the stewed tea. The small dingy café was busy and most of the tables were occupied, mostly by builders by the look of their clothing. He'd spotted Henry Morgan leaving his car in a side road just off the High Street and had followed him on foot. He had been trailing Morgan for three days now and had already come to dislike him simply because he'd had to give up most of his Christmas just to keep tabs on the man's movements. Morgan had spent Christmas Day at home and on Boxing Day had driven to his local golf club where Mark sat in the car park for over four hours before watching Morgan stagger out and fall into the back of a cab before being driven home.

Morgan was now sat at a small table in the far corner of the café in conversation with the man opposite. Mark recognised Brian Hargreaves from the description that Martin had provided him a couple of days ago. Although Mark couldn't hear what the two men were talking about it was obvious from their mannerisms that the conversation was becoming quite heated. At one point Morgan banged the sugar bowl down on the table causing other customers to look up. PC Mark Hayles was quite enjoying the scene. It was time for some action. The young PC scribbled a few notes down on the writing pad he'd hidden in the newspaper. It was a trick he'd seen in an old Columbo movie and he felt quite chuffed with himself for copying the idea. He couldn't wait for chance to tell his girlfriend that he'd spent the last few days in plain clothes following a gangster. He was excited about how impressed she would be even though he would have to exaggerate somewhat.

The sound of two chairs scrapping across the wooden floor made him look up.

He watched as both Morgan and Hargreaves made their way to the exit.

Slipping a five pound note under the plate to pay for his tea and sandwich Mark waited until the two men had turned away from the café before following.

Neither, Morgan or Hargreaves appeared to be in any rush to get anywhere as they strolled past the small parade of shops before taking a right turn into a side street. Mark was puzzled; he knew the area well, well enough to know that they were heading into a cul-de-sac where the only exit was a local park. Mark hung back until the two men had entered the park and disappeared from view. By the time he reached the park entrance he could just see Hargreaves' head above a clump of bushes some hundred yards in front. He paused for another minute to allow himself a bit more space between him and the two men. Sticking to the footpath he rounded the corner of the park just where it opened up in front of the pond. He could see Morgan sitting on the park bench facing away from him, staring at the pond, but there was no sign of Hargreaves. Just as he turned to retrace his footsteps he felt a sharp pain in his neck before blackness overcame him.

Martin had tracked down two of Felicity's friends who were renting a flat on the outskirts of Glastonbury in a small village named Pitsley. Apart from two rows of adjacent terraced houses Pitsley consisted of a chemist, a bakery, a greengrocers shop and 'The Bear' public house. It was in 'The Bear' that the two girls agreed to meet him. As soon as Martin entered the lounge bar all conversation in the pub stopped. There were only about a dozen customers in the place, the vast majority looked under age and the smell of drugs was rife. Mia Godwin and Sam Bowden were sat at a small table at the back of the pub. By the time Martin joined them most of the other customers had already left.

'It's good of you to meet me,' he said trying to wedge himself into the bench on the opposite side of the table.

'That's OK,' replied the girl who turned out to be Sam Bowden. Sam wore a pair of faded jeans, a blue tee-shirt and a denim jacket. Her wavy blond hair looked as if it hadn't seen a comb in weeks. Mia, who Martin guessed was under age, sat chewing gum. She was wearing a tartan mini-skirt that exposed shapely long legs and a skimpy white blouse that failed to hide the fact she wasn't wearing a bra.

Martin took out his notebook and placed it on the table.

'Now, what can you girls tell me about Felicity Morgan,' he asked.

Mia was the first to reply. 'She was a slag. She stole my fella while she was still going out with someone else.' She trapped the chewing gum between her teeth and blew it into a bubble before it burst. Then using her fingers pushed the remains back into her mouth.

'So I gather you didn't like her much?'

'She was alright, just a slag. Didn't expect her to end up dead though. I hope that prat Simon doesn't try and get back with me now that Felicity's not on the menu.'

Martin got the impression that he wasn't going to get anything constructive out of Mia Godwin so directed his next question at Sam Bowden.

'How long have you known Felicity?'

'Since school, we all went to Parkfield together. She was the clever one though, got that from her dad.'

'You mean Henry Morgan?'

'Yeah, right old whizz kid at figures he is, always going on at her about becoming a bloody accountant or something like that. Slimy git though, always undressing you with his eyes. I suppose that's how he got his kicks.'

Martin tried to ignore her remarks and continued with his questioning.

'Do you know if Felicity was still seeing this Simon fella?'

'Simon Reynolds, his name is.'

Mia popped another bubble before taking a sip of coke, leaving a ring of chewing gum around the glass.

'Do you know where I can get in touch with this Simon Reynolds?'

'He's a boxer, trains down at Harry's gym in Wells. You'll find him in there most days and nights.'

Martin pencilled a few details in his notebook.

'I don't suppose you want to add my telephone number in your little book?' said Mia leaning provocatively across the table. 'We're going to a New Year's party in Glastonbury. You could always pick me up on the way. I'd be ever so grateful.'

'Err, that's very kind, but I already have a partner,' Martin replied.

'Ah well that's a shame,' Mia replied. As she sat back she placed her feet on the edge of the bench and tucked her knees under her chin, exposing far too much thigh.

'So was Felicity murdered or was it an accident?' she asked.

'That's what we're trying to determine.' Martin looked from one girl to the other. It was apparent they had assumed Felicity was murdered.

'Do the police think her father killed her?' It was Sam who asked the question.

'What makes you ask that?' Martin suddenly felt he was on to something.

Sam suddenly looked nervous and the confidence had drained from her face. She glanced at Mia before replying as if looking for support.

'Well, it's just that everyone knew that her father used to knock her about,' she muttered.

'Is this right?' Martin directed the question to her friend Mia.

'He hit her a few times. I saw him hit her once.'

She blurted it out as if it was a secret she'd held back for too long.

Mia grabbed Sam's hand and the two cocky teenagers no longer looked so sure of themselves.

Deciding to leave the questioning there Martin excused himself, thanking the girls for their assistance. He could hear them muttering to themselves as he left the pub.

17

Mandy met Wesley in the hospital reception and briefed him of the current situation before leading the way to the private room where Lady Hargreaves had been taken. They stood watching the doctor administer an injection into Lady Hargreaves' arm before he checked the monitoring device she was attached to. Mandy whispered to Wesley the results from BT and the CCTV footage of the person receiving the call made from Annie Griffin's place. Wesley was about to reply when the doctor spoke. 'Ah, good morning, you must be Inspector Wesley.'

The two men shook hands.

'What's your opinion, doc?' Wesley asked as the doctor walked around the end of the bed to make notes on the clipboard that hung from the frame.

'Strange one this,' he replied. 'Some form of paralysis for sure, but at this moment in time I can't tell you what's caused it. We may know more when the blood test results come back.'

'Is it some kind of virus?' enquired Mandy.

'I really can't say. It's too early to tell. Strange thing is that the woman hasn't got a high temperature, which is something one would normally expect in these circumstances. We'll keep the patient in the isolation ward until we have results of the blood tests and I'll give you a call as soon as I have something to tell you.'

Both Wesley and Mandy nodded as the doctor left the room.

'So what's our next move?' Mandy asked.

'We try and locate Brian Hargreaves. In the meantime I'd like you to pay another visit to Sally Morgan. Ask her why she's never mentioned that her husband spent two years in Bowden Manor nursing home following a nervous breakdown. It may be nothing but yet again it may explain his recent behaviour. PC Mark Hayles is currently keeping tabs on him. Check in with Mark but do make sure the two of you aren't seen together.'

'OK, sir. I assumed Henry Morgan was still in hospital.'

'No, the doctor released him Christmas morning, that's why I've asked Mark to keep tabs on him.'

'Do you think there's a reason for Sally Morgan not to have mentioned about her husband's breakdown?'

'Maybe she didn't see it as being important, and maybe it's not, but I get the feeling that we're not getting the whole story.'

'I'll see what I can get out of her,' said Mandy. 'I'll touch base with Mark just to find out where Henry is.'

'I'm beginning to wonder if our Henry has a bit of a temper on him,' said Wesley. 'Martin called me a few minutes ago as he's been speaking to a couple of friends of Felicity's. They reckon Henry Morgan hit his daughter on several occasions.'

Mandy raised her eyebrows and pursed her lips.

'Are you suggesting that could be a reason why Felicity left home to rent a room?'

'It's just a thought,' he replied shrugging his shoulders. 'We'll catch up later. I'm heading over to Glastonbury. It seems that Martin may also have found out who our latest victim was.'

Wesley found Martin sat on the steps to Glastonbury Abbey tucking into a portion of chips rapped in newspaper.

'Hi, sir,' he mumbled with a mouthful of chips. He went to stand up.

'Sit down son, finish your lunch.'

Wesley sat on the step beside him and helped himself to a chip.

'So who is our latest victim?'

'The name's Ted Drake. Well, that's the name he'd registered as. He'd been staying at the Sawyers Arms just up the road at the far end of the town. According to the landlord he hasn't seen him for several days. He turned up just over a week ago, paid rent for two weeks in advance in cash. One of the barmen says he spoke to him a couple of times. It would appear that Ted Drake was a bit of a loner. He tried to sell the barman a couple of watches but the fella says they looked real cheap. I've taken a look around his room but couldn't find anything. No passport, no bank cards, no ID of any kind. There was a small amount of cash in the dressing table but that's all. By the look of the clothes he had I would say it's safe to say that he didn't have much money. I've just phoned the station and they're checking records to see if we've got anything else on him. Do you want another chip?'

Wesley looked down at the greasy remains in the paper.

'No thanks. So at the moment we don't have anything else on this fella?'

'No only that the guy at the Sawyers Arms says our Mr Drake had an accent but he couldn't be sure where it was from.'

'Not much to go on eh?' Wesley sighed.

'So what else has been happening?' Martin asked as he screwed up the paper before placing it in a nearby rubbish bin.

Wesley bought him up to date with events regarding Lady Hargreaves and Brian Hargreaves' phone call as they strolled back towards the car park.

'I sure hope Lady Hargreaves is OK.'

'So do I son. The last thing we need is another death on our lap.'

'So, it appears that Brian Hargreaves may not be our local villain eh? I mean, if he's speaking with TV celebrities he must have friends in high places.'

'Yes, that's what worries me,' Wesley replied. 'I think I need to make a call to Scotland Yard before we put any pressure on Brian Hargreaves. I need to know exactly what we're dealing with here. Maybe they're already keeping tabs on him for reasons unknown to us'

'It would help if we could find him first,' Martin replied throwing a few remaining chips into the waste bin.

Mandy ran across the car park the moment Wesley and Martin arrived back at the station and had the car door open even before the ignition was switched off.

'I've got some bad news sir,' she panted. 'PC Mark Hayles was found unconscious in a park on the other side of Wells a short time ago. He was found by a member of the public. He's been taken to hospital.'

'Bloody hell,' cried Wesley. 'What's going on here?'

'I'm afraid it's worse than that, sir,' Mandy replied. 'He was still unconscious when he arrived at hospital. The paramedics say he's in a bad way.'

'What? OK, I'm on my way there now. Did you speak with Sally Morgan?'

'Not yet. She wasn't at home when I called. I'll try her again in a while.'

'Sure OK. Martin, I want you to man the station.'

Martin jumped out of the car as Wesley clambered into the driver's seat.

'I'll call you from the hospital. See what else you can find out about Ted Drake, if that's his real name. He must be related to someone. It may simply be a case of him being in the wrong place at the wrong time but we need to check it out. Mandy, grab your bag, you can come with me.'

While Wesley sat in the car waiting for Mandy he reached for his mobile to phone Jane, informing her he was on his way to the hospital and that he might be late. He suggested she make her own way to the New Year's Eve party at Dr Meadows'. He explained the day's events in brief.

'Can you describe this Ted Drake fella?' Jane asked.

He read out the description as noted by Martin.

'Why are you interested?'

'I'm certain that's the name the man gave who knocked here a couple of days ago. He tried to sell me watches and a few other items of jewellery. Mrs Adkins just up the road said he knocked at her place also.'

'Why didn't you tell me?' Wesley asked.

'Sorry love, but it didn't seem important. He just appeared to be one of those annoying door to door salesmen.'

'What day was this?'

'Hmm let me think. It must have been the day before Christmas because

I'd just got home from work and Mrs Adkins caught me at the top of the road.'

'That's interesting,' Wesley replied.

'Why do you say that?'

'Because his body was found less than twenty-four hours later and he had nothing on him to identify him let alone a case full of watches and jewellery.'

'Oh John, do you think I was the last person to see him alive?'

'No you certainly weren't. Whoever killed him roughed him up something terrible before dumping his body on the side of the road.'

Wesley couldn't see Jane as she placed her hand over her mouth.

Jane agreed they would meet at Dr Meadows' later and said she would offer his apologies for being late. Being an Inspector's wife she had become accustomed to making excuses for Wesley's late or sometimes non-appearance at social gatherings.

When Wesley and Mandy arrived at the hospital there was a message for him to call a Doctor Roger Walker. The receptionist placed the call and asked Wesley to take a seat in the corridor. She introduced herself as Mrs Jenkins, a colleague of Jane's. As usual the hospital was busy with patients and hospital staff rushing to and fro. Mandy noticed that Wesley looked nervous but decided not to comment. Jane had informed her some time back about Wesley's fear of hospitals since his wife had passed away and how each visit reminded him of the past. Mandy walked over to a drinks machine returning with two plastic cups of a brown looking fluid.

'It says coffee on the cup but I can't guarantee it's going to taste like coffee,' she said handing it to him.

'Thanks, Mandy.'

Wesley forced a smile and Mandy noticed he was sweating. Fortunately they didn't have to wait long as just a minute later a small grey haired doctor wearing half rimmed glassed that were precariously perched on the end of his nose burst through the door almost colliding with a nurse heading in the opposite direction.

'Ah, you must be Inspector Wesley,' he said offering his hand. Although he was a small man of slim build he had a grip like a vice.

Wesley's first thought was that the man was Dr Crippen's double.

'Please follow me. We can talk in my office. It's more private there.'

Having taken the lift to the third floor, Wesley followed the doctor to the far end of the corridor where he opened a door into a lavish looking consulting room. The two side walls were stacked floor to ceiling with cabinets crammed with books and the huge window behind the desk looked out across the countryside that lay behind Wells High Road.

'Please, both of you, take a seat.'

Wesley sat in the leather chair in front of the desk while the doctor peered through his glasses to read several notes in front of him. Mandy pulled up another chair from the side. The doctor was reading some notes aloud to himself so Wesley gave a polite cough to remind the doctor that he too was a busy man.

'Ah yes, sorry Inspector. Just half an hour away from my desk and suddenly the whole world wants something from me.'

'I know the feeling there,' Wesley replied.

'Yes I'm sure you do.'

Doctor Roger Walker removed his glasses and proceeded to talk whilst cleaning them with his handkerchief.

'The patient who was brought in earlier today, Lady Hargreaves, is conscious and still very poorly but I'm confident she will make a full recovery in time.'

He blew over his glasses before continuing to clean them.

'However, I regret to inform you that the young constable is not so good. He remains unconscious and I'm afraid that the longer he stays like this there may be a danger of brain damage.'

Wesley sat forward in the chair.

'What happened to him doc? Are you saying this is not a simple case of him just passing out?'

The doctor replaced his glasses and peered across the table with a concerned look on his face.

'I have had blood tests carried out on both patients, Inspector, and I'm sorry to have to inform you that there are traces of Thallium poisoning in both samples.'

'What?'

Mandy's reaction was to grab Wesley's arm but she withdrew it almost immediately as soon as she realised what she'd done.

'Thallium, Inspector. It's a toxic element often used in rat poisoning. Both patients have it in their bloodstream. Unfortunately in the young constables case there is a more concentrated amount. Upon close inspection I'm more than confident that he was injected with the poison earlier today. This would have resulted in the symptoms he's experiencing right now.'

'You mean someone has tried to murder him,' Wesley replied.

'Both him and Lady Hargreaves; or just render them unconscious for a while. Either way Inspector, it appears we have someone who is willing to inject people with thallium poisoning.'

'Jesus Christ! What are their chances of survival?' Wesley asked.

'In Lady Hargreaves' case, as I say, I think it's safe to concur that given time she will make a full recovery although it may take several days, even weeks. A lot depends on how her body reacts to a full blood transfusion.'

'What about PC Mark Hayles?'

The doctor removed his glasses and toyed with them between thumb and forefinger. 'The next twelve hours are important. Ideally he'll regain consciousness but the longer he doesn't, well, I'm afraid it could be fatal.'

Wesley sat back in the chair and swallowed as he felt the bile rising in his throat, Mandy held her hand over her mouth trying to control her emotions.

'As I say the next few hours are critical. The human body cannot generally survive the amount of thallium that he has in him right now. I've administered anti-agents and we're in the process of carrying out a full blood transfusion but I can't be sure that the poison hasn't already damaged his internal organs. I'm sorry, Inspector.'

By the time Wesley and Mandy left the hospital neither was in the mood for attending New Year's Eve parties.

The following morning there was a solemn mood in the office and a look of disbelief on everyone's face. Wesley had just received a phone call from the hospital at six a.m. saying that PC Mark Hayles had passed away.

Following his admittance to hospital the previous day he had never regained consciousness. Wesley sat with his head in his hands as Mandy tried to hold back the tears. Martin banged his hand against the wall and stared out of the window behind Wesley's desk. Wesley had been through this kind of situation before but it never got any better, and he knew that for some of his staff this was the first time a colleague had been killed whilst in the line of duty. One of the young cadets was inconsolable and Bill Coombes the desk sergeant had taken her downstairs to get some fresh air. It was several minutes before anyone spoke. The atmosphere in the rest of the station was no different and the sign on the reception desk said "Ring bell for Emergencies only."

Wesley was the first to break the silence. 'I'm driving over to see Mark's parents even though I understand they were called to the hospital just before he died. Then I'm going to drive over to Alison's. She knew Mark from her early days as a young cadet. They were at college together. I need to tell her face to face,' said Wesley. 'She's not expected in the office until this afternoon so she should be at home. After that I'll visit the hospital to see Lady Hargreaves.'

'It's not fair,' Mandy sobbed. 'He was only a kid.'

Martin and Wesley looked at one another, what was there to say. Martin asked to be excused saying he needed fresh air. Wesley nodded to acknowledge his request. He knew from experience that everyone had their own way of handling these situations.

'Has there been any sighting of Brian Hargreaves?' Mandy asked whilst toying with her handkerchief.

'Pardon, err, not yet, but we have just about everyone across the county looking out for him. I'll speak with HQ and see if we can widen the search.'

They both sat in an accepted silence with their own thoughts for several minutes before Martin knocked and came back into the room. Wesley could see that the man had been crying.

'What do you want me to do?' asked Martin, 'apart from punching holes in your wall.'

'Take a trip over to Wells CCTV centre. Find out if there's any cameras near the park where Mark was found. If there are, see what you can find. Most parks have CCTV these days, whether they're actually recording anything though is a different matter.'

'Do you want me to stay here?' asked Mandy.

'No, I want you to pay another visit to the Morgan's, see if anyone is at home.

If Henry Morgan's car is there don't go in, just call me. If Sally Morgan is home ask her to explain why the Treasury have been looking into his affairs and what's his interest in Melcham Hall. We know he's been quite a regular visitor there recently. Also, ask Sally Morgan why she's never mentioned her husband's illness. He was locked away for two years in a mental institution. I'm fed up with their bloody secrecy. If she refuses to co-operate then bring her in. A few hours in one of the cells might get her to change her mind. I'm sure she knows far more than she's letting on.'

'There is one thing you ought to know,' said Mandy. 'The phone call that Brian Hargreaves made from Annie Griffin's place as you know was made to a call box situated on the corner of Whitehall and Downing Street. With the help of the guys from the CCTV control room at Whitehall they've managed to identify the person who took the call. It was James Harper, the famous TV Broadcaster and Chat show host.'

'Bloody hell,' Wesley replied as he stood up. 'What the hell's going on? That's all we need, a damn celebrity to be involved. We might as well set up the recording studio downstairs.'

An hour later, having just left PC Mark Hayles' parents, Wesley was sat with WPC Alison Bolt. Alison was still coming to terms with the news of Mark's death.

'He was only twenty-three,' she stammered looking into her empty coffee cup. 'I remember his mum; she used to teach at the local senior school that Mark and I attended. I've known Mark since we were about twelve years old. Christ, life isn't fair,' she sobbed.

Wesley placed a comforting arm around her.

'We'll find whoever did this.' He was really at a loss for words.

'But that won't bring him back will it?' Alison replied.

'No, it won't.'

Although he was gasping for a cigarette he thought it would be ill timed if he asked if it was OK to smoke in her flat.

'So you've decorated this place all by yourself?' said Wesley thinking of something to say to change the subject.

'Sorry, sir?'

'You've decorated the flat yourself?'

'Oh yes. It's a skill I learnt from dad. He can turn his hand to anything. He wanted to build his own house once but mum refused to move.'

'Jane won't even let me near the tool shed. She knows how bad my DIY skills are.'

Alison forced a smile as Wesley stood to leave.

'I fully understand if you need time off,' he said placing a hand on her shoulder.

'I'm alright, sir. I'd rather keep myself busy. I've come across a pile of letters that may be of interest. They're love letters from Lady Hargreaves to someone in France. I came across them in one of the bedrooms at Melcham Hall. I might get the bus back over there.'

'Do you think they're related to all of this?'

'I don't know, sir, but it's possible I guess.'

'OK, well if you're sure you're fine. I'm off to the hospital to see if I can get anything out of Lady Hargreaves. I'll call you later.'

'Do you mind if I pop in to see Mark's parents, sir?'

Wesley shook his head.

'I think it would be good, for you both,' he replied. 'Do that first. Melcham Hall can wait.'

There was no sign of Henry Morgan's car so Mandy parked up and walked straight up the garden path with a determined look on her face. She pressed the buzzer and knocked hard on the door. Sally Morgan answered almost immediately as if she was expecting a visit. She ushered Mandy into the lounge. The woman looked as if she had been crying and her appearance was that of someone who hadn't slept for some time.

'So, how can I help you?' she asked taking a seat opposite Mandy.

Mandy noticed how Sally's hands were shaking and the way she continually fiddled with the buttons on her cardigan.

'I wanted to speak with you regarding your husband. Is he here?'

'My husband? Oh, why would you want to speak with him?' Sally Morgan asked trying to force a smile.

'You tell me,' said Mandy. She wasn't in the mood for playing games.

'I'm sorry, but I don't understand.'

'Mrs Morgan, I'll come straight to the point. Why have you never mentioned that your husband spent two years at Bowden Manor nursing home?'

The question seemed to have struck Sally Morgan like a bullet. She sat open mouthed staring at Mandy as if she was in shock.

'Mrs Morgan? I asked you a question.'

'How did you find out about that?' she finally asked.

'We were looking into your husband's business affairs and found a gap in his employment. The rest was easy.'

'But it's confidential,' Sally Morgan replied sternly.

'Not when we're carrying out a murder investigation,' Mandy replied.

'But what has Henry got to do with our daughter's murder?'

'That's what we're trying to find out,' Mandy replied. 'I believe your husband has quite a temper.'

Sally Morgan stood up and began wringing her hands together in a nervous fashion.

'I think you ought to leave now,' she stammered.

Mandy sat back in the chair looking composed.

'Please sit down, Mrs Morgan. If you don't wish to answer questions about your husband here, we can always go down to the station to discuss things.'

'You can't take me to the station. I've done nothing wrong. I've got nothing else to say.'

'Then you leave me no alternative than to ask you to accompany me to the station,' said Mandy leaning forward in the chair.

'On what grounds?' Sally Morgan asked raising her voice.

'On the grounds of withholding information related to a murder enquiry and your refusal to co-operate with police enquiries.'

'This is outrageous,' she replied.

Mandy could see from the woman's body language that she was beginning to wilt so pressed home her authority.

'Mrs Morgan, please sit down or we'll drive to the station right now.'

With reluctance Sally Morgan slumped in the chair and folded her arms in an act of defiance. However Mandy knew from experience that the woman had backed down. Mandy held Sally's stare for a few moments letting her know she was in charge of proceedings.

'Your husband worked for the Treasury I believe?' Mandy asked.

'You obviously know he did, so why ask?'

'What made him leave his post?'

'He retired.' Sally raised her chin as she gritted her teeth.

'That's not quite right is it, Mrs Morgan? My information tells me that your husband was asked to leave following an investigation into the financial running of the treasury office.'

'I wouldn't know anything about that. Henry never discussed his work with me,' she replied defiantly.

Knowing that there may be an element of truth in the woman's reply Mandy decided upon another line of questioning.

'Can you tell me why your husband has been making regular visits to Melcham Hall recently? Some of the visits took place prior to your daughter being employed there.'

Sally Morgan looked down at the floor and took a while to reply.

'I don't know. That's news to me. Oh, I won't lie to you. Yes, Henry has been spending a lot of time away from the house, sometimes for hours. He told me he was playing golf. But….'

'Go on Mrs Morgan,' prompted Mandy.

'I needed to contact him the other day as a matter of urgency as the bank were asking him to authorise a transaction on a property that we've been looking to buy.'

'Yes, go on.'

'Well, I telephoned the golf club to ask to speak with Henry. They said he wasn't there. They said he hadn't been there for weeks.'

'Why didn't you tell me this before?'

'It didn't seem important?'

'Mrs Morgan, your husband tried to commit suicide just a few days ago and now you're telling me that you don't know where he is?'

'Henry has always done his own thing. He could be anywhere as far as I know.'

'Did he ever hit Felicity?'

The question seemed to slap Sally Morgan in the face. Her eyes widened and her jaw dropped before she broke down in tears and slumped forward in the chair placing her hands over her face. Mandy sat silent, she was sure there was more to come. She was hoping that the communication floodgates would now open and was convinced that Sally Morgan still knew a lot more than she was letting on.

'I'm just popping out to the car to make a call. We can talk more when I return,' said Mandy.

Sally Morgan didn't reply. She sat staring into the distance.

18

Although the reception desk at Wells hospital had been as busy as ever this morning there was an unspoken recognition of the knowledge that PC Mark Hayles had passed away. Jane's colleagues and other hospital staff had expressed their sympathy to Jane even though she hadn't known the young lad they all knew her husband was Inspector Wesley and that the young constable's death would be something felt in the Wesley home. Jane was in the back office filing a number of patient folders in a grey metal filing cabinet when her friend Rachel entered.

'Morning, Jane. I'm so sorry to hear about the young policeman. I've only just arrived but Maureen caught me as soon as I walked through the door. Did he work with your husband?'

'Indirectly, yes,' Jane replied. 'He was based at Wells police station but he was helping John on a case.'

Jane sighed as she closed the filing cabinet. She had finished her early morning shift and planned to visit Gerry Callow at the bookshop in Glastonbury even though she wasn't really in the mood now.

'Do you think the young policeman's death has got anything to do with Lady Hargreaves?' asked Rachel.

Jane had a puzzled expression.

'Lady Hargreaves? I don't see how. What makes you think that?'

'Well, I know I shouldn't gossip, but Gill Humphries was just telling me that the substance they found in her blood stream is the same stuff that killed the young policeman.'

'Really, are you sure?'

'That's what she said.'

'Do you know what the substance was?'

'Yes it's something called thallium.'

Rachel wasn't sure she should have mentioned anything to Jane now and looked rather embarrassed. 'I hope I haven't said the wrong thing.'

'No of course not,' Jane replied. 'I was just trying to remember where I last saw that name written somewhere.'

After leaving Alison to visit PC Mark Hayles' mother, Wesley decided to pay a quick visit to Rowan Lodge to speak with Annie Griffin before driving over to the hospital.

Annie was delighted to see the Inspector and promptly offered to put the kettle on.

'That's very kind of you, Annie, but I'm in a bit of a rush and wanted to ask you a favour.'

'Oh, of course Inspector, what is it?'

'I'm just on my way to the hospital to see Lady Hargreaves, she was taken unwell yesterday and I was wondering if you would like to come with me. I understand you haven't seen her for a while and thought that perhaps seeing you might cheer her up.'

'Why, Inspector, I'd be thrilled. I don't get out very often these days and I know it sounds sad but even a visit to the hospital sounds enticing. Let me get my shoes and coat.'

Wesley sat in the front room whilst Annie gathered her belongings. He was glancing around the room in an idle fashion when his eye caught the smouldering embers of the coal fire. The few remaining coals were struggling for their last breath and a thin pitiful trail of smoke drifted lazily towards the chimney stack. What interested him though was the burnt paper in the hearth around the fire place. It was obvious that Annie had been burning correspondence of some sort. Hearing Annie approaching he tried to dismiss it from his mind. There were times when he thought he saw too much into things.

Sometimes there was a complete innocence in people's activities.

On the way to the hospital Wesley explained how Lady Hargreaves had collapsed the previous day and said she was being kept in for a few days for observation. He made no mention of thallium poisoning and how poorly Lady Hargreaves actually was, although he was tempted to ask Annie if she knew what thallium was used for. Due to heavy traffic it took them nearly thirty minutes to get to the hospital and throughout the journey Annie continually pointed out places of interest or went into great detail explaining what had previously been located along the way, muttering words of discontent at some of the new estates that seemed to be popping up everywhere.

'Governments and councils are destroying our country.'

'Haven't they always,' Wesley replied.

As usual the hospital was busy and Wesley had difficulty finding a parking spot, eventually parking in a 'no parking' zone, something that was becoming a bit of a habit. They had only just exited the car when a security guard came marching towards them. He was stopped in his tracks as Wesley thrust his ID under the man's nose explaining the urgency of their visit. Wesley left the deflated guard to trudge back to his portakabin to await his next victim.

Exiting the lift on the 2nd floor, Wesley held onto Annie's arm and escorted her along the corridor to the private room where Lady Hargreaves was located. The nurse who accompanied them opened the door and motioned for them to enter the room stating that the patient was comfortable but they were only to spend a few minutes with her. Wesley led Annie across the room and around the side of the bed nearest the window. Lady Hargreaves was lying on her back, propped up by pillows with tubes connected to her arm and mouth.

There was a cardboard sign pinned to the headboard that read "Nil by mouth."

The nurse said although Lady Hargreaves had regained consciousness for a while, she was still extremely sleepy and wouldn't be surprised if she failed to wake at present. Wesley assured her they would make no attempt to wake her and asked if they could be left alone for just a moment. Closing the door quietly behind her, the nurse left the room. As soon as Wesley turned around back towards the bed, the look on Annie's face answered his question immediately.

'This isn't Lucy Hargreaves is it?' he whispered.

Annie shook her head as she placed her frail hand tenderly on the woman's forehead.

'The last time I saw this girl was over ten years ago just before she moved to France.'

'Can you confirm her identity for me?' he asked.

'Yes. This is Kate Melcham, Lucy's sister. What on earth is she doing here?'

'That's what I would like to know,' Wesley replied. 'Not only that, but if this is Kate Melcham, where on earth is Lucy Hargreaves?'

Having spent several hours viewing CCTV footage in Wells, concentrating on the area around the High Street and near the vicinity of the park, Martin had drawn a blank. There was no footage of anyone looking like Brian Hargreaves or Henry Morgan and no sighting of PC Mark Hayles. To make things worse, a number of cameras were misaligned showing only footage of paving slabs or grey snow laden sky. Martin left the CCTV centre in a despondent mood and headed back to his car. On the way he spotted the small coffee shop where PC Mark Hayles had last reported seeing Morgan and Hargreaves. Deciding to stop for a drink and a bite to eat before returning to the station he crossed the road and entered the drab shop. The elderly woman who served him spoke broken English with a foreign accent that he found difficult to understand so he pointed at his order from the menu. When she returned with his order, a black coffee, orange juice and toasted ham and cheese sandwich he showed her his ID and gave her a description of the two men, asking if she had seen them. To his surprise she replied, yes.

'These two men, they have been here several times,' she said in broken English. 'They always sit by the window. I only remember them because they always whisper to one another and the small man spends most of his time watching the door as if he's expecting someone else to join them. They act very strangely.'

'Have you any idea what they talk about?' Martin asked showing the woman his police ID.

'I cannot say, they talk very quietly, almost secretive.'

Martin produced a police ID photo of PC Mark Hayles from his pocket.

'Have you ever seen this man?' he asked.

The woman studied the photograph for several moments before answering.

'I think he was in here yesterday but he wasn't dressed as a policeman. He was wearing what you call civilian clothes.'

'Do you remember what time this was and when he left?'

'I cannot be sure what time he came into the café but I do know he left at two o'clock shortly after the two other gentlemen left.'

'How can you be sure of the time?' Martin asked.

'Because I was just clearing the tables, which is something I always do before finishing my shift.'

'OK thanks,' Martin replied. 'You've been really helpful.'

'Are these men in trouble?'

'Let's just say we would like to know of their whereabouts,' said Martin and handed her his card. 'If you see them, please give me a call, but under no circumstances are you to mention that I have asked about them.'

The woman took his card and placed it in her apron pocket.

'I will keep a look out for you,' she replied before departing to serve another customer.

After visiting PC Mark Hayles' mother to pass on her condolences and promising to stay in touch, WPC Alison Bolt took the bus to Shepton Mallet before beginning the long walk from the bus stop to Melcham Hall. The early winter sun had now disappeared behind a blanket of dark blue cloud that seemed to be enveloping the horizon. She quickened her pace the moment she felt the first drop of rain. By the time she reached the front door rain was sweeping across the drive, being fed by a chilly easterly wind. Alison closed the door behind her and shivered. It wasn't just the cold weather but something about the house that made her feel cold. Standing in the middle of the hallway she called out to ensure no one else was in the house. After checking both the kitchen and front parlour she made her way upstairs going directly to the room where she had found the letters on her last visit. Kneeling in front of the door she placed the lock pick into the door lock and lost her balance as the door gave way the moment she leant against it. As soon as she got to her feet Alison could see the destruction. Someone had ransacked the room. Bed clothes had been ripped off the bed and the mattress had been turned over and shredded. A small bedside table was overturned and the dressing table that had contained the letters was teetering to one side as one of the legs had been broken in half. Alison ran over to the dressing table and tried the drawer where she had previously found the letters. The lock had been broken away and what contents remained had been ripped to pieces. There was no sign of the letters. She closed the drawer and was about to leave the room when she heard the sound of a car engine start up. Darting to the window she just caught a glimpse of Brian Hargreaves' black jaguar as it sped around the side of the house, with slush and gravel being thrown up in all directions. Alison ran out of the bedroom and down the staircase and threw open the front door, but she was too late. The rear lights of the black Jaguar were just visible as the car sped up the hill heading out of the estate. Once back in the house, she made a call to the station asking for Wesley to be informed of the situation.

Jane had taken the bus from the hospital into Glastonbury and jumped off at the entrance to the market. She wanted to cheer herself up and decided that a little therapeutic shopping may help. Two stalls in particular were almost giving away Christmas wrapping paper. Jane was talking to the fishmonger when she felt a tap on her shoulder. She turned round to face Gerry Callow's beaming smile. Jane leaned forward to kiss the gentle giant on the cheek, his enormous frame completely obscuring her from the rest of the market.

'So I've caught you buying my present, eh?'

'You should be so lucky. All I've managed to buy so far is wrapping paper. In any case, how are you? And, may I ask, what are you doing outside on such a cold day?'

'Jane, you sound like my doctor. Next thing I know, you'll be bringing him here to spy on me.'

Jane had to wipe the tears from her eyes as they both laughed so much.

'Are you looking for anything particular or just browsing?' she asked.

'To be honest, the shop has been quiet all day so I thought I'd close up for lunch and take a stroll around the market. I was just on my way back to open up again.'

'In that case I'll walk with you. I was going to ask you if you might have a book about poisons.'

Gerry knitted his eyebrows, a look he always gave when he was confused about something.

'Don't worry, I'll explain on the way.'

'You knew this wasn't Lucy Hargreaves didn't you?' said Annie as Wesley pulled up a chair for her.

'I had an inclination,' he replied. 'You see, not only did the local delivery boy say that Lucy hadn't recognised him, the hairdresser said that Lucy hadn't been in for her regular appointment. On top of that you yourself mentioned that the woman you spoke to over the phone didn't know that your husband was cremated. Lucy would have known but Kate may not have remembered.'

'How clever you are, Inspector.' Annie patted him on the hand.

They both looked at the woman who seemed to be mumbling something in her sleep. Wesley couldn't understand anything the woman was saying but he caught a glimpse of Annie's face as she smiled and took hold of Kate Melcham's hand.

'Do you know what she's saying?' he asked.

Annie nodded her head.

'Voulez-vous danser avec moi?'

'What does it mean?'

'Translated, it means, would you like to dance with me?'

Wesley scratched his head looking totally confused.

Annie looked up with a broad grin on her face.

'Many years ago, Inspector, we had a French boy with us. He was a dancer, and toured throughout Europe with a small dancing troop. Unfortunately, in later years we eventually lost contact.' For a moment Annie sat lost in thought and Wesley could see Annie's eyes misting over. Then she suddenly seemed to compose herself and spoke like someone who had come to a decision about something.

'Antoine used to teach Kate and Lucy how to dance, swim in the river, ride, sing, and play croquet. He could turn his hand to most things. Lucy was never really interested but Kate loved the arts and liked nothing more than to perform for her parents. She would dress up and join Antoine in a short dance routine. Antoine would always begin the routine with "voulez-vous danser avec moi?"

Although Annie smiled, Wesley could see the concern in her eyes and the love she felt for the woman lying in the bed. He didn't understand why Kate Melcham would be repeating those words now but felt that it wasn't the right time to explore that avenue of questioning.

'I'll just speak with the nurse then I'll come back to collect you,' said Wesley placing his hand on Annie's shoulder.

Standing outside the room Wesley puffed out his cheeks and sighed. He'd felt like he was an intruder listening to someone's past, listening to stories he shouldn't hear. He strode down the corridor until he found the nurse's office where Nurse Jenkins was sat at a desk littered with paperwork.

'I'm glad I'm not the only one who spends half their life writing notes,' said Wesley.

'Ah Inspector, please, sit down.'

Wesley pulled up a chair as Nurse Jenkins made some space on the desk.

'You have the look of someone who wants to ask a question,' she implied.

'I do have a question for you and some information.'

Nurse Jenkins removed the tiny glasses from the end of her nose, toying with them in her hands.

'Please put me out of my misery, Inspector and tell me what information you have for me.'

'Your patient is not Lady Hargeaves. The woman lying in bed is in fact her sister, Kate Melcham.'

Nurse Jenkins laid her glasses down and leaned her elbows on the desk before placing her hands together in the form of prayer.

'Are you sure about this, Inspector?'

'Yes, positive. I previously had reason to believe that the woman wasn't who she was pretending to be and that's now been confirmed.'

'I have to say, Inspector, in all my years as a nurse I've never come across this situation before.'

Wesley smiled. 'I think it's a first for me too.'

Nurse Jenkins extracted one of the folders from the pile on her desk and scribbled out Lady Hargreaves' name, replacing it with Kate Melcham.

'May I ask Inspector, if we have Kate Melcham here, where on earth is Lady Hargreaves?'

'I wish I knew. I'm hoping Kate can provide us with the answer. That brings me on to my question. What are Kate's future health prospects?'

'The doctor informed me this morning that he expects Kate to make a steady recovery but it could take months before she's back to normal.'

'Ah, so she's going to be fine, that's good....'

Nurse Jenkins held up a hand halting him in mid-sentence.

'I have to inform you though that there is always a slight possibility of brain damage as the brain was starved of oxygen for a short period. Kate will remember things but only in time. If you need information from her you are going to have to be patient.'

When Wesley returned to collect Annie he stopped outside the door to the private room and peered through the observation window. Annie had both of her hands clasped over one of Kate's. He watched as Annie repeatedly whispered the words "voulez-vous danser avec moi?" But she was also saying something else to Kate which he couldn't make out.

Having dropped Annie back home he was driving into the station car park just as Alison stepped off the bus from the adjacent bus stop. Once in the building, Wesley checked to see if there were any other messages for him whilst Alison headed for the canteen in search of refreshment. He called her into the office as soon as she reappeared.

'So have all of these love letters now disappeared?' Wesley asked taking a sip of the hot tea.

'Yes sir, and from what you've just told me about Kate Melcham, I would hazard a guess that there's a connection here somewhere.'

'What makes you say that?'

'The phrase you just quoted, sir. "Voulez-vous danser avec moi?" It was in one of the letters I managed to read when I first found them.'

'Now that is interesting,' he replied. 'Do you think the secret lover could have been Antoine?'

Alison shrugged her shoulders.

'I don't know but it's more than just a coincidence don't you think?'

Wesley sat back in his chair holding a cup of tea in both hands.

'What if, the letters weren't written by Lucy Hargreaves but actually written by Kate Melcham to Antoine.'

Alison continued before Wesley could speak.

'I know she would have been younger than him, but maybe she had a crush on him. Maybe, that's the reason she moved to France? I mean; to be near him?'

'But she would have only been a young girl when he left,' said Wesley.

'Young girls grow up,' Alison replied as she placed her empty cup on the corner of Wesley's desk.

'OK, so let's assume Kate Melcham fell in love with Antoine. If he's still in France, why did she come back here? According to O'Hara she simply vanished overnight to return to the UK. What was the attraction?'

'Maybe Antoine is now living here.'

'I just don't get it,' said Wesley. 'The other thing that we seem to be forgetting here is where on earth has Lucy Hargreaves disappeared to?'

'I think we have enough evidence to warrant a full search of Melcham Hall, sir. There's something we're missing here,' said Alison.

'I agree, but first I need to speak with the Scotland Yard. Whatever Hargreaves is involved in he obviously has contacts in high places so we need to be careful where we tread. Can you bring the rest of the team up to spec while I make a quick phone call.'

Terry Austin had already switched off the lights and was about to lock the door to the lab when he heard the phone ringing on his desk. He sighed before reluctantly switching the light back on. Knowing that only a select number of people knew his number he guessed the call to be urgent.

'Terry Austin. Who's this calling?'

'Hi Terry I'm sorry to bother you,' said Wesley who sounded quite sincere.

'Inspector, what can I do for you? You do realise that my stomach is crying out for food and that I haven't had a beer in nearly twenty-four hours.'

'I'll make it up you,' Wesley replied.

'In that case I'm all ears,' Terry replied and pulled a chair out from under the table.

'This Ted Drake fella, have you carried out a blood test?'

'Not yet why? You've seen the body. Someone beat the shit out of him.'

'Do me a favour. Can you check for Thallium poisoning?'

'Thallium? Why Thallium? That's a rat poison. Not easily detectable unless given to someone in a large quantity. You'd have to really dislike someone to poison them with that stuff. What makes you ask?'

'We have another corpse in the hospital, PC Mark Hayles. The doctor has informed me that he died from Thallium poisoning. On top of that, another woman is in intensive care, again with traces of Thallium poisoning in her blood.'

'Jesus Christ! I'll get on to it straight away,' Terry replied.

'Terry, before you go. Have you any idea where someone would get hold of this stuff?'

'The answer to that is from just about any farm in the county. It was commonly used as a rat poison, not so much these days though.'

'I should have known better than to ask.'

'You know life is never simple my friend.'

Wesley thanked Terry for his help then began working his way through a pile of paperwork, something he'd put off for a couple of days. An hour later and the pile looked no smaller than when he'd started and added to his woes was an email demanding that all expenses claims and reports were up-to-date and submitted by the end of the week.

A phone call to Scotland Yard didn't provide him with any answers either. Brian Hargreaves and Henry Morgan were both known to them for fraudulent activities but neither was currently on their radar.

19

Having parked the patrol car in a side road just off the High Street in order to avoid the double yellow lines everywhere, Martin eventually found the sign he was looking for. Above one of the shops, a small window display read "Harry's Gym". He knew he wasn't as fit as he used to be and stood panting for breath after running up the short flight of steps. The moment he pushed open the door the smell of stale air and body odour filled his nostrils making him feel a little nauseous. The area above the shop had been converted into one large open space where two full size boxing rings took centre stage. In the first ring, several young boys were sat on the floor listening to someone teaching them the art of sparring. Martin walked around the ring towards the back of the room where a group of teenagers and two adults were watching the training session in the second ring. Martin approached one of the adults, tapping him on the shoulder.

'Excuse me but I'm looking for Simon Reynolds.'

The guy who turned around was a little shorter than Martin but thick set and muscular and his face bore all the marks of a boxer, with a flat nose and scarring around his eyes. 'Not someone to pick a fight with,' thought Martin.

'He's up there,' the guy said pointing up at the ring, 'the fella with the black hair. What's he in trouble for this time?' he asked staring at Martin's ID.

Martin suddenly realised that he hadn't even considered looking as to whether Simon Reynolds had a record. In any case it was too late now.

'I just need to have a chat.'

'He'll be down in a minute.'

Martin watched intently as Simon Reynolds battered his sparring partner into repeated submission before a young lad who was sat on a nearby stool acting as a time keeper rang the bell calling time on their sparring session.

'There's a copper here to see you,' the guy next to Martin shouted the moment Simon Reynolds backed off of his opponent. Several people in the gym took a glance at Martin before sloping away. Simon Reynolds jumped down from the ring and walked towards Martin with a fierce look on his face.

'What do you want? I'm busy.'

The tone of voice told Martin that he wasn't a welcomed visitor.

'Can we have a chat?'

'Yeah, sure, go on, chat.'

The small crowd of teenagers that remained burst out laughing. It was obvious that Simon Reynolds was a bit of a local hero.

'I would prefer for us to have our discussion in private,' Martin replied.

'Oh, la de da,' Reynolds replied causing some of the lads to hold their bellies as they roared with laughter.

'We can always talk down at the station,' boomed a voice from behind the boxer. Reynolds spun round to come face to face with Wesley.

'And who might you be?'

'Inspector Wesley, to you son.'

Reynolds patted his boxing gloves together as if warming for a fight but hadn't expected the reaction from Wesley who stepped forward to stare into Reynolds face. The two men stood almost nose to nose like two fighters publicising their forthcoming boxing match.

'As I said, we can talk in private here, or go down to the station where I'm sure we can find you a nice quiet cell to have a chat.'

Reynolds smirked, but he was unsure of himself.

'You think you're clever you pigs, don't you?'

Wesley inched closer to whisper in the man's ear.

'If you ever call me a pig again I'll teach you how to box, London style. Then your little fan club here can carry you out to the ambulance.'

Reynolds tried to hold his ground and looked around for support but the group of teenagers had started to disperse. Simon Reynolds held his arms out straight and called to an old man who was sat nearby.

'Harry, take these damn gloves off.'

The guy with the flat nose and scarred face untied the boxing gloves before removing them and placing them on a small table that was stood against the wall.

'We'll use the office in the corner,' said Reynolds.

The office was no bigger than a broom cupboard with just about enough room for a small desk and a chair. Three sides of the room were covered in shelving containing an assortment of boxes containing items ranging from skipping ropes and boxing gloves to toilet rolls.

Wesley sat on the edge of the desk, directing Reynolds to the chair. Martin stood in the doorway, ensuring that no one else could listen in on the conversation.

'So what do you want from me?' asked Reynolds folding his arms.

'Does the name Felicity Morgan ring a bell?'

'That slag. What's she done now, got herself pregnant by jumping some frustrated kid?'

'She's dead.'

Reynolds forced a smile.

'Do what?'

'She's dead.'

'Are you having me on?'

'I don't joke about murder.'

'Now hold on a minute.' Reynolds shot up from the chair. 'I didn't murder her. Christ, she weren't worth that.'

'Sit down, son,' commanded Wesley.

Reynolds reluctantly sat down on the edge of the chair, his bravado fast disappearing. After answering several of Wesley's questions it was apparent he was nowhere near the Melcham estate around the time in question. He'd taken part in a boxing exhibition in Taunton and had spent the night at a local motel, sharing a room with one of his sparring partners. Martin noted the details which would be checked out later.

'So you hadn't seen Felicity for a couple of weeks?'

'No, we only went out a couple of times. She didn't really fancy me she just liked having a fella on her arm.'

'And you liked to oblige?'

Reynolds smirked but thought better than to make further comment.

'Can you think of anyone who might want to cause her harm?'

Wesley stood up and walked around behind Reynolds who could feel Wesley's breath on his neck.

'Think carefully, son.'

When Reynolds answered it was with a voice that had suddenly lost all confidence.

'Felicity did the rounds, if you know what I mean. Sometimes, she'd cause a bit of hassle because of her sleeping habits but I don't think anyone would have disliked her to take it that far.'

Wesley handed his card to Reynolds.

'If you think of anyone call me.'

Wesley turned to leave but hesitated in the doorway.

'Oh just one other thing, son. Felicity was pregnant when she died.'

By the time Wesley and Martin left the building, Simon Reynolds was sweating more than if he'd just done ten rounds with his sparring partner.

'I didn't know you were coming over here,' exclaimed Martin once they were back in the High Street. 'I thought I was going to get a beating but you scared the life out of Simon Reynolds.'

Wesley took a drag on a roll-up before replying.

'He's just Billy big spuds in a small pond, Martin. Remember, I used to plod the streets where people like the Kray twins hung out. Kids like Simon Reynolds don't begin to live in the same league.'

An hour later they were back in the office and Wesley had just informed Martin that the person they thought was Lady Hargreaves was in fact her sister Kate Melcham.

'Well I guess it explains a few things,' said Martin. 'First there was the lad from the local shop who said she didn't recognise him. Then Annie Griffin questioned who she had spoken to over the phone that day, and I remember when we were over Melcham Hall how she seemed scared of the dog. It was almost as if the dog didn't recognise her either.'

'Yeah I guess it all fits,' Wesley replied.

Martin advised Wesley that two people matching the description of Brian Hargreaves and Henry Morgan were seen in a café near the park where PC Mark Hayles was murdered but at the moment there was nothing to be found on CCTV.

Mandy was sat in her car listening to their conversation on her mobile phone outside Sally Morgan's property and explained her conversation with the woman.

'That was a clever piece of detective work, sir. You said there was something wrong about Lady Hargreaves.'

'Yeah but we need to find her.'

'So have we had any sighting of Henry Morgan? Does his wife know where he is?' Wesley asked.

'No sir. Sally Morgan says her husband left the house yesterday morning and she hasn't seen him since. None of the patrols have sighted him either.'

'Why on earth has she not contacted the police before?' asked Martin.

'She says it's not the first time he's stayed away. Apparently it's been happening quite often over the last year or so.'

'Does she never query where he's going?' Wesley asked.

'She says his answer is always the same, he's going out on business that he can't discuss.'

'What woman would put up with that?' commented Martin.

'A woman who knows more than she's letting on,' Wesley replied.

'Put a tag on the house phone and keep an eye on her. She just might lead us to Henry,' said Wesley. 'Let me have an update this afternoon.'

'Will do, sir,' Mandy replied and hung up.

'Martin, I want you to concentrate on finding Brian Hargreaves. Use all the manpower we have at our disposal. Extend the search to airports and ports. I want to know the moment we get a sighting. Is that understood?'

'Yes sir.'

Gerry Callow was sat on the floor at the back of the bookshop with a pile of books on either side of him.

'What's the interest in thallium then?' he asked.

Jane was reluctant to explain what she had learned from Rachel so decided to give another reason. A little white lie would hurt.

'I found an old jerry can in the shed the other day with a label stuck to it that simply says 'Poison - Thallium - treat with care.''

Jane was sat behind the small desk that Gerry called his office. It was no bigger than a child's school desk and Jane had to admit that Gerry looked ridiculous sat behind it. The computer she was using must have been as old as some of the books in the shop as it continually lost connection and when

Jane did manage to log back in and type the word thallium, the software seemed to spend ages searching its database before timing out.

It was Gerry who was the first to find anything. He had opened an old copy of 'Farmers Weekly.'

'Ah here we are, Jane.' He read out loud. 'Thallium poisoning, also known as the "prisoner's poison" since thallium is colourless, odourless and tasteless, and is a slow-acting poison.' He then muttered something to himself that Jane couldn't catch.

'What else was that? You're mumbling.'

'Oh, sorry, Jane, there's not much else really. It just says that farmers used to use it a lot in the olden days as a rat poison.'

'Can you print that out for me? I'd like to show Wesley when he gets home.'

Jane had to admit that the shop was now looking a lot better. It was obvious that Gerry had been making an effort to turn things around. A number of the local bookshops were struggling these days especially since the introduction of the kindle but Gerry's decision to concentrate on the second-hand book market and historical section appeared to be paying off.

'When are they delivering the new sign for the bookshop?' she asked.

'Hopefully any time now. They originally said they'd have it here before Christmas.'

'Are you going to advertise the fact the shop's name is changing?'

'I never thought of that,' Gerry replied.

'It's worth trying to get an article in the local paper. It can only attract interest.'

'Jane, what would I do without you?'

Wesley was sat deep in thought long after the rest of the team had gone home.

There was still no sign of Hargreaves and Mandy had sat outside Morgan's house all afternoon with no luck either. She'd arranged for the Morgans' phone to be tapped but no one had phoned the house and Sally Morgan hadn't made any calls to anyone. Mandy had informed Sally Morgan that their discussion was far from over. He looked up at the wipe board on the far wall and tried to fit the pieces of the jigsaw together in his head. Something didn't sit right but he couldn't put his finger on it. Suddenly his line of thought was broken by the ringing of his office phone.

'Wesley speaking.'

'Ah Inspector, I'm glad I caught you. I hope I haven't called at an inconvenient time.'

Wesley recognised Terry Austin's voice straight away.

'Hi, Terry, no of course you haven't. What have you got for me?'

'I've done that blood test you asked for.'

'And?'

'You were dead right. Ted Drake, or whatever his name was, was poisoned before being beaten to death.'

'Thallium?'

'Yes.'

'Enough to kill him?'

'Hard to say, Inspector, but without treatment, then my guess would be yes.'

'Terry, is this a mixture than can be bought anywhere, you know what I mean, over the counter?'

'Well it can, but not with this level of concentration. Whoever administered this to the poor guy certainly made it themselves. This stuff is about four times more potent than anything you'd buy in a shop.'

'Are we looking at someone from a chemical background?'

'I can't answer that, Inspector. However I can safely say that whoever produced this stuff either knows exactly what they're doing or they're simply off they're rocker.'

'What else is it used for apart from being a rat poison?' asked Wesley reaching for his tobacco pouch.

'In the old days Thallium salts were used in the treatment of ringworm, other skin infections and to reduce the night sweating of tuberculosis patients. One obvious side effect for patients though was hair loss.'

'What?'

Wesley sat back in his chair with the phone stuck between his head and shoulder as he continued to roll a cigarette.

Terry noticed the concern in Wesley's voice. 'What's wrong, Inspector?'

'Just a couple of days ago, Lucy Hargreaves' hairdresser said that although she hadn't seen Lucy for a number of weeks, she did remember the fact that Lucy appeared to be losing large clumps of hair.'

'That is interesting,' Terry exclaimed. 'And you now think she was being poisoned?'

'It's too much of a coincidence. Isn't it?'

'You could be right. In any case I'll leave that one with you. If there's anything else I can help with just give me a call.'

'Terry, before you go, I'd like to ask one last question. The tattoo you found on Ted Drake's arm?'

'What about it?'

'Is there any way of telling whether it was done here in the UK or whether he had it done overseas?'

'Sorry but that's almost impossible to say as suppliers import indelible ink from all over the world these days. The only thing I'd say about the guys tattoo is that it's high quality. It wasn't done in one of those cheap and nasty back street tattooists that are springing up everywhere these days. It's quite new too. At a guess, it was done no more than two or three years ago. There's hardly any fading.'

'OK, thanks Terry, you've been a great help.'

Wesley hung up, sat back in his chair, lit his roll-up and prepared himself for his next phone conversation which was to be with James Harper.

Wesley tapped in the number on his desk phone and waited for a reply. His call was immediately answered by James Harper's secretary who said that Mr Harper was expecting his call and that she would put him through straight away. Wesley had spoken with dignitaries and celebrities on several occasions during his career but usually at formal meetings, never to discuss a murder enquiry.

The line clicked twice before he heard the secretary's voice again.

'I have Inspector Wesley on the line for you,' she said.

'Inspector Wesley, how can I help you?'

James Harper's voice oozed confidence but also that air of impatience.

'Good evening Mr Harper, thank you for accepting my call. I'm currently investigating a murder enquiry and one of the people I'm interested in speaking with is a man named Brian Hargreaves. I believe he may be an acquaintance of yours?'

'I see. Carry on, Inspector.'

Wesley knew he had to tread carefully if he was going to get any information from this guy.

'I believe Brian Hargreaves can assist us with our enquiries, but the trouble is we've been unable to locate him. I was wondering if you could assist me with locating him.'

'What has been supposedly done, Inspector?'

'At this moment in time I'd rather discuss the details with Brian Hargreaves in person but I'm sure you're aware there have been two recent murders, one on his estate and one on the road that passes the entrance to his estate.'

'And you believe I know his whereabouts?'

Wesley hesitated a second before answering.

'I know Brian Hargreaves telephoned yourself just a couple of days ago so I was hoping you might know what he's involved in or where I should look for him?'

'Involved in? Please explain, Inspector.'

Wesley knew he had touched a nerve.

'Mr Harper, if you don't mind me saying so, Brian Hargreaves seems to be the common denominator to a lot of things happening on my patch right now.'

There was a silent pause before James Harper spoke.

'I think we need to talk, Inspector, but not over the phone. Are you familiar with the Lord Taverners bar in W1?'

'I have been there on one previous occasion, yes.'

Wesley remembered going there when he was a young constable assisting the fraud squad. His job that night had been to check everyone's ID who visited the place.

'Good, tomorrow at midday. I'll meet you in the bar. I'll tell the doorman to expect you. We won't be disturbed there.'

The line went dead before Wesley could reply.

'Another long day,' Wesley thought to himself. 'Three hours there and three hours back.'

20

Brian Hargreaves closed the door behind him, walked across to the small kitchen window and closed the curtains. 'Where is that idiot Morgan?' he shouted out aloud to himself. They had always agreed that the old farmhouse was where they would meet if things became difficult. Hargreaves reached for the empty mug on the kitchen table and hurled it against the wall, pieces of china spraying across the flagstone floor. His patience had run out. He reached inside his jacket pocket and extracted a packet of cigarettes. Fumbling with the box he dropped two on the floor before he managed to place one in his mouth. He lit the cigarette and inhaled deeply before coughing profusely. It was only the third packet of cigarettes he'd smoked in over twenty years but right now he needed something to calm him down. He crossed the hallway into the front room and pressed the 'on' button on the television only to receive a dark grey screen. He'd forgotten that no one lived at the farm any longer so the television licence would have expired long ago. The farm had belonged to his father-in-law before he handed it down to his daughters. However when Kate sauntered off to France saying she wanted nothing of her father's inheritance the farm was handed over solely to Lucy. It had been run as farm for a few years following Lord Melcham's death but when the last tenant passed away it was left to fall in disrepair. Lord Melcham had stipulated in his will that the farm should never be sold, as his family had owned the land for generations. Hargreaves had argued with Lucy on several occasions about trying to change the will because it would have been possible to build twenty or more houses on the site. Being less than five miles from the Melcham estate, Hargreaves thought it was the last place anyone would think of if they were looking for him. He checked his mobile again but there were still no messages. To pass the time he decided to wander around the farmhouse. He vaguely remembered the layout having visited the place a few years ago with Lucy when they were considering having the place renovated. Unfortunately, at the time, the builders said they would be better off knocking the place and building something new but there was insufficient money to even consider that option. Having made his way upstairs he opened the door to the main bedroom where the door hinges screeched in opposition to his entrance. Once inside the room he felt as if he had just stepped into the past. Two gas mantles on either side of the fireplace dated the farmhouse. Several small black and white photos still stood on the dressing table. He picked one of them up to study it more carefully. It was a group shot of three people standing at the back of the farmhouse. He recognised his father-in-law immediately. He was taller than everyone else and stood in the middle of the group with his arms around the shoulders of the two women on either side of him. Lucy was smiling at the camera apparently enjoying having her photo taken but Kate appeared to be staring at something on the other side of the camera, a frowned look on her face. Leaving the room he crossed the hall into one of the back bedrooms. It was empty apart from a single bed and a standalone wardrobe that had lost its door in times gone by. He was pacing the room getting impatient when all of a sudden he heard the sound of footsteps on the flagstone floor downstairs before he heard footsteps on the stairs, the bare wooden boards squeaking to announce the intruder. Hargreaves looked around the room for something to defend himself with as his foot kicked something solid. He looked down and almost laughed when he saw the chamber pot protruding from under the bed. Standing behind the half opened door he listened as the intruder walked across the landing into the front bedroom before he heard the shuffle of footsteps as the person changed direction. He could sense someone's presence on the other side before the door was pushed back. As the intruder stepped into the room the chamber pot came crashing down onto the person's head. Hargreaves then threw the chamber pot on the bed and sprang across to where the intruder lay unconscious. Kneeling down he flipped the body over before sagging back in horror. He quickly felt for a pulse but there was none. He looked down at the dead body of Henry Morgan.

'Oh Christ, you bloody idiot,' cried Hargreaves putting his hands to his face as Henry Morgan stared at the ceiling with sightless eyes.

After drinking a large mug of black coffee with two sugars, Sally Morgan looked a little more composed, she obviously wasn't expecting another visit. Mandy had decided to call in on her on the way home and now sat opposite playing the waiting game. She knew Sally had more to say. The move paid off. Almost as if she were talking to herself Sally explained her husband's mental illness and the time he spent in a nursing home. She said she knew that he had been under investigation by the fraud squad when he'd worked for the treasury, but she could handle that. What caused her most concern was the knowledge that he'd been having an affair with Lady Hargreaves.

Mandy placed her own mug on the glass coffee table and sat on the edge of her chair. The announcement came as quite a shock.

'Carry on,' said Mandy.

Sally Morgan explained how they had met with the Hargreaves at a party held at Melcham Hall some eighteen months ago. Looking back, she says there was something between them then, but at the time she shrugged it aside as Henry simply trying to impress. It was almost a year later when she had borrowed Henry's mobile to make a quick call that she noticed he'd made numerous phone calls to Melcham Hall and to a mobile number that she didn't recognise. It was only when she challenged him that he confessed to having an affair with Lady Hargreaves, although he said that the affair had ended and that he was sorry.

'Did he really stop seeing her?' asked Mandy.

Sally Morgan shrugged her shoulders before blowing her nose.

'I think so. He stopped going out so much for a while, and if he was away for a few hours he would always phone to say where he was.'

'Do you any idea where he is now?'

Sally Morgan stared across the room, her eyes had misted over.

'No, but I just know he's in trouble,' Sally replied.

'What makes you think that?' asked Mandy leaning forward.

'Brian Hargreaves keeps phoning asking to speak with him. I keep telling him that Henry's not here and that he left his mobile phone in the house.'

Suddenly something clicked in Mandy's head and a thought sprung to mind. 'Has Brian Hargreaves a hold over your husband because of the affair he had with his wife? Or is there something else you haven't told me yet.'

'I think you ought to leave now,' Sally replied standing up. 'Whatever my husband is up to now, it's up to you to find him and bring him home. I'm going to have a lay down; you see I'm not sleeping well. I'm just praying that one day I'll wake up and find out that this has all been a nightmare and that my daughter is safe and well and we're a family again.'

Brian Hargreaves isn't a fit man and after dragging Henry Morgan's body downstairs he's sweating profusely and can feel his heart trying to burst through his chest. Leaving the body lying on the kitchen floor he made his way across the courtyard behind the farmhouse and pulled open the barn door. The smell of rotting hay and food waste almost caused him to wretch. He shrieked as a large rat ran from under an old upturned wheelbarrow and brushed his leg as it made its escape for freedom through the door.

'Get a grip on yourself!' he shouted.

He eventually found what he was looking for in the far corner of the barn under an old workbench that seemed to be defying gravity by staying pinned to the wall. The two petrol cans were still full and heavy. By the time he got them across the courtyard he felt as if his arms were being wrenched from his shoulders. It took him several minutes to take the rusty lids off before he kicked the first one over, standing back to watch the petrol seep across the flagstone floor. Dragging the other can to the hallway he laid it on its side until half the content had escaped before picking up the can and pouring the remaining content down the staircase. Back in the kitchen he stood in the doorway, lit a cigarette and inhaled deeply before throwing the match to the floor. The spark was immediate. By the time Hargreaves walked out of the farmhouse it was a blazing inferno.

Kate Melcham lay on her back looking at the ceiling trying desperately to focus on the strip light above her bed. Had she been dreaming? She tried to recall her last movements but everything was a scrambled blur. Turning her head to the left she viewed the metal stand from where two saline bags were hung, the plastic tubes hanging down like an octopus's tendrils. It was only then that Kate noticed one tube going into her arm and another that lead to her nose. Suddenly she became scared. What on earth was happening to her? She tried to call out but her voice was barely a whisper. She then tried to sit herself up but she didn't have the strength. Her tears came in floods as she began to sob and it took her several minutes to compose herself enough to try to think. She had a vague recollection of a woman looking down on her asking if she was alright and then being lifted onto a stretcher. Where was the woman now? Who was she, and what was she doing in Melcham Hall? Kate tried to focus again on the room she was in. How did she get there? Her fingers found the panic button that lie on the bed. Kate squeezed hard as she began to vomit.

Back in Rowan Lodge, Annie Griffin shuffled across the room to the fireplace and slumped down in the chair. She was tired, very tired, but there were still things to be done. She emptied the contents of the plastic bag onto the hearth in front of the fire then by using an old long handled metal prong that she normally used to toast her bread with she pierced several photos at a time before dropping them onto the hot coals. Although Annie knew this day would eventually arrive it didn't make the task any easier. But a vow is a vow she muttered to herself as she watched the photos shrivel and burn.

Wesley and Jane had spent the previous evening talking about thallium poisoning and the death of PC Mark Hayles. The subject brought home the realities to the danger that Wesley's work often placed him and his colleagues in. It was a subject that he and Jane rarely discussed as Jane was all too aware how passionate Wesley is about his job. This morning he'd left a note for Martin to identify any local stockists that sold thallium but appreciated that in this day and age someone could have possibly purchased it online.

Having taken the train up from Wells, Wesley had decided against walking around London. The train had been full and he'd spent most of the journey sat opposite a young mother whose three children never stopped arguing. By the time the train arrived at Charing Cross he was grateful to get off. It had been more than two years since he'd been in London and he'd forgotten how busy the streets were with workers and shoppers alike. His time spent walking the beat in the capital seemed another lifetime ago and brought back too many memories. It was only a few miles along the Embankment where his first wife Christine had been killed by a drunk driver, an incident that had mentally scarred him for life.

After leaving the station he made straight for the Lord Taverners public house. It was an exclusive address where the rich and the famous marked their social time. After showing the doorman his ID he was directed to the lounge bar, a room that reeked of colonialism with mahogany wood panelling covering every wall, supporting every book shelf. The mahogany inlaid chairs with their rich tapestry covers and the solid looking mahogany tables built for the sole purpose of supporting drinks delivered by distinguished grey haired waiters in black suits and purple coloured silk waistcoats. Wesley acknowledged the brandy placed in front of him and made a feeble attempt at straightening his tie. He couldn't remember the last time he'd wore a tie and didn't think he'd ever own a shirt where the top button could be done up. Good old Jane had saved his day again with a bit of last minute shopping. Fiddling with the collar of his shirt he looked around the room. Several of the other tables were occupied, all by men wearing expensive looking suits, talking in whispers. Wesley wondered just how many business deals were agreed around these tables. He only had to wait another minute before James Harper entered the room escorted by the largest man Wesley has ever seen. Wesley paced his crystal cut glass on the table and stood up to shake hands.

'Inspector, I'm glad you could make it. I hope it wasn't too long a journey for you.'

James Harper had a firm handshake. Wesley was tempted to say that he didn't think the appointment was a request, but rather more of a demand.

'Please, take a seat.'

Wesley noticed that the giant stood just inside the doorway, blocking anyone's exit and giving himself a complete view of the room. A glass of whisky was placed on the table without Harper even raising his arm. Nothing like the service in the Phoenix thought Wesley.

'So, have you always worked in the South West or are you familiar with the sights and sounds of this lovely city of ours?'

Wesley had no intention of providing Harper with a detailed description of his work experience except to say he knew London quite well.

'So, tell me about Brian Hargreaves,' he asked coming straight to the point.

Wesley spent the next few minutes bringing the man up to date with recent events. Wesley watched Harper swill the whisky around the edge of his glass before answering. It was almost as if he was weighing up Wesley first.

Wesley took a sip from his own glass and noticed his hands were clammy. It was rare for him to feel nervous about anything but James Harpers' aura seemed almost overpowering.

Harper ran his fingers along his lower lip, it was something that Wesley had seen him do on television when he was interviewing a celebrity.

'Where should I begin,' he said almost forcing a grin and placing his glass on the table. 'Several years ago, no that's many years ago, in the grounds where Melcham Hall now stands, there used to be another building.'

'You mean the old Abbey?' said Wesley.

'There was an Abbey yes.'

'I don't follow you.'

James Harper smiled and leant back in his chair crossing his legs.

'There are other ruins that remain on the Melcham estate which used to belong to a certain Abbey. Over the past two hundred years descendants of the Abbey have continued to, shall we say, protect their own.'

'I'm afraid you've lost me,' said Wesley.

Harper uncrossed his legs and leaned so far forward over the table that Wesley almost felt engulfed by the man.

'My ancestors built the Abbey, Inspector.' His words hung in the air, almost threatening. 'Lord Melcham was aware of its existence when he purchased the estate. Unfortunately he showed a complete disrespect for the Abbey and for those associated with it.'

Wesley scratched the side of his forehead, a trait of his whenever he was confused about something.

Harper smiled, seeing the confused look on Wesley's face. 'I haven't the time to provide you with a history lesson relating to the Griffin Abbey except to say that when Brian Hargreaves married into the Melcham family he was informed of the Abbey's existence and the justice it still sought.'

'I appreciate you informing me about some Abbey but that doesn't help me find Brian or Lady Hargreaves,' said Wesley looking perplexed.

'I assume that you're asking me what has happened to the original Lady Hargreaves,' Harper replied.

'Well, yes. I mean, I have evidence to prove that the woman currently in hospital, who has been playing the role of Lucy Hargreaves is in fact her sister Kate.'

'Carry on, Inspector.'

Wesley was aware that Harper was quite an expert in the question/answer game and was eager not to get himself cornered. Harper leaned back in the chair taking another sip of whisky.'

'Well, if that's the case, where the hell is Lucy Hargreaves?' Wesley took another sip of his brandy and sat holding the glass in both hands on his lap.

James Harper seemed to enjoy making him wait for an answer. 'My understanding is that Lucy Hargreaves is being looked after, Inspector. Members of the Abbey are watching over her.'

Wesley almost dropped his glass.

'But I don't understand, you're telling me she's been kidnapped?'

'Kidnapped, no Inspector, Lucy is where she wants to be. Since Lord Melcham's death, Lucy Hargreaves has become sole beneficiary of the Melcham estate which includes the land on which the Abbey once stood.'

He paused for a moment to take another sip of whisky.

'Because of recent threats made to Lucy we have taken precautions to ensure her safety.'

'What recent threats?'

'People in such positions are always being pestered by those who are, shall we say, not quite so well off.'

'So are you telling me that you know where she is?'

'Yes.'

'Why have the police not been informed of this?'

James Harper shrugged his shoulders.

'Quite simply, Inspector, because no crime has been committed.'

'But why is her sister Kate standing in her sister's place? Surely she's under threat?'

'Until the recent attempt to poison her we thought not. You see, Kate has no right to the estate or any of the properties or investments once owned by Lord Melcham. Lord Melcham wrote her out of his will when she eloped to France some years ago.'

'So why would she stand in for her sister?'

'When Kate heard of the threat to her sister she immediately left France and came home. The sisters made up for their past differences and Kate said that the least she could do was to stand-in for her sister until the threat went away.'

'Do you know who's made these threats?'

'We have an idea, Inspector. That's all I'm prepared to say.'

'I'm sorry Mr Harper but I have to remind you that we're dealing with a murder case here.'

James Harper leant forward across the table before speaking. 'Inspector Wesley, I can assure you that I'm aware of your enquiries, but let me make myself quite clear. The Abbey will protect Lucy Hargreaves, at all costs.'

Wesley needed time to digest what he was hearing but knew that time was something that Harper wasn't going to give him.

'I assume you know the whereabouts of Brian Hargreaves then?'

Harper's response was delayed as he seemed to ponder the question before answering. 'Unfortunately, Inspector, I don't. I was hoping you would be able to enlighten me. I've not spoken with Brian for several days.'

'When was the last time you spoke with him?' Wesley was getting tired of the question answer session.

'When you obviously saw me on camera, Inspector, I do hope it's a good shot of me.'

'So you're telling me that was the last time you two spoke?'

'Yes.'

'May I ask what the conversation was about?'

'You may ask.' Harper gave a slight shrug of his shoulders as if to say I'm not going to divulge the conversation.

The following silence was broken when Harpers bodyguard, if that what he was, walked across to whisper something in Harper's ear.

'I'm afraid I'll have to cut short our little chat, Inspector. I'm due on a live television programme at three o'clock in Shepherds Bush.'

'So I take it that you're not prepared to tell me what you and Brian Hargreaves discussed.'

'Our conversation was a family related matter, Inspector, and family matters must remain private.'

When Harper stood to leave Wesley remained seated.

'Have a safe journey back to the West Country, Inspector. It was nice to meet you.'

Wesley watched Harper and his giant sidekick leave the room before slamming his glass down on the table.

PC Martin Philips stood next to one of the Fire Officers looking at the smouldering remains of the farmhouse.

'The old place went up quick didn't it?' Martin asked. 'I only got a call twenty minutes ago.'

'Any place burns quickly when it's dowsed with petrol,' replied the commanding officer as he walked up behind them.

'So it was no accident then?'

'Certainly not, the whole place reeks of petrol. We'll keep pouring foam over it until we're sure there's no danger of it reigniting.'

Just then another member of the fire crew, standing near the smouldering remains called across to them.

'You might want to take a look at this, sir.'

Martin followed the commanding officer around what had once been the side of the building trying to avoid stepping on the hot ground. The Fire Officer was pointing through the remains of a doorway.

'What have you got?' the commanding officer asked.

'Looks like a skeleton, sir. Well, what remains of one in any case.'

Martin strained his neck to take a closer look. The smell was appalling.

'I'll get forensics over here straight away,' he said.

'There's something else out the back,' shouted another crew member approaching through the smoke. 'An old Jaguar; completely burnt out. It was parked right outside the back door.'

'Was there anyone in it?' Martin asked.

'I'm pretty sure the answer is no, but we'll confirm once we can get close enough.'

Once he was back in the car Martin placed a call through to Wesley to advise him of the situation and said he would stay there until forensics turned up.

Wesley said he would probably lose reception while he travelled on the train so they agreed to catch up when Wesley arrived in the West Country.

21

It was early morning and a dull grey overcast sky that threatened another heavy downpour did little to lift Alison's spirits as they entered the Melcham estate.

Using the spare key WPC Alison Bolt opened the front door to Melcham Hall.

It looked as if no-one had returned to the house since she last saw Brian Hargreaves speeding away. A pile of mail including sales leaflets and several copies of the local newspaper were piled up against the inside of the door. Although the house still gave her the shivers she felt more relaxed knowing that PC Martin Philips was parked out of sight just a hundred yards away. Alison made her way upstairs heading towards the bedroom where she had previously found the love letters before they were removed. Nothing had changed. The room was still in a complete mess. She stopped to check all the other bedrooms before making her way back downstairs. Just as she stepped over the mail on the floor to open the front door Alison noticed a brown buff envelope that seemed to stand out from the rest of the mail. The name on the front had been typed. It was addressed to Lady Hargreaves and there was no postmark. Alison was tempted to open it but thought it better to take it back to the office and let Wesley check out the content. She held the corner of the envelope trying not to erase any possible fingerprints. PC Philips had just ended a call on his mobile when Alison jumped in the car, placing the envelope in a clear plastic bag.

'Anyone interesting?' she asked hoping for some snippet of information about Martin's love life. It was then that she noticed the stunned look on his face.

'What is it?'

'That was Terry Austin from the lab. The remains of the skeleton found at the farmhouse yesterday belonged to Henry Morgan, not Brian Hargreaves.'

'Oh God,' said Mandy raising her hand over her mouth. At that moment Martin mobile vibrated with a text message. He read the message with some urgency.

'That was Wesley. Terry Austin phoned him too. He and Mandy are on their way to see Sally Morgan.'

'Oh that poor woman, Alison remarked. 'Mandy said she was distraught enough before this. Apparently Henry Morgan had been lying to her about where he'd been, and it's a sure bet he was involved in something illegal. He'd already been done for fraud.'

'Let's get back to the office,' Martin replied thinking of his rumbling belly.

'I haven't eaten since yesterday so I think you ought to treat me to a fry up in the canteen.'

The thought of all that greasy food made Alison's belly rumble but for the wrong reasons.

Brian Hargreaves watched the police car exit the grounds of the Melcham estate and waited in the layby until he was sure the road ahead was clear.

As he turned the aging Range Rover into the estate passing Annie Griffin's home he was sure that the front room curtains moved.

'That bloody old woman doesn't miss a thing,' he said to himself.

Leaving the car right outside the front door in case he needed to get away fast he ran up the steps to the front door and let himself in. Not stopping to check the mail he ran straight through to the library and unlocked the small writing bureau. Pulling open the bottom drawer he pushed aside a bundle of papers until his hand grabbed what he was looking for. The revolver had a full round of bullets, more than enough to get the job done. Tucking the gun into his waistband he relocked the bureau and made his way across the hall into the kitchen. In a small cupboard next to the fridge he extracted a small bottle of brandy, unscrewed the cap and took a large swig. The brandy felt as if it were burning the back of his throat and made his eyes water. He then took another swig before returning the bottle to the cupboard. Wiping the back of his hand across his mouth he quickly searched the kitchen for food. Deciding that a packet of biscuits looked the only safe thing to eat he extracted two and placed the remains of the packet into his jacket pocket. It was just as he turned to leave the kitchen he heard the front door close.

Brian Hargreaves reached for his revolver, slipped the safety catch and walked briskly but quietly around the kitchen table and stood with his back to the wall near the doorway. His senses told him that someone was in the hallway although he heard no footsteps. Time seemed to stand still and the pulse in his forehead felt as if it were about to explode. There was a slight movement to the kitchen door as if it had been caught by a draft coming from somewhere. 'Maybe another door being opened?' he thought.

Puffing his cheeks in order to try and relax a little he took a small sideways step and leant on the corner of the door frame. This allowed him to turn his head far enough to peer into the hallway. There was no one in sight. He listened for movement but all he could hear was the ticking of the grandfather clock that stood opposite the staircase. Moving slowly into the hallway his hand was sweating where he was gripping the gun so tightly. He crossed the bottom of the staircase to the opposite side of the hallway. Standing with his back to the wall he had a clear view of the staircase and the landing above. The door to the library was to his right. Placing the gun in his left hand he reaching forward and turned the door handle. There was a single click as the lock opened.

'Why don't you put that silly gun away and come and sit down.'

Brian Hargreaves peered into the room where upon he immediately recognised the person sat in the leather armchair.

'What the hell are you doing here?' he cried.

Sally Morgan had broken down in tears as soon as she'd seen Wesley and Mandy walk up the garden path. Upon opening the front door she collapsed in Wesley's arms. Looking somewhat embarrassed he held her tight as the sobs raked her body. It took Wesley another few minutes to get Sally back into the house by which time a number of neighbours had appeared in the little cul-de-sac to see what was going on. Meanwhile Mandy had walked across the road to see if any of the neighbours knew Sally Morgan well enough to provide support.

'I'll just put my husband's dinner in the microwave and then I'll be over,' said a middle aged woman who announced herself as Mrs Hopkins without even asking what the trouble was. Returning to the house Mandy nodded to Wesley that she would make them tea. Sally Morgan was sat on the settee wiping her eyes with a handkerchief, one hand still clasping Wesley's arm. Wesley had informed her that human remains found at a local farmhouse were that of her husband. She had replied that as soon as she had seen Wesley and Mandy pull up outside the house she knew that something was wrong.

'I've been dreading this day for some time,' she stammered.

Upon hearing Mrs Hopkins at the front door, Mandy lured the woman into one of the bedrooms along the hallway to advise her of the circumstances before she had the chance to speak to Sally.

'Oh my God, the poor woman,' she cried. 'First she loses her daughter and now you're telling me that her husband is dead too. What on earth happened?'

'I'm afraid I can't tell you any more at this stage,' Mandy replied. 'I just need to know that someone will be here with Sally.'

'Of course, that's no problem. I'll have to leave a note for my Burt to tell him where I am. Otherwise he might think I've gone off with some fancy man.'

She placed her hand on Mandy's shoulder and forced a smile.

'Bless her,' Mandy thought to herself. 'The woman is desperately trying to lighten things up.'

When Mandy re-entered the lounge with drinks she found Wesley and Sally stood by the patio door.

'I was just showing the Inspector the work my husband had been doing in the garden,' said Sally. 'He'd just finished building a lovely patio area over on the right there,' she said pointing. 'That's where we get most of the sun in the summer.'

'It's very nice,' Mandy replied handing the teas around.

'Ah thanks. Do you mind if I go outside for a smoke,' asked Wesley.

Sally unlocked the patio door and slid it open as Wesley stepped outside and walked across the lawn to the new patio area. He placed his tea on the ground, retrieved his tobacco from his coat pocket and began to roll a cigarette. He couldn't help but wonder why Henry Morgan had suddenly just decided to concrete half the garden. Surely that was the kind of thing one did when you first move in. He noticed the new garden shed too with its new concrete walkway wrapped around it. Back inside the house Wesley had a quiet word with Mandy while Mrs Hopkins sat talking to Sally.

'There's little point in questioning Sally any more right now. It's obvious she didn't know where her husband was or what he was doing. The neighbour says she'll stay with her for a while. Either you or Alison can pop back later.'

They said goodbye, leaving Sally explaining to Mrs Hopkins what their plans had been for the New Year.

'What are you thinking?' Mandy asked as Wesley negotiated the new one way system that encircles Wells.

'The garden, it bugs me. Maybe I've been a copper too long but something doesn't feel right.'

'What do you mean, sir?'

'Why would someone concrete half of their garden years after being in the place? Surely it's something you do when you first move in?'

'Maybe they didn't have the money,' Mandy replied shrugging her shoulders.

Wesley shook his head.

'We've looked at Henry Morgan's finances. He's been loaded for years.'

'Perhaps he just didn't fancy mowing the lawn so much,' Mandy remarked with a smirk on her face.

'Maybe he was hiding something,' Wesley replied looking serious.

Mandy noticed the envelope in his hand.

'What's that, sir?'

Wesley pursed his lips before replying.

'It's a letter that Felicity Morgan wrote but never sent. It's addressed to her mother. I was going to give it to Sally but I don't see the point now. I think she's been hurt enough already.'

Having returned home from another busy morning at the hospital, Jane was pleased to be back at home. Jasmine Cottage had been their new home for almost two years now and it was everything she and Wesley had ever wanted, except that it was a typical country Cottage and therefore rather small and dated. That was why she and Wesley had recently agreed to have an extension built which would give them a larger kitchen, new patio doors instead of the old wooden thumb latch door, along with a downstairs toilet.

The building work was due to start tomorrow so she decided that today was a good time to start putting a few things out of their way, especially Wesley's vast array of bottles that contained his numerous attempts at home made wine.

It was as she was carrying the last of the bottles down to the garden shed that contained the colourless liquid that Wesley hoped would eventually one day turn into a lovely wine that an idea sprung to mind.

Twenty minutes later, Jane was walking back home with a small packet of soluble thallium tablets she had purchased from the local hardware store.

Carefully removing the cork from one of the wine bottles she poured a small amount into an old milk bottle before replacing the cork. She then dropped one of the thallium tablets into the milk bottle and waited to see what happened.

The result was as she had expected. There was no sign that the poison had been added. The tablet had dissolved but the liquid content had remained colourless, cloudless and odourless, except for the faint aroma that a white wine offers.

'So, this is one way that Lady Hargreaves could have been poisoned,' Jane exclaimed.

As soon as Alison saw Wesley arrive back in the office she handed him the envelope addressed to Lady Hargreaves.

'I've had the team check for fingerprints but there are none,' she said.

Wesley nodded as he opened the envelope. He extracted a single sheet of A4 size paper. There was one line of print in the middle of the page. It read ۞۞۞. Wesley handed it across the desk for the team to look at as he examined the brown buff envelope.

'So we have no idea when this was delivered?'

'No sir. There was a pile of mail, mostly junk mail lying on the floor. It could have been there for a couple of days. I also checked with the post office to ask if the local postman had been handed the envelope to deliver but he says no.'

'Good work, Alison.'

'What does it mean?' asked Martin.

'I'm not sure, but one thing I do know. It's exactly the same as the tattoo that was engraved on Ted Drake's arm. The problem is that he obviously never posted it because he was already dead.'

'Someone could have removed it from his body then posted it,' Mandy suggested.

'Sure, that's possible. But what the hell does it mean?'

'I'll search the internet,' said Martin, 'it's a shot in the dark but worth a try.'

Wesley agreed and handed the note over.

Martin noticed he was still in a pensive mood.

'What's wrong, sir? You seem thoughtful.'

Wesley informed them about the recent work that had been carried out in Henry Morgan's garden.

'Maybe they just wanted a change of scenery,' said Martin.

'What are you thinking, sir?' asked Alison.

Wesley explained that what was niggling him was that people didn't suddenly concrete half of their garden, it was something people did when they first moved into a property.

'Perhaps Henry Morgan has hidden buried treasure there,' Martin commented laughing.

'Perhaps he buried something or someone,' Wesley replied chewing his bottom lip.

'Do you really think he's buried something in the garden then poured concrete all over it?' asked Alison raising her eyebrows.

'Maybe I've been watching too much television, but yes I think there is a possibility,' Wesley replied.

'So do you want us to start digging up the garden?' asked Martin trying to wipe some of the dinner stains off his shirt.

'Not yet. I think we have a little more delving to do first.'

Wesley got up from his desk and walked across the room where he stood looking out of the window down onto the street below.

'I think this case has a far wider history than any of us ever imagined,' he said without turning around. He was reluctant to inform the rest of the team at this stage of his meeting with James Harper although Mandy was already aware.

They spent the next hour going over everything they knew. While everyone added their comments Mandy updated the board with the latest information. They were still discussing the information to date when Wesley received a call from his superior reminding him that he was due to sit in on a conference call with all regional heads in ten minutes.

'I've got to join a call in a minute,' he sighed. 'Let's catch up later. Is there anything else anyone wants to add?'

'I was going to pop in to check on Annie Griffin on my way home,' said Mandy.'

'That's fine, thanks.'

'Oh and just to remind everyone that my holiday starts at the weekend,' she blurted out embarrassing herself in the process.

'Get out of here before I change my mind about your leave,' said Wesley just before everyone started to laugh.

'How did you get in the house? I had closed the front door.'

'I've always kept a spare key, just in case of emergencies.'

'You have no right to enter this house without my permission,' Brian Hargreaves shouted.

'We can always discuss the issue with the police, if that's what you'd prefer,' replied Annie Griffin sitting back on the armchair. It had been some time since Annie had been inside Melcham Hall, some time since she'd been invited.

Hargreaves set the safety clip back on the revolver and tucked it back into the waistband of his trousers.

'I could have shot you,' he exclaimed.

'Oh I don't think so. Shooting someone is not in your nature is it Brian?'

'What the hell do you mean by that?'

'Poisoning someone certainly, blackmailing someone too, but not shooting. You've never liked the sight of blood.'

'What are you on about woman? I think it's time you left this house. I want you off my property. In fact I want you out of that damn lodge too. You've been living there for free for far too long.'

'I think you'll find I have a legal right to live at Rowan Lodge,' Annie replied with a smirk on her face. 'Lord Melcham saw to that.'

Hargreaves closed the library door and leant back on it with his arms folded.

'Tell me what you want then get out.'

'I want to know who killed Felicity Morgan and Antoine Bergerac.'

'Felicity's death was an accident. Henry pushed her and she fell backwards breaking her neck.'

'What about Antoine Bergerac?'

'Antoine Bergerac? Who the hell are you talking about?'

'He was the body found dumped in the ditch just up on the main road. Apparently he was working around these parts under the name of Ted Drake.'

'Never heard of the man,' Hargreaves replied fumbling with a packet of cigarettes.

'Hmm strange considering his body was found near the estate.'

'So I'm responsible for any idiot that passes the estate now am I?'

'You don't remember Antoine do you? He stayed at Rowan Lodge many years ago, he taught Lucy and Kate to ride. He was a dancer in those days but he could turn his hand to just about anything.'

Hargreaves lit his cigarette, took a long drag and sat on the edge of the window ledge from where he could view the entrance to the house.

'I can't believe Lucy never mentioned him. He taught her sister Kate how to dance when they were children.'

'Get to the fucking point,' Hargreaves shouted as he stubbed the remains of the cigarette on the polished wooden floorboard.

'Antoine was a member of the Abbey, and they do not take kindly to one of its members being murdered.'

'The Abbey? What Abbey? What on earth are you talking about?'

Annie stood up and walked slowly across the room and opened the door to leave. Although she was getting on in years she still carried an air of authority.

'The trouble with you Brian Hargreaves is that you were never interested in the Melcham family or the history to this estate. Your sole objective was to extract as much money as you could get your hands on. You think you've been clever but I can assure you that the Abbey will come for you and you will assist us to regain what is legally ours.' Annie closed the door behind her leaving Hargreaves staring open mouthed.

Wesley was sat at the kitchen table rubbing his eyes.

'You look tired, dear. Why don't you have an early night for a change?'

'An early night eh, that sounds good,' Wesley replied with a grin on his face.

'I meant to sleep,' replied Jane placing his dinner on the table.

They ate dinner in silence. It was Jane who spoke first as she pushed her plate away. 'I was experimenting today.'

'Eh? I don't follow you.'

'With thallium.'

'You've been playing around with a poison?'

'Yes, listen. An idea came to me when I was moving your wine bottles out to the shed. I'd been thinking about that poor policeman and about Lady Hargreaves and the fact that she was being poisoned. Well, it struck me that it would be difficult to poison someone without them knowing about it.'

'Go on.' Wesley pushed his plate aside, he was intrigued.

'When I was last at the book shop speaking with Gerry, he'd discovered that when dissolved, thallium becomes a clear, colourless, odourless liquid.'

'Jane, what are you trying to say?'

'Do listen, I'm trying to explain. I purchased a box of thallium tablets and dissolved one into a small amount of one of your attempted white wines.'

'And?'

Jane walked across to the sink unit and retrieved the milk bottle, which she then handed to Wesley.

'Don't drink it, just smell it.'

Wesley looked at the small amount of clear liquid in the bottom of the bottle and raised it to his nose.

'White wine; needs a few more days to ferment though.'

'It sure does, because it contains a tablet of thallium in it.'

'What?'

'Don't you see, John? Someone could put this stuff in someone's drink every day without the person knowing, until it's too late.'

'Are you suggesting that Lady Hargreaves was being fed this stuff every day without knowing?'

Jane shrugged her shoulders as she took the bottle from him and poured the contents down the sink.

'You're the detective, you tell me.'

Wesley sat deep in thought while Jane washed out the empty bottle before placing it in the recycle bin. She had another question for him when she returned to the table.

'Have you been able to find out who killed Ted Drake yet?'

'Not yet, but we know that wasn't his real name. His name was Antoine. He originated from France but he was over here just after the war, touring with a dance group.'

'Why do you think he came back?'

'I'm not sure to be honest, however my gut feeling is that he had an affair with either Lucy or her sister Kate when they were younger and being down on his luck thought he would return to Melcham Hall to seek her attentions once again.'

'Didn't you say the other day that Lucy Hargreaves is missing?'

'Yes she is. We now know that her sister Kate had returned from France and has been pretending to be her sister.'

'That's awful,' commented Jane. 'Why on earth would someone do that?'

Wesley wiped his mouth with a tissue.

'For money I suppose or for revenge? Apparently she was short of cash and living quite a basic life in France after her father wrote her out of his will. She's the person who O'Hara tried to locate for me.'

Jane stood up and began collecting the empty plates from the table.

'The root of all evil,' she said.

'What is, your cooking?' laughed Wesley.

Wesley never saw Jane pick up the tea towel but felt the slap on the back of his head.

'Actually can you do something else for me,' Wesley asked.

'Can you see what you can dig up about an Abbey being located on the Melcham estate?'

'An Abbey?'

'Yeah, apparently there are some old ruins on the Melcham estate which used to belong to an Abbey before the Melcham family bought the estate.'

'What has an old Abbey got to do with the case?' asked Jane.

'That's what I want to find out,' Wesley answered.

'I hope I'm getting paid for this.'

'I'll pay you in kind,' Wesley replied smiling.

'Ah well, short changed as usual,' laughed Jane.

Mandy turned the car into the Melcham estate and pulled up outside Rowan Lodge. As she opened her car door she spied Annie walking towards her.

'Hello Annie, how are you?'

‘Hello Mandy, I’m fine. What brings you here?’

‘I was just on my way home but I thought I’d call in just to see how you were.’

‘That’s very kind. Would you like to come in?’

‘Thanks. I’ll only stop a minute. It’s been a long day.’

Annie led the way entering the back door. She rarely used the front door. A country thing so Mandy had learnt over the years. Mandy also noticed that the door hadn’t been locked.

‘Take a seat, I’ll put the kettle on,’ said Annie.

Mandy loved the smell of Annie’s kitchen, homemade cakes and pastries. It reminded her of when she was a child when she used to watch her own mother cook. She loved nothing better than opening the front door when returning home from school to smell her mother’s cooking.

‘So I guess that lovely Inspector Wesley is keeping you busy,’ commented Annie as she placed tea and biscuits on the table.

‘I’ll worry when he doesn’t,’ Mandy replied with a grin. ‘Have you been for a stroll around the estate?’ she asked.

The question seemed to catch Annie by surprise.

‘Oh err, yes. Just a short stroll my dear. I need to keep these old bones moving.’

‘I suppose you know we’re still looking for Brian Hargreaves,’ said Mandy selecting a biscuit.

Annie stole a glance at Mandy before replying.

‘Yes, yes I heard. I think it’s the only thing they’re talking about in the village these days.’

The two women sat talking for twenty minutes discussing local news and the rubbish on television before Mandy said she ought to make her way home.

‘It’s getting chilly now,’ exclaimed Annie. She stood up and wrapped her cardigan around her. Something caught Mandy’s eye but she wasn’t sure what it was.

‘Are you OK dear,’ Annie asked.

‘Oh yes, sorry. I was miles away. It’s time I was off to bed,’ Mandy replied.

Back in the car Mandy was about to switch on the ignition when it dawned on her. It was the brooch. The brooch on Annie’s cardigan was the same design as the tattoo found on Ted Drake’s body. Mandy quickly reached for her mobile to advise Wesley.

22

Brian Hargreaves woke with the headache from hell. Shortly after Annie had left Melcham Hall he'd gathered as many clothes and personal belongings as he could find and driven down to Taunton where he'd booked himself into a small Bed and Breakfast under the name of Woodrow. Having found a little backstreet bar just a few hundred yards from the hotel he descended the steps to the door entrance which was below street level and made his way to the bar. The place was dimly lit, and there was a distinct lack of decoration. Green and white striped wallpaper adorned two of the walls, smoke stained and peeling away in several places. The solitary barman whose appearance was that of someone who hadn't seen either sleep or daylight for months sauntered along the bar and raised his head as if to question what Hargreaves wanted.

'I'll have a large scotch, no ice.' He placed a ten pound note on the counter.

The same scene was repeated another three times before Hargreaves was aware of a woman who had just entered the bar. He knew she didn't enter via the front door as a brief shaft of daylight would have exposed the grim interior.

She smiled as she sat on one of many empty stools, crossing her legs as she turned to face him. Hargreaves guessed she had to be in her late forties, early fifties although she still had quite a figure. The grey skirt she was wearing had ridden up exposing her thigh. She knew he was looking at her and knew she could make some money tonight. After downing a large gin and tonic in just a few minutes she eased herself off the stool and brushed part him as she made her way to the toilet. He was aware of her perfume and the feeling arousing in him. He had just called the barman over to get another drink when the buxom woman reappeared and sat herself down next to him.

'And one for the lady,' he said.

'That's very kind, usual please Frank.'

It was only when Frank walked away after serving them with a large scotch and a large gin and tonic did the woman converse.

'I guess you're a tourist? I haven't seen you around here before,' she said.

Hargreaves was aware of how close she was sitting as her leg brushed his when she turned around on the stool.

'Yeah, a tourist, just down for a couple of days,' he replied taking in the dark blue eyes, the red lipstick and the fact that her blouse was undone to the point that her breasts were virtually exposed.

'Are you looking for company?'

'Could be,' he replied raising his shoulders in a nonchalant way. He was hoping that she couldn't see how nervous he actually was. Raising her glass in one hand she dropped the other by her side where his leg was and began running her fingers along his thigh.

'Want to come up to my room?' she asked. 'You can see the sea from the bedroom window and it's far more comfortable.'

I bet that's a view that many tourists have seen thought Hargreaves as he followed her up the stairs. The rest of the night was a complete blur. At seven o'clock the following morning he sat on the side of the bed. He remembered them having sex for the first time but as the wine continued to flow his recollection of the hours that followed were hazy to say the least. Wearily lifting himself off the bed he walked into the bathroom and flicked on the naked tube that was located above the mirror. He almost didn't recognise the face that stared back at him. He had aged several years in just a few weeks. Throwing cold water over his face he then wiped away the sleep and lipstick from his face. The naked woman lay half uncovered still fast asleep. He was tempted to wake her and continue where they'd left off but changed his mind, dressed quietly and left the room.

Wesley was up and about early, it was still only 08:30 and he'd already been to the office to pick up the drawing he'd received from the mortuary of the tattoo on Ted Drake's arm and was on his way to visit Annie. The morning had started bright and sunny but soon rain clouds had appeared on the horizon and as Wesley sat in the morning rush hour traffic, small drops of rain started to patter his windscreen. By the time he was heading out of Wells the heavens had opened and he was struggling to see more than a hundred yards in front.

Annie had the front door open before he'd even knocked. She had heard the car pull up and had been expecting a visit.

'Good morning, Inspector, do come in.'

Wesley took his jacket off in the hallway and removed his shoes which were already caked in mud even though he'd only walked twenty yards from the car.

'A nice drop of rain we're having,' commented Annie as if it was something that had been expected.

'Yeah, nice if you're not out in it,' Wesley replied.

'Let me make you a hot drink, then you can tell me the reason for your visit,' she replied.

Having placed his jacket on the back of a chair to dry in front of the open fire Wesley joined Annie in the kitchen. 'I'd like you to take a look at a drawing if you would, and tell me what the connection is.'

'The connection, I don't understand?' Annie had a quizzical look on her face as she placed two mugs of tea on the table.

Wesley slid the sketch across the table. Annie picked it up and held it close to her face, squinting. She placed the drawing back on the table and pulled up a chair opposite Wesley.

'You recognise it don't you?' asked Wesley even though the look on Annie's face had already answered the question. 'The tattoo, it's the same symbol as your brooch.'

'Where did you obtain this drawing from?' she asked.

'From the mortuary, the tattoo was found on the deceased man's arm. It was the person found in the lane not far from here.'

Annie almost dropped her mug. She grabbed at it with both hands and held it firmly, seemingly completely oblivious to how hot it was. Wesley played the waiting game, knowing that often in situations like this it was better to wait until the other person spoke first. Annie took a while to compose herself.

'I know only a handful of people who would have this symbol somewhere on their person.'

'What is it, and why would Ted Drake have it the tattoo on his arm?'

Annie started to laugh. A laugh that carried no merriment, no joy, a laugh that hid the pain she felt.

'His name wasn't Ted Drake; that was his alias. His real name was Antoine Bergerac. He'd come back to this country in search of love.' Annie paused. 'How did he die, Inspector?'

'He was poisoned before being beaten to death.'

For the first time he'd known her, Annie suddenly looked fragile.

'I think you need to tell me what's going on here, Annie. I need you to explain how you knew who this person was.'

Annie and Wesley had moved into the front room and Annie sat looking into the fire watching the flames lick the back of the chimney as several trails of smoke drifted lazily upwards into the void of the chimney stack. Wesley imagined that she had done this many times over the years. When she eventually looked up there was a pain etched on her face that Wesley hadn't seen before.

'Inspector, I've experienced many things in my life, including the cruelty and destruction that war brings. I've seen how jealousy destroys and how love can sometimes turn to hate. I've witnessed how people can change when their world is turned upside down, but the answer you seek I cannot provide.'

'Cannot, or will not?'

'Cannot, Inspector.'

Annie took hold of a metal poker that stood on the hearth and poked at the coal causing some pieces to flare and other to fall away as ash, as in life and death.

'Many years ago, when Lord Melcham was just a teenager and my husband and I were still in our youth, I was called upon to undertake an oath that will remain sacred with me until the day I die.'

Wesley fidgeted in his chair as he felt a sudden chill in the air.

'Are we talking about the Abbey?' he asked.

He could see Annie's aged body stiffen although she never looked up.

'James Harper mentioned an Abbey,' Wesley continued. 'I assume we're talking about the same thing?' He was hoping that the mention of the celebrity's name would bring a response.

'What you showed me is the emblem of the Abbey. Apart from that, Inspector, my lips are sealed.'

Wesley was unsure how to press the matter further but thought he would give it one more try.

'Annie, this is a murder enquiry. Felicity Morgan and Antoine Bergerac were both killed for one reason or another as was PC Mark Hayles, and now Henry Morgan whom we suspect may have had something to do with these murders was found burned to death. I need to find out why these people were murdered and who is responsible.'

'What did James Harper say when you asked a similar question?'

'He told me that the Abbey would protect Lucy Hargreaves at all costs.'

'Then you have your answer, Inspector.'

'At all costs, Annie? Does that include kidnap and murder?'

Annie replaced the poker next to the fire and stood up holding her back.

'I'm tired, Inspector. I need to rest.'

Wesley followed her to the front door. Annie hesitated as she opened the door.

'I'm not a murderer, Inspector, nor do I condone such acts, however I have a duty to serve the Abbey and nothing will deter me from that.'

'I just don't get it. What has the Abbey got to do with all of this?'

'Look up your history books, Inspector. The truth will be revealed.'

Wesley heard her close the door behind him and suddenly felt isolated from the case. It was evident that he was dealing with something much larger than he imagined or anticipated. As he sat back in his car he realised he had a message on his phone. He read the brief text then placed a call. PC Martin Philips answered almost immediately and gave him a run-down of the situation.

'OK,' Wesley sighed. 'Keep Sally Morgan entertained. I'm on my way.'

PC Martin Philips had just pulled into the station car park when he spotted a woman pacing nervously up and down the pavement outside the police station.

'Can I be of assistance?' he asked as he approached.

He noticed how agitated the woman actually was, constantly wringing her hands and biting her lip.

‘I need to speak with Inspector Wesley. It’s a matter of urgency.’

‘May I ask what it’s about?’ Martin replied concerned at the level of anxiety the woman was now expressing.

‘It’s a personal matter. It’s about my husband Henry. It’s about murder.’

Suddenly Martin’s senses kicked in. Could she be referring to Henry Morgan?

‘Come inside and I’ll find out where the Inspector is and find you somewhere private.’

Having finally enticed the woman to give her name, Martin had sat her in Wesley’s office before heading to the outer office to make a phone call.

When Wesley arrived back at the station he found Martin manning the control desk as the desk sergeant was busy dealing with a drunk down in one of the cells. Martin was being shouted at by an elderly woman who was ranting and raving at him about her missing cat and the fact that the police seemed to be doing nothing about finding the person who has obviously kidnapped her. Brushing past Martin, Wesley patted him on the shoulder, trying not to smile as the woman continued her ranting. He found Sally Morgan sat in his office. As soon as he entered the room Sally jumped up from her chair, the two of them almost colliding in the glass doorway.

‘Inspector, I need to talk to you,’ she blurted out before he could speak.

‘So I understand.’

Wesley guided her back to a seat and closed the door quietly behind him.

It was obvious that Sally Morgan had a lot to get off her chest and Wesley was an expert at listening. Over the next thirty minutes Sally Morgan explained that her husband, Henry had been having an affair with Lady Hargreaves and it was on one of the occasions he’d visited Melcham Hall that their daughter Felicity saw them together. Apparently Henry was unaware that Felicity had obtained a job at Melcham Hall and on the morning in question Felicity had entered the library to find her father and Lady Hargreaves in a compromising position. Felicity had screamed at her father and run out of the house threatening to tell her mother what she had witnessed. Her father had chased after her and eventually caught up with her on the estate, close to Rowan Lodge. He was unable to calm his daughter down and a struggle pursued during which Felicity fell backwards, breaking her neck. Her limp body told him she was dead. In sheer panic he hid her body in the garage, before later moving it to the coal shed behind Rowan Lodge.

‘The rest is history,’ said Sally Morgan wiping her eyes with a tissue.

‘Why didn’t you tell me this before?’ Wesley asked.

Sally Morgan stared at him with a vacant look in her eyes as if all the energy had been drained out of her body.

‘I wanted to kill Henry myself,’ she replied jutting out her chin as if in defiance of the way she was feeling.

'When were you first aware that your husband was having an affair?'

Sally Morgan's response was to laugh hysterically.

'Which affair is that, Inspector? Henry had been having affairs for years. He admitted to seeing Lady Hargreaves the day Felicity died but he'd been with her before and several other women before that. He didn't have to tell me. A woman knows.'

Sally Morgan looked as if she was about to say something else but then decided to say nothing. Wesley stood up and pushed his chair back against the wall.

'Wait here, Mrs Morgan. I'll fetch WPC Alison Bolt in to take a statement.' He hesitated as he opened the door. 'I don't suppose you have any idea what else your husband was involved in?'

Sally Morgan folded her arms, a look of defiance on her face.

'My husband was not a murderer, Inspector. Felicity's death was an accident, and no, I have no idea what else he was involved in.'

Jane had opened every window in their Cottage. Although it was January and there was a cold chill to the air, the sun had decided to visit today and a crisp clear blue sky meant that it was the perfect day to open the property up, especially as the builders were beginning work on their new extension today.

Built in 1818, Jasmine Cottage had had little work done to it which although had helped it to retain its character and charm meant that some elements were now in need of repair. One of these was the damp course on the kitchen side of the building. However, the new side extension would deal with that and provide them with a larger kitchen and downstairs toilet. The new patio doors would also provide them with more light and allow for a better view of the back garden and surrounding countryside. Jane was in a happy mood and had been up early to move a few things into the lounge, away from the kitchen. The kettle had already boiled twice in anticipation of the builder's arrival when there was a knock at the front door. Colin Jones had been a builder all his life, starting in the trade with his father when he was only twelve years of age. Now fifty-eight he'd decided it was time to slow down a little and had employed a young lad to help with the heavy work. Colin was happy to sit having a cup of tea with Jane whilst the young lad, Danny, was busy carrying tools into the house and around to the back garden. Jane heard how Colin had grown up in the village and how much the place had changed over the years. He even told her who had lived in Jasmine Cottage before the last residents, and went into great detail about how his granddad was responsible for building both the village hall and the grocer's shop. He omitted to tell her how much time his granddad used to spend in the local pub.

'So do you have any children?' Jane asked as soon as she could get a word in.

'Aye we do. We have a young lass named Elisia. She's just turned eighteen, a bit of handful at that age as you can imagine. We had her late in life really, we were told we couldn't have kids then just a few weeks after my poor old mum passed away, my Penny says she's pregnant. Strange how life works out ain't it?'

It was rather a statement more than a comment.

'I can imagine a teenager is hard work these days,' Jane replied.

'We did have a boy too, young Billy, but we lost him to pneumonia when he was a baby.' He placed his cup on the table and stared out of the window to where Danny was busy piling up some bricks.

'I was hoping he'd grow up working with me but it wasn't to be.'

'I'm sorry,' said Jane, uncertain whether to make further comment.

'Have you got any children, Mrs Wesley?'

'Oh please call me Jane. No, we haven't.'

'Well you're only young, it's not too late. A home breathes when it's got children running about.'

Jane blushed. It was a subject she and Wesley had never discussed.

Colin stood up and carried his cup across to the sink.

'Ah well. Best make a start.'

Jane busied herself with washing up and making the bed before she settled down in front of the computer to see what she could find about an Abbey existing on the Melcham estate.

She tapped the name into Google and hit enter.

'That's strange,' she thought to herself. The only responses to Melcham were Melcham Hall and Lord Melcham. She scrawled through two screens of data about Melcham Hall where there was small reference to the Hall being an Abbey in previous times, but there was no mention of a Griffin Abbey. Jane checked the spelling and tried a number of variations but there was nothing there.

She was muttering to herself when Colin Jones stuck his head around the door.

'Sorry to disturb you, Jane. We're just going to the yard to pick up some timber and a few other bits n pieces. You OK there, sounded like you were talking to yourself.'

'I was to be honest. Damn computers can be so frustrating when you can't find what you're looking for.'

'Are you looking for something in particular?' he asked.

'Yes, I'm trying to find out what happened to Melcham Abbey. Apparently there was an Abbey on the Melcham estate many years ago,' Jane answered.

She could see the quizzical look on Colin's face.

'Melcham Abbey you say? Never existed as far as I know, but there was a Griffin Abbey. I remember my granddad telling us kids never to go near it.'

'A Griffin Abbey, are you sure?'

'As sure as the day I was born. It used to stand in the grounds of the

Melcham estate, just down the hill from where the new Melcham Hall is now. A dark imposing place it was. Haunted they say.'

'What happened to it? Why was it destroyed?' Jane asked intrigued.

'I'm not sure I know, Jane. My old dad said there was a lot of speculation when the place was vacated. He said some of the residents died when they were forced out. Apparently most locals won't even talk about it.'

'Oh, really? How strange? What I don't understand is why there is no mention of it on Google. It's as if the place never existed,' Jane exclaimed.

'Maybe that's what people are meant to believe,' Colin replied shrugging his shoulders.

'Ah well, I guess it's now a ruin so there's little point in worrying about it,' Jane replied. 'There won't be anything to see.'

'I can get you in there,' interrupted Danny, poking his head around the doorframe.

'But it's just a ruin, isn't it?' Jane answered.

'Above ground yes, but a couple of rooms still exist below ground under the remains. The entrance is probably overgrown now and covered by weeds and whatever but there are steps that definitely take you inside, so long as you can find them. We used to play there as kids. Like Colin said, even my old dad used to warn me to keep away but as the place was a ruin even in those days we used to go over there to play hide and seek, or take girlfriends.'

'Hmm, well, yes,' Jane replied blushing. 'Do you think you would be able to find the place now?' asked Jane.

'Sure, no problem, but I don't think it's somewhere for a lady would want to go,' Danny replied.

'No, but it might be somewhere Inspector Wesley would like to take a look at,' said Jane smiling.

Kate Melcham had been drifting in an out of consciousness for three days and was still confined to bed by means of numerous tubes and connectivity to a monitoring device that appeared to be scrutinizing her every movement.

The nurse had raised the bed slightly so that Kate was now able to peer around the room and more importantly for her, she could now see who was entering the room each time someone came in. Raising her left arm as far as the drip would allow she brushed her hair away from her eyes and squinted at the clock on the far wall. It read 11:30 but she had no idea what day it was. A sliver of daylight was filtering into the room through the half-open blinds. She reached for the glass of water from the side table and took a sip, every little move seemed like a massive effort but at least she was able to feed herself now. She could even move her toes. She tried to recall events from the past few days but she found it hard to concentrate, her mind seemed to want to wander from one thing to another, and just trying to think hurt.

Kate looked up when she heard a small bleep. It was the door sensor to her room. A blurred vision of a man dressed in a white uniform appeared just inside the doorway, too far away for Kate to be able to see any clear features.

'Hello,' said Kate.

The person never answered but seemed to be observing her from a distance.

'Are you a doctor?' she asked in a drowsy voice. Just then she heard voices further away, a muffled sound of several people talking at the same time. Within the blink of an eye her visitor had disappeared and the bleep told her that the door had closed again. A couple of minutes later, two nurses were stood either side of the bed. One was replacing a drip whilst the other had brought in what looked to be some form of liquidized food.

'You have more colour about you today,' said one of the nurses who pressed a button somewhere under the bed to raise it a little.

'Yes, she does,' the other nurse replied as she took a reading from the monitoring equipment.'

'Where has the other doctor gone?' Kate asked in a slow drool.

'What other doctor, my dear?' asked one of the nurses as she tidied the bed. 'No one else has been in to you today.'

'He was there just now, by the door,' Kate replied.

The two nurses looked at one another.

'No one else has been in today. You must be thinking about Doctor Jacob who came in to see you last night.'

'But I heard the bleep,' Kate answered yawning.

'Try and get some rest now, one of us will be back in this afternoon. Just press the buzzer on the table if you need anything.'

By the time the two nurses had administered Kate's needs and left the room, Kate was asleep.

Nurse Jenkins was just finishing her shift and made her way to the nurses' changing area before leaving the hospital while Nurse Chapman finished her rounds before stopping off at the office where she found Carl Owen, the hospitals IT expert. Actually he was the only IT guy in the administration unit. Being just eighteen years of age and good looking, some of the nurses would make him blush with their comments and smiles.

'Hi Carl,' she said leaning over his shoulder giving him a slender hug.

'You're the IT expert around here, I was wondering if you'd be able to help me.'

Nurse Chapman pulled up a chair and sat alongside him, she was so close her leg rubbed against his. She knew he would help her.

'Sure,' he stammered, 'how can I help?'

'Are you able to tell when someone swipes their card into a room? I mean, if I went into see one of the patients every day would you be able to tell how many times I'd swiped my card?'

'Yeah, that's easy. Just tell me the card number or the door number.'

'The door number is N9. It's one of my patients, Kate Melcham.'

She watched as Carl typed his username and password into the in-house security system. In order he then selected a particular floor, unit, and door number.

In a few seconds a new screen appeared providing a list of times the door to N9 had been activated.

'May I take a quick look?' she asked.

Leaning across the young lad Nurse Chapman followed her finger down the list of times shown. She noted the times she had been into the room today and the last time she had entered with Nurse Jenkins, then she went back up. That's when she found it.

PC Martin Philips had just returned from the mortuary. Terry Austin had asked him to collect a parcel for Wesley as he was going to be driving past the building.

'Hello there,' said Alison as she approached from Wesley's office. 'Where have you been?'

'On an errand for the boss,' he replied with a smirk.

'Ooh Billy big spuds,' she replied laughing. 'I expect Mandy is now lying next to a pool somewhere drinking cocktails and studying the local talent.'

'Good for her,' Martin replied, 'she deserves a holiday. She's been through a lot lately.'

'Do I get a hint of concern there?' Alison asked winking.

'Just saying.'

Martin found Wesley sat at his desk reading through a report.

'If you've also come here to tell me that I shouldn't smoke in the office I'm going to ban all overtime,' said Wesley without even looking up.

'Actually I've brought you something from Terry Austin,' said Martin standing nervously in the doorway.

'Give it here and shut the bloody door,' Wesley replied striking a match to light his roll-up. He tore the sticky tape off the wrapped parcel and dropped the contents on the table. There was a note inside pinned to one of the items. Wesley opened it and read out aloud. 'Please find enclosed jacket taken from the body of PC Mark Hayles. Having analysed the skeletal remains of the body found in the recent fire at the farmhouse I can confirm that a DNA sample taken from the remains matches that found on the enclosed jacket. Both DNA samples belong to Henry Morgan.'

'So Morgan killed Mark?'

'Sure looks that way,' Wesley replied relighting his roll-up.

'In that case Morgan must have had access to the thallium,' said Martin.

'Either that or Hargreaves supplied it I guess?'

Just at that moment Wesley's office phone started to ring.

'Hello, Wesley speaking.'

'Hello, Inspector. This is Nurse Chapman from Wells' hospital. I hope I'm not interrupting anything.'

‘Of course not, how can I help?’

‘Well, it’s just something that our patient Kate Melcham said this morning that led me to look at our in-house security records. These identify who goes where in restricted areas in the hospital. Kate said she had a visitor earlier today but it was at a time when neither myself, nor Nurse Jenkins had been in to see her, and Doctor Jacobs is not due in until teatime.’

‘Can you tell from the system just who the visitor was?’ Wesley asked rubbing out the remains of his roll-up between thumb and forefinger.

‘That’s the problem, Inspector. The swipe card that was used isn’t showing as being registered to anyone, yet someone did go in the room.’

‘Is there any CCTV we can check?’

‘That’s why I called, Inspector. Carl Owens, our IT lad, has just been running through the video footage taken from the past two hours and there is a side view of a man dressed as a doctor seen leaving the building some three minutes after the rogue entry.’

‘Do you recognise the man?’ Wesley asked.

‘No, I admit it’s not a great angle but he doesn’t look familiar. I’ve shown it to several people and no one recognises him.’

‘OK, I’ll send one of my lads over to take a look. Tell Carl Owens to expect him in the next hour.’

‘Thank you, Inspector. I don’t want to waste your time but I’m concerned that someone may have breached our security.’

‘You did the right thing Nurse, we’ll be over as soon as possible.’

Wesley replaced the receiver and brought Martin up to date asking him to get over to the hospital straight away.

23

WPC Alison Bolt left the waiting room having taken the statement from Sally Morgan. She wasn't convinced that Sally had told her everything she knew, experience left her with a nagging doubt that something was missing. She had informed Sally of her obligation to provide the police with every bit of information that she could and that having previously withheld information she could still face prosecution for withholding evidence. Alison almost felt sorry for the woman she'd left crying in the interview room, but then thought of PC Mark Hayles who had lost his life earlier in the investigation and this hardened her resolve to let Sally Morgan stew for a while. They now had evidence to suggest that Henry Morgan had murdered Mark.

'What do you think, sir?' Alison asked when Wesley had finished reading the statement.

Wesley pursed his lips.

'Like you, I just get the feeling that Sally Morgan still knows more than she's told us. However, we're not going to get any more out of her now by keeping her here. Let her go, but ask one of the other constables to keep tabs on her for the next twenty-four hours. If she is keeping something to herself it's because she's planning on doing something or meeting someone. Make sure the tab is still on the house phone too.'

Brian Hargreaves slammed the car boot shut and jumped behind the steering wheel. 'Damn that nurse' she said to himself. His attempt at getting to Kate Melcham before she recovered had failed. He switched on the ignition and hit the pedal as the Range Rover screamed out of the hospital car park causing an oncoming truck to swerve to avoid a collision. Turning left onto the main road he headed east, deciding he needed to get away from the West Country and lie low for a while. It took him an hour to get onto a congested M5 motorway heading towards the Midlands. By the time he reached Coventry it was rush hour and traffic came to a crawl, the sky had changed to dark blue and a few spots of rain began to appear on the windscreen. He rolled his neck around his shoulders trying to ease the tension as he felt the beginning of a migraine starting. To his relief it only took another fifteen minutes to reach the Orion Hotel that sat just two miles off the motorway. Having booked in, and purchased a snack he made his way to

Room 103 after the receptionist had assured him that it was one of the best rooms available. He quickly showered and switched on the TV checking all the local news channels to make sure there was no mention of his name. He almost jumped out of his skin when his mobile rang. Extracting the phone from his jacket pocket he checked the caller's number. It was unknown. He waited for it to stop ringing before switching it off. He spent the next couple of hours watching TV and pacing the room, chain smoking his way through a packet of cigarettes. When his mobile vibrated he knew he'd received a message. He read the content and quickly posted reply confirming where he was staying.

Back in Wells, the young police admin officer put a call through to Wesley.

'Hargreaves is not answering his mobile, sir, and it's now switched off. All I can tell you is that he's located somewhere in the Midlands. Unless he switches the phone back on though, we've got no way of tracing its exact location.'

'OK thanks. Make sure we keep monitoring it and keep me updated.'

Wesley opened the front door to find Jane on her hands and knees washing the flagstone flooring in the hallway.

'Hello Mrs Wesley, how pleased I am to find you in such a position.'

Jane blushed before even looking up at him.

'Another comment like that and you can finish cleaning this lot,' she replied with a grin on her face. 'Your dinner is in the microwave, I'm not eating tonight as I'm going to yoga class with Brenda.'

Wesley placed his coat on the coat rack on the wall and turned towards the kitchen.

'You can get those shoes off before you go in there too,' said Jane.

'I suppose you'd like me to strip naked before I eat dinner?'

Jane looked up with a smirk on her face.

'I'm glad I'm not eating, the thought of that would have put me off my dinner.'

Wesley dipped his hand in the bucket of dirty water as he squeezed past and flicked water in her face.

'You'll pay for that,' Jane laughed.

'Promises, promises.'

When Jane entered the kitchen she found Wesley staring at the microwave.

'Don't tell me you don't know how to operate it,' she said laughing as she set the timer for three minutes.

Looking embarrassed Wesley thought it better to change the subject and crossed the kitchen to peer out of the window where the builders had left most of their equipment.

'So how's the building work coming along?'

Jane suddenly remembered what she'd been speaking to the builders about. 'Oh John, I'm sorry, I forgot to mention that while I was logged onto the computer looking for information about Melcham Abbey, Colin the builder asked me what I was looking for as he'd overheard me talking to myself. When I told him, he said there never was Melcham Abbey but there used to a Griffin Abbey on the Melcham estate.'

'A Griffin Abbey?' replied an astonished Wesley.

'Yes, and the young lad Danny, who's been digging the footings at the side of the house all day, said to tell you he knows how you can still get in there even though to all intents and purposes it's just a ruin now.'

'Oh my God,' Wesley answered.

'What's wrong, John? Have I said something that worries you?'

Jane walked around the kitchen table and took his hand in hers.

'The name Griffin, that's Annie's surname. She's the old lady who lives in Rowan Lodge on the Melcham estate.'

'Oh what a coincidence,' Jane replied.

Wesley didn't believe in coincidences. There was something wrong. He could feel it in his bones.

Wesley had just finished eating when his mobile rang.

'Hi, sir, it's Martin. I hope I haven't disturbed you.'

'Not at all, I was just waiting for Jane to make me a cuppa.'

Wesley smiled across the table in response to Jane two fingered response.

'We've had a close look at the hospital CCTV and I can confirm that Brian Hargreaves walked out of the hospital three minutes after the time of the rogue entry to Kate Melcham's room. We have a clear picture of him walking across the car park.'

'Well, well. So Brian Hargreaves pops up again, eh? This time he's trying to get to Kate Melcham. That can only mean that he was either trying to warn her off or worse still, do her some kind of harm. Either way, it suggests that she's got something over him.'

'Someone must have disturbed him,' Martin replied. 'According to the swipe card system software, he was in the room with Kate for less than a minute.'

'Thank God they did, otherwise we may have had another murder on our hands.'

'We've also done a complete scan of the car park both on foot and on camera but there's no further footage or sign of him,' said Martin.

'OK good work son. We know that he's since left the area as we've managed to track his mobile to the West Midlands, so I've asked our colleagues over there to keep an eye out for him. The only problem is that we don't know what he's driving now. Still, he can't hide out for long.'

Wesley hoped he wouldn't regret that comment.

'I've increased the security at the hospital, sir. We have a constable stationed outside Kate's room 24/7 now. Are you planning to speak with Kate tomorrow?'

'Yes I am, if the damn doctors will allow me enough time with her. Apparently she keeps slipping in and out of consciousness, although I'm told she is slowly improving.'

'Well that's got to be a good sign,' Martin replied.

'Yeah totally agree. It's time you got yourself off home. I'll meet you in the office first thing tomorrow.'

'OK, sir. Have a good evening. I hope Jane makes that cup of tea for you.'

'I think there's more chance of you buying the beers tomorrow.'

Wesley woke with a heavy head. After he'd finished speaking with Martin the previous evening he and Jane had paid a visit to their local pub where the beers had slipped down too easily. Jane's yoga class had been cancelled so she took the opportunity to visit the local with Wesley. They had deliberately not talked about work once they arrived at the pub although the discussion on the way had been about the existence of Griffin Abbey. The pub had been busy and they'd had to stand at the bar for half an hour before Jane noticed two women vacating a table by the window. Jane grabbed a chair while Wesley took a handful of empty glasses to the bar. When he returned he found Jane reading a leaflet that one of the women had left on the table. It was a timetable of the events at the local church.

'We really ought to show our faces,' Jane remarked, using a pen to underline a couple of dates.

'Yeah I know,' Wesley sighed. 'It's just a case of finding time.'

'I can't remember the last time I heard you sing in church.'

Jane couldn't hide the smirk on her face.

'It's probably the last time I managed to empty one.'

Just at that moment their friends and neighbours, Keith and Dawn Harrington entered the pub and immediately made their way over. What started out to be a quiet evening turned out to be a heavy session that Wesley was to pay for.

Still nursing his hangover Wesley left a message at the station to say he'd be in later as he wanted to speak with the builders regarding the Griffin Abbey. He failed to mention that it also gave him time to take another couple of paracetamol.

Young Danny Coles was the first to arrive. Wesley approached him at the side of the house where Danny was checking the excavations from the previous day.

'Good morning, son' said Wesley, 'how's the extension coming along?'

'Oh good morning, yeah it's good. I was just looking at how much rain had settled in the bottom of the footings. We had quite a downpour last night.'

'Yeah I know. Jane and I were caught in it walking back from the pub,' Wesley replied rolling a cigarette. 'Tell me, what do you know about the Griffin Abbey?'

'You mean the place we were discussing with Jane yesterday? It's mostly a heap of ruins now; well certainly what's left above ground is anyway.'

'Sorry, I don't follow.'

'I'm afraid I'm too young to know much about the history to the place, Inspector, but as kids we used to sneak into the Melcham estate and play amongst the ruins of the old Abbey. Above ground there's nothing left but rubble except the remains of a flight of steps that lead to nowhere, but below ground there are a couple of rooms that used to appear almost untouched, kind of stuck in a time warp. I've no idea what they're like now though.'

'Can you still get to them?' Wesley asked exhaling cigarette smoke high into the air.

'I guess so,' Danny replied shrugging his shoulders. 'To be honest I haven't been over there for years. The whole place is probably overgrown now so it may be hard to find the entrance.'

'Would you be able to take me there? I'm intrigued.'

'Has this got something to do with the recent murders?' Danny asked.

'I'd rather not comment at this stage, son. Let's just say I'm intrigued.'

Danny leant his shovel up against the side of the house and wiped the dirt from his hands onto his already mud splattered jeans.

'OK sure, no problem. When did you want to go there?'

'Whenever is convenient, Danny. I appreciate you're busy and Jane would kill me if she thought I was stopping you from working.'

'I can take you over there after work if you like?'

'That would be great. I'll pick you up from here at say seven o'clock, if that's OK with you?'

'That's fine, Mr Wesley. That gives me time to pop home and get something to eat first. Now I'd better try getting some of this rain water out of the footings otherwise your extension is going nowhere.'

Wesley turned back just as he was about to leave.

'Oh and just one other thing, Danny. I'd prefer it if no one else knows about this. If it's still possible to gain access to the place I don't want a load of other people traipsing around the place.'

'I understand, Mr Wesley.'

The rehearsals for his next show seemed to be dragging on forever. James Harper sat pencilling a sketch on his notepad when he felt his mobile vibrate in his pocket. He checked that no one was stood behind him before retrieving the phone from his jacket pocket to read the text. As soon as he'd digested the content he knew he had to take matters into his own hands.

Kate was sat propped up in bed by two enormous pillows listening to the quiet classical background music that was playing from the radio that Nurse Chapman has kindly brought into the room earlier that day. Her relaxation was suddenly disturbed when the music stopped for the lunchtime news and the presenter mentioned a fire at Penbury Farm. The presenter went on to say that the body found in the ruins of the farmhouse had been identified as Henry Morgan, a local business man. The presenter then went on to say that his daughter Felicity Morgan was recently found murdered on the Melcham estate and police were refusing to rule out any connection between the two incidents.

Kate suddenly remembered Brian Hargreaves mentioning something about Henry Morgan when she'd questioned him about the woman's body being found in the coal shed behind Rowan Lodge. Now what was it he said? Kate pressed the panic button next to the bed sending Nurse Chapman running down the corridor.

'What's wrong Kate?' she asked leaning over the bed so that she could hear Kate's whispered reply.

Kate was still making steady progress and over the past twenty-four hours had been steadily mumbling a few words, mostly to herself.

'I want to speak with the police,' Kate slurred.

'Say that again, Kate.'

'It's the police. I need to speak with the police.'

'Do you want me to call, Inspector Wesley? He's been in to see you a couple of times.'

Kate nodded. 'Yes,' she sighed. 'I think I know who it was who visited me yesterday.'

Sally Morgan walked out of the shop and glanced up and down the High Street before crossing the road and heading towards the multi-storey car park.

Moments after she had turned into the alleyway leading to the back stairs, WPC Alison Bolt handed her car keys to a colleague, dashed across the road and entered the shop. As soon as she closed the door behind her a bell tinkled somewhere at the back of the shop and she heard the shuffle of footsteps. The elderly shopkeeper dressed in a blue tee-shirt and a pair of flowery braces that appeared to be about to burst from the strain of keeping his huge belly in his trousers, appeared through a doorway behind the counter. He surveyed Alison by squinting over the top of his flat rimmed glasses.

'Good morning madam, how can I help you?'

Alison thrust her ID in front of his face. 'WPC Alison Bolt, there was a woman in here just now. Can you tell me what she purchased?'

The shopkeeper looked aghast at the police ID before replying.

'Have I done something wrong?' he mumbled.

'That depends on what you sold her,' Alison replied.

'The lady purchased a small hand gun, ideal for a beginner.'

'What do you mean a beginner?'

'She said she had recently joined her local shooting club and wanted something to practice with. A gun that wasn't too heavy, but one that she wouldn't look out of place with in front of other club members.'

'Did she pay by card?'

'No cash, but all my customers have to sign a form to say they have a firearms licence.'

'Can you show me where she signed her signature?'

The old boy reached under the counter and brought out a large A5 sized register. He flicked it open to the page where the last signature was, then turned it around to allow Alison to read it. She followed her finger across the last entry as she read the details. It showed type of weapon, description and make, ammunition details, total cost, name and address and finally a signature. Alison took a photo of the page with her mobile before turning the book around.

'Is everything alright?' the shopkeeper asked nervously.

'Except for the name and address,' she replied. 'Next time you sell someone a firearm I suggest you check their ID.'

As soon as the shop door slammed closed the old boy took off his glasses and peered down at the register. The name and address provided by Sally Morgan related to a cartoon character living in the hundred acre wood.

When Wesley entered the station he went straight to the men's locker room where he found Martin stepping out of wet trousers.

'Nice boxers,' Wesley commented.

Martin jumped as soon as Wesley spoke.

'Sorry, sir, I didn't think anyone else was about. My trousers are drenched. I got halfway up the hill when it started to pour down.'

'Who's got the patrol car then?'

'Alison. She took it last night to keep an eye on Sally Morgan.'

'Put those trousers on the radiator then and for God's sake put on a spare pair. The sight of you walking around without your trousers is enough to put anyone off their food.'

'Yes sir.'

'And by the way, don't worry about finding a clean pair of trousers. We're going below ground tonight.'

'Sir?'

'Don't worry, I'll explain later.'

Wesley went up his office and sat down behind the desk and immediately noticed he had a message waiting on the office phone. It was from Nurse Chapman saying that Kate was asking to speak with him. Wesley met Martin halfway down the stairs.

'If you're respectably dressed now you'd better come with me. We're going to the hospital to speak with Kate Melcham.'

The drive to the hospital had already taken nearly an hour due to the council's decision to start digging a large hole along the only main road in and out of Wells, and now they were stuck behind a tractor whose driver seemed intent on keeping everyone waiting behind him. Martin could see that Wesley was getting impatient.

'I'm afraid it's one of the hazards of working in the country, sir. There are so many farms around here there's a tractor down every road,' he said trying to hide the grin on his face.

Wesley didn't respond so Martin thought it was better to change the subject.

'So where are we off to tonight?'

'Ever heard of Griffin Abbey?'

'No sir, where is it?'

'On the Melcham estate apparently, laying in ruins.'

'So what is there to see?'

'That's what we're going to find out.'

Wesley could see the quizzical look on Martin's face.

'I thought you enjoyed being below ground. We spent enough time looking under the Tor last year.'

'If you remember correctly, sir, it was me who stayed on the surface most of the time, getting wet.'

'Well now's your chance to prove yourself,' Wesley replied laughing.

He then explained what Danny Coles had told him about the Griffin Abbey and how coincidental it seemed for Annie to have the same name.

'Maybe there is something in it,' Martin replied. 'It's strange there's no mention of the place on the web though.'

The hospital was as busy as ever and they agreed to wait in reception for Nurse Chapman who was dealing with an emergency. Wesley said he would wait outside and left Martin sat next to a sweet machine. Wesley hated the smell of hospitals. It still reminded him of the day his wife was killed. A memory that part of him wanted to forget yet he knew he never could. He'd just missed Jane who had finished her morning shift on the reception desk. When Nurse Chapman eventually appeared she looked harassed and ruffled from her normal appearance.

'I'm sorry to keep you waiting, Inspector. We're short staffed today, on a day when a bicyclist decides to play tag with an articulated lorry. I've had to change the poor lads dressing twice already this morning.'

Wesley tried to block out any mental picture, he didn't think he could stomach it today. 'That's alright, I fully understand.'

When they entered the room Kate Melcham was sitting up in bed, propped up by several pillows. The bed had also been raised to provide more comfort. Someone had combed her hair and she was wearing a trace of make-up. The transformation was amazing and her femininity was certainly not lost on Martin who didn't stop smiling at the patient.

'Hello, Kate, how are you feeling now?'

Wesley took both of her hands in his and leaning over the bed he kissed her on the cheek. Kate smiled and squeezed his hand.

'Good, thanks,' she whispered.

'Nurse Chapman tells me that you want to talk to me. Is that right?'

Kate took a deep intake of breath before answering.

'Lucy's in danger.'

Wesley looked puzzled.

'I don't understand. Why do you think she's in trouble? I thought she was being looked after by the Abbey? Even James Harper told me that she was being cared for.'

Suddenly Kate's whole body became rigid. She opened her mouth to speak but no words came out.

'What's wrong Kate? What did I say?'

'I'm sorry, Inspector,' Nurse Chapman interrupted. 'I'm going to have to ask you to leave. My patient is becoming stressed, and in her condition that is extremely dangerous.'

With reluctance Wesley and Martin both left the room closing the door quietly behind them, leaving Nurse Chapman administering a sedative for her patient.

Martin could see the concern on Wesley's face.

'I wonder what caused that reaction, sir. I mean, as soon as you mentioned the Abbey, Kate reacted as if you'd just stuck a needle into a nerve.'

'Perhaps that what I did, perhaps the Abbey isn't what it seems.'

'Sorry, sir, I don't understand.'

Wesley scratched his head.

'It might just be me, Martin. But every time I mention the Abbey people seem to clam up. I'm not so sure any more what the Abbey's objectives are.'

'Do you think it's possible they kidnapped Lucy instead of what we're being led to believe in that they simply took her somewhere to keep her safe.'

Wesley screwed his eyes and ran his hand over his face.

'Son, I'm not sure what's going on.'

When Nurse Chapman reappeared she made it quite clear that her patient was to see no one else for the rest of the day.

'I don't know what was said, Inspector, and it's probably none of my business. However, the result is that my patient appears to have had a panic attack. I've given her a sedative which will make her sleep for a few hours. I'll keep an eye on her and let you know later how she is.'

Wesley thanked the nurse and said he appreciated everything they were doing for Kate and that it was unfortunate that he needed to ask questions if he was going to get anywhere with their enquiries.

As he and Martin were walking across the hospital car park he received a call from Alison explaining that Sally Morgan had just purchased a gun and that WPC Fielding was trailing Sally in an unmarked car. Wesley asked for

WPC Fielding to report in every hour. He then provided Martin with a brief update as they got in the car.

'I can't imagine someone like Sally Morgan handling a gun,' said Martin.

'The problem is that she probably can't, and that makes her just as dangerous if not more,' Wesley replied.

24

Annie Griffin laid the contents of the carrier bag on the kitchen table. She had just lit the coal fire and was waiting for it to take, before throwing some more photos on it. In amongst the photos was the bundle of letters that Alison had previously come across at Melcham Hall. Annie held them in her hand and toyed with the idea of untying the ribbon that kept them together so she could read them. 'No,' she thought, 'There are some things are best left in the past.' She placed the bundle of letters on the fire and stood watching as they slowly started to burn. A tear ran down her face and she brushed it aside with the back of her hand before returning to the table to gather up the remaining photos.

The phone call from Brian Hargreaves had come as a shock. Annie had known for years that he was only ever after one thing, the Melcham estate. He didn't love Lucy, all he'd ever done was to keep her in the comforts she was used to, waiting for the day when upon their 10th wedding anniversary he would be become half owner of the estate as per Sir Clive Melcham's will. The trouble was, Lucy knew about his debts and threatened to end the marriage which would have left him with nothing. That's when he'd approached Annie for advice. It was then that she saw the ideal opportunity to claim back what she believed was rightfully hers. It was just a shame that Lucy refused to co-operate and had to be confined elsewhere. Brian Hargreaves had managed to persuade Kate back to Melcham Hall on the understanding that as long as she followed his rules, her sister would remain unharmed. Annie once again saw a light at the end of the tunnel. However, it now appeared that the idiot Hargreaves had decided to take things into his own hands by attempting to poison Kate, except he had given her too much thallium causing her to collapse and be taken to hospital. Now of course, even if she survived, there was no way she would help Hargreaves any more.

It was when Henry VIII had closed all the Abbeys and monasteries, stripping them of their wealth, that he ripped the heart out of Annie's family, the Griffins. When the Melcham family bought the land they not only left the Abbey to decay and crumble, they threw the Griffin family out on the streets and stole all their possessions. But now Annie had the chance to claw them back, to regain what was rightfully hers and to be the owner of the Melcham estate, to realise a lifetime's dream. She loved Kate and Lucy but she had to do what was right for her ancestors, her own family, the Griffin family. She watched the last of the photographs burn before making a phone call to advise someone where Hargreaves was staying.

Jane was decidedly bored at home. There was little she could do whilst the builders were constantly traipsing in and out of the kitchen for buckets of water to help mix the concrete for the foundations. Gathering a few bits and pieces together she left the builders the spare house key and headed towards the bus stop. With the children still being off school, the bus was packed and the journey into Glastonbury took over thirty-five minutes. The old book shop where she used to work had now been closed for over a year and had been replaced by a second-hand bookshop run by Gerry Callow, a well-known local eccentric of enormous proportions and known to locals as the gentle giant.

The doorbell jingled as Jane entered the shop. At first she thought the shop was empty until a voice called out behind a pile of books on a far table.

'I'll be with you in a moment.'

'What kind of service do you call this?' Jane replied trying not to laugh.

A mass of black curly hair appeared at table height before the bearded face of Gerry Callow looked over the top of the pile of books.

'Jane! Give me one second. I'm just tidying the place a little.'

'That'll be the day, you'll never find a damn book then,' Jane replied bursting into laughter.

Gerry Callow ambled across the bookshop and gave Jane a huge hug. Standing over six feet four inches tall and weighing more than twenty stone, he was like a giant bear and dwarfed the diminutive Jane. Some of the local children nicknamed him "Hagrid" a character from the Harry Potter series.

'It's good to see you. What brings you into town?' he asked.

'To be honest we've got builders in doing some work on an extension and I'm in their way, so I thought what better than to pay my friend Gerry a visit and treat him to lunch.'

He let go of Jane and patted his rotund belly.

'That gives me enormous pleasure,' he replied as his whole frame shook with laughter.

'Give me two minutes and I'll close up for an hour. Trade has been quiet today so it won't hurt to close up for an hour.'

He pulled a chair out from a small recess in the back of the shop.

'Make yourself comfortable, I won't be a moment.'

Jane picked up a couple of local newspapers to read while Gerry got himself ready. She paused for a moment to look around the shop. Nothing had changed since her last visit except that Gerry had kept the shop a little tidier. In addition to a more spacious look, there were now a number of incense sticks burning in little jars on several shelves. Jane placed the newspapers on the chair and walked across to view a row of books on a shelf situated above an antiquated type writer. The label read "Local History".

Surprisingly enough the titles were in some kind of alphabetical order. Running her finger along the line she came to where book titles starting with the letter M would have been, except there weren't any.

'Looking for anything in particular?' Gerry asked appearing from the back room, now looking more respectable having combed his hair and changed his tee-shirt for a coloured shirt that wouldn't have looked out of place on the beach in Hawaii 5 - 0.

'Yes, actually I was. I was looking for something on Melcham Hall.'

'Ah well you're too late there I'm afraid,' Gerry replied stroking his beard.

Jane turned around, a puzzled look on her face.

'A woman came in yesterday asking for the same thing. There were only two books referring to Melcham. She bought both of them, didn't even ask me the price. To be honest I'd have probably given them away, they've been here since I took over the shop.'

'What did she look like, this woman?' Jane asked.

'I didn't take much notice really, quite an elderly lady. Don't tell me it's some kind of competition,' Gerry replied laughing, 'grab as many books with the word Melcham in them.'

'What were the books about?'

Gerry could sense that Jane was being serious.

'What's up, Jane. What's going on?'

Jane explained that she'd been searching the web for information about Melcham Abbey only to find out that the place had actually been known as Griffin Abbey. She turned back to look along the shelf.

'She looked in all the G's too,' said Gerry now sounding not so confident.

'Have you seen her in here before?' Jane asked.

'No I haven't, but a lady who came in just as she was leaving recognised her, because she said hello and the two of them stood talking in the doorway for several minutes. Letting all the cold air in, they were.'

'Did she say what the lady's name was?'

'Not to me but when the old lady left I'm sure she said goodbye, Mrs Griffin.'

There wasn't a spare seat in the small café. Although the food had never been exceptional it was reasonably priced but the big attraction and benefit was that it stood on the opposite side of the road to the entrance to Glastonbury Abbey and therefore was a magnet for the tourists. Jane said they would wait for a table to become free so they stood just inside the doorway, close to the front window much to a young couples annoyance who had been trying to take a photo of the entrance to the Abbey from where they were sat. They only had to wait a few minutes before a middle-aged couple with a young child vacated a table half way down the shop. As soon as the waitress had cleaned the table they ordered lunch, a jacket potato with prawns for Jane, and fish and chips for Gerry with two slices of bread. Jane couldn't help overhearing some of the gossip around her. If she was honest she'd missed working in the town, listening to everyday life. Lunch appeared quite promptly and Gerry was soon tucking into his fish and chips as if he hadn't eaten for days.

'So how's your mother keeping these days?' Jane asked.

'She's doing OK,' he replied with a mouthful of fish. 'Getting her moved into the nursing home was the best thing we've ever done. They look after her real good.'

Jane recalled the days when she first met Gerry; his mother was always clung to his arm. Now, in just a short space of time, a year or less, she was virtually house bound and a nursing home had been the only option. Gerry used to work in Woolworths on the sweet counter and Jane often thought he would have frightened most of the children because of his size but he was extremely popular and the children knew him as the friendly giant. By the time lunch was over Gerry had a splatter of tomato sauce and tea stains down his freshly ironed shirt.

'So how's the book shop going?' asked Jane after she had insisted on paying for lunch. 'It certainly looks better since we cleared some of the junk out.'

'Ticking over would be the safest answer, Jane. The poor economy has led to a reduction in the tourist trade as you know, and the few that do come down aren't spending any money. I hear they plan to increase admission prices to the Abbey next year. I just don't understand the economics. Why increase the price when already fewer people are visiting?'

Jane didn't want to get involved in a discussion about the economic rights and wrongs affecting the tourist industry so turned the conversation back to the running of the bookshop.

'Have you thought about selling anything else other than second-hand books?'

'I'd sell contraceptives to the pope to help pay the rent,' Gerry replied laughing, 'the trouble around here is that we rely mainly on tourists and they want to buy something different to what they can get at home.'

'How long have you lived in Glastonbury?' Jane enquired as she thanked the waitress for taking their plates away.

'All of my life, Jane. I was born just a couple of streets from here.'

'Then you'll know all there is to know about the town, am I right?'

'Not much I don't know. I could tell you the history of Glastonbury back to the days of King Arthur. Why do you ask, Jane?'

'I hear that old Sam Thompson is looking to step down from running that tour bus of his. Why don't you offer to drive that around town a couple of days a week? It'll get you out of the shop for a few hours and if you were able to you could situate one of the stops conveniently outside the shop.'

'Do you know, I might just do that,' Gerry replied toying with his beard.

Jane could just imagine Gerry standing at the bus terminus looking like Hagrid as he directed people onto the bus.

'What about running the shop? I'd be losing potential sales however few, if the shop was closed a couple of days a week.'

'That's something I was going to speak to you about,' Jane replied.

Brian Hargreaves sat on the edge of the bed counting his remaining cash.

He knew he couldn't get money from a cashpoint as there would be a trace put out on his card, and there was also the possibility that the bank had been told to freeze his account. He switched his mobile back on and hit the redial to the number he'd tried twice before earlier that morning. It rang several times before cutting into voicemail again. He cursed, left a message, then switched his phone off and threw it back on the bed. Grabbing the cigarette packet from the dressing table he extracted the last one, lit it and inhaled. His mind was racing. He knew he couldn't stay in the hotel forever; he only had enough cash for another two nights. If only his contact would answer. He started to wonder if he was ever going to get any further help. Then a horrible thought occurred to him. What if they thought he might squeal on them? Would they come after him? He took another long drag on his cigarette and noticed that his hand was shaking. He stubbed the remains of the cigarette out in the ashtray and threw the empty packet into the waste bin. The dirty grey curtains that draped precariously across the window gave him a little privacy but also blocked his view of the front car park. He was straining to look over the hotel entrance when a knock on the door almost made his heart stop beating. He stood in silence, rooted to the spot as time seemed to stand still. Another knock on the door was followed by someone trying to turn the handle but he had locked the door from the inside. He waited several minutes until he heard the faintest of footsteps walking away from the door. Hargreaves crossed the room in a few quick strides and put his ear to the door. He could feel the vein in his temple throbbing as his whole body seemed to go into panic overdrive. It was some while before he managed to compose himself enough to peer outside. The corridor was empty but there was a note hanging on the door knob. He removed it and closed the door again quietly. Leaning back against the door he looked down at the note he was holding in sweaty hands. The notice read, "Room service. Room not cleaned".

Hargreaves sighed and slid down to the floor with his back against the door.

'Get a grip,' he said to himself, 'get a grip'.

Wesley spent most of the afternoon catching up on paperwork, the one part of the job that he disliked. WPC Mandy Tredwell had finally taken leave and would be in a sunnier climate for a week, a break that she thoroughly deserved thought Wesley. He had sent Martin and Alison over to Melcham

Hall to take another look around. This time they had a search warrant even though it was unlikely that Hargreaves would turn up. WPC Fielding was still keeping tabs on Sally Morgan and was expected to phone in every hour. As there was still no sign of Hargreaves he'd now asked for assistance from several other counties. Terry Austin had confirmed that Henry Morgan had probably died due to a blow to the back of the head, however as the skeleton remains were in such poor condition it was more guesswork than absolute fact.

An extensive search of the remains of the burnt out farmhouse and the grounds had failed to yield any further information and Wesley was becoming frustrated with their lack of progress. He decided to make a rare check of his emails and came across one that Mandy had posted to him the previous evening. Before he started reading it, he stood up and closed the door to his office hoping for a few minutes privacy. Once he was seated again in front of the monitor he started to read.

Hi Inspector,

I know you don't look at your emails that often, your words not mine, but I do hope you get the chance to read my mail. I'm not always very good with words but felt that I had to say something. As you well know, life in the police force can, and often is, quite stressful, and we spend most of our days fully engaged on what we're doing and forgetting about ourselves. However, when you told me last week that it was time I took some leave and said you knew it was the anniversary of me losing my child, you made me realise there is more to life than work. I do try to immerse myself into my job; it helps me forget the past for a few hours a day at least. I guess I'm just rabbiting on, what I really wanted to say was thanks for being there. Since you and Jane arrived in Street, you've been like parents to me and you've helped me to regain my confidence.

Ah well, enough blubbering on, it's time I tried on the new bikini. You never know, there may be a gorgeous hunk waiting for me.

See you in a few days. Thanks for everything.

Mandy x

Melcham Hall had stood empty for several days and as Martin and Alison entered the grand hallway the atmosphere seemed to chill them both.

'I never want to live in a place as big as this,' Alison commented. 'It gives me the creeps.'

Martin didn't want to admit as much, but he felt it too. It was almost as if the ancestors were looking down on them from some of the portraits hanging on the wood panelling in front of the balcony. The silence was almost deafening. Martin was looking upwards to the right of the hallway where the wide wooden staircase swept up to the upper floor when suddenly they both became aware of a scuffling sound coming from the kitchen. Martin nodded to Alison to indicate he was going to investigate and she was to follow behind. The kitchen door stood ajar but not enough to allow anyone to peer in so Martin gave it a little push. Just as he did so a mouse ran past his feet, and ran directly towards Alison who screamed and almost stamped on it as she ran into Martin's arms; neither of them noticed where the mouse had run to. As Alison pulled herself away she looked up into Martin's eyes and blushed. Martin smiled embarrassingly before they both looked away.

'Well, if there is anyone else here they sure know about us now,' he said breaking the ice.

Alison pulled her uniform straight and gave a polite cough.

'Err yes, I suppose so,' she stammered.

'Come on, let's check out the rest of the house,' Martin exclaimed, eager to pretend he'd not been affected by Alison's action.

They explored the rest of the house in silence as they took turns to look in every room. Two of the upstairs rooms were locked but Martin managed to gain entry in just a few minutes. It was Martin who spoke first after they'd finished checking the upstairs.

'We're missing something here but I can't put my finger on it,' he said as she lent on the balcony.

Luckily he didn't see the smirk on Alison's face.

'Be professional,' she kept saying to herself.

'There are clothes in all the wardrobes and dressing tables, don't you find that strange?'

'What do you mean strange, in what way?'

'Well, surely if Lady Hargreaves had expected to go away she would have taken clothes with her; and the same for Brian Hargreaves. His wardrobe is crammed with clothes.'

'Yeah, you've got a good point there. It's as if the whole household has just upped and left. We know that Brian Hargreaves is on the run, but where the hell is Lady Hargreaves?'

'Why would anyone want to give up a place like this?'

'Perhaps the Hargreaves' aren't as well off as they pretend to be,' Alison replied.

'I don't buy it.' Martin waved his arms in front of him. 'Just look at the furniture in this place. If the Hargreaves' were desperate for money there's a hundred things in this place worth a fortune. There's got to be another reason.'

They finished their search back in the kitchen where Martin stood looking into the larder cupboard.

'Look at the stuff in here. There's enough food to feed an army. The place is so stacked with boxes it's almost as if they're hiding something.'

'It sure makes me feel hungry,' exclaimed Alison.

Martin closed the larder door and checked that the back door was locked.

'Come on, I'll buy you lunch,' he said.

'OK, but beforehand you can drop me off at Annie's place. The Inspector asked me to drop in to make sure she was alright.'

When Annie answered the front door she was surprised to see WPC Alison Bolt standing on the doorstep.

'Why come in my dear. This is a pleasant surprise.'

Annie led the way into the kitchen where she motioned for Alison to take a seat.

'What brings you over here?' she asked.

'We've just been over to Melcham Hall to check the place out,' Alison replied. 'I don't suppose you've seen anyone around?'

'If I had, I would have been straight on the phone to you,' Annie replied extracting two clean cups from a shelf above the sink to make the customary tea. 'Have you been able to trace Brian Hargreaves yet?'

'Not yet, but half the police force in the country are on the lookout for him,' said Alison.

'I'm just nipping to the toilet, keep an eye on the kettle for me, it tends not to switch off sometimes even when the water has boiled,' said Annie.

Alison sat looking around the kitchen waiting for Annie to return. She decided to remove her jacket as the kitchen was warm. It was just as she was hanging her jacket on the back of another chair that she looked down into the grate where a piece of silk ribbon lay, burnt at one end. Alison stepped forward, picked it up and put it in her trouser pocket before Annie returned.

She remembered where she'd seen the crimson coloured silk before.

When Annie returned to the kitchen Alison made an excuse that she'd been asked to respond to an emergency in the town and said her goodbyes. Annie seemed OK and she wanted to get back to the office to inform Wesley of her suspicions.

So we now know that Annie has been in Melcham Hall,' said Wesley twisting the remains of the silk ribbon around his finger.

'If she hasn't, then she must know someone who has,' Alison replied.

'Did she ask you anything while you were there?'

'Yes, she asked if there was any news on Brian Hargreaves.'

Wesley took a deep sigh before speaking again.

'Unless Brian Hargreaves has eluded us and somehow managed to sneak back in to the building then Annie Griffin must have a key, otherwise she wouldn't have been able to gain entry,' exclaimed Martin.

'Yeah, good point. It's a question I'll have to ask her,' Wesley replied. He rested his two elbows on the desk and looked questioningly at his two colleagues. 'What are we missing here?'

'That's exactly what Martin asked when we were over at Melcham Hall, sir. I agree with him too, I don't think any of these murders or attempted murders have got anything to do with money. There is something else going on that we don't know about, something more sinister.'

'So, you found nothing there?'

'Only a mouse.'

'Sorry?'

Alison's face reddened as she remembered her reaction when the mouse ran across the hallway. She shot a quick glance at Martin who pretended to be looking at the floor.

'We saw a mouse run across the hallway. It ran out of the kitchen where it was presumably looking for food.'

Wesley looked at his two red faced colleagues and guessed there was a private joke going on.

'OK, well carry on. Alison, can you speak with WPC Fielding and get an update on what Sally Morgan is doing. Martin, don't forget we're going to explore Griffin Abbey later, so I'll meet you at my place at seven. Let's hope we find something that will help to explain some of things that are going on.'

25

Wesley had only been home for an hour when there was a knock at the front door.

'It sounds like it's time for your little excursion,' said Jane heading towards the front door to receive the visitor. Danny Coles was dressed as if he was going for a hike into the countryside. Wearing a green camouflage jacket, a pair of old jeans with tears across both of his knee caps, hiking boots and a long walking stick, the only thing missing was a trail blazers badge.

'Well you're certainly kitted out for the evening,' remarked Wesley, 'come on in, I won't be a second.'

Danny took a seat in the kitchen as Wesley got himself ready, trying desperately to get his foot in one of his old boots. PC Martin Philips was already sat at the kitchen table with a mug of coffee. Wesley did the introductions.

'Do look after them,' said Jane winking to Danny. 'The Inspector isn't as young as he used to be and Martin here doesn't like the dark.'

'I sure will,' Danny replied with a smirk on his face.

'Right I'm ready. As you seem to have my interests at heart you can lead the way.' Wesley motioned for Danny to leave.

'Do be careful dear,' Jane called out after hearing the front door close.

Martin looked at Wesley with a smirk on his face but bit his lip, deciding it was best not to make further comment. Danny suggested that he drove as he knew the quickest route and his old Ford truck was more equipped for driving off track.

'There's a short cut half way through the village across one of the many old dirt tracks. It brings you out just about a quarter of a mile from where the old Abbey used to stand.'

Wesley sat in the front passenger seat and wound down the window as he lit a roll-up. It was a mild evening for the time of year and the cloudless sky allowed the full moon to illuminate the countryside around them. Martin felt cold in the cramped back seat but didn't like to say as much. Danny was aware that he had two members of the police force in his truck and for once stuck to the speed limit.

'How long have you lived around here, Danny?' asked Wesley.

'I was born in Shepton Mallet, so all my life really, except for a couple of years I spent at University down in Exeter.'

‘So has it changed much around here over the years?’

‘There’s a lot more grockles around here now, for sure.’

‘Grockles?’

‘Aye, people who have moved down from London.’

‘Oh I see,’ Wesley replied with raised eyebrows.

‘No offence mind you, the villages needed new blood. Some people around here are stuck in a time warp. If it weren’t for the new builds going up there wouldn’t be enough work for people like me. But the countryside is changing, there’s only a few farms left now. They’re all selling up, it just doesn’t pay. Most farmers just can’t compete with the supermarkets. The government has bled our farmers dry. They’ll regret it when we get to the stage of having to import all our food products.’

Wesley looked over his shoulder at Martin who shrugged his shoulders in response. It was a debate they didn’t want to get into. A few minutes later the truck slowed as they passed the entrance to the Melcham estate.

‘We could have gone in that way,’ said Danny, ‘but the Abbey is a good half a mile further up the other side.’

At the next junction he swung a left, just avoiding a large fox as it meandered across the road.

‘Bloody vermin,’ he muttered to himself.

With the boundary of the Melcham estate on their left they carried on for another mile before passing over a small bridge. Martin tapped Wesley on the shoulder and pointed to the area where they had visited a week or so before with Archie Black. As they approached the next bend Danny took a sudden left turn, appearing to be heading straight into a hedgerow. Much to Wesley and Martin’s relief there was a narrow gap, just wide enough for a car to slip through. Wesley wondered how often Danny had taken this route as the lad appeared to have no problems negotiating the twists and turns as they drove straight into the densely wooded area of the Melcham estate. He applied the brakes just as the dirt track started to dip away in front of them. The tree canopy obscured the sky and as soon as Danny switched off the ignition and the headlights, they were sat in pitch darkness.

‘Right, I’ve got a couple of torches in the boot,’ said Danny. ‘If you two want to follow me, then no one will get lost. The path up ahead slopes away quite steeply and there’s quite a drop on our left hand side so don’t go tumbling down the embankment otherwise I’ll be spending the rest of the night trying to find you and get you out.’

‘Quite a comforting thought,’ Wesley replied.

Once Danny had gathered a few things from the boot they set off with Danny in front. Martin was at the back behind Wesley, trying desperately not to slip over. His trainers were quickly proving to be unsuitable for the slippery ground and twice he grabbed a nearby bush to prevent himself falling over. They had been walking for about five minutes when Danny stopped.

'OK, we're going to bear to the right here. It's a gradual descent before the ground levels out but we're about a hundred feet above the valley floor here. Once we reach the valley floor where the Abbey ruins are located, the area is pretty flat from there on. Is everyone OK?'

'Yeah we're fine,' Wesley replied. They walked sideways for most of the descent before they eventually reach flat ground. Here the foliage wasn't so dense and shafts of moonlight pierced the woodland floor catching a variety of moths and other insects in its path.

'At least the wild boar has disappeared from around these parts,' commented Danny. 'They were known for crippling many a man.'

'I suppose we ought to be grateful,' Martin muttered looking down at his grimy trainers that were now a different shade of white and covered in twigs.

'Just a few yards and we're there,' said Danny pointing ahead.

The only visible signs of the ruin appeared to be a number of concrete boulders protruding from the ground. Thick clumps of gorse enveloped the whole area making it difficult to know where to tread.

'Hold on a second,' said Wesley as he bent down to grab a small section of gorse bush. He shone his torch at the bright yellow seeds that now covered the palm of his hand. 'So that's where it comes from,' he muttered.

'Found something interesting?' asked Danny.

Wesley wiped the remnants from his hands.

'It's just something that I've seen before. Now I know where it grows from.'

Danny continued to lead the way and Wesley was thankful they had Danny with them as he seemed to be following an invisible path across the site. The area in front of them suddenly opened up as if a giant had swung his mace and uprooted every tree nearby. Moonlight flooded the area giving it a surreal but haunted look.

'I've stood here many times,' Danny exclaimed. 'My favourite time is spring, early evening. The place feels magical somehow.'

'It sure is peaceful,' said Wesley as he sat himself on a small boulder to catch his breath.

'Is this all there is that's left of the Abbey?' asked Martin sounding disappointed.

'It's all that's left above ground,' Danny replied. 'Come with me and let me show you the best part. You see, this was once one of the wealthiest Abbeys in the West of England, long before the old Melcham Abbey was built on top.'

Carefully negotiating the uneven ground, Danny led the way until they reached the remains of a wall that ran parallel for quite some distance. At this point he shone the torch out in front of him viewing the terrain.

'Look just ahead Mr Wesley, someone else has been here.'

A few yards ahead where the gorse had given way to a broken concrete strewn pathway there was clear evidence of several footprints in the dusty soil where the concrete was missing. As Danny moved forward, Wesley stood alongside.

'Do you think these are recent?' Wesley asked.

'It's hard to tell. Where there's no gorse the ground remains quite damp. If I had to guess though I'd say someone else has been here in the past few days for sure. In any case, let's see if we can find out what they were here for.'

Danny moved forward to a point where the derelict wall had gained a metre in height and the remains of a staircase came into view. It was an eerie sight as four uneven worn steps lead to nowhere. The remaining steps had obviously crumbled away many years previous.

'Here we are.'

Just a few feet further on Danny shone the torch to their left and sure enough, virtually hidden by the uneven ground on either side, were a number of ancient worn steps leading down to a dark void.

Sally Morgan sat in front of the television watching the local news. A news reporter was standing on the opposite side of the road to the post office in Bath where an armed robbery had taken place earlier in the day. The reporter provided details of the incident saying that a post office worker was threatened with a shorn-off shotgun before getting away with sixteen hundred pounds from the till and that a passer-by had been injured when she was knocked to the ground by one of the raiders when they ran out of the post office. The image then flicked back to the newsroom where a bald headed presenter then mentioned that police were still looking to speak with a Brian Hargreaves, who was last known to be living at Melcham Hall. The presenter said that police wanted to question the man about several matters including the disappearance of his wife, Lady Hargreaves. At the mention of his name, Sally rubbed her hand over the gun that she had on her lap. She took another drink from the small bottle of brandy she'd been cradling. Sally never drank alcohol and usually preferred to stay tea-total, but today was different and the warm tasting fluid was going straight to her head, but she was in that kind of mood.

Having just destroyed the last of the books that referred to the Abbey that she had purchased from the local bookshop, Annie Griffin sat in the small wingback chair looking through her only remaining photo album. She extracted a small black and white photo of a tall blonde haired man, muscular and wearing only a tee-shirt and pair of baggy shorts. The man was stood by the edge of the flower garden on the Melcham estate leaning on a garden rake. How handsome he looked. Annie held the photo up to the light and sighed. She still missed her husband after all these years. She placed the photo on her lap and turned the page. The next set of photos showed the children playing on the steps in the front of Melcham Hall. Kate and Lucy dressed as their father always insisted, in matching frocks with their hair tied back in pig tails. Annie recalled the fights they would get in to just to be the first to show their father what they had found after Annie had taken them for one of her 'explorative adventures' around the estate. There was another photo stuck to the corner of the page. Annie gently pulled it away to take a closer look. She recognised the young man straight away, tall and slim with long wavy black hair, wearing black trousers and a flowery white shirt. There was a pencilled note on the back of the photo which read "For my one true love x"

Having replaced the photo album in the sideboard Annie crossed the room and went in search of her coat where she placed the photos in her pocket. She carried her coat into the front room and laid it on the back of the settee before picking up the telephone.

'May I get a taxi to Wells hospital please?'

'Where the hell do these steps lead to?' Wesley asked following Danny Coles.

'You'll see,' Danny replied.

At the bottom of the steps a large wooden medieval looking door appeared to bar their way. The latch handle reluctantly snapped open sounding like a gun shot after Danny had applied some considerable pressure. Keeping the latch open he leaned on the door before it eventually resisted his demands. The stale air immediately hit their nostrils. It was a stifling, stale smell that seemed intent on warning off trespassers.

'We'll have to keep the torches switched on, there's no light down here and the floor is going to be slippery,' said Danny.

'It sounds as if you've been here recently,' Wesley commented.

Danny turned to face Wesley. 'I'll be honest with you, Inspector. The last time I came here was about a year ago with my girlfriend.'

Wesley raised his eyebrows.

'No nothing like that, Inspector. I just wanted to show her how beautiful this place is. I'm really into old places, ruins, you know, that kind of thing and thought long about going into archaeology but there's no money in it.'

'Is that why you've been excavating the Inspector's home?' asked Martin trying to hide a smirk.

'Let's just get on with this shall we?' Wesley replied.

They descended another small flight of steps before the ground evened out. At this point Danny turned back to point upwards before pointing his torch to the ceiling above. As soon as Wesley and Martin followed suit, raising their torches, they stood in awe at the scene above them. The ceiling was one large painted mural. The heavenly scenes of baby Jesus, Mary, Angels, the gates of heaven and numerous biblical characters stared down upon them. The men stood in silence as their torch lights shone around the domed ceiling. Wesley nodded his head as he tried to take it all in.

'I now understand what you were saying.'

'What do all these symbols mean?' Martin asked shining his torch at the numerous multi-shaped symbols that adorned each drawing.

'I don't know,' Danny answered, 'I've never really understood them but they appear everywhere and if you look around the edge of the ceiling you'll see there are numerous griffins looking in on the scene. What do you think, Inspector?'

Wesley was staring at the symbol that appeared in the centre of the ceiling directly above their heads. It was the symbol ۞۞۞.

'I think I've seen this one before,' he replied. He lowered his torch as he searched for the sheet of A4 paper in his jacket pocket. Unravelling the paper he held it up against the nearest wall for Danny and Martin to view.

'I know this is only a pencil sketch but it sure as hell looks pretty much identical to me,' he said.

'That's because it is,' Danny replied. 'Where did you copy that from?'

'I didn't. It was drawn by the local pathologist. The same design was on the arm of one of our murder victims and someone I know is wearing a brooch of the same design.'

'Jesus,' cried Danny, 'I'm sorry, Inspector, but that's too spooky for me.'

'I think it's more than coincidental,' exclaimed Martin.

Wesley returned the sheet of paper to his pocket and continued to explore the room. The room they were in was vast, some ten metres in length and half as wide. Although the ceiling was painted with a mural of the heavens, the walls which had once been stark white were now grubby and full of pit holes as if ornaments or tapestries had long been removed.

'What was this place used for?' asked Martin.

'I believe once upon a time there were three similar rooms here, all used for worship,' Danny replied.

'Three?'

'Yeah, look at the far wall.'

Danny shone his torch at the back wall where a blocked doorway was clearly visible.

'How long has it been bricked up?' Wesley asked.

'As long as I remember, it was probably done donkey's years ago but a friend once told me that it used to lead to two other rooms, slightly smaller than this one.'

'Were these the only rooms below ground level?'

Martin hoped the answer was yes, he didn't fancy exploring any further.

'Except for the crypt,' said Danny. 'I've never found it but apparently there was one. You see, this is all that remains of the Griffin Abbey because the old Melcham Hall was built upon it.'

'I still don't understand why there is so much secrecy about the Abbey?' Wesley interrupted. 'No one seems to want to talk about it, and there's not even mention of it on the internet. Doesn't that strike you as odd?'

'My old man used to say there were several stories about the Abbey, it depended on who you spoke to, but at the end of the day you had to make your own mind up as to which were old wives tales and which were fact.'

'What happened to the people living in the Abbey?' It was Wesley who asked the question.

'Historically they were all murdered, except for those who escaped persecution. However, in more recent years I'm not sure.'

'I'm beginning to think that history tells me that we shouldn't be here,' exclaimed Martin, who was now feeling rather nervous about the whole place.

He kept trying to diminish thoughts of being trapped down there along with ghosts from the past who might be looking for revenge and was relieved when Wesley suggested they headed back up. Martin led the way, with Danny closing the huge wooden door behind them. Back outside, even Danny seemed to be glad to be standing under the moonlight, breathing in fresh air.

The three of them sat at the top of the steps while their eyes adjusted to the evening light.

'I don't understand why archaeologists aren't traipsing all over the site,' exclaimed Martin. 'Surely, this place is an archaeologist's paradise?'

'It's because they've not been allowed permission,' said Danny. 'I know a couple of local archaeologists who have tried more than once to get permission to dig this place but the Melchams' have always refused to have the place touched.'

'Can they do that?' Wesley looked puzzled.

'Apparently so, as it belongs to the Melcham estate. It's only when a site is listed for redevelopment that archaeologists have the right to apply for access to the site when there is sufficient evidence to suggest historical interest.'

'So all the time the place is left derelict then no one is allowed to touch it?'

'That's about right, Inspector.'

'Why wouldn't the Melcham family want the place opened up to archaeologists or even members of the public unless there was something they wanted remained hidden?'

Wesley started at Martin whose question was worthy of an answer.

'You're absolutely right, Martin. I think it's time we asked Kate that very question.'

'Or Annie Griffin,' Martin replied.

Brian Hargreaves switched his mobile phone on and checked for messages. There were none. In a rage he dropped the phone to the floor and repeatedly stamped on it, laughing hysterically. He slumped back on the bed, sweating from his excursions. He was trying to think of his next move but the more he tried to think the more the vein in his temple seemed to throb. Going back to Melcham Hall wasn't an option and now his only contact with the outside world wasn't answering. Leaning across the bed he reached for his jacket in search of change for the cigarette machine that was located down in the hotel reception. He grabbed the door pass before opening the door. There was no one in the corridor so closing the door quietly behind him he made his way downstairs and crossed the foyer to where the cigarette machine was next to the entrance to the restaurant. Looking through the glass doors he could see that the restaurant was still busy as people were queued in the buffet self service area. He was hungry but he couldn't afford to be spotted by someone in the restaurant.

Having obtained the packet of cigarettes he ventured back up the staircase and made his way swiftly back to his room. He placed the door pass in the slot and turned the door handle. Just as the lock clicked open he heard someone whisper his name. Turning around, the last thing he saw was the smile on the face of his attacker as the syringe plunged into his neck and blackness followed.

Kate was sat up in bed. Although her speech was still a little slurred and she slept most of the time, she had just started taking solid food for the first time since being admitted to hospital. She tried to concentrate on the TV screen on the far wall but her mind kept drifting. She remembered receiving an unexpected phone call from Brian Hargreaves when she was living in France and had a vague recollection of returning to Melcham Hall but for some reason her mind kept wanting to take her back to her childhood when she and her sister would watch Antoine. He taught them so many things, not only how to dance but he knew what each bird was called, the names of trees and flowers and was even knowledgeable about herbs and poisons. There wasn't anything he didn't know. Her thoughts were disturbed when a nurse entered the room to remove her dinner tray which she had hardly touched.

'Are you sure you can't eat any more?'

'I've had sufficient, thank you.'

The nurse placed the food tray to one side and tidied the bed clothes.

'There, that's better. Is there anything else I can get you?'

'No, I'm fine.'

'In that case shall I switch the TV off now my love?' she asked.

'Please,' murmured, Kate. 'Oh, and by the way, could you please tell Inspector Wesley I would like to talk with him tomorrow?'

'Of course, sleep well.'

Left alone again in her solitary confinement Kate lay facing the window where a cloudless sky allowed her to stare up at a full moon. She gently drifted back to sleep, back to her childhood days when life seemed so much clearer.

26

The following morning Alison was sat behind her desk proof reading a report she'd just written about Sally Morgan when Wesley arrived.

'Good morning, can't you sleep either?' Wesley asked as he pulled up a chair opposite.

'Morning, sir,' she replied trying to stifle a yawn. 'I wanted to get my paperwork up to date before I did anything else today. Not only that but I've been doing some research into the origins of Melcham Hall.'

'What's bugging you?'

'Everything, well I mean, Brian Hargreaves obviously wants to own the place. He thinks it's his by rights. Kate comes back from France, but for what reason, certainly not to marry Brian Hargreaves? Does she want to own Melcham Hall or has she come back to help her sister? Then there's Annie Griffin, a sweet old lady one would like to think, but the more I get to know her, the more uneasy I feel. Not forgetting, Antoine Bergerac. Did he come back from France just to find Kate?'

Wesley suddenly sat forward. 'France?'

'What's up, sir? What did I say?'

Wesley put his elbows on the table and his hands under his chin as if in prayer.

'I wonder if Antoine knew why Kate had come back.'

He raised an arm just as Alison was about to speak. 'Hold on. What if Antoine and Kate was already an item in France before they both came to England? What if he thought Kate was in trouble and tried to help her?'

'But, sir, didn't O'Hara say that Kate lived on her own?'

'He said that the local barman thought she was single, but maybe she wasn't.'

Alison chewed on the end of her pencil.

'It's worth asking O'Hara if he'll snoop around a bit more,' she said.

'Yeah you're right. I think I need to make a phone call. Maybe the answer lies over there.'

'Alison, can you get on to the authorities and find out when Antoine Bergerac, alias Ted Drake came back into the country and see if there are any previous travel records that may be of interest? You might want to do the same for Kate.'

‘What do you mean she’s missing?’ Wesley had just returned to his desk to answer the phone to an apologetic young constable who had sat in his vehicle overnight around the corner from Sally Morgan’s house.

‘When I took over from WPC Fielding last night, Sally Morgan’s car was still parked in the drive at the side of the bungalow, but now the car has gone,’ he stammered. ‘It was there when I last looked around four a.m. but it’s not there now.’

Wesley rubbed his tired eyes. It was apparent that the young constable had fallen asleep while he was meant to be watching the house. Wesley had spent numerous nights trawling the streets of London on similar exercises in his younger days so he knew just how easy it was to fall asleep in the early hours of the morning. He knew there was little point in screaming at the young lad.

‘OK, well there’s not much we can about it now. Put out an APB on Sally Morgan’s vehicle. Let’s hope it turns up somewhere soon.’

‘Yes sir. Sorry sir,’ was the nervous reply.

‘What’s your name lad?’

‘Parker, sir. Gerry Parker.’

‘In that case Constable Gerry Parker I suggest you head home and get some sleep, but make sure you provide me with an update at midday.’

‘Yes sir. Thank you, sir.’

Wesley placed the phone back on the receiver and sat back in his chair with a thoughtful look on his face.

‘Oh hell!’ he cried two minutes later when he realised he’d left his tobacco at home.

It was room service who found Brian Hargreaves’ body slumped on the floor just inside the door to his room. Her screams attracted the attention of several other guests who rushed out into the corridor to investigate. Twenty minutes later two police cars and an ambulance screeched into the hotel car park. The paramedics announced Hargreaves was dead and summoned for a local doctor who less than an hour later certified the death. It was the doctor’s opinion that the deceased had died somewhere between nine and ten o’clock the previous evening. Hargreaves’ wallet was found on the bedside table containing just twenty pounds in cash and a credit card. It was only when one of the attending officers relayed Hargreaves’ name back to the station did they realise he was the man wanted by Street police. Wesley had taken the call asking what had been the cause of death. It was when he was advised that it was too early at this stage to tell, as there were no obvious wounds or marks on the body that he asked for a blood test to be carried out. As soon as he replaced the receiver he passed the details to Martin and Alison.

‘Well we can rule out Sally Morgan,’ said Martin. ‘We know she was at home yesterday evening.’

‘And she would have probably shot him,’ Alison exclaimed.

‘Which means we have another killer on our hands,’ said Wesley.

Alison and Martin spent the next couple of hours updating their notes whilst Wesley did the same, updating the wipe board at the same time, adding Brian Hargreaves as the latest victim. His train of thought was interrupted by a young admin clerk stood in the doorway waving a piece of paper.

'Sorry to interrupt, sir. A fax has just come through for you.'

Wesley quickly read the details then placed the fax on the table. He took a deep sigh before speaking.

'OK, thanks son. Can you ask Martin and Alison to come into my office?'

As soon as they were sat, Wesley provided them with an update.

'It seems that whoever killed Hargreaves was no amateur. The local pathologist says he found a needle mark on the deceased's neck and an initial blood test has confirmed a high quantity of thallium in the blood stream, enough apparently to kill several people.'

It was Alison who replied first.

'So is it possible than Brian Hargreaves was innocent all along and that our assumptions have been wrong?'

'No, Brian Hargreaves was involved, to what extent I'm not certain yet but I've also just had a report back from the forensic guys over at the old farmhouse. Apart from the tyre tracks from Henry Morgan's car, the only other tracks at the back of the farmhouse belong to Hargreaves' burnt out jaguar.'

It was Martin who spoke first.

'So we're assuming that Hargreaves killed Morgan before driving up to the Midlands.'

'It looks that way,' Wesley replied. 'I want you to take a drive to the hotel, Alison. I assume the hotel room and corridor have been cordoned off while the forensic team search for evidence. I understand they've found a witness who says she saw someone driving out of the car park that evening around the time Hargreaves was killed. Check the hotel register and run a check on everyone's name. Local police have already started interviewing everyone so liaise with them to see if they've come up with anything. Make sure we get a copy of all the statements.'

'Did he have anything else on him?' asked Martin.

'There was a bag full of clothes, oh, and his mobile phone, but that was found crushed on the bedroom floor. We're not sure if he did that or whether his attacker did. I hope I'm wrong but I get the feeling this was a professional kill,' said Wesley.

'Do you mean someone was hired to kill him?' Alison asked.

'Yes, don't you think this stinks of a hired hit? Just look at the evidence. Injection into the neck, no fingerprints, and the body quietly left inside the bedroom door. Hargreaves wasn't a small guy. Had he been simply stabbed and left to collapse, he would have woken half of the hotel.'

'Have the hotel checked their CCTV?'

'Unfortunately, Alison, they say it hasn't been working for over a year.'

'So the guy somehow walks into the hotel, past the reception desk, unnoticed by anyone then slips out the same way.'

'Unless'… interrupted Martin.

'Unless what?' questioned Wesley.

'Unless the killer was already staying in the hotel, I mean I doubt if the police searched the other bedrooms.'

'Do you know, we just might make a copper out of you one day,' said Wesley smiling as he picked up the phone.

Jane was busy with the housework, trying desperately to keep out of the way of the builders who it seemed had been drilling holes into the exterior wall of the Cottage since the crack of dawn. Having just finished putting some washing away, Jane went in search of her purse as she needed to walk to the local shop to buy milk. As she opened the front door of their dust laden home, she was greeted by Gerry Callow who was ambling up the garden path.

'Gerry? What brings you here? It's lovely to see you.'

Much to Jane's embarrassment he gave her a hug almost lifting her off her feet.

'I hope you don't mind me popping over uninvited like this but I couldn't find your phone number and there's something I need to tell you.'

Jane wondered what on earth could be important enough for the man to get on two buses and spend probably the best part of an hour and a half travelling by local transport just to tell her something. Gerry Callow rarely used the telephone and had never learnt to drive, having witnessed an accident where a friend was killed by a youth joy-riding when Gerry was just eleven years old he had vowed never to get behind a steering wheel.

'I was about to walk into the village to buy some milk and a few bit and pieces as the fridge is bare. Would you like to join me for some lunch, nothing fancy mind you, there's a small café in the village. They do sell a wonderful fry-up.'

Gerry rubbed his hands over his rotund belly.

'That, if I may say, sounds delightful.'

'In that case, I'll buy you an omelette,' Jane replied. 'I took the liberty of reading your doctor's report that you'd left on the desk when I last came over to the book shop. It clearly says no fried food.'

A despondent looking Gerry still insisted in holding Jane's arm as they walked into the village, Jane couldn't help but snigger to herself, thinking of the local gossip that would be circulating the village by the end of the day. It was a crisp chilly morning and Jane had to admit that the warmth from Gerry's colossus frame was a welcome comfort. Twice she almost slipped over on the icy pavement only to be supported by Gerry's tree trunk sized arm. A cold north-easterly wind made one's eyes water and stung the face but

Gerry seemed completely oblivious of this, protected by his thick rimmed glasses and thick black beard. A group of children were having a snowball fight just inside the entrance to the park and at least two snowballs hit Gerry as they walked past the gates. The gentle giant simply laughed, making his whole frame shake.

By the time they reached the café even Jane had built up an appetite and she was relieved to find a spare table near the window and delighted when a young waitress served them so promptly. Half an hour later having devoured his omelette, Gerry sat back in the chair trying to wipe the tomato sauce and egg stains from his tee-shirt.

'That was delightful, thanks Jane.'

'I expect you're glad you made the journey,' she replied sipping her coffee.

'Just to see you, makes it worthwhile,' Gerry replied laughing.

Ignoring his flattering remark, Jane continued.

'So, are you ever going to tell me what it is that actually brought you over to see me? I'm sure it wasn't just to have breakfast.'

'Oh yes,' he replied wiping his mouth with a napkin. 'When you were in the shop the other day you were asking about books or articles about Griffin Abbey. Well, following your advice to tidy the bookshop somewhat, I removed some of the old shelving from the back of the shop last night when I discovered this lying on the floor.' He reached inside his waistcoat and produced a crumpled piece of paper which he began to flatten out on the table.

'What is it?'

'Take a look, Jane.'

He turned the page around for her to view. It was an old newspaper cutting and was an article about the Griffin Abbey with a small black and white photo in the top right hand corner. The article was headed "Strange gathering at Griffin Abbey ruins" and read that several residents were concerned about the 'goings –on' at the Abbey. The news reporter stated, "Just recently there have been reports of a group of hooded men and women visiting the ruins of the Abbey late at night. Haunting music can be heard from as far away as George Wilson's farm." The article went on to say that the police were informed but it appeared that no action was taken as no offence had taken place. Jane held the page up to her face to take a closer look at the photo. It showed the front of the old Melcham Abbey as it had been in its hey-day, but made reference to the Griffin Abbey that once stood there. What attracted Jane's attention were the dozen or so robed individuals who were stood at the side of the building, their faces shrouded by hoods. 'Hmm that is interesting,' commented Jane.

'That's not all,' Gerry replied beaming across the table. 'Look at the date at the top of the page.' It read: 1st September 1969. 'Now look at the name of the chap who wrote the article,' he exclaimed.

The name read: Graham Stanley.

'OK, you've got me,' said Jane looking puzzled, 'what's so interesting about the name?'

Gerry then extracted a second newspaper clipping from the small pocket at the front of his flowery waistcoat, unfolded it and handed it to Jane.

'Have a read of this, Jane.'

It was an obituary list from a later paper. The third name down was Graham Stanley, aged 58, died suddenly in his sleep, 2nd September 1969.

'Don't you think that's more than coincidental?' asked Gerry. 'The fella passed away the day after taking the photo.'

Annie Griffin was busy packing clothes into a small suitcase. It had been a long time since she'd last spent a night away from Rowan Lodge. The message she had received was that someone would collect her at four o'clock but before that she wanted to pay Kate a visit at the hospital. The taxi arrived ten minutes early and Annie made the impatient driver wait until she was ready. As soon as she deposited herself into the back seat of the taxi, the frustrated driver then exceeded most of the speeding restrictions on the way to the hospital. His bad mood wasn't lifted when Annie paid him the exact amount for her fare in fifty pence pieces.

Having been given authorized access to Kate's room by the hospital security guard, Annie found Kate propped up in bed but fast asleep. Although Kate still had a drip in her arm, the one into her nose had now been removed. Another tube with a suction pad placed on Kate's chest was connected to a small device next to her bed monitoring her heart beat. Kate looked peaceful and Annie was reluctant to wake her but there was something she needed to know. A question needed answering. Annie had glanced through all the magazines on the bedside unit and was about to try and wake Kate, when Kate suddenly looked across at her. It was a few seconds before she spoke as if she were assessing where she was.

'Hi, Annie, what are you doing here?'

'Hello my dear.'

Annie walked forward and placed her hand in Kate's.

'I just popped in to see how you are keeping. You're looking a lot better than the last time I saw you. The nurse tells me that you've started eating.'

'Yes, just a little. It's a start. The doctor came in this morning. He says there is no reason why I shouldn't make a full recovery in time.'

Kate swallowed and tried to manoeuvre herself up.

'You've been in to see me before?'

'Yes my dear but you were sleeping then.'

'What's going on, Annie? I'm finding it so hard to remember and I can't concentrate.'

'Don't worry my dear, it will all become clear eventually,' Annie replied squeezing her hand. 'There is something I wanted to ask you actually.'

'Sure.'

Annie felt she had to try to get Kate to talk straight away. If she fell asleep again now, then the chance would be missed.

'Kate, my dear, were you aware that Antoine came looking for you?'

Kate's eye's fluttered as if she was thinking about what Annie had said but she didn't reply.

'You were living with Antoine in France weren't you?' Annie asked.

Kate gave a slight nod.

'Did you know he was going to follow you back home?'

Annie was getting impatient. She wasn't sure if Kate understood here questions or was just reluctant to answer. She stood there for another minute but it became obvious that Kate wasn't going to answer. Her eyelids closed as her head slumped forward and Annie assumed that drug enhanced sleep had once again taken over.

'Don't worry my dear,' said Annie letting go of Kate's hand. 'I'm sure the Abbey will ask Lucy the same question.'

Kate opened her eyes after hearing the door close. She loved Annie but right now her mind was so confused, she didn't know who to trust any more.

She wanted to ask Annie how she knew how her sister was, but was scared that she might hear something she wasn't prepared for. Why was Annie asking about Antoine? She hadn't seen him since they were kids, had she? If only she could think straight, clear her mind. Everything seemed so muddled. The room seemed to fade in and out of focus as Kate slipped back into dream mode.

Wesley had just put the phone down after speaking with O'Hara. His longtime friend and colleague had agreed to pay another visit to Perpignan to try and discover if Antoine Bergerac had been living there. Wesley had explained how Antoine had turned up in Somerset using a false identity, and how he had ended up dead in a ditch. He went in search of the fax machine to send a photo of Antoine across to him. He was stood looking at the device trying to work out how to operate the damn thing when Alison appeared.

'What's up, sir?'

'Technology, that's what's up. I need to send this across to O'Hara,' he explained holding up the photo.

'Here, let me have it. What's the fax number?'

Wesley handed Alison the both the photo and the piece of paper with the number on it and watched her as she went to work on the fax machine.

'There you are, all done,' she said just a minute later.

'You're a star,' said Wesley patting her on the shoulder. 'Just let me know if you need a favour any time.'

'Well actually, sir. I was going to ask for a day off.....'

Wesley held his hand up before she could finish the sentence.

'That'll be no,' he replied with a broad smile.

'Ah well, it was worth the try,' Alison remarked handing back the photo and paper.

Wesley returned to his desk just as another phone call disturbed his train of thought.

'I hope I haven't interrupted anything,' remarked Jane. 'I thought you'd like to know that I had a visitor this morning. Gerry Callow from the book shop.'

'Why? Is he trying to sell you some of his crap books?'

Jane could sense that her husband wasn't in the best of moods.

'No dear, but he did show me something that you might find interesting. It's an old newspaper cutting from 1969. It's headed "Strange gathering at Griffin Abbey" and it shows a picture of a number of people stood at the front of the old Melcham Abbey. The article talks about their robed appearance and the fact that they were believed to be using the Abbey late at night for purposes unknown. '

'Oh, right.'

She could hear the exasperation in Wesley's voice.

'Don't puff out your cheeks dear. It makes you look like one of them fat toads.'

Jane could visual his reaction.

'Sorry, what have you got for me then?'

Wesley sat back in his chair and rolled his head around his shoulders trying to ease the tension he was feeling.

'A chap named Graham Stanley took the photo. I assume he worked for the newspaper. Anyhow, he was found dead the next morning. Don't you think that is strange?'

'What do you same his name was?'

'Graham Stanley. The photo is dated 1st September and his name appears in the obituary column of the same newspaper a few days later saying he passed away in his sleep on 2nd September.'

'I guess it could be coincidence but I agree it does sound strange.'

'Oh, and there's something else.'

'What's that?'

'Gerry has kindly said that I can run the shop for him on Tuesdays and Fridays when he's driving the tourist bus around Glastonbury. That's all, I thought you'd like to know,' said Jane as she hung up.

A smile came to Wesley's face. He'd known it wouldn't be long before Jane got back to the book shop.

'Are you OK, sir?' asked Martin as he entered Wesley's office. 'I did knock but you seemed miles away.'

'That's OK. Yeah I'm fine,' he sighed. 'Do me a favour, Martin.' He handed him a scribbled note about Graham Stanley. 'See what you can dig up about this guy.'

'Is this related to the case, sir?'
'That's what I want to find out.'

Sally Morgan drove slowly, entering the Melcham estate and continued on down the slope to Melcham Hall. A light sprinkling of snow still covered most exposed areas and she had to negotiate the slippery gravel track. There were no other cars parked outside and the double garage doors stood open revealing an empty space within. She left the car without locking it in case she needed a fast getaway. A light drizzle had begun so she wrapped her cardigan around her, feeling for the gun in her pocket at the same time. Although she had never fired a gun in her life, just holding it in her hand gave her a sense of reassurance. She only intended to use it once, on Brian Hargreaves. The bastard was responsible for her husband's death, she just knew it. Sally had convinced herself that Hargreaves had been the reason why her husband had been arrested for fraud several years ago and the reason why he'd been acting so strange lately. He was also responsible for introducing Henry to Lady Hargreaves. Taking a deep breath she pressed the buzzer next to the front door and stood back listening to the chimes within. She pressed twice again but there was no reply. The drizzle had now turned to rain and Sally could feel the cold biting into her. She walked around to the back of the building and tried to peer through the kitchen window. There was no sign of anyone around so she tried the back door but that was locked. Deciding the only way to gain entry was to smash the kitchen window Sally searched around until she found a pile of bricks that had been stacked against the side of the garage. She returned with a brick in her hand and tapped at the kitchen window with it but without breaking the glass. Then venting her anger she stood back before hurling the brick at the window. There was a sharp crack as the window gave way sending shards of glass into the kitchen. By stacking half a dozen bricks under the kitchen window she was able push away any remaining shards of glass before clambering through the window and across the sink unit on her hands and knees. By the time she dropped to the floor she was exhausted. She wiped the sweat from her brow and suddenly noticed blood on her hands. It was then she saw the dark stain seeping through her jeans at the knee. She had obviously knelt on a piece of glass crawling across the draining board. Checking that the gun was still in her pocket Sally made her way across the kitchen and out into the spacious hallway with its magnificent staircase winding its way towards the overhead balcony. She listened for any sound but the house was eerily quiet. The flagstone floor felt cold and unwelcoming as she crossed to the library. A week old newspaper lay on a small table near the fireplace, the only evidence of someone being in the house recently and a half empty bottle of brandy stood on a small coffee table in the centre of the room. Sally unscrewed the lid and downed a large mouthful of the fine blend. The warmth of the brandy caught at the back of her throat causing her to cough. Sally laughed, and almost hysterical laugh, before taking another swig. Leaving the library, Sally felt a little light headed as she made her up the grand staircase. After searching the upstairs rooms she eventually made her way back downstairs and entered the formal dining room with its magnificent oak wood table taking centre stage. A large plasma fifty inch television had been erected above the fireplace and looked totally out of place with its surroundings. Sally searched for the remote control eventually finding it hidden underneath a cushion. Aiming it at the television she toyed with all the buttons until she found a news channel. The news reporter was standing outside a hotel, rain pouring off of the blue neon sign 'Hotel Ibis'. She turned up the volume to listen.

"So it's up to the police now to find out who killed Mr Hargreaves. From all intents and purposes this looks to be a professional killing. This is Brian Pearson reporting for BBC South West."

'No!' Sally cried and threw the remote control at the screen. 'I wanted to kill him!' she shouted, extracting the gun from her pocket and releasing the safety catch.

27

Perpignan wasn't the liveliest of places at the best of times but when O'Hara drove into the village square that morning it was as if the place had been abandoned. He parked the Citroën saloon in the small market square on the opposite side from the café Noir. It was a dull grey damp morning where the air clung to skin like a wet towel. O'Hara crossed the square looking for signs of life but there were none. Stepping up to the café he peered through the window hoping to find Pierre. There were no lights on inside and the café was empty. He rapped twice on the glass door without expecting a reply. Then, just as he stepped away from the door he heard someone call out.

'Bonjour monsieur.'

O'Hara turned around to look to see where the voice had come from.

'Up here, monsieur.'

He took another step back from the shop front and looked directly overhead and immediately recognised the elderly gentleman from his last visit. The café owner looked as if he had just been woken up.

'I will be down in a moment.'

'Thanks, no rush.'

O'Hara opened one of the foldaway chairs that were leaning up against the wall behind the small plastic table on the pavement and made himself comfortable.

It was more than ten minutes later when he heard the bolt being pulled back and the door to the café being unlocked. The café owner seemed to have aged considerably since O'Hara's last visit. He was almost bent in half and seemed to be struggling to catch his breath. O'Hara stood up to greet him.

'It's Pierre, isn't it?' O'Hara asked.

'You have a good memory my friend,' Pierre replied with a rasping voice.

He shook O'Hara's hand vigorously with a strength that defied both his age and appearance.

O'Hara followed him into the café and took a seat on one of the stools by the counter as Pierre set about making coffee.

'Where is everyone?' O'Hara asked gesticulating with his arms.

The old man laughed which caused him to cough.

'We had a village thanksgiving festival last night and I'm afraid most people will still be asleep, or hung over, or both.'

He placed a freshly brewed cup of black coffee on the counter, no indication of milk or sugar being offered.

'What brings you back to Perpignan, especially at such an early hour of the day?'

'I've come to find out what I can about a friend of Kate Melcham. You may remember that I was helping the family to locate Kate when I last visited. Since then, the family have asked me to trace a friend of hers. I'm led to believe she had been living with this guy before she went back to the UK.'

'So you found her?'

Pierre's response was almost immediate and a look of concern showed in his eyes.

'I believe a colleague of mine has located her, yes. At the moment that's all I can tell you.'

O'Hara was unsure just how much information he should pass on. Pierre ran his hand across his mouth while he assessed the information.

'Tell me one thing. Is Kate Melcham safe?'

To ask if she was safe seemed a strange question, O'Hara could only answer yes.

'Is she back with her family?' Pierre's eyes studied O'Hara's face.

'Kate is living back home but she has been rather poorly so has been taken to hospital for a check-up, but I'm sure she's fine.'

Pierre seemed to assess the answer because asking another question.

'What is the name of the person you are looking for?' Pierre wiped a glass with a tea towel that couldn't contain more stains if it tried.

'Antoine Bergerac.'

The glass shattered as it hit the floor.

'I do apologise, I'm getting so clumsy these day,' said Pierre. He bent down behind the counter to retrieve a dustpan and brush. O'Hara couldn't help but think that it was more than coincidence.

'That's OK. I'm always doing that around the house. My wife goes mad. She doesn't trust me with our best crockery any longer.'

The old man swept up the shattered glass before disappearing behind a beaded curtain to dispose of the remnants. He seemed to be gone for quite a while and O'Hara was sure he heard a telephone being replaced in its cradle. When Pierre reappeared he looked more composed and poured out more coffee.

'What did you same the name was?'

'Antoine Bergerac.'

Pierre rubbed his chin before shaking his head.

'I don't know anyone of that name. He certainly doesn't live in the village. I think I know the name of everyone around here.'

O'Hara sipped the hot coffee, not convinced that Pierre was telling the truth.

At that moment two men entered the café, sitting themselves at a small table next to the window. One was tall and thin, with black greasy hair and a long weather beaten face half obscured by a thick black moustache. He wore a white tee-shirt and black waistcoat with black cords. His colleague was a short stocky man who O'Hara guessed as being slightly older. With short cropped hair his eyes looked tiny in a large face that looked as if it had received too many punches. His shabby grey suit looked as if it had never been cleaned or seen an iron. When Pierre went over to serve them, O'Hara tried to make out what they were saying but the conversation was almost a whisper. Just as Pierre returned behind the counter to make more coffee, one of the men left the table and walked out of the café.

'So how do you plan to find your friend?' asked Pierre after he had taken a coffee over to the man who was now sat on his own.

O'Hara lit a Gauloise, dropped a match into the glass ashtray and blew the smoke high into the air. He coughed as the sharp nicotine hit the back of his throat. He had been smoking Gauloises since he and his family had moved to France because they were cheaper than the brands he used to smoke back in the UK. He knew he should quit but there were days when his knee pained him so much that a quick cigarette seemed to take his mind off things. David O'Hara had taken early retirement from the Navy when an accident aboard ship had resulted in him damaging his knee to the extent that some days he was virtually immobile.

'I guess I'll start at the building where Kate used to live. Do you know if anyone else is living there?'

Pierre shook his head. 'Not to my knowledge.'

'Well, we'll soon find out.'

'I wish you luck, my friend.' Pierre had a worried look on his face and O'Hara noticed how he kept glancing across at the table where the other occupant was sat. Finishing his coffee O'Hara placed five euros on the counter and stood up to leave. As he did so, Pierre suddenly grabbed his hand and leant over the counter.

'Be careful my son,' he whispered, coyly looking across to where the other man still sat by the window.

O'Hara didn't reply but gave a curt nod to show he understood.

A plume of black smoke could be seen drifting across the country lane near the entrance to the Melcham estate, enough for a local farmer to raise the alarm. By the time the fire brigade arrived on the scene, Melcham Hall was ablaze and the first Fire Officer in attendance immediately called for additional support. Wesley first learnt of the incident when WPC Fielding almost burst through his office door.

'I'm so sorry, sir. Just thought you ought to know,' she gasped.

'Know what?'

'Melcham Hall, sir, It's burning. According to a member of the fire brigade who just phoned, the whole building is on fire.'

Wesley grabbed his jacket from the coat stand and called across the room to Martin who was hidden behind a pile of paperwork.

'Grab your car keys, son. There's a fire over at Melcham Hall.'

Wesley and Martin arrived on the scene just as two further fire engines pulled up in front of the building. An ambulance was already parked to the side in front of the garage. Parked next to the ambulance was Sally Morgan's vehicle. Wesley thrust his ID in the face of the nearest Fire Officer who pointed to his left where the Chief Fire Officer stood talking into a hand held radio. He acknowledged Wesley's presence as soon as Wesley caught his attention and signalled to say he would be over in a minute. Martin walked across the forecourt to track down the ambulance crew. The heat from the building meant that no one could get closer than thirty feet and even three fire engines were having difficulty in controlling the blaze.

'We'll be lucky to save much of the building,' said Pete Atkins, the Chief Fire Officer as he shook hands with Wesley.

'Any idea how it started?' asked Wesley.

'He or she may well be your culprit.'

He pointed across to the side of the building where two paramedics were carrying a stretcher towards the ambulance.

'The farmer who put the call in, said he thought he heard gun shots before he first saw the smoke.'

Wesley walked away briskly in the direction of the ambulance. A middle aged female paramedic looked down at Wesley from inside the ambulance where she was placing a sheet over the body.

'She died within minutes of us arriving,' she said. 'Probably a good job too, with the amount of burns she'd received.'

'Can I take a look at the face?' he asked stepping into the ambulance.

'Sure, if you feel it necessary. There's not much left of it.'

She pulled back the sheet to expose the victims head. Wesley took one look before turning away, feeling the need to vomit. Sally Morgan was almost unrecognisable.

Leaving the fire brigade with the unenviable job of fighting the blaze, and having been informed that no other bodies could be seen inside the building, Wesley trudged up the hill towards Rowan Lodge. He was surprised not to have seen Annie standing outside Melcham Hall. Rowan Lodge appeared to be empty. Having tried the front door he walked around the back which was also locked, indicating that Annie had gone somewhere. Martin had now pulled alongside in the car and began walking across to where Wesley was stood by the back door.

'Is Annie not in, sir?'

'It appears not. I'm just phoning the station to see if there are any messages for me.'

Having confirmed there were none, Wesley directed Martin back to the car.

'I've arranged for two uniforms to be stationed by the gates. Apart from the fire and ambulance crews I don't want anyone else on the estate.'

Wesley opened the car door and jumped in the passenger seat.

'Where are we going, sir?' Martin asked after switching on the ignition.

'The Phoenix, I need a bloody drink.'

On the way he explained that the person carried out of the building was Sally Morgan.

'What did you find out about Graham Stanley?' Wesley asked returning from the bar with the drinks. He almost felt sorry for Martin when the lad viewed another orange juice compared to Wesley's pint of Shepton Tribute bitter.

'In those days he was one of only two news reporters working for the Somerset press. He was well respected and had interviewed several well-known people, local artists, a famous author and several politicians in his time. I've managed to dig out his medical records. Apparently he was fit young man who played squash and spent most of his life cycling around these parts.'

'So what did he die of?'

'He had a heart attack.'

Wesley raised his eyebrows.

'And this was the day after the photo had been taken of Griffin Abbey?'

'Yes sir.'

'Doesn't that seem a bit strange to you?'

'It could just be coincidence, sir.'

'I doubt it. I'm beginning to think that the answer to all of these deaths is somehow connected to the Abbey. I think it's time I had another word with James Harper.'

Wesley downed the rest of his pint in one gulp.

'Are you thirsty, sir?' Martin asked with a smirk on his face.

'Actually I am. Cheers, I don't mind if I do.'

He handed Martin his empty glass who trudged off to the bar searching his pockets for what little money he had on him.

When Martin returned to the table Wesley was on the phone. By the time Wesley finished the call Martin could tell it was wasn't good news.

'This whole thing gets more intriguing by the hour,' Wesley exclaimed.

'It seems that Graham Stanley was cremated.'

Martin eyebrows knitted together in a puzzled look.

'Back in those days most people were buried. In fact, it was extremely rare for a Christian to be cremated.'

'So do you believe there was a reason why he was cremated and not buried?' asked Martin.

'Well, one thing is for sure. It means we don't have a body to exhume.'

O'Hara's zipped up his jacket as he crossed the cobbled square. There were one or two people wandering around now as shops were beginning to open and the local butcher's shop was serving an elderly woman who was insistent on purchasing a particular set of steak cutlets that were displayed in the window. As he went to open his car door he noticed the driver's window was half way down. It took him less than a minute to realise that someone had been rummaging around in the car. There was nothing taken, his cd's were still under the dashboard and his back pack still lay on the passenger chair but it was obvious someone had been checking him out. Deciding there wasn't anything else of any real value in the car; he grabbed his back pack and slammed the driver's door shut just to let anyone know who was watching that he'd noticed the intrusion. Leaving the car unlocked he set foot towards Kate Melcham's apartment. As he crossed the narrow street in the corner of the square he noticed someone standing at the entrance to an alleyway between two shops, just a few yards away. O'Hara recognized him immediately. It was the other man who had entered the café earlier. Avoiding eye contact he pretended to look into the window of a small print shop as he passed the man.

'This is going to be interesting,' O'Hara said to himself as he headed for Flat 15 Rue de Fleurs. Experience told him that someone in the village was keeping an eye on him. He turned away from the square and took the next right into the Rue de Fleurs. The buildings on either side of the narrow cobbled street were quite oppressive as their overhead balconies almost touched in places preventing what little light there was entering the street. The large gothic shaped door to number 15 was open but before entering the building he stopped to look at the buzzer for apartment 4. There was no longer any name showing. Leaving the front door slightly ajar to allow a shaft of daylight into the dark interior he mounted the short flight of stairs to the first floor. Apartment 4 was on the right of the staircase and the front door was open.

He moved slowly forward keeping his back to the far wall until he stood opposite the doorway. Using his foot he nudged the door open a fraction wider and peered inside the room. Whoever had broken in had ransacked the place. Furniture had been pulled apart, chair covers ripped open, items knocked off shelves and a bed mattress was lying on the floor in shreds. Making sure he didn't touch anything he walked across the lounge to look out of the solitary window. It was obvious that the window hadn't been opened in years. It led down to a small enclosed interior courtyard that provided no exit.

Deciding there was nothing to be gained by hanging around; O'Hara made a quick exit out of the building and headed back towards the café in a solemn mood. Just as he entered the square he suddenly became aware of the sound of a motorbike engine being revved up. He turned to look back and immediately threw himself sideways to avoid the speeding motorbike.

Thankful that he hadn't been run over but dusty and bruised, he sat on the edge of the kerb as he slowly regained his composure. The rider had been dressed in black leather and wore a black helmet with the shaded visor pulled down over the face so he wasn't even sure if it was a man or a woman. He looked around the square. The only person in sight was an elderly woman shuffling along the cobbled stones with the aid of a walking stick. She was bent so low the walking stick appeared to be taller than she. Reaching into his jacket pocket he extracted another Gauloise, lit it and inhaled deeply. He sat there for another five minutes before brushing himself down and making his way back to the café. A young woman was now serving behind the counter. She was tall with jet black shoulder length hair and her white shirt and black knee length skirt accentuated her slim line figure. He ordered a black coffee and asked where Pierre was.

'My father has gone upstairs for a lay down. He sleeps for a couple of hours each morning. He's not as young as he used to be,' she informed him.

'Do you know my father?'

The young woman had a quizzical look on her face as if she was assessing him, but the most obvious resemblance were the piercing jet black eyes that had the ability to penetrate the soul.

'We first met a few days ago and I'm afraid it was me who woke him up this morning.'

'Ah, so it was you who I heard when I was in the shower.'

A brief vision of the girl showering entered O'Hara's thoughts which he quickly pushed to one side.

'Yes, I'm sorry if I disturbed you.'

The woman smiled but made no further comment. The only other occupants in the café were two elderly sunburnt gentlemen. By the appearance of their clothing O'Hara took them to be local farmers. When he placed the coffee cup to his lips he noticed his hand was shaking.

'I'm getting too old for this sort of thing,' he thought.

He had sat there for another twenty minutes contemplating his next move when the young woman walked over from the counter and placed a slip of paper next to the saucer on the table.

'Your bill,' she said quietly and promptly walked away.

O'Hara look confused. He picked up the slip of paper, unfolded it and read the message. 'Call me at three o'clock. Pierre 77865.' When he left the café and walked back to his car he was unaware of the two people watching him from inside the tinted windows of a Range Rover parked nearby.

'I've been through all of Brian Hargreaves things,' said Alison phoning from the hotel. 'Apart from his mobile phone and a credit card there's nothing here. The lab boys have been given the bits and pieces of his crushed mobile but I wouldn't bank on them getting any data from it.'

'What about the other bedrooms in the hotel? Have they been searched?'

asked Wesley who was contemplating having a sandwich with his beer.

'Yes and Martin may have been right. The person staying in the room next door was registered as a Mr Boesinger. He paid for the one night only, in cash. That's not unusual, but no one saw him go down to dinner and he never asked for room service either. When the police questioned the receptionist she said he'd had a small rucksack with him and when he signed the register he put a line in the book where his car details should have been, so we're not sure what transport method he used to get to the hotel.'

'And I don't suppose anyone saw him the next morning either?'

'No, sir, they didn't, not even at breakfast.'

'I assume the whole hotel has been checked.'

'Yes, sir, and the local police have spoken with all the registered guests. I've got their statements here.'

'Stinks, doesn't it?' Wesley replied. 'OK, let me know if the lab boys come up with anything. If you are sure there's nothing else at the hotel, tell the local officer you're on your way back. Drive carefully, we'll catch up later.'

Wesley filled Martin in with the details when he returned from the bar with two rounds of sandwiches.

'I thought you were looking hungry, sir.'

'Martin, you know me too well.'

28

Having just eaten her first full meal in days, Kate sat up in bed and looked at herself in the small hand held mirror that one of the nurses had kindly obtained for her. She noted the dark circles under her eyes and the drawn look, but managed a weak smile. She knew she was lucky to be alive. The doctor had informed her that her blood stream had contained a high level of thallium poisoning that had probably been administered into her system over the past few weeks. He said that if she hadn't been treated as quickly as she was, there was a fair chance that she would have died long before paramedics had arrived. The events of the past few weeks were slowly coming back to her and she was beginning to think she didn't want to remember any more. The jigsaw of events that were forming in her head weren't painting a pretty picture and she now feared for her sister more than ever. Pulling back the bed clothes Kate sat on the edge of the bed, her feet resting lightly on the floor. It had been nearly a week since she had last stood up and the next move was going to require huge effort. She had been told to stay in bed until the nurse arrived but she felt the urge to stand up, or at least try. With one hand gripping the bed and the other resting on the now disconnected monitoring device, Kate gingerly stood up. At first she felt a little light headed and the world around her seemed to float somewhere in the distance as if it were teasing her to reach out. Biding her time she took a few deep breaths before taking the first tentative steps. By the time she had taken half a dozen steps across to the window she leant against the window sill for support, trying to control her rasping breathing. Kate pulled hard on the cord several times as the window blind slowly rose to reveal the outside world.

The weak winter sun had already slipped behind low cloud casting a grey pall across the car park below and beyond. As Kate looked up to the cumulus of clouds passing overhead tears started to run down her face. She felt weak and alone but knew deep down that she had crossed the bridge on the way to recovery and was determined to find her sister. Only twenty-four hours previous she'd began to think she would never see the sky and the outside world again. Just as she reached up for the cord to lower the blind back down, a figure caught her eye. Being unused to the natural light Kate squinted as she stared down at the figure who was stood on the far side of the car park. She gave one final tug on the cord to close the blind.

'Why was Annie watching over her?'

O'Hara stood in the phone box leaning against the glass partitioning listening to the phone ringing at the other end of the line. He was certain he had dialled the correct number. After a while he hung up and redialled, making sure he dialled the number that Pierre had given him. Once again he let it ring for some considerable time but there was no answer. He suddenly had an uneasy feeling that something was wrong. Although he hadn't really known the old man, for some reason he felt he could trust him. Walking away from the phone box O'Hara crossed the cobbled square and headed back in the direction of the café. He had just stepped onto the pavement less than a hundred yards from the café when he heard a voice. Turning round he looked back across the square but there was no one in sight, but as he turned back he almost collided into the young woman who appeared from inside a shop doorway.

'Follow me,' she said, quickly stepping into a side alley. It was the young woman from the café.

O'Hara never had time to ask questions as he was almost running trying to keep up with her. The woman kept looking back to make sure he was following as she led the way through a maze of tiny cobbled streets where sloping overhanging buildings almost defied gravity, where there was only just room to walk around a dog lying in someone's front door, where it was impossible to escape the sound of televisions and radios and the smell of cooking.

When they eventually reached a small rustic door that appeared to be cut out of the ancient wall that ran down to the harbour, the woman stopped and gave two sharp raps with her knuckles. The door was opened immediately and the woman ushered O'Hara quickly inside. As soon as the door closed behind them they were enveloped in darkness until Pierre turned to face O'Hara, holding a lit candle.

'Please, this way,' said the old man.

A narrow passageway led them into a living room that looked as if it belonged to an era long gone. There were no windows and the sparse furniture could have been taken from any museum. They crossed the room and descended a small flight of steps into another larger room where a skylight pierced the gloom casting a grey pallor across the room. O'Hara felt a cold shiver run down his spine as if someone had just walked over his grave. The old man had obviously noticed.

'I'm sorry for the cold my friend, but we are now right on the water front and these rooms are constantly damp.'

The room they were now in was obviously the kitchen. An old Aga stood on the far wall, it's only other companion being a small welsh dresser that held a sparse variety of cooking utensils and crockery. A small square shaped wooden table with only three wooden stools of similar design stood against another wall, with a half empty bottle of wine waiting for the next visitor to finish the contents. The old man moved quietly around the room lighting a series of candles whilst the young woman stood in the doorway, her eyes never leaving O'Hara.

'Will one of you tell me what on earth is going on?'

'All in good time, my friend,' the old man replied motioning for O'Hara to take a seat.

'I can't just sit here all evening,' O'Hara exclaimed as his patience was quickly fading.

'Please, sit down.'

It was the young woman who spoke.

'There is little time, and so much that you need to know.'

The way she held the gun at her side told O'Hara that she could handle herself.

Entering the office Wesley found Alison sat behind her desk shuffling a pile of papers around.

'Blimey, you got back quick. I thought it would take you at least another hour or so. The M5 can be quite congested at the best of times.'

'Actually, sir, it was quite a good journey. I got back a lot sooner than I thought I would. In any case it's given me the chance to dive into some paperwork.'

'If I had known you like doing paperwork so much you could have helped me out with some of mine,' Wesley replied smiling.

Wesley shut himself in his office and sat down to begin the chore of catching up on paperwork. He failed to understand why, in these days, when technology was so far advanced that his in-tray seemed to contain more folders and sheets of papers than ever before. It was late afternoon when Alison popped her head around the door.

'I've just received a call from forensics, sir. They say the fire at Melcham Hall was almost certainly caused by gun shots fired by Sally Morgan. It looks as if she randomly fired at anything and everything. Apparently there are bullet holes in the walls and furniture in the library, and in the hall and kitchen where the fuse box had been blown off the wall.'

Wesley looked up and sighed.

'Why on earth would she have done that? Even if she did, why didn't she just run out? That's what I don't understand.'

'Maybe she didn't have anything to run away to,' Alison replied.

Just at that moment the door to the main office slammed shut as Martin marched across the room.

'It's nice to see you're in a good mood,' commented Wesley.

'Bloody tourists,' he shouted as he slammed a pile of folders down on his desk. 'They think this place is here just to allow them to report their stolen bikes, lost mobiles, and whatever else they want to claim back on insurance.'

Wesley looked at Alison who tried to hide the smirk on her face.

'Why don't you make us all a nice cup of tea? That'll make you feel better,' said Wesley.

Martin grunted something under his breath and slammed the same door again on his way out. Alison and Wesley burst into laughter upon hearing Martin's footsteps going back downstairs. When Martin reappeared some ten minutes later with the teas, he was almost out of breath.

'We've just received a call from West-Midlands police, sir,' he panted. 'They've managed to trace a call made from the hotel room where Brian Hargreaves was staying. The call was made to the same phone box in London as before.'

'Hmm that's interesting. So we can assume that Hargreaves was looking for help from someone.'

'Do you think he was trying to contact James Harper?' asked Alison.

'Let's give Mr Harper a call and find out shall we?'

'We had to leave the café because we were being watched,' said Pierre. 'That's why no one answered your call.'

'Can you please switch off your mobile phone? That way no one can trace your movements.' The young woman gave a wry smile, the first hint of friendliness O'Hara had felt since they'd met in the square. He retrieved his phone from his jeans pocket, switched it off and placed it on the table.

'So what's this all about?' he asked.

'Have you ever heard of the Griffin Abbey?'

It was Pierre who spoke, having now pulled up a chair.

O'Hara shook his head. 'No, what is it?'

Pierre placed his elbows on the table and interlocked his fingers as if in prayer.

'Antoine Bergerac is a member of the Griffin Abbey.'

'You mean he was,' O'Hara interrupted.'

The old man raised his head and looked across the room at the young woman.

'What do you mean?'

O'Hara sat back in the chair. 'Antoine Bergerac, alias Ted Drake, was found lying in a ditch in a village called Shepton Mallet, in Somerset, several days ago. He'd been murdered.'

He watched both the old man and the young girl for a reaction.

'You knew this man personally, didn't you?' O'Hara asked.

Pierre pushed back his chair, stood up and walked across the room to where a small bureau was located. He pulled the front of the unit down and extracted a black and white photo which he then handed to O'Hara.

'Antoine Bergerac, one of the most evil men in France.'

The young woman walked across the room and placed her hand on the old man's shoulder.

'Do you know who is responsible for his death?' she asked.

'No, that's all I know.'

'You're not really a friend of Kate's, are you?'

O'Hara hesitated before answering.

'Look, I'll come clean. A friend of mine, an Inspector Wesley, originally asked me to locate Kate Melcham. Since my last visit I've found out that she has returned to the UK. However, Antoine Bergerac, who was thought to have been a close friend, has since been murdered. The Inspector asked me to come back to the village to see what I could find.'

'And what have you found?' asked Pierre.

'Since arriving back in Perpignan, I've come across a ransacked apartment, strangers watching my every move, and a veil of secrecy. Earlier, someone even tried to run me over, and now I'm faced with a woman who's carrying a gun.'

Pierre looked up at the woman standing next to him and discreetly nodded his head.

'Let me introduce myself,' she said. Stepping forward she shook her hair free from the head scarf and smiled at O'Hara. The transformation was immense and O'Hara immediately recognised her from the café.

'I'm afraid the person who tried to run you over was me,' said Maxine. 'I wouldn't have hurt you. I just wanted to frighten you off. You seem a determined man.'

'Frighten me off from what?'

O'Hara stood up. His knee was causing him pain. Maxine took a tighter grip on the gun that she now held in front of her.

'Put that away my dear,' said Pierre. 'I don't believe Mr O'Hara has come to cause us harm. Please, let us all sit.'

The old man reached over for a bottle of brandy and selected three small glasses which he filled with the dark liquid before handing them around. He downed the contents of his glass in one, before beginning his story.

'Many years ago the Griffin Abbey was one of the wealthiest known priories in the western world. Like a number of these institutions it attracted a wide range of individuals, some not so law abiding as others. It is said that the Griffin Abbey inherited it's wealth from the Griffin family who were once close associates of the Royal family. Others will tell you that they obtained vast fortunes by thieving from others. I will show you some of the written stories, you can then decide for yourself. However I am only concerned with the present, I have no control over the past. Antoine Bergerac had used several aliases during his life with one sole purpose, to find out where the Griffin treasure was buried.'

O'Hara looked confused.

'Please get the box Maxine,' Pierre asked.

'But father....'

The old man held his arm aloft to silence the woman.

'I'm an old man now and it's time we shared the secret with someone. I would die a happy man if I knew the secret would be kept safe.'

Reluctantly, but still giving her father a hug, Maxine left the room for a moment before returning with a small tin box under her arm. She handed it to Pierre who removed the lid and extracted the paper within. Unfolding the map he laid it out across the table using the brandy glasses to prevent it ravelling up. He then ran his hands across the paper as if memorising something from the past.

'See here,' he said pointing to specific area on the map, 'this is the Melcham estate, and this oblong shape is Melcham Hall.'

O'Hara followed the old man's finger as it moved across the drawing.

'Now here, on far Western edge of the estate is where the old Melcham Abbey once stood. It was built on top of what was the Griffin Abbey. Although the Abbey is now in ruins it once heralded some of the world's most valuable artefacts.'

'Mostly stolen,' commented Maxine leaning on her father's shoulder.

The old man nodded and smiled.

'I don't understand where Kate and Lucy come into this?' said O'Hara. 'Inspector Wesley told me that Lucy is currently in the protection of the Abbey.'

Pierre looked aghast as Maxine gave a stifled cry.

'Oh dear Lord,' cried Pierre. 'The Abbey would not protect Lucy or Kate, they may use them hoping to find out information, but their sole intention is to remove them once they are of no value. They see them as the final obstacle that is preventing the Abbey from regaining the Melcham estate and the treasures that are believed to be hidden there.'

'But I thought Kate and Antoine were living together?' exclaimed O'Hara, looking more perplexed by the minute.

'Antoine has been chasing Kate for a number of years,' answered Maxine, 'and its common knowledge that he was trying to win her love. However, at the end of the day he only had one thing on his mind, and that was to use her to find out where the Griffin treasures are. I think Kate had concerns over Antoine's so-called affections for her, she's no fool. I think somehow she found out what his true objectives are. Although Antoine spent most of his life living in France he was actually born in England. He knew Kate and her sister then, but Kate wouldn't have recognised him from all those years ago. He's changed his appearance and speaks with a French accent these days. His mother's name is Annie. Annie Griffin.'

Wesley, followed closely by Alison and Nurse Jenkins walked through the swing doors that led to the corridor where Kate's room was located.

A young constable who was sat outside the door immediately stood up when he saw Wesley approach.

'Good afternoon, sir'

‘Hello son, we’ve just popped over to see how Kate’s improving.’

‘I’m afraid you just missed her, Inspector. She’s just gone for a bath.’

‘Gone for a bath?’ asked Nurse Jenkins, ‘but she’s confined to her room?’

Wesley could see the worried look on Nurse Jenkins’ face.

‘That’s what she said,’ the constable replied now sounding not quite so confident. ‘She told me that you had authorised for her to have a bath and that she wouldn’t be long.’

‘When was this?’

‘Not more than fifteen minutes ago.’

The nurse pushed the door open to Kate’s room. Sure enough the bed was empty; an insulin drip was left hanging in mid-air. Nurse Jenkins put her hands to her face.

‘Oh Inspector!’ she cried. ‘Where is my patient?’

Having used her dressing gown to hide her clothes, Kate Melcham had entered the ladies toilet, changed, and was now heading for the exit. The note she’d found that Annie had left by her bedside had said she was to trust no-one and that her sister was in grave danger unless she left the hospital at her first opportunity. Leaving the building, Kate crossed the car park heading towards the main road. She was about to cross the road when she recognised the face of the woman in the passenger seat of the vehicle parked in the lay-by. Hurrying as quickly as she could, Kate opened the rear door and jumped in before the car sped away.

Martin was in the office when the call came through from Wesley.

‘Hi, sir, everything OK?’

‘No, it’s not,’ Wesley replied. He filled Martin in on all the details and asked for a missing persons report to be circulated immediately. ‘I want all available officers working on this,’ he demanded. ‘Kate Melcham is still not fully recovered from her ordeal. We don’t know how long she’ll survive without insulin and antibiotics. Alison and I are on our way to Rowan Lodge. Annie Griffin may have a photo of Kate that we can use.’

Alison was already speaking with hospital security, insisting on viewing all available CCTV footage when Wesley appeared in the hospital reception area with Nurse Jenkins.

‘I don’t think we can do any more here for the moment, sir. The hospital security people are looking at CCTV footage and will contact me if they spot Kate, or anyone who looks similar to her.’

‘In that case, let’s get over to Annie’s.’

They left an agitated Nurse Jenkins who went back inside in search of her patient with a security guard in tow, hoping she was hiding somewhere in the building even though an initial sweep of the entire building had found nothing.

‘Annie Griffin? The name sounds familiar,’ said O’Hara.

‘She is the Head of the Griffin Abbey,’ replied Pierre. ‘She is an elderly lady these days but she is still very dangerous.’

‘You also mentioned treasures, what treasures?’

O’Hara looked first to Pierre and then to his daughter. This time is was Maxine who answered.

‘During the past hundred or so years it is said that the Griffin Abbey has once again accumulated a vast hoard of priceless artefacts from around Europe, the bulk of it being stolen. It was Annie Griffin’s elders who initially formed the Abbey when her family was considered to be one of the wealthiest in England. What started as a local feud between two families resulted in the birth of a powerful and corrupt organization that has destroyed everything, and everyone, who has tried to stand in its way.’

‘Surely an old lady cannot still command such an organization?’

Maxine laughed.

‘Oh she can, and she does, although there are some influential people working for the organization these days, including people like James Harper.’

‘Are you serious, the guy who’s the famous TV presenter?’

‘Yes,’ Maxine replied.

‘There are a number of dignitaries both in the UK and France who shall we say, have turned a blind eye to some of the actions of the Griffin Abbey during recent years.’

‘Could you name these people?’ O’Hara asked, looking at Pierre then Maxine.

‘I know who they are,’ Pierre whispered, ‘but to tell you would probably cost me and my daughter Maxine’s life, and place you in considerable danger.’

O’Hara stood up and walked around the confined space of the room. He needed time to think. Pierre helped himself to another brandy but Maxine never took her eyes off O’Hara; she had learned to trust no one. As he leant back on the opposite wall and reached into his jacket pocket for this cigarettes Maxine’s hand reached for her gun. O’Hara was aware of Maxine’s movement and slowly extracted a crumpled packet of Gauloise and a box of matches.

‘You have to trust me,’ he said, ‘my only concern is Kate Melcham. I’d never heard of the Griffin Abbey until a few minutes ago and have no interest in it either except that it may be a threat to people I care about.’ He lit his cigarette and placed the packet and matches down on the table. ‘Tell me, who are the two guys who have been watching my every move since I arrived here?’

‘They work for the Abbey,’ Pierre replied. ‘Paul and Antonio, they are brothers, although you could never tell by looking at them. They would kill their own mother if they thought there was any money in it.’

‘Oh, they sound like nice guys to know then.’

O'Hara took a long drag on the cigarette, his brain working overtime with the information he'd acquired.

'Pierre, you said that the Griffin Abbey had accumulated a vast number of artefacts and were extremely wealthy, if that's the case why are they so interested in Kate and her sister Lucy?'

'You need to understand that Lucy and Kate are the heirs to the Melcham estate, on its own worth millions. A number of years ago Lord Melcham stumbled upon the ruins of Griffin Abbey where he found a vast number of artefacts that had previously been stolen from his ancestral home and many other locations. Upon finding these artefacts, some of which are thought to be priceless, he removed them and hid them somewhere. It is believed they are hidden somewhere in Melcham Hall or within the grounds of the estate.'

Pierre paused while he poured more brandy.

'So that's why these people are trying to obtain the Melcham estate?'

'Yes exactly. When Kate moved to France she became good friends with my daughter Maxine, and as a result they socialised together. About a year ago, Maxine informed me that Kate was concerned about someone who initially seemed a good friend but who seemed to know a lot about her and was becoming a bit of a pest.'

'Would this be Antoine?'

'Yes, somehow he had found out that Kate had walked out on her ancestral home following an argument with her father and he was asking quite a number of questions about the family. She confided all of this to Maxine who in turn, informed me. It would appear that one of the reasons Kate left home was because she knew of Brian Hargreaves connections with the Griffin Abbey.'

O'Hara raised his eyebrows, somewhat surprised at the information.

'Apparently, she confronted her father at the time but he wouldn't listen to her reasoning. What he did do though, was to ensure there was a restriction placed on his other daughter's marriage agreement stating that Hargreaves would not be entitled to any of the estates finances until the tenth anniversary of their marriage, and as you know, Kate was written out of the will because of her disagreements with her father.'

'I think I'm beginning to see the picture now,' said O'Hara. 'But what I don't understand is what has happened to her sister, Lucy?'

'Lucy caught Hargreaves stealing from the estate and demanded a divorce, telling him that unless he agreed to the divorce she would go to the police. She said she had enough evidence to destroy him.'

'So where is she now?'

It was Maxine who answered.

'Our guess is that Hargreaves made arrangements for Lucy to be kidnapped and for her sister Kate to stand in for her, on the understanding that Lucy would remain unharmed unless Kate decided not to help.'

'Why did he not just bump Lucy off?'

'I don't think he wanted to take the risk. If Lucy was found dead, then according to the will left by Lord Melcham the estate would be handed over to the National Trust meaning Hargreaves and his colleagues would not receive a penny.'

'Surely Hargreaves has looked for the treasure. I mean, you say the guy is married to Lucy, he must have searched Melcham Hall many times.'

'But obviously has found nothing,' said Maxine. 'The building has over twenty rooms, some of which in places like that are possibly only accessible via secret tunnels. I know that sounds rather fanciful but it's a possibility.'

O'Hara stubbed his cigarette out and scratched his head. There was too much information to take in.

'So, what if Kate had said no to taking on her sister's identity? Surely he risked losing his claim to the Melcham estate?'

'I think he was sure that Kate would help if she thought her sister's life was at risk.'

'Even so, how does Hargreaves expect to inherit anything?'

'We believe his plan was to get Kate to play the role of her sister to the extent that when they met with the family solicitor on the tenth anniversary of the marriage when the reading of the will takes place, Hargreaves would claim his rightful inheritance to the estate. Kate and her sister are so alike, the solicitor would never notice.'

'When is the reading of the will due to take place?'

'The tenth anniversary is next week.'

'Oh my God, so we've only got a few days to find Lucy,' O'Hara exclaimed.

'Exactly,' Pierre replied with a worried look on his face.

'So what was Kate's view on all of this?'

'Kate saw this as her opportunity to expose Hargreaves for the fraudster he was and decided to play along with Hargreaves. So far, we think he has believed her.'

'But if someone has now killed both Hargreaves and Antoine, where does that leave the two sisters?'

'From what you have told us,' said Maxine, 'I would say they are both in grave danger. You see, people like James Harper and his associates have a lot to lose if they can't get hold of Melcham Hall. Their hidden treasures are buried there somewhere.'

Kate hadn't seen the syringe Annie was holding, but felt the immediate prick of the needle as it was injected into her arm. Just seconds after jumping into the back of the vehicle she entered a world of total blackness.

For the next twenty minutes the Daimler sped smoothly and efficiently through country lanes avoiding any main roads on route to Frome. It was only when they turned into an un-adopted road where the car's suspension was tested to its fullest, did Annie relax. She knew they had arrived. As soon as the car came to a halt in front of Emsbury House, Annie motioned to the driver to take Kate inside. The former home of the Duke of Emsbury had remained empty for several years following the late Duke's death. It was then purchased by James Harper with the Abbey's money. A large advertising board had been erected on the front lawn displaying the name "Perigrin Solutions", sufficient to keep any nosey parkers away. Annie made her way directly to the large drawing room at the back of the house while Kate was being carried upstairs to one of the bedrooms. As soon as Annie entered the room, she saw the figure sat in the wingback chair in front of the roaring log fire.

'Ah, there you are. Good news, I hope,' said James Harper.

Annie didn't look as pleased as he thought she would, she simply smiled as she helped herself to a drink from the cocktail cabinet.

'Kate will sleep for a while. There's no point in trying to wake her for a couple of hours.'

29

Wesley banged his fist hard on the front door of Rowan Lodge. He'd already knocked twice without success and had sent Alison round the back of the building. He was about to knock again when suddenly the door was opened from within and Alison invited him in.

'The back door was unlocked, sir. There's no sign of Annie.'

'OK, let's carry out a thorough search of the house, she must have photos somewhere.'

'Shouldn't we have a search warrant, sir?' she asked.

'Annie won't know we've been here, and what's more, we can't afford to wait. Kate's life is at stake. You take the bedrooms while I look down here.'

Ten minutes later Wesley had drawn a blank when suddenly Alison came running down the stairs.

'I found these, sir. They were in one of Annie's cardigans.'

She handed over a colour photo of Lucy and Kate. They were both dressed for a formal occasion and standing on the steps outside Melcham Hall.

'This will have to do,' said Wesley. 'It looks like they were taken a few years ago though. Were there any others?'

'Just this one, sir,' Alison replied handing over a slightly larger photo of a group shot. 'This looks to be from the same occasion but look closely at the chap on the far left.'

Wesley stared at the figure until it dawned on him who it was.

'Well I never, Ted Drake, or should I say Antoine Bergerac?'

Wesley ran his hand across his chin.

'I'd like to know where Annie is. I'm beginning to think Annie knows the answer to several of our questions. Let's run these photos over to the station. We can get them copied and circulated.'

Kate opened her eyes and tried to focus, images were just a blur and her head felt like someone had hit her with a brick. She felt sick and leaned over the side of the bed to vomit. As she did so a hand gripped her arm, providing support. After emptying the contents of her stomach she gripped the friendly arm with every ounce of effort she could muster to pull herself up. When Kate turned her head around to see who the person was who was holding her the recognition was instant, as she looked into her sisters eyes. The emotion was over-whelming as the two sisters cried hugging one another. Lucy eventually helped her sister to sit back on the bed and brushed tear stained hair from her eyes.

'I never thought I'd see you again,' Lucy whispered.

Kate was still drowsy and finding it difficult to concentrate.

'Where are we?' Kate asked.

'I wish I knew. Try and sleep for a while. I'll still be here when you wake, and then we'll chat. The effects of the drug are going to take a while to wear off,' Lucy replied.

Even though Kate desperately wanted to talk with her sister she couldn't ignore the demands of her body. Reluctantly closing her eyes she fell back into a deep drug enhanced sleep.

Martin was busy on the phone contacting local police units when Wesley and Alison arrived back at the station. Wesley gave him a description of what they believed Kate was wearing when she left the hospital and handed him the photos to circulate.

'Thanks, sir. We have three possible sightings already,' he said holding his hand over the mouthpiece.

'I'm sure we're going to get hundreds,' Wesley replied. 'It's picking out the legitimate one that's always difficult.'

Wesley headed towards his office as Alison sat at her desk looking dismayed at the pile of paperwork that had accumulated in such a short period of time, while Martin did his best to administer the small team of helpers who had been called in to assist with the phones. The office was a hive of activity, fingers tapping at keyboards, telephones ringing waiting for someone to answer them, and the constant chatter of voices as people wrestled to be heard above the din.

Wesley was lost in thought when Alison tapped on his door.

'Come in, close the door and take a seat. What have you got for me?'

Alison pulled up a chair opposite, pulling her skirt down a little as she sat and toyed with a loose strand of blonde hair. Wesley watched her as she composed herself. He was impressed with the way Alison handled herself. She was always organised, never allowed her herself to get flustered and always followed up on things. Nothing escaped her attention. He knew she would make an Inspector one day, a damn good one at that.

'I've been phoning around the village, sir. I've built up quite a number of contacts over the past eighteen months, all reliable, honest people. I've been asking if anyone has seen Annie, but there's been no sighting of her for the quite some time.'

'I don't understand. She can't just disappear?'

'I appreciate Annie doesn't go out as often as she used to but she hasn't been to the hairdressers, the library, the local tea shop, or visited any of her friends for some weeks.'

'How do we know who her friends are?' Wesley implored.

Alison's face couldn't hide the crimson colour in her cheeks and she gave a polite cough.

'The last time Mandy visited Annie, she managed to take a peek at her address book which she keeps next to the phone. Mandy wrote the names and numbers down. There are only four or five names.'

She looked down at her notes, not wanting to look Wesley in the face.

'Carry on,' he said, a smirk on his face.

'Everyone I've spoken to say's the same thing. Annie's not been in contact with them for weeks.'

Wesley could sense that Alison wanted to say more but was uncertain of her convictions.

'What's on your mind, Alison?' he asked encouragingly.

'It's just that we know Annie's not at home, she hasn't been seen by any of her friends and the last time you saw was at the hospital.'

'Are you suggesting she's a missing person?'

'I was beginning to think that, sir, but I've just spoken with PC Givens, he was on duty at the hospital just before Kate walked out. He says that Annie visited Kate only an hour before Kate went missing.'

'Are you suggesting Annie's involved with Kate's disappearance?'

'I just think it's too coincidental, sir.'

Wesley sat back in his chair and sighed. 'I wish I knew. But one thing's for sure, we need to find both Kate and Annie Griffin, and soon.'

'I need to get in contact with Inspector Wesley,' said O'Hara reaching for his mobile.

'Wait!' Maxine snatched the phone from his hand. 'I'm sorry, but I believe your mobile is being tracked. It's best to keep it switched off. You can use mine.'

All three sat around the table as O'Hara input Wesley's number into the phone. It was a number he knew from heart, having worked with Wesley on a previous case. Wesley reacted to the phone's vibrations as it grumbled on his desk. He looked at the caller's number but didn't recognise it. "If it's one of those sales pitches I'll scream," he said to himself.

'Inspector Wesley speaking, how can I help?'

'John! It's David. I'm so glad I could get through to you.'

Wesley could hear the concern in O'Hara's voice.

'Hi David, what's wrong? You sound like you're in trouble.'

Wesley walked across to the open window hoping he could get a better signal.

'Don't worry about me, I'm fine. It's Kate Melcham I'm worried about.'

He filled Wesley in on what he had learnt from Pierre and Maxine, including the fact that Annie was thought to be the Head of the Griffin Abbey and that Antoine was actually her son. Wesley stood leaning against the wall rubbing the back of his neck as he tried to take in everything that O'Hara had said.

'That goes a long way to explaining Annie's involvement in all this. We were only discussing her a few minutes ago. She hasn't been seen for a couple of days. In fact, the last sighting of her was when she visited Kate in hospital.'

There was a short pause before O'Hara replied.

'How is Kate's recovery going?' he asked.

'That's another problem. Kate walked out of the hospital earlier today and hasn't been seen since. I've got the whole county looking for her.'

'Do you think she's been abducted?'

'I pray not, but she had no money on her as far as we know so I don't see how she could just disappear.'

'Oh Christ,' O'Hara exclaimed. 'Do you think Annie is involved?'

'From what you've just told me, I would think there's a very good chance, yes.'

Wesley could hear voices in the background.

'What's going on?' he asked straining to listen.

'It would seem we have visitors,' O'Hara exclaimed. 'I've got to go John. I'll be in touch.'

'Please be careful,' Wesley replied, but the line had already been cut.

Wesley stood looking down on the street below, praying that he hadn't put his friend O'Hara in a dangerous situation.

The banging on the front door was persistent. Maxine had grabbed her gun and stood in the kitchen doorway looking composed. 'The woman knows how to handle herself,' thought O'Hara who was impressed with her swift movement. She turned to face them and placed her finger to her lips, indicating silence. They could just about make out muffled conversations outside in the street. It sounded like two voices. The conversation stopped as abruptly as it had started and was followed by the sound of footsteps running down the street. The silence that followed was almost deafening, the atmosphere sucking the life out of the room. Maxine motioned for the two men to remain where they were and slipped quietly out of the room, disappearing from their view into the darkened room. O'Hara could see the strain on Pierre's face as they stared at one another. The old man tried to force a grin but it failed to hide his concerns. When Maxine returned to the room she spoke in a whisper.

'I think they have gone but they won't be far. Knowing their tactics, one will be sat in a car at the end of the street, on the corner of the square, the other will be on foot encircling the building.'

'I assume you're talking about the two goons from earlier,' asked O'Hara.

'Yes, they've obviously been to the café and found no one there, so have come to find out where everyone is.'

'Do they do this often?'

Pierre nodded his head in the affirmative.

'So what do we do?' O'Hara looked first at Maxine then back at Pierre.

'There is another way out,' Maxine replied. She walked across to the far corner of the room and pulled back a curtain that hung from floor to ceiling, exposing another doorway.

'This leads directly down to the waterfront. We have a small boat moored there that we can use.' She looked across the room to her father.

'It's OK father, don't worry. We'll be fine.'

There was a confident and determined look on her face when she turned to face O'Hara.

'When we reach the Stalburg Bridge you can jump on to the jetty and disappear into the market crowd. There is a taxi rank there. Choose any of the yellow cabs; they'll take you out of town. If you leave me your car keys I'll arrange for your car to be put into safe hiding.'

O'Hara stood to leave but Pierre remained seated at the table.

'Aren't you coming with us?' he asked.

'No, I'm too old to start running around the village. Those men are not after me. Oh, I expect they'll try to bully something out of me regarding your whereabouts, if they manage to get into the house. But Maxine will return shortly and they know better than to face her.'

O'Hara leant forward and kissed Pierre on the forehead. 'Thank you,' he said before following Maxine out of the door. As soon as they were stood outside in the narrow alleyway Maxine waited until she heard her father bolt the door from the inside.

'Follow me, but let's be quick.'

The narrow cobblestoned alleyway enclosed by buildings either side was both slippery and steep as it wound down towards the river. The cobblestones never saw daylight and were covered in a shiny green moss that looked almost fluorescent in the dim light. O'Hara was finding it difficult to keep his footing and twice almost banged into Maxine whose slim lithe figure seemed to float across the ground as she nimbly led the way. The steep path eventually gave way to a flight of steps that appeared almost vertical.

'There is no rail on one side so be careful,' said Maxine over her shoulder.

'Don't worry if I fall I'll make sure I land on you.'

Maxine looked back with a glimmer of a smile on her face. At the bottom of the steps stood a small jetty where two boats were moored, both open topped, both around four metres in length. Maxine jumped onto the first boat, turned and grabbed O'Hara's hand almost pulling him on board.

'I'll start the engine while you untie the ropes.'

The engine soon coughed into life and the moment O'Hara had released the two rope ties they began to pull away from the jetty.

'Please lay on the floor. That way no one will see you,' said Maxine.

O'Hara lay on his back looking up to where Maxine stood at the steering wheel. His eyes couldn't help but take in the slim curves of the young woman standing in front of him and he was beginning to wish the circumstances were different.

The powerful engine made easy work of the river and they made swift progress, leaving a wash behind them that caused several small boats to bob up and down on their moorings.

'We're not far from the bridge,' exclaimed Maxine some five minutes later, her voice breaking O'Hara's train of thought.

'When I give the signal, I want you to slip over the rail onto the walkway whilst the boat is still moving. That way no one will expect to see you get off. The eyes only see what they expect to see. In front of you will be a small flight of steps. Turn right at the top, cross the bridge and head into the market area. There are always numerous taxis there.'

'What about you?' he asked.

'I'm going back to look after my father.' She extracted her mobile from her jacket pocket and threw it to him. 'Please don't try to call me. I will be in touch with you when I know it's safe.'

'How can I thank you? I feel that you've saved my life.'

'You don't have to thank me Mr O'Hara. All I ask is that you help to find Kate.'

The boat started to slow a little.

'Here we are. When I give the signal please jump off.'

'Thanks Maxine.' He didn't know what else to say.

Wesley had gathered the team into his office and relayed the information to them that he'd just received from O'Hara. There was an air of disbelief when he told them the truth about Annie Griffin and how Antoine had been her son.

'That would explain her recent strange behaviour,' Martin remarked.

'And her disappearance,' Alison exclaimed.

'Do you think Annie Griffin is involved in Kate Melcham's disappearance?' asked another young WPC at the back of the room.

'Given the information that has now come to light I think we have to assume that Annie is behind this,' Wesley replied with a sigh.

'Have we got any leads to go on?'

'We've had a couple of possible sightings,' said Martin. 'We're following up on them now.'

Wesley nodded. Just then his desk phone rang. He answered it and listened to the caller. By the time he replaced the receiver there was a wide grin on his face.

'What is it, sir?' Alison enquired, anticipating some good news at last.

'That was a chap named Peter Reynolds, a member of the hospital security staff. He's just come back on shift after his three days off. He called as soon as he heard about Kate's disappearance. It would appear that Kate's hospital wristband had been fitted with a small tracking device. It's something that the hospital security team had been trialling amongst themselves, with the idea of then trailing patients at risk. Peter Reynolds has just informed me that he took the liberty of installing the device on Kate's wristband just to trial it. The fact that the patient has gone missing is just a coincidence. Assuming Kate is still wearing the wristband, the tracking system is showing her to be located somewhere in Frome, a fifteen to twenty minute car journey from the hospital. He can also tell that the location of the wristband hasn't changed for the past six hours, so we can assume that Kate's either found herself a place to hide or she's been taken somewhere where she's being held. Either way we now have a location.'

The whole office burst into gossip at the announcement.

'How accurate is the tracker?' asked Martin. 'I mean, can we pin down the location to an actual road or building?'

'Virtually yes, the details I have here provide a grid reference that Peter will explain in more detail. So, let's plan our move. Martin, identify what vehicles we have and the number of staff at our disposal. Alison, I want you to contact the hospital, organise paramedic support and keep an open line at all times with Peter Reynolds, just in case the location changes.' He scribbled a note on a piece of paper and handed it to WPC Clare Denning. 'Clare, this is the current grid reference where we believe Kate to be. Speak with Peter Reynolds, he'll explain everything. Dig out the local maps and tell me what's there and what we could be facing. We will all meet in the car park in thirty minutes.'

30

Kate wiped the sleep from her eyes. Her head felt heavy but otherwise she was OK. She was holding the cup of water in both hands that Lucy had just poured and was trying to take in what Lucy was saying.

'I don't think Annie drugged you with the same stuff that Brian had been using on me,' said Lucy. 'Look at my hair. It's falling out in clumps.'

Kate smiled at her sister. 'I'd rather have a bald sister than a dead one.'

For the first time in months they both shared laughter.

'When did you first start to suspect Brian?' Kate asked as she took a sip of water.

'I think I've always known he had a dodgy side to him. Maybe that was part of the attraction. But when I found out that he'd been selling some of the family heirlooms, that really was, the final straw. Added to which, we had no money in the bank. He was selling stuff to pay back creditors from deals that had backfired. Then one day he started to ask what had happened to the family treasures, and kept asking where we had hidden the artefacts. I had no idea what he was talking about and as the months went by he would continually ask the same questions and was becoming extremely angry because I said I didn't know the answer. With regards to our finances I challenged him as to where our savings had gone and why we he had resorted to selling bits and pieces from the family home. He never did give me a straight answer except to tell me he would try and mend his ways, but it was at that time I began to feel unwell. Then one day I overheard him talking to a man named Henry Morgan…' Lucy stopped half way through the sentence.

'What's up, Lucy?' Kate could see the tears welling in her sister's eyes.

'I'd been stupid,' she stammered. 'Brian and I hadn't been an item for a number of years and when this guy started paying attention to me, well, you can guess the rest.'

'Do you mean you had an affair?'

Lucy nodded her head in confirmation. Kate never replied and thought it better to let her sister continue.

'One day, I overheard them talking. They were discussing what to do with a body. I thought I was going mad but the more I heard, the more convinced I was that they were actually trying to dispose of someone.' Lucy's whole body shuddered as the tears flowed. 'Oh, what did I do? I didn't want anyone to get hurt,' she cried.

'I don't understand. Who's body? Who got hurt?' Kate asked.

'Henry Morgan's daughter. She was working as a cleaner at Melcham Hall. She saw Henry and I...well you know, and she threatened to tell her mother what was going on. It was the following day that I overheard Henry asking Brian where they could hide the body.'

Kate placed her cup on the bed and placed her hands over her mouth. The realization that someone had been murdered suddenly hit her. Jumping off the bed she knelt by the window and vomited. It was several minutes before either sister spoke. When Kate did look up, she looked into the eyes of a sister who had seemed to age overnight. She pulled herself to her feet and sat on the edge of the bed, clasping Lucy's hand.

'So, let me get this right. You believe that Henry Morgan killed his own daughter?'

'Yes,' Lucy replied almost in a whisper.

'Would there be any way to prove it?'

'I don't know. I think Brian guessed that I'd overheard because the next thing I knew I was here in this place. Looking back, I'm pretty sure he had been drugging me for some time.'

'You obviously won't be aware that the girl's body was found in the coal shed behind Rowan Lodge,' exclaimed Kate.

Lucy stared at her sister, a look of sheer horror etched across her face.

It was several minutes before either sister spoke. Lucy was the first to break the silence.

'Why did you come back from France?' she asked. 'Nothing makes sense anymore.'

'Brian contacted me. He said that you were unwell and had to convalesce and that doctors had told him you were unlikely to recover. He said you would be unable to attend the forthcoming meeting with the family solicitor at which time he would be granted his part ownership of the Melcham estate and where you would officially be recognised as heir to the estate. He asked me to 'sit-in' for you and in return I would be paid a lump sum to keep quiet. He said we were so alike that no one would know. He made it quite clear that if I didn't play along with his plan then I would never see you again. He refused to tell me where you were except to say that you would be OK so long as I played my part.'

Kate paused as she toyed with a handkerchief, continually wrapping it around her fingers

'My intention was to expose him as soon as I had discovered where you were, but unfortunately I think he didn't trust me enough, because when I arrived at hospital they found my blood stream poisoned by thallium too.'

'Thallium? Isn't that the stuff that father used to kill rats with?'

'Yes, come to think of it I do believe it is.'

'So that's what the bastard was also pumping into me. I thought the hair loss was simply due to a change in hormones or something, I never imagined my own husband was slowly killing me. It all fits now. There are some days I can't even stand up because of the pain in my guts.'

'I think you need a blood transfusion as soon as possible. We need to find a way to get out of here.'

'It's no use trying the window,' said Lucy, 'it's locked. I've tried several times. Even if you could break the glass you can't squeeze through the metal bars.'

Lucy held her head in her hands.

'Are you OK?' asked Kate looking concerned.

'Yeah, apart from the hair loss, my memory has been awful, and I've not been able to concentrate on anything. I keep getting a pain across my eyes. I'm convinced now that each time he gave me my headache powder he included some of the drug with it.'

'He could have killed you,' exclaimed Kate.

'Oh I don't think he had any intention of that, not straight away in any case. He just wanted me out of the way. What did he say had happened to me?'

'He said that your migraines had become more regular and that the doctor had suggested you be taken away to convalesce but the prognosis wasn't good. My suspicions about him were confirmed when he told me that I was not allowed to visit you.'

'Is that what made you suspect, Brian?'

'Oh Lucy, I don't wish to upset you but anyone could see that from the start his sole intention was to get his hands on Daddy's estate. Although I never mentioned anything to you when I went to France, I did some research into Brian's business matters then, and it was quite apparent that he was a crook. In fact, I'm sure there was someone backing him in the early days of your marriage, someone who was possibly keeping him out of jail.'

'You mean someone with money?'

'Possibly, yes. Or someone who had power over others.'

'I still don't understand what these so-called treasures are he kept on about?' exclaimed Lucy.

'Well, I'm not really sure either,' Kate replied. 'However, I do have a vague memory of mother and father sitting in the drawing one evening when we were young. I remember watching them for a few moments when father said something like, "At least no one will think to look there for the treasures." As soon as I heard the word treasure I thought we were about to play a game of hide and seek, but they never mentioned it again.'

It was at that moment they heard the sound of a key being turned in the lock.

Kate and Lucy stood side by side staring at the door.

The two sisters' immediately recognised Annie, but neither of them knew who the man was who stood beside her.

'Ladies let me introduce you to, James Harper.'

Both Kate and Lucy looked confused. It was Kate who spoke first.

'Annie can you explain what the hell is going on? Why are we being held here? What do you want from us? Father let you stay in the Lodge, put a roof over your head. I don't understand. I thought you loved us?'

Annie gave a hideous laugh.

'So I should be grateful. Is that what you're saying? It was your family who stole from the Griffin family. It was your father who hid the treasures belonging to the Abbey. Do you think I should be grateful for that?'

'We have no idea what you're talking about,' Lucy replied.

'Let me educate you, shall I?'

There was fearless tone to Annie's voice.

'The Griffin Abbey stood in what are now the grounds of the Melcham estate for over a hundred years until your bloody family purchased the land, or should I say stole it. Then when your grandfather had the old Melcham Abbey built he ordered the destruction of the Griffin Abbey and had Melcham Abbey built on top. Not only did he destroy my family's ancestral home, he also made a number of my family homeless, including my own mother and father.'

'But what has that got to do with us?' cried Lucy, 'we weren't even born.'

'Your grandfather ruined my family and to add salt to the wound he then hid the treasures they possessed. Before I go to my grave I want the Griffin treasures handed back to the Griffin Abbey, to where they rightly belong. James, here, is my step-son. He will take over the Griffin Abbey when I'm gone.'

'James is your step-son? I didn't think you had any children at all?' said Kate.

Annie curled her top lip with a look of disgust.

'Oh, I had a child of my own. One of the conditions that allowed my husband and me to stay in the Lodge was that we were never to raise a family there. When Anthony was born, he was taken from me and handed over to a family in France, where he grew up. I only saw him half a dozen times throughout his entire life. You knew him as Antoine.'

'No!' Lucy screamed. 'You're making this up. It can't be true.'

Kate pursed her lips and screwed her eyes as she tried to digest the information.

'That makes sense now,' Kate exclaimed. 'That's why he kept pestering me about the estate. You were using him to get to our inheritance.'

'You would have nothing to inherit if your family hadn't stolen from us,' cried Annie.

'So where do you fit into all of this?' Lucy asked Harper.

'Annie's husband, Fred, was my father. Oh don't look too shocked. My own mother died during childbirth and Fred wasn't in a position to look after me. Although he put me up for adoption, he put money aside each week to pay for my upbringing and education. When he passed away, Annie contacted me and the rest is history.'

'That doesn't explain your interest in the so called treasures of Griffin Abbey,' exclaimed Lucy.

'Annie asked for my assistance, on the understanding that I will eventually succeed her as the heir to the family fortunes.'

'And you're prepared to murder for them?' said Kate.

'You need to be more careful of your choice of words my dear,' he replied.

'But we don't anything about these so-called treasures and artefacts. We were told about them,' exclaimed Lucy.

'I don't believe you, either of you,' replied Annie. 'You both need to think very carefully about your answers. Time is running out.'

The two sisters stared at Annie, a woman they both thought they knew.

'Now if you'll excuse us I have an important conference call to attend. Please make yourselves comfortable. We'll speak later.'

He led Annie out of the room and closed the door. The sound of the key turning in the lock told Kate and Lucy they weren't going anywhere.

Maxine switched off the ignition and moored the boat before ascending the steps leading from the river back to the house. As she approached she noticed the side door was open, and immediately knew something was wrong. She unclicked the safety catch on her gun and stealthily crept up to the doorway. There was no sound from within so crouching low with the gun in both hands she stepped inside. She saw her father straight away. His body was slumped on the floor on the opposite side of the table. Maxine ran across the room and knelt down beside him to feel for a pulse. She found one but it was weak. She quickly searched the rest of the house but it was empty, the intruders had gone. Placing the gun in the back of her waistband she leant over her father's body to check his injuries.

'Papa, can you hear me?'

Pierre's eyelids fluttered before his eyes opened a little. A large bruise had already formed over his left eye and his bottom lip was split. He forced a grin.

'Oh papa, what did they do to you?'

Several times he moved his lips and licked at them with his tongue before he answered.

'I'm OK. Those two goons, Paul and Antonio, aren't very good at their job. I think they've broken a couple of ribs but that's all. I didn't tell them anything. They shot the lock away; we'll need to get it fixed.'

Maxine didn't need to be told who her father was talking about. He raised his left arm and reached for her shoulder.

'Help me up, Maxine. I'll be OK once I'm sat in the chair.'

Once she had got him into the chair she helped to remove his shirt before cutting an old bed sheet into strips and wrapping the material tightly around his rib cage. The old man's breathing was laboured and he looked tired.

'Come and lie down in the other room. You need to sleep, father.'

By the time Maxine had retrieved a blanket to place over him, Pierre was sleeping. She gently pushed his hair away from his eyes and ran her fingers across his cheek. For the first time in her life she realised how frail he looked and she suddenly thought of her mother and wished she was still there to look after him. Their mother had been the head of the house and Maxine took after her in so many ways. A café owner all her life, she had become the person who people would talk to when they had troubles. She had the ability to listen with a sympathetic ear but also could always offer words of wisdom, words of advice.

What would she have said to Maxine now, if she was still alive? Would she try to deter her or simply acknowledge what needed to be done?

When Maxine stood up there was fierce burning look in her eyes, a look of revenge. As she made her father comfortable there was a glimmer of a smirk on her face.

WPC Clare Denning opened the map and spread it across the car bonnet.

'If these readings are accurate, Kate is currently located here,' she said pointing.

'According to the map there are four large Victorian houses on this side of the road. All four lay back from the road and all appear to have approximately half an acre of ground. The only way in is from the main road.'

'I've spoken with Inspector Yates at Frome, they're happy to assist and will arrange for the road to be blocked off as soon as we get over there,' said Martin.

'Good work,' Wesley replied, 'how long will it take us to get to Frome?'

'About thirty minutes, sir.'

'Then we had better get going. Clare, you come with me and Alison. Martin, you take the rest of the team in the patrol car. Have we arranged for paramedic assistance?'

'Yes, I spoke with Inspector Yates, he's organizing that from their end,' Alison replied.

'Good girl, in that case unless anyone has any questions let's go. You lead the way, Martin. You know the area better than anyone else.'

Taking the B3139 they headed north-east until they turned onto the A371 to avoid heavy congestion. After passing through Shepton Mallet and Melcham Hall, Martin turned onto the A362 into Frome.

Inspector Yates and his team were parked in a layby outside the busy town centre. Yates jumped out of his vehicle as soon as Martin pulled the patrol car off the road. A giant of a man, he dwarfed Wesley as he made his way past the parked vehicles.

‘Wesley, it’s good to meet you.’ Even his handshake left Wesley wincing.

‘Good afternoon, thanks for your assistance, it’s much appreciated,’ said Wesley.

‘There’s nothing better than the thrill of surprising the enemy, is there?’

Wesley could see the excitement on Yates’ face as he briefed him of the situation.

‘At this stage we are only assuming that Kate is being held against her will,’ Wesley replied. ‘Having left the hospital with no money or credit cards she must have been driven here by someone. I’m just hoping that that someone is a friend rather than an enemy.’

‘Well, there’s one sure way to find out.’ Yates rubbed his hands together like someone just spoiling for a fight.

‘I’ve just spoken with hospital security,’ said WPC Clare Denning. ‘If the tracking device is accurate, then Kate is in the first of the four big houses at the start of Ferndale road.’

‘I know where that is,’ Yates answered.

‘Are we far away?’ Wesley asked.

‘About two minutes by car. I’ll radio ahead and get the far end of Ferndale locked down. If we enter from this side, we’ll leave one vehicle blocking the road and another blocking the drive. Most of the entrances to the properties along there are un-adopted roads, so we might as well park up and walk from the main road. At least that way they won’t hear the cars approach.’

Wesley nodded. It sounded like a good plan. Just as Yates turned around to head for his vehicle Wesley placed a hand on his shoulder.

‘Are any of your officers armed?’

‘I’ve got one marksman, but don’t worry Wes, I’ve always got by with these,’ he replied waving his fists in the air.

Wesley wanted to laugh but he could just imagine Yates doing exactly that.

‘What do you think is going to happen to us?’ asked Kate.

‘I don’t know,’ Lucy replied. ‘They can’t keep us here forever and Brian needs you or me to attend the meeting with the solicitor. Talking about Brian, where the hell is he?’

‘I know the police were looking for him but I haven’t seen him for several days. They’d been to the house a few times asking what we knew or had heard about the death of a young woman.’

‘Do you mean Felicity?’

‘At first I had no idea, but yes, she was eventually identified by her parents.’

‘Oh my God, so do you think Brian killed her?’

‘I’m not sure really, Lucy.’ She grabbed Lucy’s hands. ‘I think the police suspect either Brian or that Henry Morgan chap.’

‘Do you mean Felicity’s father?’

'Yes.'

'This is like a nightmare.' Lucy put her hands over her eyes as she tried to block everything out of her mind. Kate stared at her sister, how she had lost weight, how drawn she looked and how fragile. It was all Hargreaves' fault.

She guided Lucy back to the bed and sat down beside her. As she scratched her wrist where the hospital wristband had been rubbing, something fell to the floor. It was a tiny metal looking object. She reached down to pick it up and toyed with it between her fingers.

'What's that?' asked Lucy looking up.

'I don't know it just fell off my hospital wristband.'

'Here, let me take a look.'

Kate placed the tiny object into the palm of Lucy's hand. Suddenly Lucy started to giggle.

'What are you laughing at?' Lucy looked confused.

'It's a transmitter. The hospital must have attached it to your wristband. If it's still working they'll know exactly where you are.'

Just as Wesley got back into the car his mobile rang. He didn't recognise the number of the mobile that O'Hara had just purchased and was hesitant to answer but decided it may be important. He was glad he did. For the next few minutes he listened intently to the information that O'Hara gave him and tried to take in what he was saying about Annie.

'It all makes sense now,' he replied before giving O'Hara an update on events in the UK. 'So where are you now?'

O'Hara explained that Maxine had dropped him off in a nearby village and that he was going to hire a car to get home. He would arrange for someone to collect his own vehicle later, in case it was being watched.

'I'm sorry to have put you through all that,' said Wesley, 'I had no idea this was going to turn out to be like this.'

'You owe me again,' O'Hara replied laughing. 'Keep me informed as to what happens. I need to get out of here. Use this number if you need to contact me.'

The convoy of vehicles turned into Ferndale Road with one car stopping on the main road and two others blocking the entrance to the property. The light was beginning to fade casting long shadows between the trees and hedgerows that lined the un-adopted approach. Yates led the way with Wesley alongside, followed closely by Martin and two of Yates' colleagues, with Alison and two paramedics taking up the rear. Yates stopped for a second, listening to the message on his radio.

'There are two officers around the back. There's no other exit, whoever is in there are in for a surprise.'

Yates rapped his huge knuckles on the front door, the sound echoing throughout the house. 'Over to you, Inspector,' said Yates. 'You know these people.'

He rapped on the door again. Seconds later, footsteps could be heard from within followed by the sound of someone sliding back a bolt. When the door was opened, James Harper peered out into the evening light.

'Mr Harper, good evening, we meet again,' said Wesley.

Yates just managed to get his foot in the door as Harper attempted to close it.

'We have visitors!' Harper shouted and turned to run but Yates was exceptionally quick for a big man and rugby tackled the man to the ground. Suddenly there was a scream from one of the upstairs rooms. With Harper already securely pinned to the floor, Wesley led the way upstairs followed by Martin and Alison. Two other colleagues began a search of the ground floor.

Two of the bedroom doors were open but the one facing them at the end of the corridor was closed, with a light shining through the gap underneath.

Wesley banged on the door. 'It's the Police, open up!'

'We're in here,' Lucy cried, 'Kate's hurt.'

Wesley turned the handle but the door was locked.

'I'll open it,' exclaimed Yates striding forward. James Harper was already being escorted to a police vehicle by two of his colleagues.

Yates' shoulder hit the door with a shuddering thump and the door burst open, one of its hinges splintering away from the door frame.

No one could have envisaged the scene they saw. Kate was lying unconscious on the bed at the far end of the room. Lucy was standing near the window with a syringe held against the side of her neck.

'Come any closer and I swear I'll inject the poison into her,' shouted Annie who was stood behind Lucy, one hand gripping her hair, the other holding the syringe that was now clearly exposed, being attached to the back of her brooch.

'Annie, what on earth are you doing?' said Wesley. 'There's no need to kill anyone.'

'She's injected Kate,' cried Lucy, 'she's killed my sister!'

'I administered Kate a sleeping drug, she's not dead. I was going to do the same with Lucy until you lot ruined everything,' Annie replied pulling hard on Lucy's hair to keep her close.

Wesley's mind was racing, he had to calm Annie down and get her to release Lucy.

'Annie, let Lucy go, we can talk about this. There's no need for anyone else to get hurt.'

'Do you take me for a fool? You're not going to let me walk away from here. I may be an old lady but I'm not stupid.'

Alison had been standing in the doorway behind Wesley but now moved forward with her hands held out in front to show she wasn't carrying a weapon.

'Why don't we take you home to the Lodge? We can sit and talk in private,' said Alison, 'just like we did before.'

There was a deafening silence in the room as Annie seemed to be considering Alison's suggestion. What followed was thirty seconds of chaos. The window behind Annie smashed as pieces of glass showered the room. Lucy screamed as Annie released her grip to look behind her. Yates was quick off the mark and took the opportunity to launch himself at Annie who crashed backwards into the wall next to the window, dropping the brooch with the deadly syringe.

Wesley kicked the brooch out of Annie's reach whilst Lucy ran forward into Alison's arms. In an instant the paramedics were in the room attending to Kate.

Yates placed cufflinks on a bewildered looking Annie and handed her over to a waiting WPC who escorted the battered and bruised woman out of the room, bypassing Martin as he entered the bedroom.

'Where the hell did you go?' asked Wesley.

With a smug look on his face, the young PC held his hand in the air to display the brick he'd thrown at the window.

'I thought the window breaking behind her would distract Annie long enough for someone to tackle her.'

'You're not just a handsome devil,' said Alison, whose face immediately turned crimson, regretting what she'd just said.

'I didn't think you'd noticed,' Martin replied.

Wesley gave a polite cough. 'When you two have finished with the compliments we'll get out of here shall we?'

The paramedics had lifted Kate onto a stretcher and were already carrying her downstairs. Lucy was now in the capable hands of WPC Clare Denning following on behind.

'This is some dangerous piece of equipment,' exclaimed Yates, holding the tip of the brooch, carefully avoiding the sharp needle.

'I've got a horrible feeling that we'll discover that Annie has used the brooch to kill before now,' said Wesley.

31

The following morning the villagers of Perpignan were only talking about one subject, the tragic accident where two men had died when their vehicle had plunged into the river during the early hours of the morning.

Maxine was busy running the café whilst her father was asleep, recovering upstairs. She spent the day listening to the locals describe how Paul and Antonio had died. At the end of the day when she closed the café, there was a knowing smirk on her face.

Three days later after being checked over by doctors, both Kate and Lucy were allowed to go home, except that the bulk of Melcham Hall had been burnt to the ground.

'Why don't you come and stay with my wife and I for a couple of days?' said Wesley. 'I know Jane would be thrilled to have you stay over, and you can rest up for a while.' Both sisters happily agreed and left the hospital with Wesley heading for the peace and quiet of Jasmine Cottage. Wesley had telephoned ahead to make Jane aware of his idea and she immediately set about preparing the spare bedrooms. That evening following dinner both sisters had an early night and slept soundly for the first time in months.

The following morning Wesley had a late breakfast, spending most of it talking to Kate and Lucy in between one of Jane's famous fry ups.

'So do you think Annie is responsible for Brian's murder?' Lucy asked pouring more tea. Alison had broken the news about his death to her in the hospital the previous day.

'I think there's a good chance that Annie was involved, especially given the method of killing, but my money is still on James Harper.'

'The whole thing makes me shiver,' Kate remarked, the strain of the last few days clearly showing in her face.

'What I find frightening is that we both grew up knowing Annie and Antoine and yet we had no idea the Griffin Abbey even existed,' said Lucy.

'I wouldn't get too stressed about that,' said Jane as she walked across the kitchen with more toast. 'It's often the things under our noses that we don't see.'

'Listen to Miss Marple,' joked Wesley. For the first time he'd known them, both sisters smiled, a natural smile, and he realized just how attractive they both were.

Following breakfast Wesley left them getting ready to join Jane for a trip into Wells for some therapeutic shopping. When he arrived at the station things weren't quite so jovial although there was an air of relief that Lucy and her sister Kate had been found alive. Wesley sat behind his desk and picked up the sheet of A4 from his notepad, reading the contents.

Hi Wesley,

I eventually made it home safely and have organized for my car to be picked up.

Maxine and her father Pierre are both busy working back at the café. There has been no sign of the two guys who had been following us. ***(He omitted the fact that two bodies had been recovered from the river the previous evening).***

Martin informs me that you've made a couple of arrests over there. I hope that clears everything up. I haven't made any mention of the past forty-eight hours to the wife and kids, it is better that way. The next time you telephone please say it's just because you're coming over on leave, I much prefer a quieter life these days. Send Jane our love.

Cheers pal.

O'Hara

Wesley folded the paper and placed it in his pocket. There are some things in life that money can't buy.

Annie Griffin was sat in the interview room staring at the floor. WPC Clare Denning was stood against the far wall next to the door. Doctor Ian Meadows was also sat at the table alongside Brian Harding, Annie's QC. Wesley took a seat opposite Annie alongside WPC Alison Bolt. He nodded to Alison who pushed the button on the recording machine.

'It's Thursday 5th January , time 09:15, present in the room are Annie Griffin, WPC Clare Denning, WPC Alison Bolt, Inspector John Wesley, Brian Harding and Doctor Ian Meadows.'

'Shall we start from the beginning?' asked Wesley, leaning his elbows on the table.

Annie Griffin had aged ten years overnight and Doctor Ian Meadows had been called in as there were concerns over her health. He reluctantly agreed that she could be interviewed but stated that the old lady was showing signs of stress.

Annie confirmed her name, age and address. She explained how she had grown up on the Melcham estate knowing that her ancestors had once owned Griffin Abbey. She stated that the Melcham family were to blame for everything that had happened as they were the ones who stole from her family. She added that although Lord Melcham had always treated her well she believed he had stolen the artefacts and treasures that had once belonged to the Abbey, robbing her of her rightful inheritance. In announcing this she gave an almost hysterical laugh that made Wesley look across to the doctor.

A minute passed by before she continued. Anthony (Antoine) had been born out of wedlock and had been given up for adoption from the day he was born.

She knew that when Lord Melcham passed away the Melcham estate wasn't as comfortably off as it had once been and this was proved by the financial irregularities being performed by Brian Hargreaves and an ex-partner, Henry Morgan. It was when her son Anthony had witnessed the, albeit accidental murder of Felicity Morgan, that she saw her opportunity to get her hands back on what was rightly hers. She knew by telling the police about the body in the coal shed that they would start prying into Hargreaves' affairs and that that would take the spotlight away from her. However, things had taken a turn for the worse when her son Anthony decided that he didn't want a share of the Abbey's treasures, he wanted it all. It was then that she knew she had to have him removed. Brian Hargreaves had knocked him unconscious and given him a beating with an old croquet bat to make it look like a mugging. She was sorry too for the death of the young policeman who had been trailing Hargreaves but he got too close for comfort. Annie took a sip of water, refusing the offer of tea or coffee. When Wesley asked her why Hargreaves was killed she grinned. She said the man was a fool, that he spent his life making mistakes, expecting other people to bail him out. He had phoned her to say he had accidentally killed Henry Morgan and needed to go into hiding. She laughed again and said she even told him what hotel to stay in, so all she had to do was tell James Harper where he was. At first he'd seemed excited about helping the Abbey. It was the Abbey that had previously kept him and Morgan out of jail by paying owed taxes in return for their help. She said Morgan had over stepped the mark when he'd had a brief affair with Lucy which was witnessed by Morgan's daughter. That's what had caused Henry Morgan to argue with his daughter. Felicity was going to expose him.

An hour into the interview and Annie was clearly getting tired. Doctor Ian Meadows gave a polite cough and pointed to his wrist watch. Wesley nodded that he understood.

'Just one more question, Annie. We know you used the syringe on the back of your brooch to keep the poison in but tell me where did you obtain the poison from?'

'Its high concentrate thallium, a potion that my father created many years ago, mixing thallium with oil and water. When a certain amount is injected into a human or animal it gives the appearance of a heart attack. I provided

Brian Hargreaves with thallium salts to use on Lucy, far less dangerous but none the less lethal over a period of time.'

'Hence the hair loss,' said Alison.

'That's quite right,' Annie replied. 'You've been doing your homework, Inspector.'

Doctor Ian Meadows gave another polite cough which Wesley knew he had to respond to.

'Annie Griffin, you are charged with the attempted murder of Lucy Hargreaves and your assistance in the murders of Brian Hargreaves and PC Mark Hayles, your involvement in holding Lucy Hargreaves and Kate Melcham against their will, and in diverting the course of justice. You will be taken down to the cells where you will be held until tomorrow morning when you be taken from here to Wells Court to stand before the Judge.'

Wesley read out the time and date the interview ended.

He stood up as Annie was led away by WPC Clare Denning followed closely by the doctor. As soon as Annie had left the room, Wesley made a phone to Inspector Yates. James Harper had admitted to murdering Brian Hargreaves and aiding and abetting Annie Griffin in the abduction of Lucy and Kate. Yates said that when interviewed and cautioned, James Harper had blamed Annie Griffin for everything. Wesley thanked Yates for his help before hanging up.

'Alison, will you do me a favour, find Martin, then meet me at the front of the building. I think it's time we all had a drink.'

Wesley sat back on the uncomfortable pub bench and began to roll a cigarette. Alison was sat beside him reading a local newspaper she had just retrieved from a nearby table. They both looked up when Martin arrived with a tray of drinks and three packets of crisps.

'Blimey we are splashing out,' commented Wesley snatching the cheese and onion variety before anyone else nabbed them.

'Before we take a drink, sir, can we raise our glasses to Mark?' said Alison.

Wesley looked across the table and noticed the tears welling up in her eyes.

'I think that's the best suggestion I've heard in a long time.'

The three colleagues reached across the table to touch glasses in tribute to their fallen colleague. 'God bless you, Mark,' Wesley announced.

Martin was the first to speak to break the subdued silence.

'What I don't understand is how and why James Harper got involved.'

Wesley placed his beer glass down on the table.

'I was speaking with Lucy a short while ago. It appears that James Harper's father was in fact Fred Griffin, Annie's husband. James was his son from his first marriage. James' mother died giving birth to him.'

'So when did Annie ask him for help?' asked Alison.

‘We still need to find that out, but I believe she knew some time ago that she was not going to be able to manage things by herself and she didn’t trust Hargreaves, so she got Hargreaves and his side-kick Morgan to get in touch with Harper. In return for keeping them out of jail by funding their financial discrepancies, he ensured they worked for Annie.’

‘So who killed Felicity Morgan?’

‘That was her father, Henry. I’m pretty much convinced it was an accident. He struck her and she fell backwards breaking her neck.’

‘But what caused them to argue?’

‘Felicity had caught her father in a compromising situation with Lucy Hargreaves. Lucy has admitted she’d had a brief affair with the man. Unfortunately Felicity opened the wrong door at the wrong time and caught them at it. She threatened to tell her mother and, well, the rest is history.’

‘So he placed her body in the coal shed?’

‘No, I think Brian Hargreaves was responsible for that. He put her body in an old wheelbarrow and pushed it as far as he could towards Annie’s place, before carrying the rest of the way through the trees and dumping it in the coal shed. I don’t think he expected the body to be found as quickly as it was. I think his intention was to hide the body there for a few days before deciding where best to dispose of it.’

Alison shook her shoulders as a shiver went down her spine.

‘It’s sounds so awful, sir. Apart from the victim, it’s hard to imagine what was going on in Morgan’s mind. I mean, he’d just killed his daughter.’

‘Do you think Hargreaves meant to kill Henry Morgan, sir?’ asked Martin.

‘That’s something we’ll never know the answer to,’ he replied.

‘What I’ll never understand is how someone like Annie who appeared to have so much love for Lucy and Kate suddenly turned so violent towards them,’ Alison exclaimed.

‘That’s something I spoke to Doctor Meadows about. It’s come to light that Annie was treated for schizophrenia several years ago and her medical records show she’s had a couple of relapses in the past,’ replied Wesley.

‘That would certainly explain her behavioural changes,’ said Martin.

‘So what are Lucy and Kate going to do now?’

‘For the time being they’re staying with Jane and me. They need to get their lives back on track. I understand Kate is selling her apartment in France and is going to settle down back in the UK.’

Epilogue

Three months after the fire had virtually destroyed Melcham Hall, the insurance company handed Lucy Hargreaves a cheque for the sum of £800,000 and work began on rebuilding the ancestral home. Lucy wrote a new will stating that she and her sister Kate would only ever be the sole beneficiaries of the estate.

It was during the rebuilding work when workmen found a hidden trap door under the flagstone kitchen floor. In the gloom of the basement below they came across a shield with the ۞۞۞ symbol emblazed across the middle encircled by Griffins. The legendary creature with the body, tail, and back legs of a lion; the head and wings of an eagle; and with eagle's talons as front feet. The Griffin was thought to be an especially powerful and majestic creature.

Alongside the shield was a small wooden box, which when opened was found to contain an ancient leather-bound book. Upon examination the book was identified as being written in Occitan, the ancient language of the Languedoc.

The treasures that Annie and her family had sought amounted to a wooden shield and a priceless book. Neither of which could ever be converted into ready cash.

When the rebuilding of Melcham Hall was complete, Lucy ordered the surviving rooms of the Griffin Abbey to be restored to their former glory and the shield to be erected in a glass case at the entrance.

The Griffin artefacts had been found hidden behind a false wall next to the room where the domed ceiling depicted the drawings of baby Jesus surrounded by the winged creatures. By identifying the materials used in building the false wall, the restoration team confirmed that it had been erected less than twenty years ago.

The assumption was made that Lord Melcham had returned the artefacts to their rightful home shortly before his death.

The site has now been opened to the public with proceeds going towards the continued restoration of the Melcham estate.

Annie Griffin was convicted of attempted murder, aiding and abetting the kidnapping of Lucy Hargreaves and Kate Melcham for purposes of regaining unlawful ownership of the Melcham estate. She confessed to coaxing Brian

Hargreaves into assisting the Abbey in their quest to regain the Melcham estate.

Annie Griffin was sentenced to eight years imprisonment but never served a day of her sentence. Annie died of a heart attack the night after being sentenced. The post mortem found a high dosage of thallium poisoning in her blood.

On 3rd September 1969 Edwina Stanley had received a cheque for £5000 on the understanding that her husband Graham would be cremated. The cheque, which was paid directly to the local newspaper where he was employed, was eventually traced back to Peregrine Solutions. The owner of the company was identified as Annie Griffin.

James Harper, the famous TV Broadcaster and Chat show host made front page headlines of the national papers when he was found guilty of the murder of Brian Hargreaves, of detaining Lucy Hargreaves and Kate Melcham against their will and playing a part in their abduction. The press also commented on the fact that along with making large sum payments to Brian Hargreaves and Henry Morgan to hide financial irregularities within a number of private companies, James Harper was also being investigated for tax evasion. He was sentenced to twelve years imprisonment.

The case file showed that Felicity Morgan died as a result of a struggle with her father and her death was recorded as death by misadventure.

Wesley had placed the letter written by Felicity to her mother that was never sent, in the case file. In it, Felicity stated she was pregnant and named Brian Hargreaves as the father.

Henry and Sally Morgan were both cremated the same day. The small service at Wells crematorium was attended by only a handful of people including Inspector John Wesley and WPC Mandy Tredwell.

It was recorded that Brian Hargreaves was responsible for the murders of Antoine Bergerac, PC Mark Hayles and Henry Morgan.

When the police were finally able to retrieve data from his mobile phone they found an unsent text message that read, "The silly girl said she was pregnant. That would have ruined everything."

Maxine had telephoned Kate to say that she and her father had decided to sell the café in Perpignan and move to the South coast where her father could enjoy his retirement. She said a cheque they had received from an unknown benefactor had provided them with the opportunity of a lifetime. A new rent free home; and private health care for her father. Lucy and Kate were the unknown benefactors.

When the extension work had been completed on Jasmine Cottage, Wesley and Jane held a party to celebrate the new look to their home.

Martin's arrival with Alison, started tongues wagging and Mandy, now refreshed from her holiday looked more relaxed than ever.

Colin Jones, the builder arrived with his family and his young assistant, Danny. Danny was immediately attracted to WPC Clare Denning, both being the same age and was trying to impress her with the way he had led Wesley to the Griffin Abbey, elaborating on how dangerous the adventure had been.

Gerry Callow had closed the book shop early, arriving before the other visitors. It gave him time to set up a small display of ancient books and magazines in Jane's kitchen. Since the day that Jane had given him a few ideas on marketing, he'd taken the opportunity to promote his bookshop everywhere he went and was now beginning to enjoy having a captivated audience.

With the assistance of historical records and a typed glossary of information he explained how a religious sect had founded the Griffin Abbey and went on to describe the events that originally led to the Abbey's ruin, started by Henry VIII's dissolution of the Abbey's and Monasteries. In later years because some of its members were wanted for questioning in relation to a number of 'incidents' including murder and financial irregularities, the family dispersed around the globe and went into hiding. A small contingent decided to remain in the UK including Annie Griffin's parents. Seeing the continual decline of her empire, Annie's mother had already sent her daughter away, providing her with a false identity. It was only when both parents and her husband died, did Annie revert to using her maiden name of Griffin.

The last people to arrive at Jasmine Cottage were David O'Hara and his family. With introductions made to new acquaintances, and hugs and handshakes given to old friends, everyone settled down to listen to a diversity of stories and adventures. Wesley took a seat on the low wall at the edge of the new patio and placed his arm around Jane's waist. Jane turned to look at him and smiled. There was no need for words.

Other Inspector Wesley Novels

Full Circle: *Published 20 Sep 2011*

Normandy 1946. In a remote village a young boy is left scarred by witnessing an act of horrific cruelty. Satanists destroy his innocence and set him on a path which plays out decade later in London.

When Inspector John Wesley is handed a letter by private investigator David O'Hara, neither can foresee the sequence of events to follow, or the dangers they will face. Things become personal for Wesley when a close friend disappears. A web of ongoing corruption and murder takes him half way across Europe where both colleagues and loved ones are endangered.

With help from O'Hara, and the police throughout Europe, he pursues those responsible. The trail eventually leads back to Normandy, where it all began. Having spent most of his working life in the police force, Wesley thought he had experienced everything there was to fear. That was, until he came face to face with the Devil.

Tor Murders: *Published 26 Jul 2012*

When Inspector Wesley moved down to the West Country he hoped for a quieter life than the one he'd left behind in London.

Then Suzie Potter is found strangled on the side of the Tor that stands high above the ruins of Glastonbury Abbey. When a second body is found less than twenty fours later, the nightmare is about to unfold.

As Wesley starts to interrogate the owners of Abbey House, even neighbours begin to act suspiciously. A young student is also reported missing and it becomes apparent that what lies below the Tor may hold the answer.

A labyrinth of tunnels, secrets, lies, intrigue and jealousy that stretches back into the past soon casts a tragic pall over the town. Wesley's powers of investigation are tested to the limit before the Tor and local inhabitants reveal their secrets.

To read the opening Chapters of any of the Inspector Wesley novels go to www.davewatson.info

Lightning Source UK Ltd.
Milton Keynes UK
UKOW05f1359060913

216632UK00001B/24/P